PRAISE FOR *THE LEGEND OF SHEBA*

"Tosca Lee's *The Legend of Sheba* is a tale of lush prose, rich setting, and meticulously researched historic detail. The queen of Sheba may be a figure obscured by the millennia, but Tosca Lee brings her to life—and she is strong, capable, and irresistibly seductive."

—Allison Pataki, *New York Times*
bestselling author of *The Traitor's Wife*

"I didn't think I could admire a novel more than I admired *Iscariot*, but Tosca Lee has outdone herself with *The Legend of Sheba*. As luscious as the ancient Arabian kingdom and as fascinating as the queen who ruled it, *Sheba* captivates with beauty, depth, intelligence, and cunning storytelling skill."

—Erin Healy, bestselling author of
Motherless and *Stranger Things*

"*The Legend of Sheba* is an enthralling, impeccably researched novel full of wisdom that will appeal to both religious and secular audiences. The vivid beauty of Lee's prose is unsurpassed. I felt as though Sheba herself was speaking to me, and her struggles and triumphs were my own."

—Rebecca Kanner, author of
Sinners and the Sea

"*The Legend of Sheba* is no fairy-tale romance of a woman swooning for a king. Tosca Lee has once again proven to be a fearless, dare I say, reckless storyteller as she gives us an unbridled retelling of a queen strong in wisdom and heart. It will leave you reflecting far beyond the turn of the last page."

—Pam Hogeweide, author of
Unladylike: Resisting the Injustice of Inequality in the Church

"A wild camel ride through the desert full of twists, turns, and surprises . . . A luxurious royal feast of eloquence, imagery, and theme. It's a beautiful story brilliantly told. Tosca Lee has the heart of a poet, the mind of a scholar, and the imagination of a storyteller."

—Josh Olds, LifeIsStory.com

"As a meticulous researcher Lee consistently strives to make her stories not just believable but eye-popping with realism. *The Legend of Sheba* leaves no novel stone unturned—action, intrigue, romance, and even mysticism make this a novel that must be read in a single sitting. The verbal tapestry of a minor biblical narrative will have readers examining the story of Sheba and Solomon in a completely new light."

—Dr. Joe Cathey, Professor of Old Testament
at Dallas Baptist University

"If Cecil B. DeMille were still around, he'd want to make Tosca Lee's *The Legend of Sheba* into a movie. It's an epic masterpiece. A timeless tale that takes readers to heights of love and battle few have seen before. And, just like a favorite movie, you'll want to experience the richness and depth of *Sheba* over and over again."

—Michael Napoliello Jr., Radar Pictures

THE LEGEND OF
SHEBA

RISE OF A QUEEN

A NOVEL

TOSCA LEE

HOWARD BOOKS
A DIVISION OF SIMON & SCHUSTER, INC.

NEW YORK   NASHVILLE   LONDON   TORONTO   SYDNEY   NEW DELHI

Howard Books
A Division of Simon & Schuster, Inc.
1230 Avenue of the Americas
New York, NY 10020

First Howard Books hardcover edition September 2014

HOWARD and colophon are trademarks of Simon & Schuster, Inc.

For information about special discounts for bulk purchases, please contact Simon
& Schuster Special Sales at 1-866-506-1949 or business@simonandschuster.com.

The Simon & Schuster Speakers Bureau can bring authors to your live event. For
more information or to book an event, contact the Simon & Schuster Speakers
Bureau at 1-866-248-3049 or visit our website at www.simonspeakers.com.

Interior design by Jaime Putorti

Manufactured in the United States of America

10 9 8 7 6 5 4 3 2 1

Library of Congress Cataloging-in-Publication Data

Lee, Tosca Moon.
  The legend of Sheba : rise of a Queen / Tosca Lee.—First Howard Books
hardcover edition.
    pages cm
  1. Sheba, Queen of—Fiction. 2. Bible. Old Testament—History of Biblical
events—Fiction. 3. Queens—Sheba (Kingdom)—Fiction. I. Title.
  PS3612.E3487L44 2014
  813'.6—dc23
  2014012494

ISBN 978-1-4516-8404-9
ISBN 978-1-4516-8406-3 (ebook)

FOR THOSE WHO RISE UP TO THE JOURNEY.

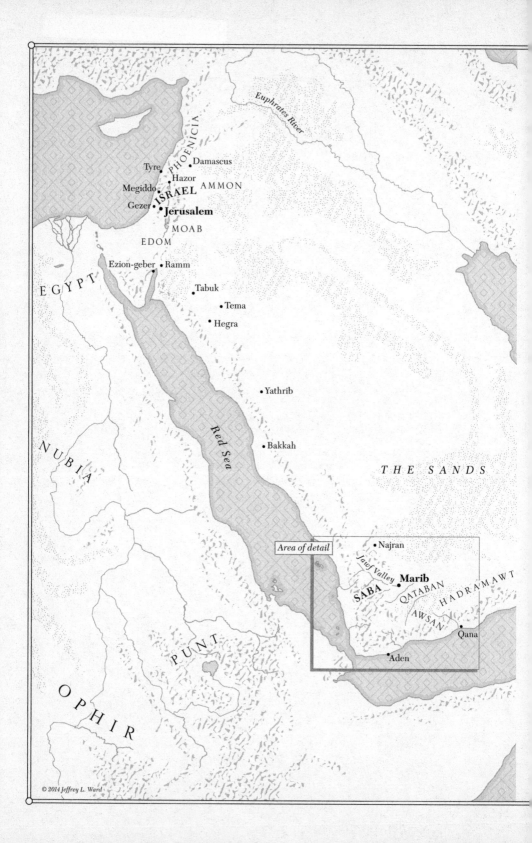

Euphrates River

PHOENICIA
Tyre •   • Damascus
• Hazor
Megiddo •   AMMON
Gezer • **ISRAEL**
      • **Jerusalem**
      MOAB
EDOM
Ezion-geber •   • Ramm

EGYPT

• Tabuk

• Tema

• Hegra

NUBIA

Red Sea

• Yathrib

• Bakkah

THE SANDS

Area of detail
      • Najran
Jauf Valley
      Marib
SABA • QATABAN   HADRAMAWT
AWSAN
      • Qana
• Aden

PUNT

OPHIR

© 2014 Jeffrey L. Ward

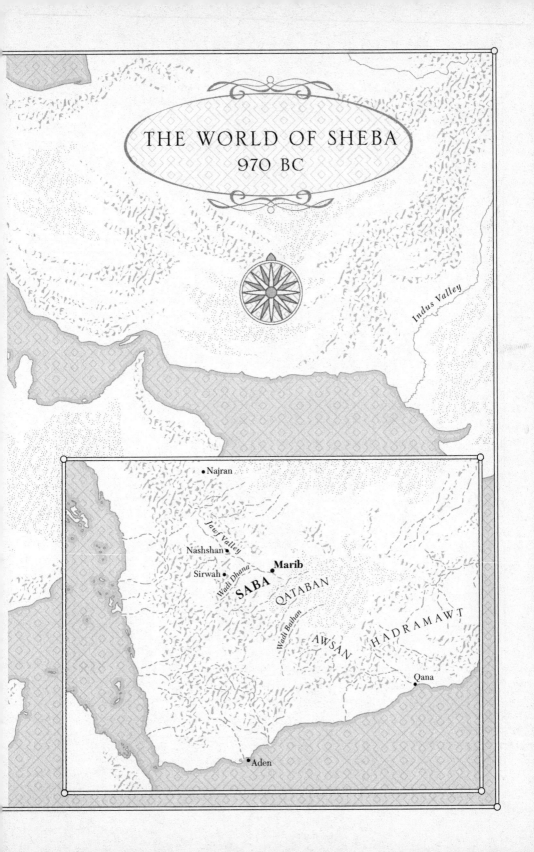

THE WORLD OF SHEBA
970 BC

Indus Valley

Najran

Jawf Valley

Nashshan

Sirwah

Wadi Dhana

SABA

Marib

QATABAN

Wadi Bayhan

AWSAN

HADRAMAWT

Qana

Aden

There is the tale that is told: A desert queen journeyed north with a caravan of riches to pay tribute to a king and his One God. The story of a queen conquered by a king before she returned to her own land laden with gifts.

That is the tale you are meant to believe.

Which means most of it is a lie.

The truth is far more than even the storytellers could conjure. The riches more priceless. The secrets more corrosive. The love and betrayal more passionate and devastating, both.

Love . . . The very word is a husk shriveled beneath the sun of the desert waste, its essence long lost to the sands. So will my tale be to those who traveled her barren routes, my footprints as though they never were. Nor will the mountains remember me or the waters of the Wadi Dhana speak of me as they swell the fertile floodplain. Far from the desert, the inexorable silt has its way in the end. It is a mercy.

Across the narrow sea, the pillars of the great temple once bore my name: Bilqis, Daughter of the Moon. Here, to the west, the palace columns bear another: Makeda, Woman of Fire. To those I served as priestess and unifier, I wore the name of my kingdom:

Saba. To the Israelites, I was queen of the spice lands they called
Sheba.

They also called me whore.

The history keepers will no doubt tell their own tale, and the
priests another. It is the men's accounts that seem to survive a
world obsessed with conquest, our actions beyond bedchamber and
hearth remembered only when we leave their obscurity. And so we
become infamous because we were not invisible, the truth of our
lives ephemeral as incense.

It is harder for queens, who have no luxury of meekness. History
does not know how to reconcile our ambition or our power when
we are strong enough to survive it. The priests have no tolerance
for those of us driven by the divine madness of questions. And so
our stories are blackened from the fire of righteous indignation by
those who envy our imagined fornications. We become temptresses,
harlots, and heretics.

I have been all and none of these, depending who tells the tale.

Across the sea in Saba, the mountain rains have ceased by now,
the waters of the mighty Dhana turned to steam on the fields at
dawn. In a few months the northern traders will sail in the quest for
incense and gold . . . bringing with them news of the king who sends
them.

I have not spoken his name in years.

Yes, there is indeed a tale. But if you would have the truth from
me, it begins with this:

I never meant to become queen.

ONE

My mother, Ismeni, was born under the glimmer of the Dog Star, when men become disoriented by its light. They said she enchanted my father, that he made her his consort with a clouded mind. No king would choose a wife from his own tribe when he could strengthen alliance with another.

But I saw the way their gazes followed her whenever she appeared in the palace porticoes, their conversations drifting to suspended silence until she passed from sight. On the rare occasion that she took her seat beside Father's in the Hall of Judgment, the chamber swelled like a tide drawn by the darkened moon. Bronze-skinned with brows like dove's wings and lips for whispering prayers, my mother was the most exquisite thing in all of Saba. The trickle of rain over the highland terraces couldn't match the music of her beaded hems nor the best frankincense of Hadramawt compete with her perfume.

Drowsing on her sofa in the hot afternoon, I would twine my fingers with hers and admire the turquoise of her rings. I hoped my hands and feet would be as slender as hers. It was all I hoped; it never occurred to me that any other aspect of her beauty might be granted a mortal twice on this earth.

Many days we received gifts from my father: rare citrus imported from the north, sweet within their bitter rinds. Songbirds and ivory combs from across the narrow sea. Bolts of fine Egyptian linen, which my mother had made into gowns for me to match her own.

But my greatest treasures were the songs she sang like lullabies murmured against my ear. The ritual prayers she taught me as we knelt before her idols, the sweet waft of incense perfuming her hair. Never once did she chide me for clinging to her when she donned the robes of the thing called "queen." Never once when she went to my father at night was she not curled around me again by morning. Beyond the palace, Saba sprawled from the sheer edge of the coastal range to the foot of the desert waste. But I was content that my world stretched no farther than my mother's chamber.

In the evenings I sat before her jewelry chest and adorned my ears with lapis, my shoulders weighed down with necklaces as she reclined by her table. It was covered in gold, a glowing thing in the low light of the lamp that seemed to gild anything near it—the side of my mother's face, the silver cup in her hand.

And then I would dance as she clapped her hands, bracelets chiming on my ankles—the dance of the monsoon rain running through the wadi ravines, and the gentle sprinkles of summer coaxing millet from the winter-brown earth. Of the highland ibex, my arms curved over my head like great crescent horns, and the lions that stalked them, which always made her laugh. And then she would leap to her feet and join me, the tiers of carnelian beads at her neck jingling with every stamp of her heels.

"You will be more beautiful than I," she said one night after we had fallen onto the cushions.

"Never, Mamma!" The thought was impossible.

She held out her hand and I lay down against her.

"I was never so fair at your age," she said, kissing the top of my head. "But beware, little Bilqis. Beauty is a weapon you can only wield once."

Before I could ask what she meant she slid a heavy bangle off her wrist. It was as wide as my hand and crusted with rubies. "Do you see these stones? They are harder than quartz or emeralds. They do not break under pressure, or soften with age. Let this remind you, my dove, that wisdom is lasting and therefore more precious." She slid the bracelet onto my arm.

"But—"

"Hush now. The Sister Stars are rising—a time for new things." She touched the amulet at my throat, a bronze sun-face inscribed on the back for my protection. "How do you like the idea of a young prince brother?"

I nestled against her, toying with the bangle. My nurse made me burn incense before the alabaster idol of Shams, the sun goddess, every month since I could remember in prayer for this very thing.

"I would like that."

I said it because I knew it would please her. What I did not say was that I would like it far better than a sister, who would vie with me for my mother's attention. That I could share her with a boy knowing he would eventually leave us for my father's side—and the throne.

I vowed to pray daily that my mother's baby would indeed be a boy.

Ten days later my mother suffered a seizure and hit her head on the marble bench inside her bath. That night I was told she had abandoned me for the afterlife, taking my unborn brother with her.

I screamed until I collapsed against the edge of her table. I called them liars and begged to see her, flailing against anyone who tried to touch me. My mother would never leave me! When they took me to her at last, I threw myself over her, clutching her cold neck until they pried me away, strands of her long hair still tangled in my fingers.

After they closed up the royal mausoleum at the temple of the moon god, Almaqah, her face was before me constantly. Sometimes I could smell her, feel the softness of her cheek against mine as I slept. She had not deserted me. I stopped speaking for nearly a year after her death. Everyone thought I had gone mute with grief. But the truth is that I would speak only to her.

I whispered to her as I lay in bed every night until her voice faded the following summer, taking some vital part of me with it. I was six years old.

Hagarlat, my father's second wife, was neither young nor beautiful. But her presence in the palace renewed ties with the tribes of Nashshan to the north, and control of the trade route through the immense Jawf valley. If the dams and canals that channeled the summer monsoons were the lifeblood of Saba, the incense route was her breath, every exhale of her roads profitably laden with frankincense, bdellium, balsam, and myrrh.

I was eight when my half-brother broke the peace of the women's quarter with his angry wail just before the first rains of spring. Father offered gold figurines of Hagarlat and my brother at the temple feast that year, inscribed with the appropriate curses should anyone remove them. I felt betrayed by this blasphemy; my mother was interred on that sacred soil.

But even the appearance of an heir could not appease his council ,for whom my father would never compare to his militant sire. My grandfather Agabos had been a killer of men. Thousands fell to the machine of his ambition as he campaigned to unite the four great kingdoms: Awsan, Qataban, Hadramawt, and Saba to rule them all.

It was Agabos who had married the princess from across the narrow sea through whom his children received the royal darkness of their skin.

But my father, the only one of Agabos' sons to survive his campaigns, was more interested in advancing the worship of the moon god Almaqah throughout the federated kingdom than the boundaries of Saba itself. That year, he appointed himself high priest and presided over temple banquets and ritual hunts until even my young ears could not help but hear the murmured discontent sweeping through the palace halls like a furtive swarm of bees.

I distrusted Hagarlat. Not because she encouraged his zeal, or because she had the face of a mottled camel—or even because she had brought the squalling thing that was my brother into the world—but because she had usurped my mother's chamber along with her jewels and made the name Ismeni seem a distant thing in the minds of everyone but me.

The palace had become foreign to me with my stepmother's servants and uncanny priests filling its halls with their rough tribal tongue. My new relatives and even their slaves looked through me when they weren't ordering me about, and the children I had grown up with had long distanced themselves from me during my year of silence. "Stay away from me!" one of them, a boy named Luban, said when I tried to get him to sneak out to the stables. We had spent hours feeding the camels and hiding from my nurse the year before my mother's death. He was by now several inches taller than I and the laughter in his eyes for me was gone. "Your mother is dead and Hagarlat is queen. You're just a bastard now."

I blinked in astonishment at the scorn on his round face.

And then I blackened his eye.

"I am the daughter of the king!" I shouted, standing over him until someone pulled me away.

I went that evening without supper, but I had no appetite. I had seen young friends of dead unions become the servants of the offspring who replaced them, before. I never thought it would happen to me.

"You are a princess. Do not forget who you are," my nurse said to me that night. But I did not know who I was. Only that she and her daughter, Shara, were all that remained to me now.

Though no one else called me "bastard"—at least to my face—I did not miss the eyes that turned away, the dwindling choice of fabric for my gowns, the gifts from my father that grew more intermittent before they ceased altogether.

One day I strode boldly into Hagarlat's chamber, where she was dictating the celebration to take place for my brother's first birthday, bolts of dyed cloth and rare silk laid out across the settee. "Where are the things my father sends for me?" I demanded. I heard the intake of breath around me, saw from the corner of my eye the horrified expression of my nurse.

Hagarlat turned, astonishment scrawled as clearly across her face as the henna on her forehead. Green jasper dripped from her ears. A thick, gold girdle hung from her burgeoning waist. I thought she looked like a decorated donkey.

"Why, child, has he forgotten you? And he sends so many gifts here. Ah, what a mess your face is." She reached toward my cheek. Just as my lower lip threatened to quiver, I saw it: the ruby bangle that once belonged to my mother—the same one given to me before her death.

"Where did you get that?" I said. My nurse pulled me away, hissing at me to shush. "That is mine!"

"What, this?" Hagarlat said. "Why, if it means so much to you, have it." She took it off and tossed it at me. It fell on the floor at my feet.

"Forgive me, my queen!" my nurse said. I ducked the circle of her arms and snatched the bracelet from the floor. One of the rubies was missing, and I frantically began to search for it until my nurse hauled me from the chamber.

I avoided the palace as much as I could after that. I escaped to the gardens and lost myself by the pools, where I hummed my mother's songs. Lost myself, too, in study with the tutor my father assigned to me, ostensibly to keep me out of trouble.

Within three years I had devoured the poetry of Sumer, the wisdom writings of Egypt, and the creation stories of Babylonia. I called on the palace scribes and read court documents over their shoulders when they would humor me, my father's chief scribe allowing me to admire the proud lines of his script and even producing the battle accounts of my grandfather when I plied him with a jug of wine pilfered from the cellar. I waited anxiously for the traders to return with new treasures of parchment scrolls, tablets, and vellum—even palm stalks etched with their commercial receipts.

For the first time since my mother's passing to the shadow world, I found joy. My toddling brother, Dhamar, would become king. And I would slip past the palace halls with their political squabbles and private intrigues to the stories of others come alive from far-flung places. To escape all . . .

But the gaze of Hagarlat's brother.

Sadiq was a serpent—a fat man with a languid gaze that missed nothing and a knack for convincing my father's advisors of his usefulness. The maidservants and slaves gossiped often about him, saying he had been born under a strong omen—which really meant he had come into considerable wealth with his sister's marriage to my father. It seemed half the palace was taken with him, though I couldn't fathom why.

But Sadiq was taken with only one person: me.

His eyes followed me through the porticoes. I felt the slither of them on my back and shoulders, felt them bore into me anytime I appeared in the alabaster hall.

I wasn't the only one to notice.

"I wouldn't be surprised if Hagarlat asked your father to give you to Sadiq," my nurse said one evening after tut-tutting over my unkempt hair. Shara, the closest thing I ever had to a sister, stared at her mother and then at me. She had grown to resent Hagarlat's family since their arrival in the palace, if only out of loyalty to me.

"He wouldn't," I said.

"And why not?"

"He already has Sadiq's loyalty."

Even then I held no illusions about my future. I would be married to some noble or another in a matter of years.

But not Sadiq.

"Hagarlat's love of her brother is no secret," she said, fiercely combing my hair. "And neither is her ability to secure favors from your father."

"He's not even a tribal chief!"

"He's the queen's brother. He'll be master of waters by year's end, mark me."

I looked at her, incredulous. The master of waters oversaw the distribution of flow from the great wadi dam, the sluices of which irrigated the oases on either side of Marib. It was a position of power over the capital's most influential tribes. Only a fair and respected man could arbitrate the inevitable conflicts over the allocation of waters.

Sadiq was neither.

"He'll do nothing but collect bribes."

"Bilqis!"

"It's true. Sadiq is a worm sucking the tit of his sister!"

My nurse drew a sharp breath and was, I knew, on the verge

of warning me to prudence. But before she got a word out, Shara dropped the bronze mirror that she had been polishing. It fell with a thud to the carpet.

"Clumsy girl!" her mother snapped. Shara didn't seem to hear; her wide eyes were fastened on the floor.

My nurse hesitated and then gasped and dropped the handful of my hair she had begun to plait. She swept aside, her head bowed so low that I thought her neck would break.

I slowly turned on my stool.

There, in the arched doorway of our shared chamber, stood Hagarlat. The hem of her veil was pinned back from her face, a rainfall of gold fell from each ear. Two of her women stood in the antechamber beyond. I rose to my feet.

For a moment, neither of us moved. Nor did I move even to bow when she walked quietly toward me. She stopped just before the mirror and bent to retrieve it as though it were a wayward toy. Appraising it once, she took the cloth from Shara's startled hand, passed it over the surface, and then handed the mirror to me.

"So you may see more clearly," she said. And then she walked out, dropping the cloth behind her.

The instant she was gone, my nurse and Shara turned toward me as one, their faces pale, nostrils flared with fear. I didn't ask how the door to the outer chamber had come open. It didn't matter.

I was betrothed to Sadiq within a week.

I threw myself at my father's feet in the audience room of his private chamber—the place where he might be not a king but a man.

"I beg you, do not give me to him," I cried. I clasped the fine leather of his sandals, pushed up the hem of his robe to touch my forehead to the top of them.

"Bilqis," he said with a sigh. I raised my head even as he looked away. The lines around his eyes seemed more pronounced in the low lamplight of the chamber, the characteristic kohl missing from the rim of his lower lashes. "Can you not do this thing? For Saba—for Almaqah, over all?"

"What do I care for any god?" I said. "The gods do what they will!"

"Are you a goddess, that you, too, should do what you will?" he said softly.

"She did this because she heard me speak ill of Sadiq. I repent of it!" I dropped my head, clutched at his feet. "I will apologize. I will serve in her chamber. But please do not do this!"

He reached for me, to draw me up. "Hagarlat would see our tribal bonds strengthened. And why not? Your brother will be king. Do you really think the queen so petty?"

I jerked away from him. "Do you not see that she hates me?" I stumbled back, away from the low dais and into the pool of lantern light before the throne. I opened my mouth to renew my appeal but stopped when I saw how he stared at me.

For a moment his mouth worked, though no words came out. There was a pallor to his skin that hadn't been there before.

"Ismeni . . . ?" he said faintly. His hand lifted, fingers trembling in the air.

"Father?"

I went to him again but when I tried to clasp his knees, he flinched away.

"Father, it is I, Bilqis!"

"It is late," he said, eyes turned toward the latticed window. Torchlight glowed up from the royal gardens below.

"Please, my king. I was your daughter once. If you have any love for me—"

"It is settled." His voice was strained. The lamp flickered and I saw it then on his face: the grimace of the years since my mother's death. Love eclipsed by the dark moon of pain.

Sadiq seemed to be everywhere after that. He stood in the porticoes when I went out to the gardens. He loitered near the fountains as I went about my lessons. And though he did not approach me beneath the gaze of the ubiquitous guards, his eyes were as ever-present as the scorching sun.

I quit attending meals in the hall. I began to avoid my lessons. The sight of him, from the way he wore his ornamental dagger high up in his belt as though it were his very manhood to the number of rings on his fingers, repulsed me. I would feel different in time, my nurse assured me. But my only comfort was that I would never be alone with him until we married in three years.

Sadiq, however, was not a man of honor.

I was twelve the first time he laid hands on me.

The soft scrape of the door woke me. I was alone and at first glance by light of the waning lamp, I thought it was Baram, the eunuch. He, too, was paunched around the middle and soft-chinned, and the only man allowed in the women's quarter.

And then I saw the gleam of the dagger's hilt.

He crossed the room in three strides and I bolted up, screaming for Baram. Sadiq struck me hard across the face.

I fought him as his weight fell on me, the scabbard of his dagger digging into my ribs, but he was twice my size. "Baram and the women are attending my sister, who is even now miscarrying your new brother," he said hotly against my ear. He was putrid with perfume and wine. "And none of them will stand against the new master of waters."

His hand closed around my throat. His other tugged up my gown. I clawed at him until I nearly lost consciousness and then squeezed shut my eyes.

I lay in bed the next three days.

My nurse called for the physician, who could find no fever in me. Only the stupefied torpor of one who no longer wished to live in her own skin. Sadiq had managed to leave no mark on my neck or face—just the scrapes of his rings against my thighs.

I wanted to rise only to walk into the desert waste until the sands consumed me, but had no will even for that. As night came on the fourth evening, I called for my nurse. I would ask for the deadly nightshade that Hagarlat used to dilate her pupils. Or for the honey of rhododendron nectar.

But she just blinked at me and said, "Why, child? Why do you want these things? You are beautiful already and such honey will only make you ill."

I couldn't bring myself to give voice to the words.

She gave me qat to chew instead, but even the stimulant leaves would not rouse me from my bed.

The second time Sadiq forced himself on me, I said, "My father will have you killed. I will accuse you before the entire council!"

"Will he? They will ask you, 'Did you cry out? Who heard you? Why did you not come immediately to your king father the first time?' When I claim you tried to seduce me and voice concern about your honor, whom do you think they will believe?" And I knew he was right: he was brother to the queen and master of waters. I was the daughter of a woman born under a bad omen, too often alone.

"When they send for the midwife and she finds you not intact, I will have no choice but to publicly set you aside for the sake of my honor, and the queen's."

I should have been filled with righteous fury. I should have accused him before my father if only to escape him—and any other man, as no man would marry me without a hefty bribe after such a public scandal. Instead, I was overcome with shame like the rot of worms beneath the skin.

I begged Shara not to leave my bed at night. But she could not deny the queen if called for. Sadiq raped me twice more in the months that followed, even as clouds gathered over the highland terraces and the first gusts of the coming season shook the trees on the hills.

The rains came and I kept to my bed. The torrents swept down the hills through the afternoon, carrying trees and earth and any building in their way into the wadi ravines. At last I slept through the night, exhausted by my vigilance of the weeks prior. For now, at least, I was safe; the master of waters was away from the palace, monitoring the floods and the condition of the canals with a labor force ready to repair any breach in the sluices.

Sometime before dawn, I rose and walked to the window. I was a wisp beneath my shift, having lost the young curves I had only begun to come into. Clasping the sill, I threw open the latticed shutter. The first servants were in the yard; I could make out their shadowed forms against the faint hue of dawn. As I had on so many nights since my mother's passing, I sought out the Sister Stars. But that morning the moon obscured one of them. I stood at the window long after the sky had brightened and the stars began to fade, watching it pass before their company.

For the first time in years, I prayed. Not to Shams, the sun, who had failed to protect my mother . . . but to Almaqah, the moon god who had received her.

Save me or let me die.

That was all. I slid the ruby bracelet, the most precious thing I owned, from my arm and laid it on the sill before the fading crescent.

Later that day, men came rushing into the courtyard, their shouts rising to the open window of my chamber. Not long after, a great, singular wail went up from the hall of women, so loud that it carried to my chamber.

My nurse brought the news an hour later: one of the sluice gates had buckled. Sadiq had been carried away in the flood.

I raised my eyes heavenward.

I am yours.

Sadiq's body was never found. A month after his death, Hagarlat accused me before my father. Her face was drawn, her clothing hanging on a frame turned gaunt. I had grown into my own gowns once more, as though I had acquired the lushness she had lost in her grief.

"That girl is a curse to this house." Her voice broke. "She cursed my brother as she has cursed me!"

"My queen, you are overwrought," my father said, sounding weary.

"Am I? My brother—her betrothed—is dead and I have miscarried twice since coming into your household. Her own mother gave birth to only one girl and died with your son in her belly. I tell you that girl brings death to everyone near her!"

When my father finally looked at me, I knew he saw the shadow of the woman he had married not for treaties but for love. And I understood at last why he had not sought me in my grief, or summoned me in the years of my withdrawal since her death.

"Wife," he said, lowering his head.

"You will send her away or I will leave this court and take my son with me lest she kill him, too, as she did her own mother and unborn brother! My mother had seven children by the time she was my age, and my sister five sons. But not once in four years have I carried another to term. Would you cost us the lives of our other unborn children as well?"

I turned on her with a hiss. I was like the branch, no longer green, that splinters beneath the weight of a single bird. I was prepared to be reckless, to curse her, her son, and every hoped-for issue of her womb, and every tenant of her tribe with their camels and goats down to the last rabid dog.

But the breath I had drawn to curse her came out as a soft chuff of wonder instead. For one insane moment, I nearly laughed.

There was nothing she could do to me, nothing that could be taken from me that had not already been taken or that I had not been willing to shed—down to my very life—myself.

I, who had no power, did not need to utter a word. She had lost all supremacy over me. And in that moment, she knew it, too. I watched the color drain from her cheeks.

"Yes," I said to my father. "Send me away. Let me go across the narrow sea to the land of your mother's mother before you. And give me priests and offerings for the temple of Almaqah there, and I will take them in your name."

Was that relief that flitted across his face?

I could not begrudge him his quick agreement. Almaqah had been his salvation, too.

That fall I boarded a ship with my tutor, a retinue of priests, new ministers for the growing colony, and a wealth of incense, offerings, and gifts for the temple in Punt. I was not allowed to bring my nurse or Shara with me—Hagarlat had seen to that—and so bid them both tearful goodbyes, kissing their necks and commending them to the gods.

I was resolved that I would never return to the palace at Marib with its dark corridors and darker memories. That I would live my life in Punt—and in peace—all my days.

But Almaqah, once summoned, had other plans for me.

TWO

I had been dreaming of the fog that descends over the highlands before the monsoon rains. Fog like milk stirred by the first gusts of the coming storm before the dull roar of the flood rushes down the mountain. A flood brimming with froth, capricious as its change-ling color—first white, then yellow as it fills with silt. Waters deadly enough to carry away a camel or even a house as they rage into the wadis toward the sluices and the waiting fields below.

"Makeda."

I opened my eyes, stared up through the fine gauze of my bed toward the ceiling. Serpents of lamplight played about its tiles, cast-ing shadows through the canopy meant to keep out the relentless mosquitoes.

The cicadas were singing. Even with the shutters closed I could hear their deafening chorus. In the place between the dream world and this one, they might even be taken for incessant sheets of rain, lulling one back to sleep . . .

A kiss lit against my temple, soft as a moth. I reached up, eyes closed, to catch at a tendril of hair, twine it around my fin-ger, hold it against my nose. A warm knee slid against me. The last of the incense on the burner had gone out, leaving only the sachet of sheets musted with desire spent hours ago in the spring heat.

"Makeda." Whispered now. It was the name given me by my grandmother's family—a name I had embraced upon coming to Punt and leaving the ravaged Bilqis behind.

I pulled him toward me, searched for that salty neck. He groaned, held for a moment as though he would speak, and then covered me.

Even then I thought I heard rain, falling in drumming pulse and then in thundering flood. Until we fell still and I drowsed again.

"Makeda."

I sighed, the deep breath of the contented.

"You must wake."

I opened heavy eyes as he leaned upon his elbow and smoothed my damp forehead, the black fall of his hair framing his face. Maqar, whose noble father had served mine on royal council. Maqar, the warrior who had come two years ago bringing with him more Sabaean settlers to work the gold mine and bolster the garrison.

Maqar, my love.

I drew him down against me with a sleep-laden sigh, crossed my arms around his back. "It is still night."

"Yes," he murmured against my cheek, the short hairs of his beard tickling me. This time when he pulled away, I couldn't coax him back. "Come, Princess."

A rustle of bedsheets and I was alone on the mattress.

"Where?"

We had left the palace in the middle of the night countless times, sneaking away like children to bathe in the garden pools by starlight or make love in the orchards until the first light of dawn as curious hoopoe birds watched from the moringa trees.

"A great new adventure."

"Can't you see you've exhausted me?"

He laughed softly. "I thought it was the other way around."

"You are the urn that never empties."

"And you are the well that never dries. But come now."

I lolled onto my side. Standing like that he might have been a bronze statue in any temple alcove. By every known and unknown god, he was beautiful.

"Tell me you love me." But when the corner of my mouth turned up in a smile, he did not reciprocate.

"You know I do." But a strange shadow drifted through his eyes. Was it a trick of the lamp, sputtering in the last of its oil, or had the lines across his forehead deepened?

The bed curtain fell behind him. He began to gather his clothes.

I gave a quizzical laugh. "What adventure is this that will not wait until tomorrow night?"

"You will see."

A soft scrape sounded outside my chamber. The eunuch given me by my great-aunt always slept outside my upper-story door. Why did he stir at this hour?

I pushed up on my elbows, fully awake now.

Maqar returned, my embroidered caftan in one hand, his other extended to me.

I frowned and rose from bed.

"Quickly," he said, stepping out through the curtain again. I watched as he wrapped and belted his sarong over those lean hips. When he reached for his sword I knew we would not be bathing. I slipped into the gown.

Maqar came and knelt with my slippers, sliding one and then the other onto my feet. Just before he rose, he looked up at me. Those were the same eyes that had followed me as though I was the sun itself when he first arrived to captain the garrison—and soon after, the palace guard. But tonight there was more, some strange hope within them.

"My love, what is this?"

"Come." He stood, and handed me my veil.

Outside, Yafush was not only awake but waiting, torch in hand, firelight glancing off his rich Nubian skin, the gold ring glowing in his ear. I glanced from him to Maqar. Since when did my lover act in concert with my bodyguard?

Suddenly I wondered if Maqar had arranged to secretly marry me this night. How many times had we talked about that very thing in our garden bed beneath the stars?

A princess did not choose her own husband. But neither had my father, in the six years of my exile, made any other arrangement. For all I knew, Sadiq had shared the secret of my ruin before his death. For all I knew, Hagarlat had orchestrated the entire thing. The thought had occurred to me.

Maqar, my healer, knew I had not come virgin to his bed. Nor had he ever asked about my first tearful flight from it. When I went into his arms at last, I found myself grateful for all that had conspired to bring me here, the beauty of these days far outweighing the horror of those nights. Maqar's noble ties were wasted on me, an exile. And I could not win him favors—Hagarlat's kinsmen had all but taken over the council and Saba's most prestigious positions. But he would never want for wealth through me, here in Punt. And I would not want for love.

All of these thoughts occurred within the space of my first three steps beyond my chamber.

A secret wedding. I smiled to myself. No more questions, then.

I followed them down the corridor to the ground floor courtyard and out through the colonnade. The gardens were lit, cicadas in full symphony. I reached for Maqar's hand. He lifted my fingers to his lips without looking at me.

I glanced sidelong at Yafush. One might not know at first sight of his muscled arms and impassive face that he was not a man intact. But what had Maqar said to him, that his brow was so somber? Was this not a joyous occasion? Why then did neither of them look glad to lead me where they did?

Something was wrong.

By the time we passed through the smaller north gate, my heart was drumming against my ribs and I had no more romantic notions about moringa trees or weddings.

I refused to go farther.

"Where are you taking me? Tell me now."

Maqar turned, and for a moment I didn't recognize him. I had never seen him without a smile for me playing in his eyes if not on his lips. But now in the torchlight—this was not the face of a man about to marry his lover, but a man wrestling with something within himself.

"To the temple. A ship arrived yesterday at port."

A ship? It was late into the season for ships, even from Egypt. "What has that got to do with us?"

"It is better that you see and hear for yourself."

I looked from him to the rocky plain, its uneven grade flinty by moonlight, the faint glow of torches on the hill beyond snakelike along the temple path.

"Makeda," he said, and hesitated. When I turned back, anguish was plain upon his face. "Only remember: I have never played you false."

I stared at him, amazed by this statement.

"I think you'd best go to the temple, Princess," Yafush said.

I glanced between the two of them, but they would say no more. "Neither of you will speak? Then let us be done with this charade!"

I gathered the hem of my gown and struck out ahead of them, heart pounding in the cage of my chest.

I ascended the temple path, past the stone steles of my ancestors, my footfalls too loud against the drone of insects, each step both too swift and slow at once.

A figure waited atop the hill, black against the evening sky. A priest, by his robe. The chief priest by the glow of the moon against his shaven head. Was he party to this as well? He raised his palm in blessing as we arrived, his voice gravel against the night.

"Princess."

The fortress temple rose up behind him, its ibex friezes shrouded in shadow. The carved wooden doors lay open. Torchlight shone from within like a great, glowing eye.

What waited through those doors here, in the dead of night?

When I looked at Maqar, his only response was a silent nod. And I understood that whatever waited inside, I must meet it first.

For a wild moment I actually entertained the thought of running back down the path—not to the palace, or even the gardens, but the dark field of steles. There, at least, I need only confront the scorpions. But it was as though the act of coming here had barred the way back already.

I lifted my gaze to the moon, full and high in its zenith.

And then I walked into the temple.

Five forms stood within the inner court. I blinked against the torchlight as their faces coalesced from the shadows.

Hassat, head of the council in Punt and distant kin to me. Beside him, Nabat, captain of the garrison. Neither gave any indication he had stirred from his bed this night, if he had gone to it at all. Next to Nabat stood three men in Sabaean dress, their daggers tucked in their belts against their bellies, swords on their hips.

"Princess," Hassat said, inclining his head.

"Councilman Hassat," I stammered. Even without knowing what to expect, I was surprised to see him waiting here, apparently for me.

"I apologize for summoning you here like this."

I clasped my hands together to stop their shaking.

Hassat moved toward me, firelight playing over the severe panes of his cheeks. He indicated the three others. "These men have come to you at great risk."

"Indeed—" I paused to clear my throat, which had all but closed up. "Indeed, if you have come from Saba. It is nearly time for the rains." Only a fool crossed the sea during the rainy season . . . or a man on desperate errand.

"Princess," one of the others said. "I come from the noble tribe of Aman."

"Of the great Jawf Valley," I said slowly, the place name having become foreign to my tongue.

"A formidable clan with ties to the powerful traders of Gab-aan," Hassat said. "And this man is Khalkharib, blood kin of your father's most senior councilman, who walks now in the shadow world. And this one is Yatha, kin to your father's councilman Abamar."

A trickle of sweat slid between my breasts. The tribal lands of these three men formed a nearly perfect north–south line through Saba between the mountain range to the west and desert to the east.

"I have not laid eyes on your kinsmen in many years," I said carefully. "Though I know my father has trusted them well. But what do you want with me?"

"Plague has come with the traders' caravans to Marib," Hassat said.

"I'm sorry to hear it."

For a moment, no one spoke.

I looked from one of them to the other in rising confusion.

At last, the one called Yatha stepped toward me.

"Princess, sickness has taken the palace. Your king father is ill. He was ailing before even this. We have not known since we left whether he lives or dies."

I staggered a step. But when I turned toward Maqar, who had entered behind me, I spun back.

"The king was alive when you left. Then why have you come? Better that you had waited until there was news of my father, whether he lived or died!"

"The monsoon is coming. We dare not wait."

"And so you come to say only that he is ill?"

But no. They would not have risked the crossing only for that.

Did I imagine it or had the cicadas fallen silent? Was there less magic in the shadows of these walls, as though the sanctuary itself had become mere limestone and mortar at the arrival of this envoy?

"There is more," the man from Aman said. "Hagarlat has seen to it that her tribe-kin occupy every position of power."

"I am aware."

"But there are many tribes, ours included, who will not stomach the rise of the Nashshans and their allies. The king is advanced in age. Whether he lives days or even a year more, there will soon be war for the throne."

"But my brother—"

"Is only ten and a Nashshan pawn."

"And yet he is the heir!"

Maqar came to stand at my side. Very quietly, he said, "Makeda . . . he is not the only heir."

I stared at him as my skin went cold in the stifling air of the sanctum court.

"The tribes of Aman to the north and many as far south as Hadramawt are ready to support your claim," Yatha said.

I heard these words without comprehending them.

"As will Punt." This from Nabat, silent until now. "Who would see the granddaughter of Agabos on the federated throne."

Is this how it is done?

"My brother is the grandson of Agabos," I heard myself say. "Why would Punt support the claim of one sibling over another?"

"Hagarlat has no loyalty to Punt and we have none to her," Hassat said. "She cares only for the gold and goods we export and the tariffs her kinsmen reap from them as they travel the trade route north through Nashshan lands."

"But my father—"

"Forgive me, Princess," Khalkharib, the tallest of them, said, "but your king father may even now lie dead. If you do not return, others will assert their right—by force if not by bloodline. No one will expect your return until after the rains. If we move quickly, we will prevent war and secure your throne."

"Saba has not had a ruling queen in generations!"

"Almaqah willing, she will have one again. Our tribes are ready. We have prepared for this moment for years."

An hour ago I had been drunk with sleep and the contentment of life in Punt, and Saba had been a distant thing, the torrent of her rains remembered only in dreams. But now it came to me: The strife of the northern tribes in their struggle against Nashshan's increasing influence. My own tribe's desire to retain power and the southern bid for new favor. How swiftly they moved! And for what?

The promise of future favors owed or hope of a marriage alliance with the throne?

Then I understood. They did not mean for Saba to have a ruling queen, but for its queen to bring one of them to kingship.

And here stood Maqar . . . conveniently sent to me two years ago by his father with a company of warriors.

I stared at him with new eyes and he shook his head just perceptibly. And though I heard his unvoiced thought, I saw only a stranger wearing that beloved face.

Who am I, if not his lover?

A queen?

A pawn.

"My men assemble at the port even now," Nabat was saying to the others, and then they were talking all at once about provisions for the return.

"My father may yet live!" I said, cutting them off.

Khalkharib glanced at me as though just remembering I was there.

"By the time we return, Princess, he may not. And Hagarlat and her Nashshan councilors will have seized the federated throne and begun to raise force enough to defend it. The monsoons are coming. Almaqah has smiled upon us. But we must leave immediately."

That night, I railed against Maqar.

"What else have you kept from me? What other schemes have you worked behind my back these last two years?"

He caught my fists when I came flying at him, and pulled me against his chest. Zabib, my maid, flinched as though to make herself unseen even as she scurried about the chamber packing my jewelry, my gowns, my precious wealth of scrolls. Dawn was breaking, the morning sky ominous. Outside my door palace slaves and armed men carried my belongings to the convoy waiting in the palace courtyard—an escort arranged I knew not how long ago, and without my knowledge.

"You call my brother a Nashshan pawn. And yet here you are—you and these men come to summon me after plotting behind my back for years! Any one of you might have been found out at any time. You do not know Hagarlat as I do! How long has my life been in danger, and I, none the wiser?"

"Makeda," he said urgently, holding me tight. "Every man here has been sworn to your protection. The garrison. My men here in the palace. Yafush, who sleeps outside the door of your chamber—"

"You, who sleep in it. What a fool I've been! And to think that for a moment tonight as you took me from this chamber I thought you meant to marry me in secret!" I laughed, the sound cruel, but then covered my eyes in angry humiliation.

"I have dreamed of nothing else."

"Even now, how sincere your declarations ring," I said bitterly.

"Because they are true! But how could I marry you, knowing that this day would come—even as I wished it never would?" His hands fell away from me. "How could I?"

"You've lied to me all this time!"

"No. Almaqah knows I would marry you this instant if you would have me."

"How convenient that you then would become king. Tell me, was that the intent of your noble father all this while? Did he instruct you in the way you should seduce me as well?"

"Makeda." His expression was anguished. "Please . . ."

"Tell me that wasn't his design the entire time, as he plotted with the others to see me to the throne."

"The allies had long made a pact that there would be no offer of marriage treaty, lest their motives come under suspicion by Hagar-lat. Not until—"

I slapped him. After a stunned instant, I slapped him again.

"How clever everyone has been! And I thought myself forgotten all these years until tonight. And without even an hour's warning from you. For all the nights I gave myself to you, you might have at least done me that service in return."

He turned on me, voice raised. "How should I have told you? Can you not see that I have been torn? How should I make you believe me? Tell me, and I will do it!"

"It's too late. And now those men come to collect me and I am to go obediently at their summons? Well I won't do it!"

I yelled at Zabib to stop her packing, to put my things away.

All around me, the sanctuary of this chamber—a place of refuge, study, and peace, and later, of evenings laden with the discovery of love—felt laid bare. Here, I had wept in Maqar's arms the first time he had come to me, not as a thief, but as one to heal with word and caress and sigh. Here, I had hoped to spend the rest of my life in languid contentment poring over my ever-expanding library of scrolls, away from the specters of my past.

And now here it all was, disassembling before my eyes as the mountains of Saba loomed in the distance.

Humiliating tears slipped down my cheeks, hot and salty as the long Red Sea.

"Makeda . . ." He took me by the wrists. "My love."

"Don't speak to me of love. I beg you. Give me that mercy."

He pulled me toward him with desperate strength. "Tell me what you would have me do!"

I wanted to tell him to go—to go and return across the sea with them and leave me in peace. But even then I couldn't bear the thought of these walls without him. I had welcomed exile because it was safe. But it had been beautiful because of him.

"Send these men away," I said. "Live with me here, as we did before. Let it all be as it was. If you are true, stay with me though I will never be queen."

"How long will I be able to keep you safe when another is on the throne—another whose first priority will be to hunt down any competitor for it? Did you truly think your life would be safe if your brother wore the crown?"

"Then let us steal into the countryside and forget that we ever slept within the walls of any palace! We'll grow an orchard and plant fields. We will live our days in peace . . ." But even as I said it, I knew my conviction was as false as the illusion of my freedom all these years. That I pleaded not with him, but with the god who had freed me once from Saba and now cruelly called me back.

"I can't return. I cannot. I cannot . . ." I covered my eyes with shaking hands, not knowing if I said it to him, or to the god.

He took me by the shoulders. "If you wanted, I would run away into the countryside and live out my days with you in hiding. Say the word, and I will do it. But you would never be safe. We would never be in peace. We would live our lives looking always over our shoulders and you would grow to resent me."

"Never."

"Yes. Because the only place you will ever be safe is on the throne. And a day will come when you will wonder if your true place was where the gods had pointed. Do you think it is a mistake that you are firstborn to a king? That your parents came from the same royal clan? Do you not see you were meant for more? So you will not be a pawn. Then don't let them make you one! You are smarter than they are, more learned than any sage. And you loved Saba once."

Yes. I had. Before my mother left me for the afterlife and I gave up my voice. Before Sadiq poisoned my chambers and Punt became my sanctuary if only because it was not the Saba I had come to know.

This morning I had dreamed of her rains. In days to come, I would wonder if it had been an omen. I had never been able to banish the past but had lived always in fear of its tendrils, even as I invited traders from the ports to dine with me in exchange for their stories. From the safety of Punt's halls, I had followed the exploits of the council, the shifting politics of the tribes, and news of the growing cult of Almaqah and the temples my father built in his name. Almaqah, the god of the thundering bull and lunar cycle to whom I had sworn myself so many years ago.

Saba had found me in my dreams. Saba had found me here. I might have left Saba, but it had never left me. And now I saw that a part of me, more wise and seeing than my waking mind, had prepared for this future all along.

Somewhere outside the shrill song of a flycatcher caught the air. I closed my eyes.

"You asked what I would have you do."

"Yes. Name it!"

"If I become queen, I will never marry you. To marry you would be to wonder all my days. I want something of certainty in this world. And so you will not be my husband, and never my king. Now what is your answer?"

"That you will be a better queen than the kings before you."

I dropped my head to Maqar's shoulder. His arms closed around me more gently than before. At last, he exhaled a long and shaky breath as though he had held it all this time.

"Stay with me," I said.

"I will serve you all my life."

An hour later I walked out of that chamber, I thought, forever. I was not a queen. Not yet. But I was no longer the princess I had been. That morning I boarded a ship on the edge of the narrow sea and assumed again the name by which Saba knew me: Bilqis.

And so my days of obscurity came to an end. I was eighteen years old.

THREE

When I closed my eyes, I thought I could smell the frankincense weeping from the trees. It was said the perfume of Saba wafted out to sailors on the Red Sea and throughout the southern gulf. Here, in the Markha Valley, one could almost believe it.

"Princess."

I opened my eyes on the tents and camels of twelve hundred tribesmen sprawled near the edge of the great waste.

Overhead, the sky was churning. And yet, the heavens had held. It was a sign from Almaqah, they had said days ago on the southern coastal plain. There my priest, Asm, who had come with me from Punt, had sacrificed a camel—one we could not afford, and therefore one Almaqah must honor.

Maqar, mounted at my side, pointed. Riders, on the northern edge of the valley.

"Come," I said, refastening my veil. I guided my camel down the ridge.

To leave or enter Saba was to risk all—through treacherous mountains after the hot hell of the coastal plain, only to be laughed at by baboons. Through an ocean of sand in the vast eastern waste, graveyard to innumerable would-be invaders. The only traversable way in was from the north through the oases of the Jawf, and then only if one had kin-ties to the tribes or riches to trade . . . or south from the seaport through the valleys, and then only if one had a ship. It was never the sea that safeguarded the cradle of Saba—along with her wealth—but always her mountains and sands.

I had wept on landing in the southern port. Not in relief that our company had made the crossing before the rains or that we had been met by the southern tribe of Urramar with much-needed supplies and camels. But because I had not thought I would ever be glad to see Saba's high mountain ranges again.

Maqar was right. I had loved Saba once. And now, like a lover returned, I was broken at the sight of her.

But my return was not without cost. Sadiq came to me in nightmares for the first time in years as we entered the mountain passes of Qataban. I tossed in a sweat, shuddering beneath my woolen mantle in the late spring chill.

"Get out!" I said the night Maqar woke and tried to comfort me. I had followed him from the tent moments later, retching in the dirt.

Hagarlat haunted me through the high plateaus, and my father's morose face down the descent to the great Baihan Valley. And though Maqar forgave me my outburst, neither did he touch me.

I was beside myself. Punt was a shadow land beyond the narrow sea and Saba had greeted me with demons. And so I plunged forward, the only direction available to me now: north, toward the capital.

Just as we reached the edge of camp, something sailed over the rim of the mountains against the brooding sky. I squinted at the languid flight of a vulture as clouds unfurled overhead.

In the camp, tribal accents punctuated the air, sharp and guttural as the thunder rolling beyond the horizon. Chieftains, in urgent conversation under the canopy of the command tent.

Lightning flashed, shocking the landscape. In the valley itself, the air was eerily still.

One by one, the nobles fell silent as I approached the tent. Among them, a new man perhaps a few years younger than my father, in rapid conversation with Khalkharib just an instant ago.

Twelve sets of kohl-rimmed eyes assessed me at once. Did I waver as I walked toward them, did my step falter? How did they perceive me, these men who knew nothing of me but my bloodline? Did any one of them see in me a queen—or only a means to their own power?

I looked at each of them in turn, the newcomer last of all.

"This is Wahabil," Khalkharib said. "His tribe is kin-tribe to your own." He had not needed to tell me; I recognized the old sunburst of the goddess Shams on his dagger's scabbard immediately. I greeted him as kin, touching my veiled nose to his. He was stocky, no taller than I, with uncharacteristically light eyes and a wispy beard that did not disguise his jowls.

"My men wait in the next valley," Wahabil said.

"Have you brought word of my kinsmen? I had thought to receive—"

"A rider has arrived from Marib," Khalkharib interrupted.

I stared at him before slowly turning to Wahabil.

My heart became a cudgel.

"The king your father is dead," Wahabil said. "Hagarlat has set her son on the alabaster throne. We refuse him allegiance. Your kinsmen gather at Sirwah even now."

Silence.

Wahabil slowly leaned forward, hands on his knees. "Hail, Queen."

Khalkharib perfunctorily followed suit, along with Nabat and the man from Aman. And then Yatha, and the chieftains of Urramar and Awsan, and another from eastern Hadramawt who had joined us on the coastal plain, and four others whose tribes I had suddenly forgotten. One by one, they fell forward, their murmurs filling the too still air.

Beyond the canopy, those near enough to see and hear shouted and came to fall forward in groups and then in waves, their murmurs rising to the ominous sky, seeding the clouds with my name.

Hail, Queen! Queen Bilqis.

I instinctively turned toward Maqar, but found him bent nearly to the dry wadi floor, the neck I had adored so many nights bowed low.

The gust came, sweeping through the valley, sending the canopy shuddering as the sky broke to the south.

"Gather the men," Khalkharib said, over the oncoming storm. "We march on Marib."

That night, the voice of my mother, lost so many years ago, returned. Just a croon at first, in my sleeping mind's ear. A song like wind through the tent flap, the trill of rain against the rumble of a highland storm. It was the lullaby of Saba, of her mountains and ringed plateaus, the music of her terraces in the spring deluge trickling down to her fields and orchards.

It was my mother's song. And it was mine.

In the Baihan Valley we gained men from the tribes of Kahar and Awsan. We moved swiftly, skirting oases already populated with water hens; Hagarlat had no doubt summoned her allies weeks ago and word of my arrival would soon reach her spies, if it had not already. Word had already traveled between outlying settlements, from which tribesmen came to eat at our fires or summon us to theirs for "fat and meat," curious for news or a glimpse of the returning princess, the would-be queen. The richest of them slaughtered goat and lamb—sometimes up to a dozen animals to feed a portion of our number even as they ate nothing themselves—one of them sending his four sons to join us in the morning, yelling, "Remember your servant Ammiyatha! Remember Ammiyatha with favor!" Meanwhile, smaller wadis had become watercourses nearly overnight from the lowland rains, rivers running toward the waiting fields where workers labored to shore up breaches in canals.

We were followed by widows with naked children, old men with bent backs and one tooth left in their heads, boys wandering with young, hungry siblings, their loincloths no more than tatters. They, too, came to eat by our fires, these poorest and forgotten kinsmen of tribes afflicted by sickness or wells gone dry through winter. I assumed each time that they were given something to eat—a bowl of frothing camel's milk, at the least—but when I saw several men turn away a young mother and her children, I was incensed.

"Saba is flowing with frankincense worth its weight in gold," I fumed at Wahabil. "How is it possible that anyone living in the envy of nations goes hungry?" I went after the young woman and her children and brought them to my tent.

"The men turn them away as their supplies run thin," Maqar said to me later, in low tones. "Already some of the men of Urramar have had to slaughter a camel."

"Give her my portion if no one will feed her, and one of my blankets as well."

Despite my words, I did not go hungry that night. I later learned Wahabil and Maqar both had given their food to the woman, who slipped away before dawn.

The initial trek inland had felt like one unending cycle of back strain from riding and stony beds within a snarling landscape of camels hobbled and couched for sleep. I failed to feel in those first, stunned days more than the mounting spring heat beneath the sti-fling clouds, the hardness of the saddle, the chill through my cloak at night. And the flies, which were relentless, biting camel and human alike.

But as the sky descended over the western highlands, heavy and pregnant with rain, I realized that I no longer fell into the sleep of the exhausted when I lay down, but lay awake listening for the cough of nearby cheetahs in the evening, the violent squawk of the peregrine at dawn.

And as the distance to Marib tightened like an invisible cord, I found myself strained not by the weeks of travel behind me, but the crucial days before me.

If we were defeated, I knew very well what would become of me. These kinsmen and allies staked their own lives in ready gamble for the benefits they might reap. But what of my priest, Asm, who had come with his acolytes at my request? Of my eunuch, Yafush, who slept outside my tent, and Maqar, who discreetly joined me within it? What end awaited them if we failed?

Almaqah deliver us all.

But it was not just the question of our fates afield. I had already been fighting, since the shores of Punt, a war of oppositions. Gone these six years from Saba, I was a queen who did not know her ene-mies or the true loyalty of her allies. A queen whose nobles meant to broker power in my council until one of them married me and I was queen in name only.

I had had to fight even to ride alongside them if only to be privy to their discussions—to ride at all, in fact, threatening to set fire to the litter brought for me. Clearly, I had been meant to accompany them like the sacred ark my grandfather's army bore into battle—a symbol by which those who carried it proclaimed sovereignty . . . but a thing with no power of its own.

Almaqah had called me back to Saba. Almaqah must make me clever.

I spoke seldom but listened to everything. I learned quickly who was—and was not—among my expected list of allies. Who had the best spies. Which nobles the others looked to first. Whose men had the best camels, most kin-ties, deadliest feuds.

Thread by thread, I began to decipher the lacework of loyalties, ambition, and grudges that had knit me at its center years before my knowledge. With every company of tribesmen who joined us, I did the thing I had done now for years: I studied. I learned. Whom I must exercise the greatest influence over. Whose backing I required before all others. Whom I could trust. Whom I must not.

But knowledge did not lessen the nobles' distinct forbearance whenever I approached or smooth their stilted answers even as they bowed their heads—except when it came to the fluent reminders of their contribution to my cause.

"The tribesmen of Kahar come to you with axe and spear and sword," their chieftain said in his accented Sabaean. "Six hundred men I bring you. A hundred animals will we sacrifice to Almaqah for your health when we return to our territory and you are queen. And you must not forget us either."

I felt by now that what had started as blood right had become a long list of bartered favors to the point that I had never felt so indebted in my life.

"Yafush," I whispered, late one night, rolling up the corner of my black tent flap. In this sea of men sleeping by dying fires and couched camels, my tent was practically indistinguishable from nearly fifty others like it.

The eunuch, who faced always away, did not turn. "You are rest-less, Princess."

I lay down, the broad slope of his shoulder like the western range against the stars. He never strayed far from my side, standing over me even when I squatted to relieve myself beneath the privacy of my cloak—the same way any Sabaean man did, which Yafush, the eunuch, never failed to call womanly.

"I see the way they look at me," I said softly. "I am a thing—a crown to be worn on another head."

"That is good."

"Why?"

"They, too, will protect you with their lives. At least for now."

A man murmured in his sleep from a neighboring fire, the sound cut short by a gruff complaint.

"Tell me about the Egyptian queen Hatshepsut."

"You know already about this queen."

I did—had read every account of the Egyptian monarch who sent the first expedition down the Red Sea to trade with my ancestors in Punt. The female Pharaoh who styled herself king. I had dreamed mottled dreams of her, of the false Pharaonic beard, delicate fingertips curled around the flail of her office, of the sun god Amun, her divine father.

"Tell me what your people say about her," I whispered.

He rolled slightly onto his back at last without turning to look at me. "They say she made herself like a man. And that the Pharaoh after her erased her every image. You must not let that happen, Princess."

"There's little I can do about that if I am dead."

"A woman cannot rule like a man, Princess."

"And why not?"

"Because she is a woman."

"You say this to me? Your own people have queens."

"A queen must rule as a woman, Princess."

I was silent for a moment, understanding the enigmatic Nubian at last.

"Tell me, is it true she was the daughter of Amun? How can a woman be the daughter of a god?"

"She is the Pharaoh. If Amun, rather than her father, puts her on the throne, whose daughter is she?" He smiled, his teeth white in the darkness.

I smiled, started to let the tent flap fall, but then caught it.

"Yafush . . ."

"Yes, Princess."

"Will you not call me 'queen' now?"

"You are a woman of many names, Princess."

I stared up at the darkness in my tent nearly until dawn, thinking of what Yafush had said. If I was discounted as a woman but must not be made masculine, then I must become something else entirely.

The next day I had Asm, my priest, proclaim me High Priestess and Daughter of Almaqah before our entire company. He had frowned when I first told him.

"Princess, why do you ask this thing?" he said.

"Who do you think will provide the gold for the temple when you are chief priest? I am not asking."

For the first time since my arrival on the southern shore, I set aside my soiled tunic and donned my carnelian robe. I unwound my hair and hung my heavy crescent collar around my neck. I put on my rings, the weight of them foreign to fingers dried and cracked with travel, and set my gold headdress with the fall of delicate filigree on my brow.

All morning the sky had progressively darkened to the west. The moment Asm held the gilded horns over my head and proclaimed me High Priestess of the Moon, Daughter of the Bull, a rumble sounded from the far range as though the mountains had calved from the edge of the earth. At the time I thought nothing of this; it was the season, and the highlands had gathered clouds for days. Under the weight of so much cloth and gold, I would have counted the gale of any storm a blessing in the mid-morning swelter.

I was not prepared for the startled ripple that shuddered through the tribesmen. For the tens and then hundreds who sank to their knees. I saw from the corner of my eye how Khalkharib stared and Wahabil fell low . . . my priest, stark-faced, and Maqar, palm outstretched as though I were not the woman who had slept a hundred nights in his arms, but a god.

Afterward, Asm, who had wanted to wait to conduct the rite at the temple complex in Marib, proclaimed the moment a sign, and said he would never question me again.

"Tell me, Daughter of Almaqah, did you have a vision?"

I shook my head and he seemed to accept this with some disappointment. I did not tell him that I had not been looking for signs. That the rite, for me, had been claim and dread bargain, both. Daughter of Almaqah. Even my father, high priest before me, had not dared to identify himself as the son of the god. He had not needed to, using his throne as a vehicle for the cult, rather than the other way around.

Now my triumph or failure would be shared by the moon god himself—the name of Almaqah irrevocably burnished or tarnished by the outcome of this march for generations to come.

If I was the moon god's thrall, he would also be mine.

I buried a precious jade necklace in the clearing before we broke camp.

See me to my throne.

That afternoon, the sky roiled and broke over the mountains.

At the eastern end of the Harib Valley we were met with nearly seven hundred tribesmen who pledged ready loyalty to me. Half that number were my kinsmen, the faces of those few I had once known—cousins, slaves, and uncles—grown unfamiliar. The kinsmen of Khalkharib and Maqar, led by his father, Salban, comprised the other half.

I saw the way they pretended not to search my face behind the veil. The way one of them stared into my eyes before he lifted his palm. So they had heard, by then, the story of my installment as High Priestess. And somehow I felt that we met as greater strangers because of it.

It was a relief to me when one of them said, "Cousin, do you remember how we used to play in the palace? You were four and I was five and I would catch lizards for you. Now, I will cut down north men for you!" I said that I did and embraced him, but part of my memory of those years had long burned away.

We were by now within the western fringe of the Sayhad, the desert that formed the southwest corner of the waste. There was fodder here, where the great wadi once ran into her thirsty sands—bindweed, salty tamarisk, and last year's sedge.

From here, a man traveling north and east might ride for a month, losing himself among the dunes and calcified flats to exhaustion, dehydration, or madness before he ever encountered another soul. The vast sands had protected Saba's eastern border from the beginning of days, legions of invaders buried beneath the swell of its granulated waves.

That night, as the tribesmen divided into feeding families, a handful of men came out of the desert, tossing sand in the air to signify peace. They were dwellers of the waste's deadly refuge who might enter the sands for months at a time—the men they called Wolves of the Desert.

"They say there is a well near here, sweet from the rains this time of year," the man of Aman said to me later. He nodded to the east, toward the desert beyond. "They have come to water their camels after months of brackish wells in there. But they are more thirsty for news and had not heard about the death of your father or your arrival here. If you offer those men camels or knives they will join you."

"I will send someone to talk to them. And where are my allies your kinsmen?" I said. My cousin—my father's nephew—had reported that Hagarlat's allies might number five, even seven thousand or more.

"They will come," he said, pushing a bundle of qat into his mouth before he left my fire.

"I no longer trust him," Maqar said after slipping into my tent. The moon was dark—a fine night for an ambush. But so far, the scouts had seen nothing.

"Because he is a north man?" I said, as we reclined against a pile of saddlebags. I smoothed the hair from his face. It was the first time I had touched him in days.

"No. Because he does not look at you as the others do."

I laughed. "How should he look at me?" The tribesmen were hard and weathered men. Maqar, too, was a warrior, and a maker of warriors, but at twenty-five still untouched by the flint that so quickly struck war in other men's hearts.

"You don't even realize it, do you? You are otherworldly. I have never seen you like this, as you were on that day. Do I dare touch you, Daughter of Almaqah?"

"You must." I leaned back against him and his fingers lit like a breath against my cheek. Outside, it had begun to rain.

"Makeda . . ."

"It is Bilqis now," I murmured, capturing his thumb with my lips.

"And yet, I will always think of you as Makeda, even when you are my queen, long after you've married some noble or even the Pharaoh in Egypt. Long after you've forgotten Punt, and me."

I bit him, if not hard. "Never say that. Besides, have you not heard the rumors? I cursed my betrothed and so he died. And do you think Khalkharib and the others have not seen you coming into or leaving my tent? They know I am no virgin, if they did not know it before."

"They will quickly forgive both when you are queen."

"It doesn't matter. If not you, then no one." I did not say that I had begun to rethink my vow that I would never marry him. Time enough for that.

His laugh was soft and, I thought, sad. "So you say now. But the day will come when your councilmen will advise you to make alliance with someone far more powerful. And if they do not, I will."

"You swore to stay by me."

"And so I will, even if not in your bed."

"Why do you say these things?" Had I wounded him so much those first nights after our return? "There are other ways to make alliance. You said yourself, I am clever. Do you think I could give myself so easily—or at all—to another, knowing you are near? No. I will not let you go."

He was quiet as I lay back against him, but it didn't matter. I would prove my words with time. I could not imagine life—here or in Punt, or anywhere—without him.

But then . . . a pit twisted in my stomach.

"Surely you considered this possibility," I said slowly. "That I would hold to you, even if I became queen as you meant me to."

"Can you really ask that now?"

For a moment there was only the thickening patter of rain. When I said nothing, he sat up abruptly.

"You said you would never make me king and I accepted it. And it has cost me more than you know. Do you not see the way they look at me? The way your nobles go silent whenever I approach? They are too cautious to show their disdain, but it is there because I have your favor."

"They are jealous!"

"Even so, I say you must marry for treaty out of love for you, when I want only to possess you! What more will convince you? I give you my pride, my body, my life!"

I leaned up and clasped his shoulders. His words shamed me. "Forgive me," I said. And then, in a whisper: "Forgive me." After a long moment the stiffness slowly left his frame.

"The politics of these tribes is infecting us both," I said. "And you and I . . . have slept too long apart."

I smoothed back the fall of hair from his neck. He turned his head and even in the darkness I knew the question in that gaze. And then I was in his arms and clasped tightly, the patter of rain drowning out his sighs.

FOUR

I gathered with my tribal leaders at dawn in a broad patch of scrub on the desert's edge. Six cairns in crude imitation of Marib's temple pillars marked its use as an open air sanctuary by nomads and travelers.

Niman, my cousin, had provided the ibex kid bound before us. Niman himself might have been king, had his father survived Agabos' campaigns. But none of Agabos' sons had survived except for my father, and so the throne had passed to him. The kid bleated intermittently, the young starts of its horns curving slightly toward one another, forming a perfect crescent atop its head.

Niman had also brought another item I thought never to lay eyes on: the *markab*.

I had seen the *markab* only in depictions of my grandfather's victories on the bronze temple door. But now here it was, as though lifted from the frieze of legend itself.

An open-frame ark of acacia wood decorated with gold and ostrich plumes, the *markab* was both battle standard and war trophy. Gold horns rose up from the base on either side of it—their exaggerated crescents evoking the moon god's familiar, the bull. My grandfather's army had carried the ship, as its name meant, into battle, a bare-breasted virgin riding within it, and no tribal force had ever captured it. But the *markab* had become lost in the last years of his reign, or so I had heard.

A hush fell in camp at sight of it as ten men carried it overhead and twenty more jogged alongside, reminiscent of the day when warriors shackled themselves to its frame so that they might defend it and the virgin battle queen to their last breaths. When they brought it to the clearing, I saw the fittings by which it could be mounted atop a camel.

I was guided into the clearing by an acolyte at each arm; an hour earlier Asm had given me the bitter datura, the root of the moonflower, to drink. I had retched immediately and refused the rest, then vomited twice more.

I knelt before the *markab*, mouth acrid, my unbound hair falling to the earth and coiling atop my thighs. A robed figure towered above me, blotting out the sky. Asm. The gilded skull of Almaqah's bull seemed to hover atop his head, its eyes black and endless holes, the nasal cavity like a toothed grimace so that I almost screamed at first sight of it.

He spoke, and though I knew the gravel of his voice well, it seemed the skull formed the words with phantom bovine lips as the mountain rumbled to the west.

"We make the gift of blood—water, salt, and ocher of life—that you hear the petition of your daughter. Almaqah, god of moon and thunder, hear your servant and answer!" His hand lashed out. Five runes hovered, impossibly, in the air before they skittered to the ground. Two of them lay upturned: the liver rune, and the blood rune.

"Almaqah, hear and answer," murmured the tribesmen surrounding the clearing, worshippers of Amm and Sayin, Athtar and Wadd—gods of sun, moon, and morning star, of field and rain and thunder—the gods of their territories and ancestors and clans. Every tribesman swore by the gods of the lands they visited, as I had sworn by Sayin on the coastal plain and by Amm in Qataban. But we were in Saba's sovereign territory now.

Saba and Almaqah, over all.

The priest turned to the east, where the pale sliver of the waxing moon had begun its day-rise over the desert. The crescent knife shimmered in his hand, twin to the sickle in the sky.

"Almaqah, grant victory to your daughter and swiftness to the swords of these, her kinsmen and allies. Reveal whether they march on Marib this day! Grant clear omen and be remembered for your favor to your people. Grant victory, that you may be worshipped forever. Saba and Almaqah, over all!"

The tribes strike their own deals with the gods, I thought abstractedly. *As all men must.* But my bargain, struck days ago, had been between the god and me alone.

Asm was kneeling over the kid, holding it by the head. I didn't remember seeing him move. The knife flashed downward, impossibly fast, and curved slowly upward again. For a suspended moment, blood brimmed in a macabre smile across that creamy throat before spurting a red arc into the air.

An acolyte fell to his knees to catch the blood in a golden basin and I watched it fill until my vision dotted like the crimson splatter on the bowl's edge. There was no wind; the metallic tang of it was in my nostrils until I could taste it.

I stared, transfixed as the life of the animal grotesquely failed before me, the bound legs lifted so stiffly from the ground falling limply to the dust at last.

When Asm moved to carve open the belly, I told myself to look away and thought that I had, even as I watched the acolyte pull on the edge of that gaping wound.

Reek of bowel . . . rend of flesh like the ripping of so many threads . . . Asm, bloodied up to his forearms, cutting free the liver . . .

With dread amazement I watched him examine and then delicately slice it open, peeling it apart like a fruit.

"The omen is favorable," he announced. "We march on Marib today!"

A shout went up from the tribesmen, shocking the pulse that drummed too quickly, too loudly in my ears.

"What of the outcome?" one man called out.

The priest passed the red mass to the one acolyte and accepted the bowl of blood from the other. I realized, belatedly, he had come to kneel before me.

"Daughter of Almaqah, look into the bowl and tell me what you see."

I tore my eyes from the black sockets of the skull.

There, the bowl. So much blood. I leaned forward, peered into that red well, the welter of life and death. And for a moment it seemed that I was not in this clearing, or even here, on the edge of the desert, but in the palace. That I was a girl clinging to her dead mother, strands of her hair caught in my fingers. That I was twelve again, and desperate for salvation, the rubies of my mother's bracelet as deeply crimson as the flecks of blood against that golden rim . . .

My vision shrouded, closing over me. A sharp ringing deafened my ears.

"My queen, what do you see?" Asm, from very far away.

"Incense. Frankincense," I heard myself say.

I reached for him, but he had gotten to his feet. I fell forward, flailing for purchase. My hands landed on the edge of the bowl, sending it over.

"The spice road," I heard him say as though from a distance. "The spice road!" he roared. "Almaqah grants prosperous reign!" The tribesmen erupted in shouts—all except Maqar, who seized me by the shoulders, my hands outstretched between us, fingers dripping blood.

He caught me up in his arms, calling for water, something for the queen to eat. When he looked down at me next, his face was clouded as the western sky. I touched his face.

We had mended things silently, if desperately, in our nomadic bed through the night and again, just before dawn. And I had sworn to myself in the quiet moment of sunrise that we would be married by summer's end. I did not care what his father's intent had been. He could have the satisfaction of thinking he had contrived it. It did not matter; the gain was mine.

A man came running from camp. I struggled to stand, only then seeing the blood I had smeared across Maqar's cheek and chest. "Tribesmen, coming in from the north!" the man shouted. "Hundreds!"

All around us, hands instinctively went to swords, but the man from Aman loudly announced, "You see, my queen!" He jutted his chin toward the large company on the horizon. "My men have come."

As the men made ready, I paused near the *markab* to slide a finger over the gilded horns. I plucked idly at an ostrich feather. The gold leaf was very fine, very smooth, without even a nick. As was the acacia wood, as far as I could tell. The feathers were pristine—too pristine and new to have ever entered the field of battle so long ago . . .

Very clever.

We rode west out to meet the tribesmen of Aman on the plain of Marib. The man had been right; there were hundreds. They joined our number, filling our right flank. It was by now almost noon and rain had begun to fall, matting hair to head and veil to face. More men had come from nearby villages throughout the morning and we

were by now nearly four thousand in number, a unified royal escort,
a show of militant accord.

Ahead of us, across the Wadi Dhana, which ran parallel us to
our left, the edge of Marib's southern oasis lay green against the
encroaching sands of the desert. My heart began a steady drum.

I had not thought to see these fields again or to ever count it a
blessing if I did. But now my spirit surged at sight of the raging wadi,
that watercourse of dreams come to life once more. And there—the
temple within the southern oasis, connected to the capital by a narrow causeway over the waters.

When we broached the eastern edge of the smaller north oases,
Niman abruptly turned in his saddle. Raising his spear, he shouted,
"Saba and Almaqah, over all!"

Those nearest us took up the refrain, and within minutes it
became a cry four thousand strong, drowning out rain and waterway
both.

But just when we should have seen the walls of Marib rising up
from the western horizon, the horizon itself seemed to waver, like
heat waves over a dusty road. For a moment, I thought it the afteref-
fect of Asm's tea—what few drops I had actually retained of it. And
then I saw.

Lines of north men. Lines and lines of them.

Nabat signaled a stop. A short blast from a horn issued midway
back, carrying the order.

Maqar drew close and said, low, "Have your priest usher you
across the causeway to the temple. Now." And then, to Yafush:
"Keep her safe."

I stayed Yafush with a hand. "No."

Maqar leaned in urgently. "You cannot safely watch the outcome
of this. Not against so many men!"

"I will not run for walls as others fight in my name."

"Go now, while there is time," he hissed.

"And what—wait for some report? A messenger, to say whether I am queen or not?"

"This is meaningless if you are killed! I will come for you myself when it is over. You will enter the city in triumph. But until then you at least will have sanctuary there."

He did not need to finish his sentence for me to hear the rest of it: *If we fail.*

"And what would I do with sanctuary? Live out my life as a priestess, never to set foot outside those walls again?" I shook my head. "I will not leave my *markab*. And I will not leave you."

"Forget me! I must be nothing to you now! For the sake of Saba—"

But something—something too long latent, and too long forgotten rose up in me. Righteous, furious indignation. A refusal to renounce my birth name or birthright again out of shame or fear . . . or to ever cower again. Every thought of disgrace, every dread terror of the past, fell away from me like a shell all at once.

"Do you not think I knew the danger when I agreed to return? That I might have been killed the moment we set foot onshore, or any moment since? I am my mother's daughter and I will not hide!" I said, my voice rising in volume. I ripped off my veil. "I am the daughter of the king, the anointed of Almaqah!" And then I was turning, shouting back to those around me. "I am the granddaughter of the great Agabos, the unifier of Saba! Whose *markab* do you think that is? It was his. It is mine. It is ours!"

Cries from behind me, swords raised to the air. Ahead of me, Khalkharib and the others had turned back to stare. It did not matter that it was not the lost *markab* of my grandfather. It would be now. I rose up in the saddle.

"Can men defeat the chosen of the gods? *We* are the children of Almaqah, who has promised prosperity in measures unseen to come! Saba! And Almaqah! Over all!"

The shouts rose to a roar.

Beside me, Maqar's face was stark. His mouth was moving, his whisper inaudible, but somehow I heard the words that fell from his lips.

Who are you?

A horn sounded. The lines of north men had begun to advance, closing half the distance between us. Ahead of us, Nabat was studying them intensely, seeming to murmur to himself. Khalkharib, beside him, leaned forward in the saddle and then said something swiftly to Nabat.

Nabat shouted back to us through the din. "They are too few! We have the advantage!"

"We have every advantage," Niman said with a dark grin. "Saba and Almaqah!"

In the split moment before the men surged forward, the field fell away. There was only Maqar, looking at me with that same unreadable expression of one who knows and does not recognize another, at once.

And then the ranks rushed forward, carrying everything and everyone with it like the monsoon raging down the highland ravines.

We surged across the northern oasis. A thousand men on camels seemed to flow past me. Three thousand on foot closed in their wake—tribesmen urbanized by city and village returned in an instant to fierce nomadic roots like the tamed animal turned feral at the first scent of blood.

Perhaps it was the lingering effect of the datura, but even though I knew I had never ridden so hard in my life—and not even as fast as those tribesmen streaming past me with beautiful ferocity, their colors and those of their camels streaming behind them in violent mosaic—for a moment I thought I floated, the she-camel beneath me so much like the rolling of waves and not the jarring walk I had lived with for weeks . . .

Yafush closed in tight against me, grabbing for my reins, Maqar against my other side, sword drawn. I, armored in linen and silk, and armed with only my dagger.

Ahead, the first line of north men seemed to falter and break to one side. At a sharp double blast of the horn, my archers—kneeling in the saddle—sent a volley straight for them. Far ahead, men fell at random, like gaps in a line of teeth.

But there—they were wheeling, the line not breaking so much as sliding like earth from a hill, toward the left flank. Nabat was bellowing at Khalkharib, who seemed not to hear as confusion spread like a gust through our number.

I was slowing, the sheer loss of speed like pain, as ahead of me the same men who had fondled their camels like beloved pets around the fires shouted their names now as war cry.

Something was wrong. I looked back at the great gap opening in our company—not the forward separation between those mounted and on foot, but between the right flank and middle. There was a long moment of confusion . . . and then the sudden clash of blades and lightning of iron where there should not have been.

Maqar shouted toward the clamor.

I squeezed shut my eyes and opened them, willing them to see truly. I stared as the right flank shrunk in on itself, collapsing against the men of Qataban. What had happened?

And then I knew.

The men of Aman had betrayed us.

Ahead, the mounted charge had reeled left toward the onslaught of north men. In moments, we would be flanked.

"Princess!" The voice of Yafush, who might go days without speaking, startled me. Never had I heard it raised in alarm. He grabbed for me and I knew he meant to spirit me from the field before the north men reached the causeway and my escape became impossible. I jerked on the rein, too late. The large Nubian had grabbed a handful of my tunic even as my camel darted ahead.

I swung, airborne, crashed hard against the side of his mount. We fell back and Maqar's head swiveled toward us. With a last look at me, he abruptly broke right with his father's men.

Yafush hauled me over the neck of his camel, bent low as the volley came at last. Men staggered to the earth around us, arrows protruding from chest, thigh, and throat.

I craned to see the widening gap in our number as Nabat and the men of Saba crashed into the oncoming north men and the Qatabans fell back against the traitor tribe of Aman.

I took all of this in, vaguely aware that I couldn't breathe, jarred by every footfall of the loping camel.

Yafush veered from the field toward the narrow causeway as a clot of north men rushed to intercept us.

Maqar. Where was Maqar? In the breach I saw the fallen, camels nosing at their unmoving masters or milling among the wounded. There—the robed figure of Asm, clutching at his leg.

And then I saw it. Aimless, head lashing to the side: the white bull camel carrying the *markab*.

With a violent twist that rent my gown from my shoulders, I tumbled free. No airborne moment this time—the earth tilted and slammed the breath from my body. I groped in the mud, gaping for air with lungs that refused to expand. Pain shot through the iron case of my ribs. For a moment I thought I had been struck with an archer's arrow.

Somewhere, the cry: *Saba and Almaqah!*

The rain was in my eyes, stars where there should be none in a twilight that did not exist.

I spotted Yafush surrounded by north men, the clash of their swords a distant thing in a world slowly losing sound. I thought: *I die*. Better here, like this, than before Hagarlat's court. Mud against my cheek.

But Maqar was on that field. Asm. Yafush, and thousands of men in a bargain I had struck with Almaqah himself.

Get up.

Breath, when it came, was an excruciating wisp, my rebellious lungs incessant at last.

The clamor of the field came roaring back.

I rolled and pain shot down my arms, sent my heart hammering into my ears. I shoved up from the ground, heavy and weightless at once, the earth spinning beneath me. Before me in the oasis, bodies sprawled like bloodied runes.

One object towered over them all: a golden ark atop a flash of white, reins trailing in the muck. I staggered . . . and then ran, nightmare slow, for the *markab*.

I grabbed for the bridle, missed as the snarling bull swung away, and then dove for the reins. I jerked his head around and down with all my weight. An eternity passed as my foot found purchase on his neck—I could not afford to couch and mount him—and then I was lifted up. I grabbed hold of the acacia frame, clawed my way into it, the reins wound around my hand.

"Daughter of Almaqah!" It was one of the tribesmen. I had no chance to see his scabbard—only that he was visibly in pain but holding up his riding stick to me.

I grabbed it and, clasping the acacia frame, urged the bull into a run.

Chaos. I made for the broken flank, heart thundering. I screamed for Maqar and, when I could not find him, for every god whose name I knew. A rallying shout—ahead of me, the renewed cry.

Almaqah!

I did not see the line of north men falter. Barely registered the blast of my kinsmen's horns. With all my strength, I got to my feet in the *markab*.

One sight—one face—mattered to me now.

Only at the last moment did I catch sight of Maqar, hair matted to his gore-smattered face, going down just as the tribe of Aman buckled.

They say that I called down the power of Almaqah from the crescent-horned cradle of the *markab* as though it were a throne. That I ripped my gown, like the war-virgins of old, shouting encouragement to my warriors until the north men fell.

The truth is that Yafush reached me as I collapsed from the camel. That even after they bore me into the city and proclaimed me queen, I lay in bed with broken ribs for weeks, unwilling to wake.

My lover was dead. The crown was mine.

Hagarlat, my half-brother, Dhamar, and their influential nobles were strangled at the order of Wahabil, my new chief minister. I gave permission to Niman and our tribe-kin to raid Nashshan, Aman, and their allies in retribution. They surrounded their wells, claimed thousands of camels, and took as many slaves to be sold as far as Damascus with the first traders' caravans.

My kinsmen returned exultant but I felt no triumph. I had gained a kingdom poisoned with regret.

I drifted between consciousness and the merciful sleep of the physician's draught. I spoke often with Maqar in those hours until he became not a man but an ibex, his blood in a golden bowl.

At last, I woke and dashed the bottle of draught to the floor.

When Asm presided over the sacrifice of five hundred bulls and three hundred ibex at the temple in celebration, I sent a young virgin in my stead to gaze into the morbid cauldron. Asm, I knew, was puzzled that I would not divine it again and I never told him the truth: the day in the clearing I had called for incense, knowing myself close to fainting.

But as I gazed into the bowl, I had seen nothing.

FIVE

Marib, jewel of Saba, sat at the crossroads of the world. Her caravan route stretched from the highlands of southern Hadramawt north to Damascus, her sea routes from Ophir to the eastern Indus River. Anyone dealing in passage of spices, slaves, gold, ivory, incense, textiles, jewels, or exotic animals had dealings with Saba's roads and ports. Which meant they now had dealings with me.

In my first months as queen, I sent colonists from Saba north to the great Jawf Valley, where I bestowed on them the choice fields of the traitor tribes of Nashshan and Aman. They, in turn, provided labor for the building of garrisons and new temples at the oases. The trade route—that all-important artery through the heart of Saba's unified kingdom—was secure.

I took into my service men from the tribes and kin-tribes of those who had fought for me and a handful of Desert Wolves. I summoned the most powerful nobles of the tribal kingdoms to ritual feast within the temple complex to make pacts of federation within its auspices.

The rains had come in abundance; the fields were green with sorghum and millet. At desert's edge, the tamarisk and mimosa were in pink bloom, the sands awash with blue heliotrope.

I funded a corps of engineers to repair the canals and stave off the ever-present silt. I consulted with Wahabil on the appointment of new ministers and vice-ministers of trade and treasury, and councilmen to the colony of Punt across the sea.

I dedicated a bronze figure of Maqar to the temple and had it installed opposite those of my mother and father—and had those of Hagarlat and my half brother ritually relieved of their curses and removed. But unlike the statue of my father, which listed his many services to the cult of Almaqah, and my mother's, which eulogized the glory of the gods in her beauty, Maqar's bore only the word "heart" in reminder of what Almaqah had taken from me.

I did not allow myself to think of Maqar by day. But at night, Shara, my childhood friend, held me as the tears broke like an earthen dam. I clasped the alabaster jar with the dust of his grave to my chest. It was meant to be drunk with wine for the soothing of grief, but I could not bring myself to do it, the wine in any cup too like the blood in the bowl.

It did not help that the aged eyes of Maqar stared out at me from the thin eyelids of his father, Salban, each time my council convened so that I could barely meet his gaze anytime he spoke. Nor when my councilors began to debate the merits of my latest marriage proposal and the question of an heir.

"I am barely upon this throne," I said one day. "Would you see me gone from it so soon that you plan for my death?"

"Never, my queen." The portly Abamar of Awsan bowed his head. "May you reign a hundred years."

"And yet," Salban said quietly, startling me. He had remained mercifully silent on the matter to date. "You considered alliance with another clan once before. Will you not consider it now?"

My fingers went cold.

I had spoken my earlier intent to marry Maqar to no one but him.

"I presume . . . that you mean my brief betrothal when I was a child," I said, very carefully. I would not speak Sadiq's name.

He inclined his head—too late. The question so long put to rest that night before Maqar's death had reared up within my heart once more.

"Almaqah has set me upon this seat, as I have set you upon yours," I said, looking meaningfully from one man to the next. "Almaqah will make the future known. For now, we have far more pressing matters."

That summer, as gum flowed in the trees of the foothills and the frankincense farmers went out to make their cuts in the papery bark, I accepted young women from the noble families of Saba and Awsan to tend my chambers, men to oversee the stables, and priests and priestesses from entire pantheons of gods to serve my household.

I did all these things, barely reckoning the hour of the day, and the month only by the capricious moon through my window as I lay down each night.

That autumn, as tears of white resin were gathered from the frankincense trees and the rains returned again, grief ceased its nightly visit. Duty remained in its stead. I slept rarely, and when I did it was only to dream of a body-strewn field, the ibex in the clearing. At times I thought I heard the keening of souls as I woke to the wind howling through the stone mouths of the lions beneath the palace cornices. In a sweat, I went to my table to pore over the accounts of disputes settled in my name and the temple tithes gathered for public works.

"My queen," Shara said, pushing up from the silk pillows of the bed where she slept beside me. "Will you not rest? The records will not have changed by tomorrow."

"Soon," I said, as I did every night.

I could not tell her that I dare not. That the office I wore like a leaden mantle had been purchased too dearly and I must wield wisely this power I resented so well. Worse, Salban's comment had brought to barbed life the question of Maqar's intention I had thought long buried. A thousand times I nearly sent for his father, to demand answers to questions dignity forbade me ask. It was a riddle with no answer at any rate: no confirmation of Maqar's duplicity could ever dissuade me of his love, no denial ever put my heart to rest.

And neither would return him to me.

I knew only one thing for certain: I was queen now. And I knew nothing to do but labor all hours or go mad.

"My queen," Wahabil said one early evening as I met with my privy council. I glanced up with a start, only then realizing that I had nodded off where I sat.

"Forgive me," I said. "Pray continue."

"We have held you hours in session. Perhaps a short recess," he said, nodding to the scribe sitting in the corner. To my right and left, the others made to rise.

"No," I said sharply. And then, "Councilor Abyada is newly married. Let us finish our business and speed him to his young wife, where his mind is, no doubt, already." Chuckles from around the table.

"Ah," Abyada said, with a cant of his aging head, "it is true. And yet, I am not a young man and she is vigorous for want of a child. I beg you, delay me, that I may rally my strength."

I smiled but said, "We will continue."

Farther down, Niman and Khalkarib exchanged glances. Yatha studied his folded hands.

"Well?" I said.

Wahabil slowly rose from his seat at the far end of the table, walked its length, and came to lean in before me, obscuring the others from view.

"My queen," he said quietly, laying a ringed hand on the table's polished ebony, "you are exhausted."

"Nonsense," I said. "I do not have the benefit of that fine qat you and Yatha favor so greatly."

Polite laughter from the others. But Wahabil straightened and shook his head.

"We worry for your majesty. You wear yourself away. The servants say you hardly sleep, refuse all but the smallest amount of food . . ."

"My servants are women, councilor. No doubt your own mothers and wives say the same of you. They are not interested in land disputes or the condition of the dam or the southern canals or trading vast sums of myrrh for Egyptian horses."

"And yet it is apparent to us as well. My queen, if there is some unease that keeps you from food or rest, let me send for the physician, I beg you."

The table was silent as I felt the weight of their eyes upon me. Niman, my cousin. Abyada. Khalkharib and Yatha. Nabat, captain of my guard. Abamar. Their forbearance and impatience in varied mosaic.

"I assure you I am well," I said. "Perhaps we should take that recess after all."

"You are the unifier of Saba. Your person is precious to the kingdom, especially as you are without an heir. You must look to your well-being. If not for your own sake—"

I slammed my hands on the table and stood.

"What do you want of me? What have I not given to you, to Saba, that is mine to give? In what way have I failed you that you chastise me? My duty! My obedience! Myriad lives! What more do you ask?"

"My queen," Wahabil said, "perhaps if you were to marry, it would ease your burden. And the security of an heir—"

"I will not speak of marriage!" I said, dashing a pile of parchment along with my gold cup to the floor.

I was shaking with a fury I did not understand, welled up from a source I had long thought dry.

"You, who summoned me because you did not want a Nashshan pawn on the throne." I stared at each man in turn. "Do *not* think to make a man among your nobles king through me. I am queen, and by Almaqah, I will rule!"

With a last look around the table, I shoved back my chair. "This meeting is finished."

That night, Asm came to visit me in my private chamber—the same one that had once belonged to my king father.

"Wahabil sent you," I said wearily. Outside, drizzle fell in a constant drone. I could just make out the dull roar of the corbel lions through the sputter of a rainy season nearing its end.

"No man may send the chief priest of Almaqah anywhere," he said. "But he did ask."

I looked away.

"Have you come to chastise me, too?"

It had been my custom in Punt to visit during the dark moon, to observe the nightly sacrifice for Almaqah's return to the sky. But I had not walked that narrow temple causeway since the ritual feast months ago.

"For what would I chastise you? Almaqah's Daughter must do as she will."

I gave a soft laugh.

"You do not believe that?"

I did not know how to say that being queen was a death sentence of loneliness. That I felt every finger's breadth of the ever-widening gap between those closest to me and the isolation of my own counsel and the thoughts I could not, dare not, share.

Nor would I say that I had never felt more a slave or less remembered to the gods.

And so I said nothing.

"Perhaps she must remember who she is."

I considered Asm where he lounged on the low sofa adjacent mine. He had never adopted the silver hem and hood of the other priests, his simple robe lending gravity to his position more than any flamboyance would have. He had seemed ageless to me always, nearly immortal except for the injury to his leg that day on the field, and the limp he would now walk with forever. The low flicker of the lamp on the gold table between us—my mother's table, reclaimed from Hagarlat's apartment—illuminated the rich earthen hue of his skin. It was the color of Punt and my kinsmen there, their skin a bare shade darker than my own.

"She is the queen," I said at last, reaching for my wine.

"And beloved by her people."

"They love me for what I might do for them," I said. "Because they want land and trade tariffs and disputes decided in their favor." I glanced up and he gave a slight shrug of acquiescence. "So, I think sometimes, must the gods say of us as we intone prayers of supplication. The barren woman for children, the sick for health, the farmer for rain, and the merchant for fair weather and safety."

"The queen, for the favor already evident upon her."

I was silent a moment before I said: "I did not know favor came at such cost."

The priest said quietly, "There is always a price. Do you yourself not reserve your best favor for those who prove their devotion through the costliest ways? Those who send men to march for your throne even though they may die . . . who go at your bidding to build your garrisons and offer routes through their land with the best terms at their oases?"

"If what you say is true, then our worship is nothing but the brokering of deals. No man who comes into my hall does so without hope of some gain. And neither do we offer devotion except for hope of what we want. No wonder the gods scorn our attempts to control them with our piety. No wonder they strike us when we least expect it, if only to prove that we cannot," I said bitterly.

"Do you truly think the gods so petty?"

"It is the only thing that makes sense to me," I said. "That they act out because we have never given them what they truly want."

"And what is that?"

I shrugged. "We do not ask about the hearts of gods, whether they care to be known. We spill blood in their names, which we make fearsome. But we do not seek to know them. We do not offer love. Not truly. I understand something of that now," I said, gazing dispassionately at the alabaster burner on the table, the thin tendrils of incense disappearing before my eyes, going nowhere.

"And I think they must be the loneliest of beings," I said softly. "Or perhaps, being gods, they have no desire to be known, and mine is an entirely human affliction." Outside, the rain had stopped.

When he said nothing, I glanced at the priest and found him staring at me with strange amazement.

"How is it that you ponder such thoughts, that you enter the mind of the gods?" he said.

I blinked. "I think them always! These thoughts are with me day and night! But surely you have thought these things yourself and can speak to this. Speak then. Tell me how the gods rid themselves of the desire to be known and accept our transactions instead—how I may go one hour without crying out to them: *Why?* Why did Almaqah take Maqar from me? Why, when I might bear it that no one truly knows me as long as he does!"

Though my affection for Maqar had been no secret to him, I was mortified hearing the echo of those words from my lips. "And yet I know what you will say—that then I would love Almaqah only because he gave me what I wanted. And that is true. And that is no love. I am as guilty as anyone in bemoaning the lack of what I will not myself give!"

Asm said nothing as my heart thudded between us in the silence.

"Isn't it true?" I demanded.

He gave a faint shake of his head. "The gods are unknowable. As intercessors, we are tasked only with predicting and placating the whim of Almaqah—"

"Yes, with statues and feasts and blood on the altar. Yes, yes, I know," I said, setting down my wine, untouched all this time. "But why? What need do they have for all our striving? Is it arrogance that demands our dread adoration? Or is it fear that if we do not sing and praise and build countless temples in their names, they will cease to exist? Whatever the reason, I wonder now if they take from us that which we love so we *must* seek them, if only to scavenge for meaning in this existence. *Why? Why?* I ask it day and night!"

He was looking at me then as though at an oracle, a strange mixture of bafflement and reverence tattooed across his face. And though we sat only two arms' breadths apart, I felt the distance between us as a league.

"For the first time," he said, very softly, "I envy you the office you carry like a weight, that you may understand the minds of gods better than any of us."

And that was the worst of all. Where was I to turn if not to him?

"Don't you understand? I know nothing! I ask and hear only silence. For all I know, Almaqah has abandoned me. I, who build temples in his name. What have I done to cause such offense that he would take Maqar?"

Or what had Maqar? Had he deceived me and Almaqah killed him for his duplicity? But I had seen the last look on his face. He had thrown himself into the melee. Why? For atonement? For love?

And the worst of it was this: there was no oracle or sacrificial liver, no star or rising constellation from which I could extract the truth. And the priest before me could no more decipher the mind of Almaqah than I.

"It is the story I told myself after I abandoned worship of Shams," I said, wiping hot tears from my cheek. "That any living thing could wither beneath the same heat with which the sun gave life. But the moon arrived in the cool of night to preside over lovers and dreams, to give life to seeds as they slumber in the soil. Now I know that seeds molder in the dark, and the moon falls on peasant and queen alike. Just as the sun. In which case no man is favored at all, and the gods do as they will and we are the ones who assign meaning to their actions. Either that . . . or they exist not at all."

He was silent.

"Will you not say I am speaking sacrilege? I say this to my own priest! You, who have not even a platitude for me. Do you not condemn me?"

"I will not patronize you with platitudes," he said at last, very quietly. "You are the Daughter of Almaqah. You wear his favor. If he will not speak to you, to whom will he speak?"

He left me soon after that, clearly disturbed, and I could not help but feel that I had somehow infected him with my turmoil. And I did not know if that was a good thing that he might seek answers for both our sakes . . . or if such answers were unknowable and he went away troubled when I might have let him go in peace.

That night, I expected my every question, fully realized now that they had been heretically voiced, to torture me until dawn. Instead, I lay down to my first full evening of sleep in months. It was as though having spoken them I had exorcised their poison, if not their barbs, for a time.

SIX

Perhaps in a gesture of conciliation, Wahabil offered to oversee the royal banquet for my chief traders. It was fall, and soon the caravans would turn north carrying Saba's famous incense along with textiles, spices, and precious stones imported from Ophir to the west and Hidush to the east.

I set my steward and treasury at his disposal for the event. When I described my vision, however, his eyes widened.

"My queen, the cost of this banquet alone—"

"This is no banquet," I said, drawing him aside. "It is a message—one that must travel to the corners of the world."

The Libyans had grown for years now to military prominence in Egypt. The kings of Assyria and Babylonia—a true Babylonian, after the Elamite king before him—had had fifteen years to establish their policies. The king of Phoenicia had been trading cedar and artisans for grain and oil even longer than that. If I had learned one thing of kingship in all the accounts I had read, it was this: there was nothing so appealing as alliance and trade with a sovereign whose reputation was known after years on a stable throne—and nothing so uncertain as one recently come to reign.

Especially if she was a queen.

It was crucial that I meet these traders whose names I had only heard or read about in the records, who carried Saba to the world. I would gather them to court to feast them with meat and fat before their journey. Or so I said.

But the truth, which Wahabil understood, was that I meant to wage a cunning campaign—not with swords and axes, but luxury. And not on a field, but from a palace.

I had made an inadvertent promise in the name of Almaqah that day in the clearing, and now I meant to ensure the prophecy of the bowl—with or without the god's participation. Sabaean frankincense would perfume the temples of a thousand nameless gods and myrrh embalm the bodies of Egypt's dead immortals in return for textiles, wine, iron, horses.

But I would add to Saba's wealth in new ways.

I would send our best goods across seas of water and sand and receive in turn not just the wealth of nations, but scholars and artisans from far-flung lands, come to experience Saba's fabled kingdom. The day would come that poets and astronomers adorned my court as brightly as gold and silver did now. We would exchange knowledge with the farmers of Egypt's famous wheat fields, the mathematicians of Babylonia, masons of Phoenicia, and textile makers of Hidush. Unification had been the hallmark of my grandfather, and worship of Almaqah the legacy of my father. Knowledge and learning would be mine.

"You must make me beautiful," I said to Shara that night.

She laughed, and the brittle sound surprised me; I had not heard it once since my return. The years of my absence had not been gentle with her, but left an austere creature in their wake. Fine lines spidered out from her eyes like canals scratched into dry earth. Her narrow hands, when they were not occupied, fluttered together like two birds. I never asked what had befallen her after her mother's death, nor would she tell me except to say that she had briefly been the concubine of some man. I did not doubt Hagarlat had had some hand in that—the stories of her cruelties were many. Twice Shara's prayers of gratitude had drifted into my dreams those first nightmar-ish weeks of my return. When I had recovered, I offered her any life she chose, and she had chosen to stay with me.

"Shall I make the sun brighter as well?"

She lingered at my jewelry chest, collecting bracelets, earrings, and rings until her arms were glinting with gems.

"And you—I will not have you in the plain clothes you favor. That is not the Shara I remember. No, you will wear a gown from my wardrobe, and I will choose your sandals and jewels. Saba's low-est slaves will wear the finest linen before the eyes of emissaries and traders. And you will be as a queen in any other country. They will carry tales about you to the courts of kings!"

The color left her face and she dropped several of the pieces she had been holding. I went to her and took her by the shoulders. She was trembling.

"Shara, what's this?"

She glanced up, gaze stark.

"Swear something to me," she said. "As my milk sister if not my queen."

I blinked. "Anything."

"Do not give me away."

"Give you away?"

For the first time I almost demanded to know what Hagarlat had done to her. What the man she had been given to had done to her—and where he was now so I could repay him for the thing that made her look at me like this.

But instead, I took the things from her arms and laid them aside. Parting the two hands that had flown together, I clasped them tightly. "I will not give you away. I swear it. You are all I have in this world." I kissed her then and drew her against me. And as I laid my hand against her hair, something serrated and fierce sliced through me that I had not felt even for Maqar. I had wanted comfort, security for Shara since my return. But that night, I saw now in her the woman used and cast away. The widow. The orphan. The arthritic man. She was the farmer, toiling in the field beneath an unforgiving sun. The woman confronting death in childbed. The priest, looking heavenward for signs from an impassive god.

I could not cool the sun or make the ground yield. I could not ward off death or make the gods speak.

But I was her queen, and I could protect her. No . . . more than that.

Now the kernel already within me took root: I would elevate Saba in learning—not only for my legacy as queen, but because in so doing I would raise up even her humblest people. One day women like Shara would feel nothing but pride in the company of any foreign emissary and count herself his superior because she dwelled in a kingdom flowing with wisdom to match its wealth.

I let go of her, startled by this thought. Shara, too, seemed like a different creature when she allowed me to lay an embroidered mantle over her gown, and slip amethyst bracelets on her arm and jasper rings on her fingers.

"You are all I have as well," she said, and I thought she looked like a queen.

That night, as the doors opened before me and the music of flute and tambourine filled my ears, I stepped into a hall brimming with the richest merchants and traders of Saba come to impress the new queen with their faraway dealings in exotic commodities. But I had turned the tables. I did not miss the way their necks craned. The way they glanced this way and that as though following a flock of birds from one wonder to the next.

I tried to see the spectacle before me as they might: The lanterns imported from the faraway silk lands glowing from the ceiling like a hundred distant suns . . . The alabaster luminaries like so many miniature houses on the steps to the dais throwing light from their carved windows onto the giant silver disc behind my throne until it shone like the orange harvest moon.

In the middle of the hall sprawled a long, low table inlaid with precious lapis lazuli and laden with silver pitchers of wine and cups crusted with turquoise. Jasmine and white roses flocked the great columns of the hall, pillars of fragrant white clouds.

Along the far wall, musicians of every kind shone like gods, everything about them gilded from their tunics to their skin. Even the long hair of the man playing the lyre shimmered in the light.

White smoke of purest frankincense wafted from great bronze burners wrought in the shape of ibex and bull. It curled out of their nostrils like breath, Almaqah's idols come to life.

I lifted my gaze to the lanterns above, arranged into the constellations of the evening sky, the Sister Stars suspended in timeless night. There, the hunter. And there, the Dog Star, larger than the others.

Truly, the alabaster hall had become a wonder.

Nor did I miss the stark-eyed marvel of the courtiers as I entered, silver dripping from my ears in filigree so fine it glistened like rain, gold scales trailing from my girdle to my knees as the eyes of two hundred peacock feathers stared from the hem of my gown. I had left my crescent crown behind in favor of a more magnificent headpiece: a silver ibex, eyes glowing with giant rubies, the crescent against the sun disc suspended between its graceful horns.

The veiled Shara elicited deferential half bows from those uncertain whether she was a visiting royal. Even the women who tended my chambers were arrayed in costly dyed gowns, jasper and Egyptian faience around their necks and wrists. And no courtier had ever seen a eunuch more exotic than Yafush, thick gold bands around his arms.

Twenty guards flanked the dais in indigo vests, the silver crescent of Almaqah hanging low over their chests and gleaming from the hilts of their swords.

Beyond the hall, the lattice into the outer court teemed with the eyes of hundreds come to witness the pageantry and be fed—dates and lamb, yes, but more important, the fodder of tales they would take back to their tribal kin. From my vantage I could already see servants poised among them with great platters of bread, figs, cakes.

When I had ascended the dais, a girl draped in silver, a star diadem gleaming on her forehead, brought me a drinking bowl.

"My honored guests," I said, my voice carrying to the corners of a hall gone silent. "Tonight is a night of journeys. We embark with the caravans to the far corners of the world. But ours is no ordinary passage. We are the children of Almaqah! We descend not from the earth as the people of inferior gods, but from the loins of the moon and the sun, his consort. And so we begin our journey in the heavens, in the bosom of Almaqah, where we feast in the celestial realm!" I lifted the bowl to cheers and the music began again.

Servants poured water into silver hand basins as my chamberlain personally oversaw the seating of the guests—my full council of twenty-four in the middle of the table, closest to the throne, ministers of trade to the right and left of them in colorful head scarves. There were several men after that in ornately embroidered wool, their dagger hilts crusted with cabochon gemstones and citrine sunbursts. My traders. And myriad merchants along the great expanse of sky-blue table, to either end.

"My queen," Wahabil said, coming to stand before me where I had taken my seat on the throne. I opened my mouth to congratulate him but then saw that he was accompanied by a man in a simple sarong and vest. The silver handle of the dagger peering up through his belt was obviously old, the sigil of a long and proud clan lineage.

"I present you Tamrin of Gabaan. Son of Shahr of Gabaan. Your chief trader, and your father's chief trader before you, as Tamrin's father was before him."

The man bowed low. When he straightened, I took my time noticing the elegant line of his mustache and beard, the dark kohl of his eyelids, the surprising color of his skin, which I expected to be sun-blackened as a farmer's, but was instead a warm burnished bronze. He wore no rings—no jewelry at all except for a broad golden cuff on his wrist.

"My queen," he said. "Please allow me to echo what have no doubt been the words of my kinsman, Councilor Ilyafa, and condemn the shameful actions of Aman. And to praise your just dealings with them. May Almaqah bless your reign and make your name great."

I considered him for a moment without word. He was perhaps only a few years older than I.

"Tell me, how is your father?" I said at last.

"He is like the camel released to pasture after years of toil. Fat and content," he chuckled.

"Such a powerful tribe, Gabaan," I said, thoughtfully stroking the ibex head carved at the end of my armrest. "And how . . . neutral." I did not need to state the obvious: that they had sent no men to aid my march on Marib. It had been a conversation of some length between Wahabil and me.

Tamrin inclined his head. "My queen?"

"A shrewd policy, given Gabaan's reliance on politic relations with the tribes of the oases." I glanced up at him. "And yet, how difficult for one to discern loyalty once neutrality is no longer necessary."

"My queen is wise. I defer to her agreements with Councilor Ilyafa as to how Gabaan's loyalty might best be expressed. As for me, I am only a trader, a nomad among nomads."

He neither flushed nor stuttered in his response. He was either practiced at conducting himself at court or a fool.

I did not think him a fool.

"What do you think of our banquet, Tamrin of Gabaan?"

Throughout the hall, my guests spoke tersely between bites of sweet bread rolled and dipped in sauces of cardamom and fennel. They did not loiter; to eat too slowly was to tempt malevolent spirits to the table.

He gestured toward the constellation of lanterns. "It is a marvel. I will tell the tale of it for a lifetime and be accused of exaggeration. But now, if you will permit, I have brought you a gift."

A younger man handed him a long, rectangular box, which Tamrin presented to me with two hands.

"It is a humble gesture, but it comes from a very great distance. Your love of learning was known to my father."

Shara accepted the box and opened it, holding it for me to see. Inside, a double scroll of fine vellum.

"Whose writings are these?" I said.

"The northern king of Israel's, translated by my father. They say the king has been taught secret knowledge from his god."

I had read some sparse accounts of this kingdom only half a century old, this tribal federation still in its urban infancy.

"And do you believe the gods teach secret knowledge, Tamrin of Gabaan?"

"They say it of all sovereigns, do they not?" he said with a smile. "I admit I do not understand his god. But I do know he is hungry for the riches and rare goods of the world."

"Is there a king who isn't?"

"Ah, but this one has wealth to buy it. Wealth to rival even Saba's own."

I laughed, the sound ringing out over the dais. Beside Tamrin, Wahabil smiled politely, fatigue around his eyes. Overseeing this banquet had taxed him sorely. I would find a way to reward him—with some rest, if nothing else.

"Every trader is also a storyteller. I see now why you are accused of exaggeration."

He acquiesced with a slight bow.

"And yet we both know only Babylonia and Egypt rival Saba in wealth," I said. "But even the Egyptians must trade everything down to the new wigs they are so fond of to buy our myrrh."

Wahabil chuckled, and Tamrin, too, though he seemed to be studying me from behind that courtly veneer.

"The Israelite has brokered powerful alliances with Egypt."

"Has he."

"He's married Pharaoh's daughter and received the city of Gezer at the crossroads of the Sea Road and King's Highway as dowry. And so he controls trade into Egypt to his south and Phoenicia to the north."

I tilted my head. It was not the practice of Pharaohs to marry off their daughters—only to accept foreign princesses for their royal sons. What did their Pharaoh see in an upstart king that caused him to disregard Egypt's political pride?

A soft cough from Wahabil. Beyond him, the guests had nearly finished eating.

"Come with me," I said, rising. My guests hurriedly got to their feet. "We will soon see about Egypt for ourselves."

I gestured for the two men to join me as I led my retinue out to the palace gardens. Gasps flew up from the first guests to emerge behind us. The grounds, lit by a thousand lanterns, had been transformed. Great swaths of indigo gauze billowed the length of the garden, dissecting it east and west, flowing like waves in the evening breeze.

West of the indigo straits, civets and lions gazed languidly from cages beneath fruit trees. Ostriches roamed within a large enclosure and songbirds chirruped in competition with parrots from an arboretum the size of my private audience chamber. Tethered to a locust tree: the white and black zebra. Gold shimmered in thin discs strung from one acacia tree to the next. Dark-skinned servants lowered platters of flatbread onto tables filled with bowls of fish in turmeric sauce, lamb and lentil stew, crumbled cheese and spiced greens. The delicacies of Punt.

North of "Punt," pyramids as high as five men rose up against a scrim disc lit from the back side by a candelabra of torches so that it shone like the rising of Ra. Naked slaves in black woolen wigs and faience collars waited on the bank of the River Nile before the temple of Isis to serve pitchers of Egyptian beer. It surpassed even my meticulous instruction; I noted with delight the papyrus swaying in the evening breeze at the edge of the artificial river, the barge as large as a litter that drifted lazily upon it.

The entire eastern half of the garden was a series of oases—those caravan stops of Yathrib, Dedan, and Tema along the incense road. Camels of the best bloodlines grazed, hobbled beneath date palms, chewing their cud out of spitting range. Three white she-camels had been couched between black tents, the flaps of which had been tied open to reveal broad and brightly woven rugs boasting platters of fish and spring onions, pickled vegetables, and exotic eggs of varying colors and sizes. Several fiercely dressed servants, in more finery than any true Wolf of the Desert would deign to wear, waited to welcome my "traveler" guests.

Everywhere, there were dancers—stomping the ground in Punt or balancing pots on their heads in the oases—and musicians playing hand drums, ouds and the sistrums of Egypt.

A great gold cauldron stood near the entrance, full of frankincense pearls. And in the middle of the "Red Sea," an island with an alabaster throne so identical to that in the palace hall—even down to its ibex-hooved feet and the leopard pelt draped over its arm—that pointing guests wondered aloud by what means it had been spirited here so swiftly.

I clapped, and the musicians fell silent.

"We have come down from the heavens as the very gods," I said, "to sail across the Red Sea to Ophir. There, to inspect the gold and exotic wildlife of Punt, to sample her delicacies to the music of her birds. Or perhaps you will travel north to Egypt to drink Pharaoh's beer, burn your offering of incense before Isis, and pray Ra rises again. Or, if you prefer, set forth this side of the sea with the caravans, through Dedan and Yathrib, all the way to Palmyra!"

I moved to the cauldron and scooped out a handful of frankincense with one of many waiting silver cups. "But do not forget to take with you the best of Saba if you expect to carry away the gold of Punt, the favor of Ra, or the hospitality of the oases! Swear by the gods of each place you visit and make offerings so sweet that even they must turn a wistful eye to Saba and sing her praises. Saba and Almaqah, over all!"

The echoed cry filled the night, and I glanced heavenward at the white disc of the moon.

Elated ululations and revelry overtook the garden. Even my council members joined in with the enthusiasm of younger men as the music began again.

I glanced back at the trader in triumph and was not disappointed. He laughed with pleasure as my guests collected their incense before wandering off in search of distant delights.

He leaned in, not so far as to arouse the ire of my eunuch, but close enough that I could hear him when he murmured, "Truly, my queen, you command wonders."

"Thank you for your gift," I said.

"Perhaps another evening you will indulge a simple trader his tales before my caravan turns north, and instruct me what tales I should carry with me. Though for my telling of this night, I will surely be called a liar. Until then, I beg you to call upon me if there is any way I may prove the loyalty of Gabaan and of Tamrin the trader to you. Gabaan loyalty, once given, is staunch. Perhaps one day you will give me the honor of proving it."

I considered him sidelong, the straight line of his nose, the way the skin crinkled around his eyes. Eyes accustomed to squinting into the sun.

"I will."

That night, as I ascended my garden throne, my mind was not in Punt, Egypt, or the oases, or on the guests pinching the slave girls before drunkenly wading into the Nile.

I found myself considering a corner of the grounds untouched by the light of the farthest lantern. A stretch of land north of the Tema oasis, beyond even Edom, a world away.

Israel. The name rolled through my mind like a word tasted on the tongue. I searched for the trader in the melee of guests but could not find him. Tamrin's stories were obviously as polished as his court manners. But no kingdom half a century old could wield such influence or boast such wealth as he claimed. No sovereign could be so favored by the ever-fickle gods.

Hours later, when I finally proclaimed the journey ended and Saba wealthier than ever, and the last of the gold discs and Egyptian scarabs and bolts of brightly colored cloth from the Indus Valley had been given to the guests, and a thousand parcels of grain each containing a silver cup had been distributed to those in the courtyard, I retired to my chamber. Waving an exhausted Shara to bed, I sat down on my sofa with my new scroll, noting the Phoenician lettering, the finely penned Aramaic.

I read past dawn, long into morning.

SEVEN

"Tell me," I said, from the seat in my private chamber. "What conceit is this?" Here, I had begged my father not to give me to Sadiq. And here, I had asked him to send me away. How much had changed.

Tamrin rose from his bow, clearly surprised. "My queen?" Once again he was plainly adorned, the cuff on his wrist and neatly trimmed beard his only ornaments, his hair held back in a simple leather thong. Across the room, Yafush stood near the door, gold gleaming from nose and neck, imposing and still and beautiful as an obsidian statue. How different two men could be!

Shara poured wine and I sat back in the carved chair as he took the customary sip, clearly perplexed over the rim of the cup.

"Have you read the scroll you gave me?" I said.

Tamrin's brows lifted. "I—have not. Well, only a portion. The king's writings are sometimes cited in the Israelite court."

"I see."

I had wanted to burn the scroll last night, this collection of sayings so clearly influenced by other, mostly Egyptian, proverbs. That was how it was done with wisdom writings such as these and I grudgingly admitted it was a clever compendium, if not especially revelatory. But his proverbs were not what had offended me.

"How long has this king been on his throne?"

"Ten years, my queen, if not eleven. But I beg you, what has offended you so?"

"There are two songs included here by this king."

I reached for the scroll on the ivory table beside me, lifted it, and read: "'In his days may the righteous flourish, and peace abound, till the moon be no more.'" I glanced up at him.

"Ah, my queen," he said with what seemed like relief. "I assure you he means no slight against your god. Many gods are worshipped on the fringe of his city by his wives and their households."

"Are you certain?" I continued before he could answer: "'May he have dominion from sea to sea and from the river to the ends of the earth! May desert tribes bow down before him and his enemies lick the dust! May the kings of Tarshish and of the coastlands render him tribute . . .'" I lifted my gaze from the scroll, fastened it on him. "*May the kings of Sheba and Seba bring gifts.*'"

Did he pale where he stood?

"I'm well aware that my kingdom is called 'Sheba' by unschooled tongues. Is this not so?"

"It is as you say."

"And where is 'Seba'?"

He hesitated. "Punt, my queen."

My stare turned stony. He immediately fell into a deep bow as I skipped ahead once more.

"'For he delivers the needy . . . pity on the weak . . . Long may he live . . . May gold of Sheba be given to him!'"

I threw the scroll at his feet.

"My queen, I profusely apologize. I was not aware—"

"This is recorded as the prayer of David son of Jesse," I said flatly. "Who is that?"

"That is the king father of Solomon."

"That is what they call him? 'Son of Jesse'?"

He straightened. "Yes. The king's father was not born to a royal family."

"How then," I said, droll, "does one become king?"

He pursed his lips for a moment. "He was chosen by one of their prophets from the sons of Jesse. He was a shepherd . . . and the youngest son."

My laughter rang out through the chamber.

"And now the shepherd's son is this great and wealthy king." I glanced at Shara, who covered what I imagined to be a rare smile as though she were not veiled.

"Yes." The trader spread his hands. "His father was an unlikely king. But this is the lore: that he was a war champion. A bandit many of his days, and a killer of men. It was he who united these tribes of Israel."

Our own rulers were unifiers of tribes. Even today, my people called me *mukarrib*—"unifier"—after the tradition of my grandfather, who knit the four great kingdoms into one, Saba over them all.

"So this shepherd king's prayer is that Saba should bring gold to his son."

"My queen, Saba's wealth is legendary. It is a compliment to your kingdom that the former king wished his son to be held in so much esteem."

"Come, Tamrin, let us speak frankly now."

He stood back as I stepped down from the dais and moved toward a low sofa. I gestured Tamrin to the one adjacent, affording him the status of a councilor.

"Ten years on the throne. Eleven, perhaps, you say," I began, as Shara set a plate of dates before us.

"Yes, my queen."

"His wife is the daughter of the Pharaoh. But it is well known the Pharaoh is weak."

"His first wife."

"How many does he have?" I lifted my cup. My own father had kept several concubines himself.

"I'm not certain of the number. Perhaps two hundred at last count."

With an effort, I did not sputter.

He smiled slightly. "It is true. The Pharaoh's daughter brought him Gezer. The Ammonite bride, control of the King's Highway from the Red Sea all the way to Damascus. There are many of these, including concubines from the twelve tribes of his nation, and wives from the vassal states of Moab, Edom, Aram, Hamath, Zobah, Canaan, the Hittites, and the Amalekites."

"Is every account of this man so grossly exaggerated—from his lands to his wealth to his wives?" This time, when I looked at him, I almost stared. How had I not noticed until now that his eyes were a very dark blue?

The trader shook his head slightly. "I fear not. I have seen his capital and the construction of his temple, and his fortifications of the cities where his garrisons control the roads from the Euphrates to the Sinai and from the Red Sea to Palmyra. With control over the trade routes passing through Gezer, he is also the middleman in the trade of horses and chariots between Anatolia and Egypt."

My eyes narrowed.

"They call him the Merchant Prince," he continued. "He has a taste for every luxury, every exotic good and animal."

"And women, apparently."

"Apparently," he said, with a slight smile.

"Why have I heard so little of him or his father, if he is so very

powerful and so very wealthy?" I had heard something of the brig-
and king David years ago, but that was all.

"Few caravans go so far north, often taking their goods only as
far as the oasis at Dedan, where they are purchased by other traders.
My father has made the full journey of months to Edom and Jerusalem several times, and I, twice, and I have seen these things for
myself. Your father had dealings with this king—indeed, he sent the
myrrh for the burial of the king's beloved mother as she grew infirm.
On my last trip, I learned she had gone to the shadow world."

I considered the man before me again, carefully taking in the
lapis of those eyes and the fine lines around them, the wide bow of
his upper lip, the slender fingers of his calloused hands. I had been
right to think that this was the kind of man who must proclaim Saba's
commercial might to the rest of the world. I noted the way he had
not lounged fully, his feet on the floor yet, a man grounded, never
quite fully unguarded.

Or a man who tolerated courtly life with seeming ease, but only
for as long as he must.

"You left my banquet early," I said.

He inclined his head. "I am a humble trader not at home with
luxury. Forgive me."

I plucked at an imaginary string on my sleeve. "What did my
father receive in return for this queen's burial incense? I assume the
king's mother was a queen, and not some shepherdess."

"The king's thanks and favorable terms."

"The king's . . . thanks."

"Yes, and favorable trade terms. My queen," Tamrin said, leaning toward me, "I will take north such tales of your kingdom, of
your wealth and the loyalty of your people. Tell me what else you
desire . . . and I will do it."

Did I perceive wrongly, or did those eyes hold promises within them, the faintest smolder? My gaze lit on the back of his hand, traveled the line of his wrist to the strong forearm, corded beneath the skin.

I leaned back against the cushions.

"You understand my purpose. Then understand this: I want our language and gods and the exploits of our water engineers carried north beyond Phoenicia. I want the world to hear of our dam and canals and the breeding of our camels. And the twin paradises of Marib that are our oases, and the walled city our capital, and her many-storied houses."

"And the beauty of her queen?"

I quirked a smile, amused. "You have never laid eyes on my face."

"Nevertheless, when I tell the tale of you, my queen, I will be accused of exaggerating as much as you have accused me in my telling of Solomon. But why do you want the world to hear of Saba's marvels? It cannot be for mere right to boast."

"You are right. But boast we must. I want to lure the world's most educated sages and skilled artisans to my capital. I am longing for the day when bronze workers and builders from Phoenicia and astronomers from Babylonia and textile workers with the secret of silk from the edge of the east flock to Saba for our abundance, and because their knowledge will be richly rewarded here."

He drew in a slow breath. "Ah, and now I see. And so I will see to it that Saba is spoken like the name of a god, with mystery and wonder . . . and the name of her queen, as a goddess."

I laughed then, and it was a very different sound from that of earlier.

"I expect that you will soon receive many gifts from Egypt now that the rains are over," Tamrin said, watching me. His eyes drifted down my veil.

"Egypt's golden days are behind her," I said.

"But her Libyan mercenaries grow more powerful by the day. Egypt has lost Nubia, but she will soon be a new and more militant kingdom."

"We have always had good relations with Egypt. But the priests rule Egypt now. We will send gifts to the temples in Thebes."

"As you say, my queen. These visions will be costly."

"Yes, and you will stand to profit. I will make you rich—richer than you are," I said. Only a man of means with nothing to prove would dress in such plain quality and carry himself so well. "But now tell me: what gods does this king Solomon worship?"

"The god of his forefathers."

"Which is?"

"They call him 'the God That Is,' the 'I Am.'"

I raised a brow.

"What is the god's name?"

"It is a god with an unpronounceable name. The god they believe to be over all gods."

"Surely this king is bound for a fall!" I chuckled. "Does he not know how well this was done in Egypt, when Akhenaten proclaimed worship of Aten alone—a god with at least a name—and how miserably it failed? Akhenaten, who is 'the enemy' in their own archive!" I had read the account years ago of the temples neglected for years after Akhenaten's death and the plague that ripped through the population. No wonder history hated him for angering the gods.

"What is this unspeakable god's symbol? Have you brought back an idol with you?"

He hesitated. "The god has no symbol. It has no idol."

I broke out in truer laughter than before. "A god who cannot be spoken or seen."

"Their law forbids the graven image of any god—including their own."

"What atheism is this, that they annihilate the name and face of the divine?"

"I assure you his priests are devout," he said somberly, "though the king's wives practice their cults in the high places he has built for them outside the city."

I shrugged. "He will not be long for this world."

"As you say." Tamrin bowed his head. "But while he is still in it, what gifts shall I prepare to bring with my caravan when we depart?"

I looked at him squarely. "None."

His brows lifted.

"Take your usual quantities for distribution, of the best quality."

"Are you certain, my queen?"

"Saba has the monopoly on the spice trade. If he wants commodities from Punt or Hidush or even the east beyond, he has to deal with us. If he wants the highest quality frankincense, he has to deal with us. I am the new queen with whom he must deal. He may send gifts . . . to us."

He hesitated. "As you say. And what message shall I take to the Merchant Prince?"

"Only your stories . . . and prices."

"And when I go to Jerusalem and tell tales of Saba and her magnificent queen to this king hungry for peaceful and profitable alliances . . . what am I to say when he proposes a marriage alliance with Saba?"

"That I have no daughter for him."

"I meant, my queen, with you."

I leveled a look at him. "I am the ruler of my country. Not a princess to be sent to his harem."

"May you reign a hundred years," he said, bowing his head.

When he had taken his leave, I removed my veil and drank long from my cup.

I did not miss Shara's sideways glance.

"I know what you're thinking," I said later, as she undressed me in my chamber after the nobles' daughters who tended my rooms had been sent to their beds.

"Tell me you didn't notice how handsome he is . . . and how he looked at you."

"I might have noticed."

She laughed, and I was grateful for the sound.

That night, as Shara slept, the rhythm of her breath like the rolling tide in and out to sea, I thought again of those slender fingers and corded forearms, the way the bow of that upper lip broadened when he smiled.

But I didn't need a lover so much as a skilled ally. A mouthpiece to the world.

A beautiful mouth, granted.

Tamrin returned three weeks later to take his leave of me at the temple on the first day of the waxing moon—a time for new beginnings and journeys. This time he wore a bronze amulet inscribed for protection, the amulet of traders. A priestess—that female incarnation of Almaqah's lunar cycle—intoned a hymn as Asm's acolyte caught the blood of an ibex in the bowl before the sacred well. The young virgin installed at the temple by my bidding swayed where she knelt, no doubt under the influence of Asm's datura tea.

"The lion will roar," she said, and repeated herself. Asm did not interpret. The omen was for the trader alone; he alone must discern its meaning, if indeed there was one.

When I raised my arms over the trader in benediction, the girl looked up at me and screamed, shielding her eyes. I ignored her, knowing she was half out of her mind, my focus solely on Tamrin, this man in whom I must place so much trust and whose journey I realized I strangely envied.

He, too, looked up at me, as though I were not a woman or a queen but something *other*.

And I felt the space between us stretch as keenly as I had the night I had burdened Asm with my questions, when my circular ruminations and terrible search for answers had not been mirrored in his eyes.

I dipped my fingers in the bowl. "Return safely and swiftly to me next year," I said, drawing the upturned crescent on his forehead.

He fell forward and kissed the strap of my sandal.

He left moments later, riding off to join the caravan of three hundred camels and as many men.

Winter came, and I forgot the Israelite king.

EIGHT

I gave blessings to marriages. I pardoned the persecuted seek-
ing sanctuary at the temple and pronounced the oaths they should
swear on the graves of dead relatives in penance. I sat in judgment
of a tribe known for raiding its neighbor's camels, and of a woman
who married two brothers and divorced one of them but had not
received back half her dowry. And again, of a man who could not
give his wife children and so took in a traveler and left them alone,
and the traveler, who claimed right to the child when he visited the
following year.

"Under whose tent was the child conceived?" I said.

"Mine," said the husband.

"Then it is your child, and as often as this man returns you will
welcome him as a brother."

I was twenty years old, and well aware of the council's constant
obsession with the question of my heir. I had received marriage
proposals from every powerful clan in Saba, including my cousin,
Niman. I refused them all.

Wahabil hounded me by the month, as regular as my menses.

"If you will not marry for treaty," he said urgently one evening,
"take a man from among the priests. Better yet, two or more of

them. Let the child be gotten by Almaqah himself. So it was done in days past, that queens bore children to the gods. For the sake of your kingdom, I beg you, or upon your death there will be war."

Though there were priests and priestesses aplenty who performed such services, I did not know how to tell him that in the two years I had lain with Maqar, I had not once conceived. That it was possible Sadiq's rough use of me a year before my courses began might have damaged me for childbearing. I did not know this for certain but could not bear the humiliation of bringing myself to speak of it—to him or anyone.

"I will think on it," was all I said, wishing I could give him some promise, if only to put him at ease.

"Is this what it is to be a eunuch?" I said that night to Yafush as he walked a step behind me in the garden. "That I do not even remember the touch of a man to crave it at all?"

"To be a eunuch, Princess, is not to lose the longing," he said quietly, "only the means to satisfy it."

I waited for him and took his arm. "I am sorry it was done to you. I think it may be sin—against the body, if not the gods."

"I think you are more of a eunuch than me, Princess."

"You are ever the comfort, Yafush."

"One day, you will remember your woman's body again. And it will remember you."

I presided over ritual feasts. I looked into the bowl once more . . . and saw only the life of the animal given to an indifferent god, if the god even existed at all. Perhaps that was the function of gods, that they were created to unite a people under one auspice greater than a throne, even if it was only an agreed-upon fiction. This thought depressed me greatly as winter came, the sun cool and flat, devoid of mystery.

The first clouds had gathered over the western highlands the day Wahabil came to say that a messenger had arrived from the northern Jawf.

Tamrin, the trader, had returned.

I received him in the alabaster hall six days later.

"My queen," he said, bowing with his retinue before my court. His skin had darkened and he wore a new gold ring on his finger.

"I trust your journey was profitable?" I said, laying my arms on the rests of my throne.

He straightened. "Indeed. Please allow me to present these small gifts from the best of my caravan."

Wahabil, standing on the dais near me, gestured Tamrin's men to approach as I leaned forward where I sat.

"My queen, from Phoenicia." Two men came forward with several bolts of cloth, that prized Tyrian purple so coveted by royals. "Cloth dyed with the sea snails found only off Phoenician shores. The precious color of kings—and queens—worth its weight in silver."

I gestured for the cloth to be brought closer, so that I could rub it between my fingers. It grew finer by the year.

"From shores across the great inland sea," he said, as a man brought forward a chest of gold pieces. Wahabil selected several items to bring to me: jewelry inlaid with precious stones, some with an odd spiral filigree more delicate than I had seen before.

"From Egypt," Tamrin said, of an array of Egyptian wigs. Upon closer inspection I could see that some of the wool had been braided with tiny gold beads.

There was a ruckus at the end of the hall. The guards stood back, several of them skittering to one side as startled cries flew up from the courtiers.

I laughed and got to my feet, hands clasped together as a man led a horse through the hall's great doors. The horse, gold in color, whipped its head to the side, red and blue tassels dancing from its bridle as the man holding her reins struggled to keep his grasp.

"Caution, my queen," Wahabil said, an arm carefully held out.

I lifted the long hem of my gown and stepped past him to see the animal for myself. We had so few horses in Saba.

"How did you possibly journey with this creature?" I said, enrapt. "Truly, if you say you were spirited here by a jinn, I will believe you."

A caravan might go for days without sight of water—no particular hardship for a camel, especially if it found fodder. But a horse was another matter altogether. Those in my stables had been brought by boat to Punt, and then to Saba across the narrow sea.

"The oases are verdant, my queen. Two camels carried nothing but grain for the feeding of it in between." Tamrin smiled, seeming to relax just perceptibly. No, the feat and sheer expense of bringing this animal back to Saba had not been lost on me.

I walked around to the side, admiring the animal, and then sucked in a breath.

"But—this is a stallion!" I exclaimed.

"Indeed. So that the queen may grow her stables."

I lifted a hand very slowly to touch that proud equine head. "Truly, Tamrin, you have worked a wonder."

"Ah, but I am not yet finished," he said, as several more men came forward bearing jars.

I walked among them as the trader indicated their contents: cardamom, coriander, fennel. A box of rare and priceless saffron. An amphora of purest olive oil.

"Nineteen more have been delivered already to your storerooms," he said. The creases around his eyes were more pronounced, light against the darker shade of his skin as one who squints hours beneath the sun. He was different, so freshly come from the caravan road, though I couldn't tell exactly what in his manner had changed.

"You will join me for dinner and tell me of your travels," I said.

He bowed low as the horse was led from the hall.

"Your journey was indeed profitable," I said that evening in the garden, leaning back against the cushions. Gone was any semblance of spectacle, an elegant but simple meal laid before us. I had heard that it was difficult for traders to adjust to their mud-brick dwellings after so many nights sleeping in the open by the fire—so much so that they might stay in the tents of their kin-tribe beyond city walls or in the company of their camels for weeks after their return. It was the second time I had received him privately—except for the attendance of Shara and Yafush, who were as ever-present as my own arms.

"Indeed." Tamrin leaned forward with a smile, a honeyed date in his cheek. He chewed it thoughtfully, as though choosing the beginning of his tale, took a long sip of palm wine from his cup, and said, "The world is hungry for the best of Saba. But they are most enamored of my newest rare export . . ."

I tilted my head. Only the quantities of spices and perfumes, of balsam and incense, and the patterns of the textiles, ever varied. Every item Saba exported was expensive, from the gold of Punt to the frankincense of Hadramawt, which must travel so many miles overland with a retinue to protect it that it rivaled the value of gold itself by the time it reached market.

"That new export is the eyewitness tale of Saba's new queen," he said, grinning.

I laughed then, the sound rising to the fig trees.

"In the oases, tribesmen of every kind come not only to gawk at our wares and eat by our fires, but foremost to receive news."

"Yes," I said. "I know something of that."

"We have not left them wanting. Soon, the tale of your beauty and wealth will reach the very edge of the world."

"You flatter."

Tamrin gave a dramatic sigh. "You say I flatter, and they say I exaggerate when I boast that the very stars descended to your hall, that incense burns day and night within it so the scent of the gods is in the nostrils of even the lowliest palace slave day and night. That ivory is as marble and alabaster as limestone, and cinnamon bark as firewood in Marib. That the queen's maidservant is so finely dressed as to be mistaken for the queen. But there is no mistaking the queen when one sets eyes upon her at last . . ." His gaze turned languid. Wine glistened on his lower lip. "No. There is no mistaking a beauty that, once seen, sears itself into the mind of the observer as the face of a fiery goddess. That such great and terrible loveliness is memorized in exquisite detail after only a single glance."

I sighed and shook my head as though he were hopeless, and he shrugged with a chuckle.

"And so it is true what they say of Sabaean traders," I said, "that they may spin whatever tales they wish about Saba, as no one but the traders will ever make the journey to test their veracity."

"I would be dubbed a liar and a fraud were it not all true," he said with a quiet smile.

This, from a man who had never seen my face.

"But I, too, crave news," I said. "Tell me of the world beyond Saba, as you saw and heard of it."

"Ah, yes. There is a new king in Athens, the city across the western sea, with whom the Phoenicians trade. The Phoenicians are fond of these people. They, too, are merchants after a sort."

"And the Phoenicians?"

"They sail across the sea, farther each year. Their navigators are unmatched. That has not changed."

Tamrin's mind seemed to be roaming as he said this, as though he were formulating other thoughts entirely. His face had grown leaner over the year of his travels, lending the blue of his eyes a glitter less hard than simply feral.

"Your gifts are too exquisite. I must reimburse you, for the horse especially and its fodder. Camels, goats, gold—name it and it is yours."

"That is not necessary," he said, picking carelessly at the plate of dates, and then from another of oiled almonds.

"I insist."

"It is not necessary . . . because it has already been done. I brought the purple cloth and spices as tribute. The gold and jewels, the oil and stallion—and the provisioning of the animal and the two extra camels to carry its fodder—are gifts from the Israelite king, Solomon."

I gave him a queer look.

"I did not know if you would have it publicly known, so I did not announce it in your hall. Forgive me. I thought it would do no harm for your courtiers to think such bounty the return of your ventures."

He was clever.

"Were such rich displays common when you returned to my father's court?"

He shook his head. "No. Your gambit has paid handsomely. You are a savvy statesman already, my queen, to open a conversation with silence."

"My gambit . . ."

"To send no message, to send no gifts. The king was greatly perplexed."

"Well then, I must hear this tale."

"I carried to him news of your father's death . . ."

"You had words face-to-face with him?"

He nodded. "Indeed. I stood before his entire court as he took me to such task that I did not know at first how to respond."

"Took you to task? You are my subject. Your manners are as honed and burnished as a blade. What you mean to say is that he has taken *me* to task."

Tamrin lifted his gaze, his expression serious.

"Tell me all of it, then, and plainly."

"I carried news of your father's death," he began again. "Of the allies who were prepared to back your claim and your march on the throne. Of the utter conquest of your enemies and garrisoning of their lands and the building of new temples to the moon god. 'Does she not send word, or gift or petition for alliance?' the king said."

I barked a laugh. Petition an upstart king?

"The king was intrigued to the point, I think, of offense. Truly, my queen, you do not know the position I was in. Here is a man accustomed to all that he demands. To the best offerings of every kingdom beneath him, neighboring him, and as far away as Tarshish. It was all I could do not to offer up my entire cargo and claim it a royal gift though it might mean the loss of all my worldly possessions and those of half my tribe." His forehead wrinkled slightly. "Instead, I told him you were a queen who spoke not with gestures or words, but commanded an army with her eyes. The queen of Saba is a mystery no man may unravel." He paused and then gave a small smile, as though in spite of himself.

"Now, finally, I have caught you in a blatant untruth."

"No." Tamrin shook his head. "It is the truth, though I did not say that you speak as eloquently as the wisest kings. And so he bade me speak of you more, as you bade me a year ago tell you about him. And I sang the same song of your beauty and of Saba's wealth such that silver has no value in a land filled with so much gold and precious commodities—both here, and in the colony across the sea. 'For Saba spans the sea to the gold mines and temples and fields of Punt,' I said. And he bade me stay with him at court for many days."

Now I understood something else I had seen in him; here was a man still basking in the attention of this king!

"For days I watched him sit in judgment on his gold and ivory throne, and I saw the tribute of nations arrive to his table, his stables, and armory."

"And how great is this tribute?"

"My queen, the gifts he sent back with me are but trifles."

"Is that so?" But then, those items—except the stallion—were trifles to Saba as well. What was it that had so impressed the trader, then?

"His wealth grows by the day. He has already broken the Philistine monopoly on iron. He has great mines near Edom, from which he exports much copper. And now he has Phoenician ships of his own that set out on the western sea from the port at Yafo to trade with Phrygia, Thrace, and Tarshish. His temple is completed after seven years of labor by Phoenician architects and artisans and workers to cut the stones. Those outside the city say that a spirit did the work, because there was never a sound of chisel at the temple site and so it was constructed in silence. The truth is that many of the stones were dressed in tunnels under the mount. Regardless, his legend grows."

"What can a king like Hiram of Phoenicia possibly gain from a fledgling kingdom that he sends so many men and builds ships and a temple for this king?" I said, incredulous. It gnawed at me. The Phoenician king would not give so generously to one obviously green—and doomed to failure, now that I remembered his nameless, faceless god. Why did so many, if the tales were true at all, seek ties to this king that they would send their daughters to him in droves?

"Solomon has ceded a territory to Hiram in payment, as the Israelite kingdom lies entirely along the eastern border of Phoenicia. And he sends great sums of wheat, barley, and olive oil to Hiram's table, as the Phoenicians cannot feed themselves." He shook his head. "He has also added forty new wives to his harem since last I set foot in Jerusalem."

"*Forty?*"

"Indeed. And now that the temple is finished, he has begun work on a great palace for himself, and another for the Pharaoh's daughter."

I stared at him, wondering if it was possible that the trader could embellish so much.

"My queen, on my oath, all I say is true."

"Come now. Let us be frank. How is it even possible for one man to lie with so many women? Forgive me, but now your tale stretches even the limit of exaggeration."

"I do not doubt they see him little, his chief wives receiving the majority of his, ah, attentions. These brides are given—and received—with dowries that specifically expand his reach and the security of his highways, or in exchange for men to build his outlying cities, or to cement the peace of neighboring tribes. He is not obsessed with the getting of sons, this king, but with the expansion of his wealth and trade. He has an enemy in Damascus who stands against him, harassing his northern frontier—"

"You said his northern border stretched as far as the Euphrates."

"Yes, well, that is now in dispute, it seems. His territory seems to stretch far northeast of Damascus, but the city itself has been taken by Rezon, the new Syrian king. And so he has fortified his chief cities even more and begun the building of one even in the desert."

So. All was not so perfect in this infant kingdom. I leaned back again as Tamrin paused, my mind in a roil.

Egypt bordered this Israelite kingdom to the south, Phoenicia to the north and west. As allies, what could the three of them not accomplish? Such nations had formed brotherhoods before—Egypt chief among them—for the exchange of gifts and envoys and marriage, and the defense of one another. Saba had her own ties with Egypt and markets in Jerusalem and Tyre, but here was a king who called the Pharaoh "father" and put the food on Hiram's table! Even a weakened Egypt had found a way to marry into power, and a king to secure her trade routes.

I pursed my lips. Here I was, pressured at every turn to marry a single man. Would that I could make as many treaties by marriage and never give up a portion of my throne! Yafush had been right all those months ago: a woman could not rule like a man.

No, we must be far more clever.

"The short of it, my queen, is this: He is a king who knows no other outcome but that he gets his way—not by war, as with his father—but by commerce."

"What are you saying?"

"My queen, he quizzed me at length about you and your court and your judgments over your people." Tamrin hesitated then, shifting uncomfortably where he sat.

"And so?"

"Then he all but commanded the appearance of your emissary in court, along with Saba's homage."

I locked him in a gaze then of such frost that he fell forward onto his knees, bowing his forehead to the ground.

"Oh, *did he*?"

NINE

Λ woman can stew a great length in the space of a year. A queen, even more—especially when she bears a grudge.

And the fact that I did bothered me. Because it lent all the tales of this king, the Israelite, credence.

If even the remotest part of the account was true, particularly the tight alliances with Phoenicia and Egypt—with whom he was literally in bed—I knew I could not afford to stand by silently. One twitch by any one of these nations might affect the security of Saba's routes or her markets.

I called Tamrin to my court six times in the next eight months. It was his off year, when other, smaller caravans carried many of the same goods north without the prestige of the queen's chief trader, who ventured farther and stayed longer in each stop along the way. One winter to depart on the long journey of months. Months spent in the oases en route, in Jerusalem, Damascus, perhaps. And the return journey of months again. And then, after almost a year of rest, the departure in winter again.

The first time I summoned him, he presented me with a new scroll. "The latest writings of the king," he said. He gave me also a small wonder: a statue of the Phoenician goddess Astarte, seated on a throne and holding a bowl.

"Is this she, whom the Phoenicians venerate?" I said.

"Yes, the goddess of fertility, sex, and war." Tamrin paused. "I suppose it is all the same thing."

I laughed.

"But you did not go as far as Phoenicia . . . ?"

He shook his head. "I acquired this in Jerusalem, where she is also known."

"By the people of the God That Is?" I said, with mock scandal.

"There are more gods in that city than temples in Saba," he said.

"But what is she doing? Is she divining?" I had never looked at a bowl the same since that day in the clearing.

"No. You will see. In this hollow you pour warm milk. Try it, and there will be a wonder."

That night I read the latest proverbs of the Israelite. Of Lady Wisdom and her counterpart, Folly. How he vexed me.

Idly, I considered the statue of Astarte and asked Shara to fetch warmed milk. She hovered over me as I poured it within the idol and set it back on the table. We stared at it together for long minutes, looking as stupid as goats, until first one drop and then another appeared on her breasts and dribbled into the bowl.

We laughed together as I inspected the idol, seeing now two holes where her nipples had been.

"Why, they were plugged with wax," I said, "and the warm milk melted it!"

Shara laughed intermittently into the night long after I had added it to the shelf of my household idols.

"Tell me the story of the paradise," I said when I summoned Tamrin next. And so he related again the tale of the first man made from the earth and the woman from the rib of the man. Of the snake that told the woman she would not die if she ate the sacred fruit.

"Is this not the same tale as Gilgamesh of Babylonia, who finds the goddess of life and wisdom in the garden—the 'keeper of the fruit of life'? Is this not the same goddess that this king writes of when he says 'Lady Wisdom'? And yet you say he worships only one god, and that not a goddess at all!"

"Their stories are strange to me," Tamrin said, shaking his head. "Yet I know this: I have seen this king judge impossible cases. And he himself told me that on the night he made sacrifice of a thousand burnt offerings his god came to him in a dream and asked the king what he should give him. And the king asked for wisdom and discernment to rule his people, and the god said it would give that as well as the wealth and power that he might have asked for besides. So it is said that the king can see the heart of a man as only a god can. That he understands nature and animals in a way no man ever could—even the ways of spiders and locusts and harvesting ants. Some of the simple folk say he can talk also to trees, birds, and fish."

I scoffed. "What are these impossible cases?" I thought of the blood feuds brought to my hall when the high councils of their own tribes and those of neighboring kin-tribes had failed.

"Two prostitutes, my queen. A scandalous story."

"Then I must hear it."

"Both have infants, but one of them dies in the middle of the night. They appear in the king's court, the surviving infant between them. 'She rolled over on her child in the night and killed it,' the first prostitute says. 'No, she is the one who killed her child and took mine as her own,' the second one says. And how is the king to know who is the liar?"

"The king could claim the child for the temple," I said. "The lying mother then has no child. And the proper mother has the comfort of knowing he is dedicated to divine service and that she will receive her reward."

The trader inclined his head. "As you say. But this king ordered a guard to take out his sword and divide the infant—half to each woman, as though it were a loaf of bread."

"Ahh . . . !"

"The one woman said that this was just, but the second fell forward, begging that the child be given to the other."

"And so the mother was revealed."

"Yes."

"Tell me. Does a wise man truly take hundreds of wives?" I said, brow arched.

Tamrin grinned. "Apparently."

With each summons, I grew increasingly demanding.

"Tell me again the story of his father and mother." And he told me, as patiently as though it were the first time, how the king's father spied one of his men's wives bathing on the roof. How he sent for her and made her pregnant, and how when her husband returned from war, he commanded him to go lie with her, but the man would not while his own men were still in the field. And so the king had him put on the front line of the battle, where he died.

"He disobeyed a direct command," I said that afternoon. "Is anything said of that? Subjects have died for lesser disobediences to kings before. You said yourself this king was a killer of men."

"Yes," Tamrin said. "And no, nothing is said of that. Because the king's god took offense and the king, by his own admission, said such a man should die."

I made him tell me again of Abraham, the man promised a son and then told by his god to sacrifice him, and how circumcision was required of him and his men.

"What does this god care for the foreskins of his worshippers?" I said, thinking back to my conversation with Yafush. "This god who creates the foreskin, but then says, 'Cut it off!' Nor do I understand the god who says one moment, 'I will give you heirs like the stars' and then says, 'Sacrifice your son!'"

Tamrin shrugged. "Nor do I. But that is the story, and the moral is that one does not question the God That Is."

"Are you certain? I know of this city, Ur, where you say this patriarch of the Israelites was born. It was the largest city in the world. If this Abraham left Ur and his children settled in Canaan, where this Israelite kingdom is today, I think there is a different moral."

"And what is that?"

I paused and mused aloud: "This tale is a lesson to Abraham's children. That his sons should not be like his new neighbors, who worship gods to which they sacrifice their children, but that they should serve their god in the way he has said. But it seems to me that this man was testing his god as much as his god was testing him."

Tamrin looked as one struck. "Surely you are the wisest of women!"

"Only a woman who pays attention. Who is the god to whom the Canaanites sacrificed their children?"

"Molech. The god of nearby Ammon." He tapped his chin then. "The king has a wife from among that people."

"I wonder," I said thoughtfully, "what his god may think of that?"

The months passed like this. Spring. Summer. The rains of autumn. At last, Tamrin came to court to take his leave.

"My camels are fed and fattened. I have gathered the best of Saba to me and you have financed me well. What now should I take to this king by way of your answer?"

I spread my hands. "Do any of my councilmen appear prepared to travel?"

"What gift or message would you have me take?" he said, and I saw something like desperation in him.

"Tell him that the queen of Saba and Daughter of Almaqah greets him in the unpronounceable name of his god," I said with a wry smile. Chuckles from the gallery of my court. "You will tell him in private that every king has enemies who wear the smiles of allies. That every ally outside his borders fashions himself a friend for as long as friendship suits. We have no alliance and I pretend no friendship, but offer dealing to mutual advantage. You will take with you the gifts I have prepared for his temple, and sapphires for his queen."

"And what will I say when he asks why your emissary does not present himself to his court and Saba does not pay homage?"

"Shall the mountains get up and go bow to the tree that boasts of its new roots? Saba has existed since the beginning of time. Her emissaries may no more be summoned than her mountains, which move only when they want and then woe to whom they fall upon. And so you will tell him he has greatly offended your queen. You will give him the gifts of our idols, the bull, and the ibex, so that he will know our gods and the god who calls Saba's queen 'daughter.' And we send, too, the golden bowl for his new palace and welcome *his* emissaries, if they are hardy enough to make the journey. We promise to show them wonders and marvels to spawn tales befitting a king. That is, if they may be persuaded to return. No one, upon entering paradise, ever wishes to leave it. And so we invite them to loiter on Saba's terraces as the very gods do, drawn by her perfume."

I knew by Tamrin's stilted bow that he already anticipated the king's anger.

I smiled beneath my veil.

TEN

Tamrin returned in early spring before the rains. He was thinner this time, his expression worn. I noted in passing the gifts that streamed into my hall—the pearl and jasper jewelry, the beaded fabrics, cosmetics, and perfume in costly jars. The hyssop, licorice pods, cassia, and saffron. The ornately hooded peregrine falcon, the sleek Egyptian cat on the golden leash. I named her Bast on the spot, for the Egyptian goddess.

"You see—even the gods attend our halls," I said, as my ministers chuckled their approval.

"My queen," Tamrin said, bowing low to me later, in private. "I have taken the tale of your wisdom and learning to the king of Israel. And also of Saba's self-sufficiency, so that we neither depend on others for food, as Phoenicia, or for skilled workers, as the Israelite king himself—though I did not say so quite as blatantly." There, finally, was the rogue smile I had come to know.

"And the king says to you, 'Fair queen, how you veil yourself in silence and then in words! How you mystify, to your own detriment. How can it be that you claim to need nothing, and that your ministers do not appear before me? I understand you were not schooled to become queen—may you grow in better wisdom. The perfume of your palace comes to me over this great distance. It is indeed the breath of the divine. But if you are sovereign of a land set apart by the gods, then I am ten times so, for mine is given to my hand by the One who placed your god in the night sky.'"

"Is there no end to his vanity?" I sputtered.

Tamrin's lips set as though carved of stone and I understood he had not looked forward to the delivery of this message, carried with him all these months.

"But that is no fault of yours. I hold you innocent of his conceit," I said more gently.

"Truly, my queen, if you only knew the questions he asked of me, and those of the scholars who flock to his court. They are all curious, knowing little of Saba. They asked much about you and I answered them sincerely, saying that you are the most prized woman in the world so that men from the far corners of it seek your alliance and your bed—men as numerous as there are peoples."

I shook my head and flicked my eyes heavenward. "And to think I feared you unwell, and yet I see you are right as rain after all."

"These sages, when they return to their own courts and schools, will take with them tales of Saba's queen. Soon the world will equate the name of Saba with beauty and wealth. This is as you wished, is it not?"

"It is." I did not say that they would take also the account of how the king presumed to school me. "Have you no new writings for me?"

"None," he said. "It is said the king writes less and less."

"Is he so troubled?"

"He does not confide in me. But I hear tell of friction among his tribes, between the north, from which he raises levies, and the south, which he favors."

"He conscripts labor from among his own tribes?"

First the ceding of territory to Hiram, and now the conscription of his own tribes?

"And he says *I* must grow in wisdom! How do his people not resent it? Did you not tell me the Egyptians did the same to his people?"

"Indeed, and they do resent it. But the conquered Canaanites, Hittites, and Amorites alone cannot provide the labor for his projects, which are many."

This was the second crack I had noted in this king's veneer.

"Come, sit, you look as though you weave on your feet."

"If you will permit me, I will not stay, having left my camels and men and come these six days' journey from them straightaway. How the king took me to task! Saying to me, 'If she asks thus, tell her thus.' Anything you may wish to know, he has told me, from the order of his birth to the fates of his brothers so that I may answer any question of yours about him. But for now I beg you, let me give you his response and return to you when I have seen my camels watered and rested. Our journey was not easy; we were set upon by bandits twice in our return."

"Who dares?"

He shook his head, as though still warding off flies. "Bands in constant movement even as this kingdom of Israel expands. There are displaced peoples everywhere, many by the hand of Solomon's father—those whom he did not exterminate. The world beyond Saba is a place of turmoil and hardship." His gaze hardened. "But we took ten of them before it was through."

"You will have more armed men when next you depart. Let me take up worry on this matter."

"We lost little cargo and only a few camels. It might have been far worse. But you, my queen, may rest knowing you remain a mystery to the Israelite king. In my days there, I answered his many questions of your grandfather, and your father the high priest before you. And of your mother and her famous beauty. And I told him that Saba is a world in itself from the narrow sea to the desert interior, where only the Wolves of the Desert survive. And that she has not one temple but many, and many gods, Almaqah chief among them. And yet after so many days of praising Saba and my queen to him, as I prepared to depart, he said as though we had only begun, 'You have said all of this and yet, is not your queen sovereign only of some mountains and desert waste, and a grove of incense trees? Why then do you boast to me of her?'" He turned his palms up as he said this.

I stared at Tamrin for a moment. After all that! Was this king possibly mad? But then . . . I turned away with a shake of my head.

"My queen?"

"He is testing you," I said, turning back to him, "to see if you indulge him or become defensive, if you open your mouth to speak, or close it with only a knowing smile. Because both will tell him something of how much you say is true."

How easily I saw it now. The king was weary of flowery speech— at which Tamrin excelled. But this king grew tired of conversation sheathed in silk. And so he pretended to have forgotten days of prodigious propaganda and prodded with rude words. He was the child who, forced to behave and smile for hours, finally sticks out his tongue. I began to laugh at that thought, knowing the feeling well. He was tired, perhaps, even of flattery, restless for what he could not venture beyond his borders to learn as I could not venture beyond mine.

Now Tamrin was really staring at me.

"What is it?" I said to him.

"My queen, he said to me, 'When you tell her this, after all the account of how you have praised her, watch her. If she is shrewd, she will wonder at my reason for saying it. If she is wise, she may laugh.

But if she is a fool, she will become enraged.' And by Almaqah, I see now that he was right, and further, that my queen is as wise as I have thought all along." He fell down low before me then.

Should I have been flattered that I proved wise? Or incensed that he had equipped my own man to put me to the test? I was not amused.

"And so he sends back my own man as jury," I said dryly. "And did he tell you to say this, too? How inconvenient that it was not carried out before the entire court. Get up."

He started to do so then froze, and fell down again onto his face.

"I have been toyed with. And now I show myself the fool."

"Better you than me. How would you like to risk your caravans and life serving a foolish queen?"

"And how I will serve her always, because she is not foolish."

"Yes. Because a foreign king told you so. Get up." He got to his feet.

"Go. See to your camels. Eat, rest. I will relieve you of this burden of speaking for the both of us from opposite corners of your mouth. I can only imagine the conversations you must have had in your head."

He exhaled, shaking his head slightly.

"Return to me in the fall."

I was incensed one moment at the king's audacity . . . perplexed the next. Preoccupied all the while. If Solomon, sitting at the crossroads, held Egypt and Phoenicia in thrall, somehow I must hold him in mine.

Through the coming months, I began to draft a response in my head written a few words at a time, stopping and beginning again. That fall, I put it all to papyrus myself.

You ask how it can be that I need nothing. I ask you: how can it be that you are so dependent on everyone else? We have a custom in Saba among our tribespeople, that we humiliate ourselves and make light of our riches. "What a beautiful animal!" one man says of the rarest white camel. "Ah, this?" its owner says. "Why, this is but a goat, and one without milk." And so you may be assured that the bird that flies to your borders from mine comes from a people whose virtues are understatement and hospitality, those same qualities that require us to give our best possessions and animals—even the very tent we sleep beneath—to anyone who merely compliments it, saying it is nothing and a trifle.

But these are not your customs, and so I will tell you without interference: Saba has no need for grain from any source but her oases. The scents of the gods grow in our own gardens because it gave the gods pleasure to plant them there. Grain and god—we have no need of anyone. The same sun that shrivels another nation's harvest warms our soil and the moon causes seeds to germinate in the dark. Gold is less precious to us—it is as the sands of the desert, clinging to sandals and eyelids and hair. Our mines are inexhaustible, our date palms unrivaled, our herds countless.

We are impervious to attack; no army may march against us and survive the sands or scale the cliffs that border the salty sea. The gods have created this fortress around us, as insular as your vanished Eden, with only the smallest of gates by which we share our goods and receive tribute from the world. In my capital we have not one paradise but two. All has been given to us in double measure. The perfume of our myrrh is divine— spiriting souls of Pharaohs and kings to the netherworld, the scent of it so pervasive when it grows as to sustain the very poorest living upon its soil well into old age, and grant him immortality in death. And how can it not? The entire kingdom smells of god so that every man is a priest, and the very insects sing hymns. Here, earthly pleasure becomes divine and we dwell in knowledge of the sublime by the sheer act of breathing. The gods are indeed unjust, having given all good things to us in abundance. Even so, through the trade of our ships and caravans, we eat of the world's table and wear her best silk and indigo and purple. We are so lost to luxury that the simplest grains and figs and linens are as novelties to us.

You ask how I can need nothing. Here is the answer. But your real question is not how a nation needs nothing, but how a woman does not. And the answer is this: I am the product of my land. I am Saba. Egypt has her Nile, but we have the monsoons, our dams and canals, the design of which was whispered to our ancestors by the gods. And so we persist since time immemorial, forever and blessed. Any war we make, or have ever made, is only and solely with ourselves, as no one may match us in vengeance or in passion.

Why, then, do you command me as some vassal, to send my emissaries to you? Did you summon my father thus—he who was chief priest to the god who rises over our mountains, which reach to the heavens themselves? I am High Priestess, the Daughter of Almaqah, who harkens to no mortal king.

And so I write to you not as a queen or priestess. And I ask of you: how do you worship one god before all others, a god without name or face? Why does a wise man call upon one god and risk angering the jealous ears of others—and why does your god ask of you such a thing? And how does one worship in a temple closed off to the heavens by a roof?

*There should not be mysteries between us. I hear from
my trader, Tamrin, that we are cousins who both trace our
ancestors to that man of the flood, Noah, whose sons dispersed
to the ends of the earth. And so surely you understand all that I
have written, and know all of these things already. And so I pen
these words to the wind, hoping only for their echo. Even the
gods wish to be known.*

I don't know why I added this last, whether the gods or my heart
commanded it stand.

ELEVEN

I watched the girls who kept my chamber. The way they tittered over petty obsessions: the best-looking of the male palace slaves. The minor officials who took them to their beds. The gifts that came for me, many of which I sloughed off on them, and where and whom they had come from.

I observed my counselors. The vendettas that drove them, their agendas in the chamber, the way they argued over the table as though the moon itself might fall from the sky if they did not have their way.

The acolytes of my new priestly school, filled with such zeal. It dictated their every waking moment in hope for—what? My priests, who clung to their mystical identity in an echelon separate and therefore superior to the secular world. How did they know their god looked down on them at all?

I saw it all with a too-clear eye: the way farmers and merchants chased abundance as though it were the very sun, and as vainly. The wives who flaunted their pregnant bellies, the barren women who covered their heads, the lovers who worshipped the idol of their romance.

Wahabil, lost to the uncertainty of the future. Shara, to the prison of her past. Tamrin, ever restless. Only my enigmatic eunuch seemed to dwell in a place of I know not what—peace? The present?—like an island among us.

Impossibly, four years had passed. I was twenty-two.

"All right," I said at last to Wahabil. It was autumn, and the last rains had gone, taking with them the scent of almond and apricot trees in full fruit. "Go to Asm. Tell him I will make the marriage to the god."

I thought my minister would fall down in relief.

"I will make arrangements for the new moon," he said.

I did not know how to tell him that he might as well make them for the dark moon when Almaqah hid his face from the earth. That it would not matter. But I only nodded and said that yes, he must do that, and no, it was not too soon. There was no point in waiting, as I was no longer young.

The night of the new moon, I sat in vigil till dawn. I did this for seven nights, resting during the day, breaking my fast only at sundown with boiled quail eggs and pomegranate. I sent gifts of bronze statues and alabaster incense burners to the temple, jars of rare nard for the priests, and gold jewelry for the priestesses in service to the god.

On the eighth night, I crossed the oasis adorned in neither veil nor jewels. I left Yafush and my women at the causeway and gave Shara my sandals that I might enter the temple grounds barefoot and unescorted as any supplicant, a bowl of oil in my hands. Before the silent priests of the forecourt, I poured the oil on the altar and drank from the sacred well. And then I shed my robe and entered the open sanctuary in only my linen shift.

I knelt in shivering prayer until the next morning. And then I returned to the palace and closed myself away, seeing no one but Shara and drinking only water until the first day of the waxing moon.

On the last night, as the moon hid its face and I burned incense on the bronze burner with the leaping ibex handle, I realized Shara was staring at me.

"Are you afraid?" she whispered.

I watched the white smoke. A wisp of life, and then no more. A moment, too fleeting and gone.

Tomorrow I would let my women paint my eyes with kohl and my face and hands with henna. I would eat honey cakes and fruit and fat. At sunset, I would don the heavy bridal veil and enter the temple. I would stay in the room prepared for me, attended by the priestesses for a week as the god came in the guise of a shrouded priest each night. All beneath the half-lidded eye of Almaqah, shining through the window of my stony wedding bower, as the god rose over me in my bed.

The incense sputtered and the smoke thickened, cloying in my nostrils, too strong. I opened the shutter, but the walls were closing around me.

I crossed the chamber, unable to breathe, and shoved open the door. Shara was after me, my shawl in her hands, calling out, "My queen!" and then "Bilqis!" But I was running down the hallway and then the stair, out toward the portico, pushing past the guards. The heavy step of Yafush sounded behind me as I tore toward the garden.

I ran past beds of oleander and long-stemmed anemone, asters like purple stars fallen from the night, heaving breath into lungs that had constricted over the course of the last four years. Ahead, on the lantern-lit way, the fronds of tall palms swayed over the garden pool. In my mind, I plunged in, falling down among the lilies to my knees until I could lie back in the water, submerged. But even I could not rouse me from my torpor and I stopped before the edge of the water to stare, breathless, into its moonless night.

Running steps—Yafush, and the guards. I wrapped my arms around myself and vaguely heard Yafush tell the guards to go back to their posts. And then Shara was there, wrapping the woolen shawl around my shoulders.

"I'm fine," I heard myself say. "I only needed some air."

I staggered then, nearly going into the pool after all, and Yafush caught me up in his arms.

I turned my cheek against his oiled chest and closed my eyes.

Back in my chamber, I took the draught Shara gave me.

"The priests need not know," she said, her face pale in the lamplight. "You won't have broken your fast, at any rate."

I nodded, no longer caring, and fell into mercifully dreamless sleep.

Someone was calling me. I heard my name again, more urgently, and stirred, my limbs like lead.

Voices. A commotion outside my door.

"My queen." Shara, shaking me.

Whom is she speaking to? I thought distantly, even as I said, "What is it?" the words formed with difficulty, slurred even to my ear.

"Tamrin. The trader. He came barging into the courtyard with his men, shouting for an audience, their camels nearly dead on their feet."

I blinked at her, trying to make sense of what she was saying.

"Tamrin?" I got up from the bed and Shara wrapped my robe around me. But it was two months too early for his return. Had his caravan been attacked? I had sent fifty armed men with him eleven months ago.

"He started a mighty argument when Wahabil said you could not see him or any man today. The hall was full of shouting. He went nearly mad, saying that he must speak with the queen—today, now."

I looked toward the window and then the water clock, shocked to realize it was nearly mid-afternoon.

I swiftly pinned back my hair. The moment Shara realized what I meant to do, she said, "Bilqis, you cannot!"

But I was yanking open the chamber door and there was Yafush, standing outside, my girls startled as birds by my appearance in the outer room.

"I think you had best come, Princess," Yafush said.

Both men's heads swiveled the moment I entered my council chamber.

"My queen!" Wahabil exclaimed even as Tamrin strode urgently forward.

"My queen," Tamrin said, falling low before me. The dust of his journey clung to his tunic and hair. When he straightened, I could see that his face had been wiped hastily clean. Behind him on the table a plate of food lay untouched.

"They said you would not see me, that you were sequestered—" He faltered and stared, and I realized that in my groggy haste I had forgotten to don my veil.

Wahabil's hands had gone to his head.

"How have you returned so soon?" I demanded, alarmed at the look of him—never had I seen him so unsettled. "Were you harassed upon the route?"

He shook his head. "Yes, but we are safe. I came ahead with a small company—your armed men are with my caravan weeks behind."

"This might have waited—" Wahabil said, throwing up his hands.

"I fear to wait!" Tamrin said.

"The gods will accomplish what they will without our machinations," I said. "There will be another cycle. I am not so old yet."

"My queen, we dare not wait for the gods but act now," Tamrin
said, clearly thinking I had spoken to him, as a positively queer look
crossed Wahabil's face.

I might have laughed at the looks on both their faces had I not
been impatient to hear why Tamrin was in such a state.

"My queen, my men and I have ridden hard for days to come to
you—" He was staring again and I wanted to shake him.

"What has happened?" I demanded. No trader ever left his
caravan.

"The king would not receive me."

"What do you mean?"

"His chamberlain received your gifts from us, explaining that
the king had urgent business and could not meet us. But when I said
I had a message for the king and that I must deliver it personally, I
was kept waiting. Five days in a row I returned with your scroll, waiting with those who had come to petition the king, waiting as though
I were one of the two prostitutes of the story!"

My scroll. The one by which I had meant to rouse his indignation but that ended with my baring, if even in code, my great isolation. I felt a flush of heat rush to my cheeks.

"When at last he received me before his court, I said, 'My lord,
you receive Saba's gifts by way of your chamberlain, but you have not
received her greatest treasure—these words penned by the Jewel of
Saba herself, which I may deliver to no hand but your own!' And he
said, 'What I have asked I have not received. Where is the queen's
emissary?'"

"And when I told him your message, that his emissaries were
welcome in Saba, he said, 'Does your queen think I tell her "Send
your emissaries" out of vanity?'"

I felt my eyes narrow. "What is that supposed to mean?"

"I begged the same question, but he would not answer."

"'Is it true,' he asked me then before his court, 'that your queen has the feet of a goat?'"

"*What?*"

"I was flabbergasted. 'My lord, who could say such a thing of the most beautiful woman in the world?' I said. 'I am here as eyewitness to say she is perfect in every way. Why do you insult the Daughter of the Moon?' 'You are neither her advisor nor her councilman,' the king said, to which I replied, 'No, but I am the voice of the queen to your court, that bids your men return with me to paradise, and even I come only for the glory of Saba and her gods, with tears each time I depart and songs of thanksgiving each time I return. But judge her words for yourself, as all that she says is wise and true.'"

"And?" I said.

"And then he dismissed me."

I blinked.

"What of the scroll?"

"I gave it over to his attendant and my men and I went away stunned."

A public snubbing. I thought back to the message I had sent him. I knew it by rote, having revised it a thousand times, speaking parts of it aloud, even, as though in conversation with the man himself. Was it possible I had missed the mark so completely?

"Does he expect me to send Wahabil himself to grovel at his feet?" I said. "We will find new markets for our goods. We will cut him off completely. If I have to ferry incense to Punt and carry it north by camel to Egypt, we will cut him out!" I would deal with his enemy in Damascus and create our own roads across the mountains into Phoenicia. We would add our wealth to Egypt's. Perhaps, in time, I would even marry a Pharaoh . . .

"There is more," Wahabil said, apparently resigned.

"What more could there be?"

"The king's court was full of Phoenicians," Tamrin said, "and the king busy with entertaining them, shut away with them often, and then gone from the city for days."

"Phoenicians?"

"I listened in on the gossip of the courtiers and asked around the city. And now I know it is the reason he did not receive us, that a great number of Phoenician artisans have arrived and many of them have gone down to the Red Sea gulf, where the wadi separating Edom from the Amalekites empties into the sea at the port city of Ezion-geber . . ." He walked to the table, drawing a map with his finger upon its polished surface, pressing his fingertip last of all to the port in the northern gulf of the narrow sea on the border between Israel and Egypt.

"Phoenicians, in the gulf . . ." I said faintly.

"When we left and passed through Edom, I took a small company of men and went to the gulf. My queen—" Tamrin shook his head. "The king is building a port city there. The Israelites have brought down timber from the forest of Lebanon where they are even now constructing a fleet of ships—a merchant ship navy."

I took a step backward as one struck.

Now I understood why the king had given towns to Hiram, and why, in his need for wealth, he felt he could snub the riches of Saba.

Solomon, the Israelite king, meant to neutralize Saba's trade and render our caravans obsolete.

Even as I raged that I would cut him out, he had already undertaken plans to do the same to me.

"Wahabil," I said, staring at the table. "Fetch the maps. Gather my council. And notify the temple that I will not make the marriage this night."

When he had left the room, I cursed and turned away, stalking down the length of the table to lean upon its surface, glaring at the faint shape of the sea invisibly drawn on the tabletop.

"There is something else," the trader said strangely, behind me. "That I could not say in the company of Wahabil."

"Anything you say to me may be said in front of him."

"Not this."

I turned my head. With a last glance at me I saw him go to a packsaddle on the inlaid bench against the wall.

"As we prepared to leave, a band of men on fine horses came to our fire as we camped near the fortified city of Arad. Their bridles were adorned with golden tassels. The king's men." He withdrew something wrapped in a hide. When he uncovered it, I saw that it was wrapped underneath in a piece of purple cloth.

It was the size, perhaps, of an incense burner, if less square. "The chamberlain who received us had the customary gifts brought out to my men where we camped beyond the city. Jewelry, cloth, spices. And a slave skilled in the playing of the lyre, which I am told the king's father played as well. I have brought him here in the case that he may shed some light on the gossip of court." I nodded, grateful for his foresight. "But the men who came to my camp that night brought one thing only. This." Tamrin came and held it out to me.

I took it from him. "And what did they say?"

"Only that it came from the king himself and that I was to deliver it to you in private. That is all."

I unwrapped the fabric—the same purple of the Phoenicians. Within the cloth, it was wrapped again in linen embroidered with a gold lion. I glanced up at Tamrin to find him staring again at me.

"Truly, my queen, I did not exaggerate your beauty, but find every praise of it insufficient now that I see your face," he said softly.

But I was in no state for flattery. I held up the linen's embroidered corner.

He frowned. "There are such lions on either side of the king's throne."

I untied the fabric to reveal the figure of a bull. A fine, ebon bull with a gold ring through its nose. I stared at it blankly, turning it over in my hands. I might have thought it his god had I known better. But he worshipped the Unnamed One. Our own artisans made idols very much the same as this . . .

There, on the back, was the blessing of Almaqah.

This was the very idol I had sent with the trader to the king.

"He throws our gifts back in our face? What is the meaning of this?" I demanded, the linen square in my fist.

"I—I don't know," Tamrin said, seemingly at a loss.

"He does not receive my trader. He returns my idol. And even now he builds Phoenician ships to neutralize our trade. But I tell you, this so-called king will regret the day he heard the name Bilqis, queen of Saba!"

I threw the idol against the wall, where it splintered.

"Go!" I said to Tamrin. "See your camels watered. Eat. For love of Almaqah, bathe."

When he had gone, I slumped down into the nearest chair. In all of this, Yafush, ever silent in the corner, had said nothing.

"I think," I said softly, "this is my doing."

"I do not think you can make a man do what he does, Princess."

I shook my head faintly. "Are you so sure? Last night as I looked into the garden pool, a part of me prayed to be relieved of this wedding to the god. And now I have had what I asked . . . It is the way of the gods, is it not, to make every prayer a riddle, so that they grant one petition but exact such cost that we wish it back? And now Saba is not only without heir, but her prosperity lies threatened as well."

What manner of man was this—this king supposedly wise and certainly as arrogant as his god? This king of an infant nation who presumed to command the queen of a land as old as time itself— why? Because he was a king and I was a queen without a king? Because arrogance demanded he take offense that I did not scrape and send an envoy to him as the others—because I did not make of myself a treaty bride?

I sifted through these questions like rune-stones, as magicians do when the proper lot has not been cast, searching to see that the one they wanted was even among them.

What did it mean that he meant to render our overland routes obsolete? With ships, he might sail along the southern coast of Saba directly to Hadramawt and the best incense in the world.

No. He did not mean to cut Saba out—only her queen.

I became aware then of Yafush standing before the wall where the idol lay broken. He had moved so silently that from the corner of my eye he seemed like an obsidian statue that had changed places on its own.

"I think you had best look, Princess."

I turned away. "I know. I will send an animal in reparation. Three," I said. I would likely be required to put the confession of my desecration in writing and make an oath over the grave of my father. To journey as far, perhaps, as the new temple of Nashshan in penance.

"I think you had best look, Princess," Yafush said again.

I glanced back to find him staring at the smashed idol. But there, something lighter peeked through the ruined body of the bull. I got up, walked over, and then crouched down in front of it. Lifting it from the floor, I pulled it apart with the distinct crack and splinter of wood. Now I could see that the idol was hollow and that inside the cavity there was a small scroll.

"What trickery is this?" I said, pulling the scroll from the cavity. It was sealed with a lion, identical to that on the cloth.

I swiftly broke the seal and unwound the scroll. As my gaze passed over the fine Phoenician script, my heart began to pound.

A scrape outside the door. I closed the scroll and gathered up the broken idol, wrapping it in the embroidered linen and purple cloth.

"Quickly," I said, shoving the bundle at Yafush, who followed me through the side door even as the main one opened and the voices of my council, raised in curiosity and outrage, began to file in behind us.

TWELVE

Inside my bedchamber, I fell down beside my table. I forgot the broken idol the instant I dropped it onto a cushion and, with shaking hands, unrolled the scroll.

Your words have come to me on the wind. How they stir me! Not in the longing of their own echo, but because they are the echo of my own.

What a riddle you are. High Priestess, woman, queen. Who are you really? What is your secret name? Who is this woman who denies me her emissaries and her flattery? She is either fearless or reckless, and I do not think her reckless. You say you write to me as a woman but do not try to entice me—a woman who will not rely on wiles, but proves me with hard questions instead. They tell me the name they call you in Punt means "Woman of Fire." How you have enflamed me.

If you have found these words, you are suspicious enough to examine your own god. Only the fearless or reckless question the gods. But no, I misspeak—not reckless, but driven by that divine madness to know what others deem dangerous. And so we are dangerous because we know no other way to be.

*And here I am, holding a conversation with myself, only
imagining that it is with you. For all I know these words will brittle
in hiding and turn to dust in the dark. But one way or another, we
will have words. Not because I command it, but because we must.
What hold have you taken over me? How dare you command the
distraction of a king in the space of a single line?*

I sat back hard, and read on.

*I have sent you a gift within a gift—a slave that plays the lyre.
His name is Mazor—a name that means "medicine." My father
played the lyre, and it was medicine to the king before him.
Mazor is a musician, yes, but he also speaks and writes both the
Aramaic of the traders and the language of my people. He knows
our stories and hymns. He was precious in my court—there is
no one like him—and I pray he is precious and useful in yours.*

*You ask about my god and my temple. Send your emissaries.
I will tell and show them great things to carry back to you. I will
answer you and you will leave my table filled. But for now I tell
you this: our temple is not open to the sky because our god is found
in all things. Your god is the god of thunder and moon but mine
created the sky. And so he is not to be found there. We do not
worship his handiwork—the moon and stars are his fingerprints—
but the dread power and promise of the god himself.*

*Send your emissary—I have given you every reason now
to do so. If you do not, you will be cut out as my ships sail far
beyond the range of your camel caravans and sea vessels. I have
in this way forced your hand. Will you be fearless or reckless in
return? Send your men. Do not be so arrogant. You are without
an ally husband. Your commerce is in danger. I do not say it
as a threat; it is the truth. You have much to gain through me.*

*But you will recoil at this statement, and so I say instead: save
your kingdom. You may, as you say, need nothing of the outside
world. But it will leave you behind in innovation, if not in your
lifetime then in the generation to come.*

*In the end, I am not a king, or even a man, but perhaps
a boy. Surrounded by courtiers, officers . . . hungry for the
world, but too often alone within it. You know something of
this, I think. I grew up in my father's harem, surrounded by
a hundred mothers. I learned the language of their sighs and
the cant of their gazes when they thought no one was looking.
Which way does your gaze go when you are alone, I wonder?
How full or empty is the god inside you when everyone else
looks to you as High Priestess? How many of your questions
have gone unanswered?*

*You are of the age that I was when I nearly tore my hair
from my head. They call me wise, but wisdom does not
guarantee peace. It only reminds us what we do not know—
what we cannot know—and of our own frailties, so that we
resign ourselves to them again, again, again, in those rare
moments that we let go of the very world we must rule.*

*Selah, Queen Bilqis. Selah, Woman of Fire. Selah, Daughter
of the Moon. Send your emissary and something for me—not
your incense, for I am surrounded by the divine. Not your
grain, for my table is full. Not your wise men, for wisdom is
given me. But something of yourself. Fire for a thirsty soul.*

~Solomon

I dropped my hands to the table. My heart was beating very fast.

THIRTEEN

I read and reread his letter, starting again before even finishing, near the window and then by light of the bronze ibex lamp.

By Almaqah, he was bold. Haughty. Brazen. And he called me reckless?

He was conceited. A self-proclaimed dangerous man—pah! But then, by the same token, a man who called himself a boy and wrote as though lost.

A man who considered himself a knower of women—I supposed he was that—even as he presumed to know me.

And why did that warm me? How could it—here was a king who presumed to wrest Saba's monopoly away from her . . . and then audaciously begged for response!

I did not understand this king!

Twice on my first reading I had nearly torn the scroll to pieces. He told *me* not to be arrogant? He presumed to dictate to *me*? This king of a tribal state no more than a generation old, already festering with tension?

I reread it again, and then twice more. I leaned against the edge of the table, trying to imagine his voice, what his words might sound like delivered from his lips.

Which way does your gaze go when you are alone, I wonder?
What hold have you taken over me?

My council was gathering. What a stir they would be in! And yet I could not face them in private turmoil myself. I had given Yafush instruction to have them question the musician, Mazor, as I was delayed for an hour. And then again, for two more.

The Israelite king was right; he was forcing my hand indeed.

But there was more between the brash lines of his script. Some longing, some emptiness that I knew all too well.

And here I am, holding a conversation with myself, only imagining that it is with you.

Was it all fabrication intended to seduce? He would play on my sympathy if he could not command me. Or my need for—what? A teacher? A peer?

No, a treaty husband. And so he would tempt my own hand to move if he could not force it.

Yes, he was dangerous, if only for his manipulation.

I nearly sent for Tamrin but stayed myself. He did not know I had found this scroll. Or had the king given some instruction about it in case I never discovered the idol's secret?

What if he had, saying to Tamrin as before that if I reacted in such-and-such a way it meant one thing, and if another, it meant something else? He had nullified my trader as a source of information then, or at least rendered him suspect so that I would not—dare not—make myself vulnerable with my questions.

How well he had done to wrap his scroll in layers! Layer upon layer, like an Egyptian onion. And what lay at the core?

I could refuse to acknowledge it. I could force his hand in this way, too, waiting to see if he sent word, more blatantly this time. But then how would he judge me if I was not as dangerous or cunning as he might think—even hope—that I was? And how would he approach me then—with more confidence, or with more caution?

I paced to the window and back twenty times. I forgot my hunger. In all this time, I had not eaten. How could I, who stood to lose everything?

And yet I had not felt so alive in years.

At last I poured some wine and sat down to read the scroll again—had he read mine as many times?—the question of my response looming before me.

"This will end in war," Khalkharib said, pushing to his feet upon my entry.

I had steeled myself, knowing they would have stirred themselves into a frenzy in my absence. Even before I entered, I heard their raised voices through my private door as I hesitated, palm upon the carved wood, unsure how to navigate the conversation of this chamber in conjunction with the unseen one of the scroll tucked within my sleeve.

"You will speak no word of the scroll," I said to Yafush when I had emerged from my chamber at last. His gaze had been placid—nothing at all like the alarm in Shara's face.

"My queen, what has happened? And why have you shut yourself away?" she said, clasping my hands.

"The upstart king likes to make noise," I had said, kissing her cheek. "All is well. But Almaqah will not have a bride this night."

Now, as my council bowed before me, maps strewn across the table between them, I felt an inexplicable calm.

Will you be fearless or reckless in return?

"We will start at the beginning," I said. "If this will end in war, it certainly does not begin with it."

"My queen," Wahabil said the moment I took my seat, "we

believe these are the routes the king means to take." He pointed to the largest map and I could see now that two crimson strings had been laid out upon it, both originating at the port of Ezion-geber at the gulf, both running south the length of the narrow sea before parting ways: one to the east along the southern coast of Saba . . . and one to the west around the southern coast of Ophir. "On this route," he said, pointing to the western line, "we assume they will make port in Egypt on the return if not the departure."

"And the other route?"

"We assume they must provision somewhere along our southern coast before sailing for Hidush. But these are Phoenician navigators. Who knows how far or wide they may sail without sight of land?"

"They cannot circumnavigate us altogether," I said, folding my hands, remarking to myself again how strange it was that I felt as composed as a statue after the wild pendulum of my emotions the last several hours.

Or perhaps it was the wine I had drunk on an empty stomach.

"The eastern-bound ships will need to take on a cargo of incense at some point in their journey," I mused. "The world will not go without our frankincense. And neither will he."

"But what is to keep Hadramawt from trading with him directly?" Councilor Abyada said.

"If the ships come to Hadramawt directly, Saba loses tithes and tariffs at every temple and oasis along the land route north," Khalkharib said. "All of Saba will suffer for it."

"But that is exactly what he means to do," Niman said. "Without the overland expense, he stands to profit even more."

"Saba will also lose the monopoly on the spice and textile market of Hidush and fall into competition with her own kingdoms," Khalkharib said. "The very existence of these ships threatens Saba's unified existence!"

"Yes," I said quietly. "I am aware."

I leaned my chin onto my hand, staring at the map as the conversation continued across the table.

"There is Punt—"

"You are assuming his ships are willing to stop in Punt."

"Forget the ships. We will ferry goods to Punt and carry them north by caravan to Egypt."

Save your kingdom.

"Egypt will not deal with us, but only directly with Solomon," I said, looking up to see who had voiced this last. Khalkharib.

"Who is to say he will cooperate with us at all? He has begun this venture without word or emissary or treaty with us!"

One way or another, we will have words. Not because I command it, but because we must.

Niman shook his head. "Khalkharib is right. It will come to war."

"He will deal with us," I said.

"That is easy enough to say!" Khalkharib shook his head as though I were out of my mind. For the first time since entering the room I wanted to slap him.

"And what if he doesn't agree?" Niman said.

"We will make him agree."

"With what leverage?" Khalkharib pressed. "He has everything to gain and nothing to lose. And what should we do—ply him with pretty words or whine like children? No. We respond with force."

You may, as you say, need nothing of the outside world. But it will leave you behind in innovation, if not in your lifetime then in the generation to come.

"We must call for the priest and draw the lots," Niman said.

"The lots!" Khalkharib agreed.

I shook my head. I myself had never seen the three arrows marked "Do," "Do Not," and "Wait." Nor did I ever want to.

I got to my feet.

"Councilors! You are swift to war. Saba has not seen war—true war—since the days of my grandfather. Our rashness will only appear as desperation, and not gain us time in the end. You are talking about years spent rallying the enemies of a king from the corners of the continent. Of plying them with costly gifts while our caravans go without distribution. Such a war will bring no ruin to Solomon, who has the armies of Egypt and Phoenicia at his side, but only to us. The Pharaoh may be weak, but Egypt is filled with Libyan mercenaries. Phoenicia's king is old. But they eat because of Solomon. They have iron and copper because of him. We are speaking out of pride, but there are other ways to conquer than to war with three nations. When the rains come down the wadi ravine, do we stand against them or harness their waters for our use?"

"Yes, but those are our waters. These are not our ships."

I moved toward the middle of the table.

"He has the skill of the Phoenicians at his fingertips. He wants to cut out Saba and deal directly with her subkingdoms. In his position, I would do the same."

Silence.

"I see for us opportunity. Far markets, and exotic imports—brought not only by camels, those ships of the desert—but by sea."

Khalkharib gave a caustic laugh. "That is all very well! Except we do not have a fleet of Phoenician ships."

"No. We don't. But he does."

Wahabil shook his head. "Even if he was amiable—which he obviously is not—we do not possess ports large enough to accommodate such ships."

"Then we need to build them."

"That could take years."

"Fewer years than a war, with enough labor. And our caravans will continue in peace in the meantime, undisrupted. Perhaps even more profitably than ever."

"How would we amass such labor? Our tribesmen are working the fields and incense harvest, shoring up canals and tending flocks and city works . . ."

"Then we will have to make treaty for it. The Israelite king did the same with Hiram of Phoenicia. Why can we not as well? You say yourself that ships—ships capable of carrying what, hundreds of men?—are being built in the gulf even now. Men capable of helping us expand our ports. Ports by which we could trade in quantities much greater than by land caravan alone."

"What makes you think the Israelite king will even consider treating with us?" Khalkharib said.

I laughed and folded my hands. "Gentlemen. We are the most persuasive of nations. I could say that we are backed by the most powerful of gods. I could tell you that our councilors are the most astute statesmen. This is true. But our argument is far more fundamental than that. The Israelite king seeks luxury. He is jealous for the best of the world. And he has a fleet to pay for. So we will persuade him with the very thing he is eager to get out from under us: our riches. He will agree because he cannot afford *not* to gain Hadramawt's incense or to lose Punt's gold. As long as temples offer prayer to gods, as long as the dead must be prepared for burial, and as long as gold is precious, there will be markets for the wealth of Saba. And we will provide it—as a nation—far better than piecemeal as individual kingdoms, and with far better terms, from Hadramawt to Punt."

Wahabil sat down hard. "My queen, from all I hear, he is as proud as he is cunning. This is the king to whom you have refused to send emissaries, snubbing since you came to the crown."

"And so how intrigued he will be to receive them at last."

"Even so, every account of this king is of a sovereign able to impress his own will upon others until they see no other way but his. They say he is imbued with the magic of his god."

I laughed again. "Truly, do you believe this, Wahabil?"

He shook his head. "I have spoken at length with Tamrin, whom I have known for many years as stalwart. Even he anguishes when the king denies him and flourishes when he showers him with the smallest attention as though this king were the very sun. What emissary will you send to match wits with him, if he is all that they say?"

"One he dare not turn away," I said. "Me."

Would I be fearless or reckless?

I would be both.

FOURTEEN

I was not prepared for the assault of their outrage.

"My queen!" Wahabil dropped his hands to the table. "You cannot!"

"And who says what a queen may or may not do?"

"It is too dangerous," Niman said. Beside him, Abyada shook his head.

"Your throne will not be safe," Wahabil said. "What is to keep another from conspiring in your absence?"

In the face of their objection, trepidation flooded me for the first time since I had entered the room.

What had I done? What had I spoken and now committed? Such bravado, once voiced, could not be taken back.

I must be clever. I must be swift.

"No one may do what I am about to do. And who has done it before?"

Even Hatshepsut, the matriarch Pharaoh, had not gone in person to Punt.

"Yes, and who has eaten a poisonous snake while it is still alive? But why would anyone want to?" Wahabil said. "If you would arrange a marriage treaty, my queen, I beg you, let your kinsmen arrange it. It is the way it is done."

Marriage again.

I didn't know whether to laugh or to scream at him.

"It is *not* such a treaty. I go as a sovereign. As one king to another. No one, even you, Khalkharib, will make our argument as vehemently as I, in the way of kings. And yet you will accompany me. You and Niman."

More protests, but even in the uproar, the pieces came to me, swiftly, without premeditation. I felt it all with a sense of elation.

Wahabil sat back, arms in the air.

"Come now, councilors," I said, standing before them. "Do you not know that you are saying this to the princess who journeyed with you from Punt's shores? Who lay down beneath the stars with you, never knowing one night until the next if we would be set upon by north men? Not knowing if the wadis would fill and wash us away as we slept? Did we not march together from the coastal plain of Hadramawt and through the valleys of Qataban to the very edge of the desert?"

Niman shook his head. "That is different."

"Yes. This journey is a stretching of the legs by comparison. A chance for me to see the northern route for myself. Of course, if you are saying that you do not feel up to the long days of travel . . ."

"I will gladly go on your behalf, as your cousin and kinsman," Niman said.

"Then as kinsmen, we will go together." I sat down again. "We are protected in Saba. But we are isolated. We depend on the accounts of our traders to bring news of this foreign court of which they seem so enamored, and to speak on our behalf. Let us see and assess this power—this threat—for ourselves. We have turned our eyes to our mountains and our wadis and mastered the rains. We have turned our eyes to the heavens and built temples to our gods. Now let us turn our gazes to the world. Let us not, in our isolation,

find ourselves years from now an antiquated paradise, set apart like
the lands of myth. One day, though it may be centuries from now,
armies will come to our borders. And we cannot afford to be as innocent as children kept too long in the cradle."

"My queen, this is not a stretching of the legs but an arduous
journey of half a year!" Wahabil said. "Tamrin will attest to its sand-
storms and bandits—"

"Do we not have those things here?" I said. "We are a caravan
nation. When did we forget that the nomad is in our blood? We live
in cities, but we are hardy and not softened by luxury. Well. Perhaps
a little." I smiled. A couple of uncomfortable chuckles issued around
the table.

"Our ancestors made no allowance for weakness, and neither do
we," I continued. "And so this is less a journey to some distant land
than a quest of remembering who we are. Lesser men make war and
invade foreign borders for want or fear. We neither fear nor want,
and we shall prove it. Let the chieftains of Edom and the Amalakites
and the Pharaoh of Egypt and the kings of Phoenicia and yes, of
Israel, be surprised. Would Solomon himself make this journey? He
dare not! His northern tribes conspire against his south. What does
it say of our kingdom, and of its queen, that she may leave with the
full confidence of returning to find it intact? That the journey of a
year is nothing to her? I dare any sovereign to do the same!"

I raised my palm before they could protest again.

"This is a campaign more clever than any war. We will make
many arrangements. We will journey with such spectacle that he will
know he has no choice but to treat with us. We will awe him not with
our weapons, but with our wealth. Our incense will be as spears. Our
gold as fire, and our ivory like arrows. Egypt has given him land and
garrisons. Phoenicia, the materials for his temple, palace, and ships
and artisans to build them all. But Saba will offer him the foreign

exotic he so craves in quantities he could never imagine, and the possibility of touching the far reaches of the world . . . without leaving his throne."

Wahabil was shaking his head. "It is too dangerous. My queen, you are without an heir. Anything could happen and Saba would be at the very war you speak against—not outside her borders, but within them."

"I will make provision of an heir . . . by adoption," I said, thinking quickly.

They all looked at me then in such shock!

"I will adopt an heir before Almaqah in the auspices of the temple. But I will do it in secret. Even you will not know whom I have chosen. I will seal the name in the safekeeping of the priests—of three priests in three temples. And neither you nor anyone will know which ones, so that only after confirmation of my death will they journey to Marib and break open the seal to announce that name," I said, deciding it all even as the words flowed from my mouth.

"That—is not done," Wahabil stammered.

"Nor is it done that a queen gets up and journeys half a world away. And yet, I will do it."

"Adoption of an heir is not unknown. There is precedent in the adoption of a kinsman," Niman said.

"And what great relief for you, that you need not know who and find yourself harassed by chieftains taking up sides, but only keep my throne safe in my absence, or my person safe as we journey together." I glanced from Niman to Khalkharib.

I saw the way Wahabil considered me then, a slight smile playing about his mouth.

"But the tribes—what is to keep them from rising up in your absence?" Yatha said. "Hadramawt stands much to gain if you fail."

I lifted my hand.

"You. Or do you not think you can control them?" I glanced around the table. "I tell you this, a mighty curse will be upon any tribe who dares in my absence. I will enact it at the temple on the day that I set out upon that road."

My heart was soaring in my chest as I said all of this. Certainly I had no intention of dying in this venture, and a part of me now felt something I had not felt in years.

Freedom.

"But now I task you all with silence," I said. "If word of my plan should pass beyond this chamber, I will ferret out the one who betrayed me. And for such treason, he will pay with his life. This journey will be many months, a year, in the planning. No one must know my intention to depart, or even that I have until well after I am gone."

Now they stared at me and I knew I must be either mad or inspired.

"How is that possible?" Yatha blurted.

"We make it possible," I said, very quietly. "And if Saba's throne should be overrun in my absence, you will be cursed along with the tribes that rise up against me. Almaqah himself will deny you your place in the shadow land beyond death. I will inform the priests, and the curse will be put in place before my departure."

Niman was openly searching around the room and Kalkharib looked frankly scandalized.

"But as Saba prospers," I continued, "so will you and your tribes. When the Phoenician ships sail, the first choice of every season's best goods will fall to you in turn. The best bull in my stables will be sent to service your she-camels and the children of your children will study in the far courts of kings. Your lowliest slave will be held in the esteem of other tribes' chieftains, and your sons will be confidants and council to the federator of our kingdoms after me.

You will want for nothing except the answers to questions that those hungry, landless, and afraid never have luxury to lay before the gods. And so your greatest problem will be that of what to do with so many offspring and how to distribute your great wealth upon the journey to your forefathers. But now . . ."

I gestured to Yafush and my eunuch came closer. It was early evening. To think I might even now have been crossing the causeway to the temple to marry the god. But the new moon had brought its own agenda.

"You will give me your vow beneath the blade of my eunuch before leaving this chamber."

Yafush unsheathed his sword and raised it, tip pointed downward over Wahabil's nape.

"My queen," Wahabil said, head bowed. "If I have ever given you cause to doubt—"

"You have not, my friend. And so give me your vow, as you live before Almaqah's Daughter and in the presence of the reborn god himself."

"Almaqah himself strike me dead if I ever betray you," Wahabil said.

Yafush moved to Yatha, who stared through his lashes, head bent, at me.

"I vow," he said.

One by one, they swore their oath to me. Of course they did. I knew this only for grand gesture; any one of them could break it in my absence a year from now. But my spirit was already traveling that incense road, journeying north toward the oases of Yathrib and Dedan, toward Israel. Not for the sake of the king, but because I could no longer contain it here.

When they were done and Yafush stood back once more, Wahabil fairly shouted, "My queen, how will no one know you are gone?"

"I will make my plan known to you. Soon, we will give this king a spectacle that will bring him to his knees."

B y every god, what had I done?

I could not sleep but paced to the window and back. I would not take out the scroll and read it again—a tenth, an eleventh time—by light of the lamp even as Shara slept.

I told myself this audacious plan was for the sake of my kingdom. But the truth was Solomon's letter had sent my nerves to jangling beneath my skin. Without it, I might have entertained the wooing of his enemies. Now, instead, I must woo—and turn—the ambitions of a king.

Perhaps tomorrow I would berate myself for having fallen reactive prey to the king's machinations. I had threatened my council and made grandiose promises that even I did not know if I could keep. I had abandoned the bedchamber of my god in order to scheme a journey to the land of a nameless other. For all I knew, rash action was exactly what Solomon had hoped to ignite in me. Well then, I would not disappoint but far exceed his expectation.

Time enough for doubt later. Tonight, I was excited as I had not been since the day I left Saba for the shores of Punt. Every great turn in my life had been marked by a journey. It was time to begin a new one. A greater one.

That night, in the hours just before dawn, I sent for the Israelite slave, Mazor. If he had been roused from sleep—and he certainly had—he did not show it, but bowed low in my outer chamber, his hair drawn back neatly at his nape, only the gray in his beard belying his age on a face that was round as a boy's.

"Are you not exhausted from your journey and hard ride here?"

"I have been well fed and rested. But even had I not, the praise of my god revives me."

How I envied him his sure devotion, even to a nameless god.

"Then play and sing for me," I said, reclining.

"In the common tongue, or that of my people?" he said.

"In your own."

He bowed low and began to play and as he sang his voice was filled with beautiful melancholy. I closed my eyes and absorbed it like oil.

He played through the first rays of dawn and long into morning, singing song after song in his strange language until I slept at last, lulled by the repetitive "yah," the long vowels from the palate softened by the tongue.

That morning, I dreamed of puzzles. Of foreign kings who both commanded and cajoled and thrones that must be left to be fortified. Of faceless gods with unpronounceable names.

For the first time in years, I slept assured of the path before me. For the first time in years, I looked forward to the future.

But now all my cunning of the past must be as nothing compared to what I would do next.

FIFTEEN

That winter, the trader of Tamrin's off year, a wiry man of the Awsan tribe of Sharah, came to the palace at my summons. It was not his normal route to travel as far as Israel, but only as far as the oasis of Tema, south of Edom.

"I am sending a company of fifty armed men to safeguard your caravan," I said. "But when you reach Tema, you must send twenty of them on to the court of the Israelite king and wait for their return to escort you south again in safety." To the captain of the cohort, I entrusted a golden ewer I had specially commissioned with two ibex head spouts facing away from one another, their graceful horns curved up and adjoined as a double handle. Beneath the one was engraved the name "Fearless." Beneath the other, "Reckless." I had the ewer filled, the mouth of "Reckless" plugged with wax, the other with a scroll upon which I had written only this:

Your questions are but a mirror; only a man who asks them of himself would pose them to another.

Am I fearless or reckless? They are two sides of one vessel. To pour from one is to draw from the other.

My emissary will depart with my royal trader in a year's
time. They weep to leave paradise. But as you cannot go out
into the world, I will send Saba to you. On that day the sun will
rise from the south.

Who am I? I am a girl whose hair has been pulled by a boy,
if only to get her attention. Well, you have it. Now what will the
girl do?

My name is Riddle. My questions are as many as the sand.

I woke early to finish the business of court. I met with my council, and by the hour with Wahabil, who must have the running of my kingdom in my absence.

Shara immediately noticed the change in me.

"How different you are!" she exclaimed, clasping my face between her hands. "The color in your cheeks rivals that of your jewels!" But if it did, it was infectious; the childhood friend who had wept in fear when I told her my plan and then wept again when I said she would accompany me seemed like one who wakes from a long sleep. Her step had lightened and her movements quickened. Twice I even heard her singing in my chamber as she laid out bolts of fabric brought up from the coffers.

For that sound alone, I would have journeyed to the end of the earth.

That spring, when the rains had ceased, I sent for Tamrin. He was quieter than I had come to expect of him, his gaze restless.

"I promise you that the king will receive you when next you set foot in his city," I said. "They will tell tales of this coming trip for generations. But you must make many arrangements now. You will have more treasure to transport and more camels to carry it. You will have, too, many more armed men." He studied me closely then, the broad bow of his lip widening.

"This in response to the king's new port?"

I nodded. "We will engage him in negotiation and persuade him with such gifts that he will give us all that we desire."

"You will send your emissary then?" New life seemed to flood his face.

"I have put you in the most difficult position with this king. This time will be different. I am going with you."

And with that, the color was gone.

"My queen . . ."

"Surely you have thought very long about what those ships mean—not just for Saba, but for your own caravans."

He nodded, and I saw the new lines around his eyes. "Indeed, my father has never wrung his hands so often or hard in his life." He gave a mirthless laugh. "Neither have I, for that matter."

I knew it was not for the wealth of the trek—no. This was a man who basked in the attention of king and queen alike but held nothing so earthly as gold precious. It was not the loss of wealth that he feared, but the hard freedom of the road.

"I will make right. For you, and for Saba."

I looked up to feel the weight of that lapis gaze. "I have never doubted you."

"But you must say only that the queen is sending an envoy to negotiate with the king. And you must prepare to carry wealth that has never been moved without an entire army."

"My queen, I cannot lessen the journey's hardship for you. And with more men and camels it will indeed take an army to move."

"As it so happens . . . I have one."

He went away a different man than he had come to me. We were all of us different, galvanized by this venture, the air of secret between us. Even Wahabil seemed driven by purpose more than worry, the creases gone from his head as he spoke sharply with the chamberlain and barked at the steward.

Only in moments did anxiety seize me. So many promises. So many grand claims. I could not fail. I must not fail. I lifted my chin in my meetings with Wahabil and the council. But taking to the garden when the palace threatened to close in around me, I knew I might fail in a hundred ways. In the journey itself, before ever reaching Israel. In my composure with this king, this devourer of the world. What if Saba's wealth fell short? I had never doubted it before, but for the first time, I found myself taking stock of stable and gold mine, of field and vineyard, of the gnarled trees that produced the pearls of our frankincense. What if I failed to engage this purported wise man, this king who so embraced riddles? Was I clever, or did he seek only to marry Saba's wealth out from under her to suit his own insatiable coffers?

I sought the moon through the pomegranate branches, past the vivid fray of red trumpet flowers. But the moon in its cold day walk only stared back.

I commissioned a great alabaster statue of myself with wide, obsidian, and all-seeing eyes for the day that my absence was unavoidably made known. I conscripted camels and armed men from every tribe. I would not travel with the palace guard, those most trusted by Nabat, but with the men who might otherwise be enlisted to march on Marib by those ambitious in my absence. In this way, they and their kin must pray for the success of the queen's caravan.

The rains came at the end of summer, long and generous. Promise loomed everywhere—for a good winter crop, for Saba.

More travelers than ever flooded the temple that year during the summer pilgrimage. Presiding over the ritual feast, I pronounced good omen, and the prediction of unprecedented wealth to the nation. A day when those sacred guests of the feast—the poor, the forgotten, and the wayfarer—would be so few as to become celebrated elite.

More claims. More promises. What had started with the air of festivity—and continued around me in the persons of Wahabil and even Khalkharib and Shara so that her skin glowed like a girl's—became a quiet gnawing in my gut.

I called for Mazor every night. I had learned by then a great deal of the Israelite language with its soft consonants born back in the throat. Knew by now the words to myriad songs written by this poet king. I had studied them eagerly, and then frenetically. Two months before my departure, I bid him play his lyre as my chamber girl rubbed oil into my hands and hair and feet. Soon they would be cracked with travel.

It was on such an evening that my cohort returned from Israel.

"Such news, my queen," he said as I received him in my private chamber. "The king himself received us and insisted we stay several days. Such strange and exotic foods, such feasting I have never experienced—"

"Yes, yes," I waved him on, impatient, my heart stuttering in my chest.

"We presented him with your gift and what care he took in turning it over in his own hands! He cried out when he found the scroll, as triumphant as a boy. But his brow furrowed before the entire court as he read it and when he tipped the ewer a fine stream of sand spilled out onto the floor. I thought he might weep, he seemed so moved at the sight of it. 'So many questions,' he said. 'Yes.' And then, 'She knows.' When he set the ewer aside he looked at it often as he inquired about our journey.

"The next night he brought us in to feast. He asked which of your emissary you meant to send to him, and the names of their tribes. We were none the wiser and said so, and he ate very little. On the third day after we arrived, there was an eclipse and an outcry in the city. The king disappeared into his chambers and did not call for us, but neither would he let us go. And so we stayed two more days until he summoned us to wish us good journey. He gave us many gifts of knives and leather and to me a fine Hittite bow. For you, he gave this."

He pulled a wrapped scroll from his belt.

Did my heart drum its way out of my chest? I indicated for Yafush to receive it, though I wanted nothing more than to snatch it from his hands.

I started to thank him—I meant to dismiss him immediately—but then he said, "My queen, there is one thing more. As we were leaving, Phoenician messengers came into the city. And so we loitered another day, asking all over the king's court after them. My queen, Hiram of Phoenicia is dead."

I let out an incredulous breath. I could not have received this news at a more auspicious time.

Now the king must renew ties with the new Phoenician king. Perhaps their prior agreements might even be in jeopardy.

Alone in my chamber, I broke the seal on the scroll and unrolled it with clumsy fingers.

Lady Riddle.

How you torture me with your words as with your silence. How you test me. How you delight and anger me at once!

Do you not know that your commercial interests are at stake? But of course you do. And so you punish me with the briefness of your reply and the cleverness of your gift, knowing the one will pique, the other delight. Do you not know I could hobble your kingdom? Do not mistake this king for a boy, but only a man with boyish thoughts. I have pulled your hair. You kick me in the shin. Take care you do not spit in my eye.

I am eager for your emissary, but I know already I will be disappointed. Do not send me your wisest man, or your cleverest, or your most skilled. I am tired of flattery and posturing and simpering. But Saba's emissaries do not simper, you say. I am tired of agreements laid out like logic, as precisely as foundation stones for a palace. I tire even of music and gold and feasting. I go away hungry from my own table.

But you know this, because you tire of it as well. My words are a mirror. But you know this, too. Of course you do. And so once again, I make my arguments, knowing I am speaking only to myself.

Tell me: Do you think your gods know you as well as I, whose face you have never seen?

How you keep me waiting. You have pegged me well and yet you do not know me. It is a dangerous game you play. Fearless and reckless is ultimately foolish. Are you a fool, my queen?

If you are wise, you will be cautious. If you are clever, you will be simple.

But if you have mercy, you will send each of your emissaries with a separate word from you of such length that they may not be devoured at once by this hungry king.

~Solomon

I read it, enraged, and then again in triumph. Let him presume to know me even as he called himself unknowable, this king who was said to discern the hearts of men.

Well, I was no man. And soon we would have words at great length indeed.

SIXTEEN

Two weeks after I received word from Solomon, a veil covered the sun.

I had been walking in the garden with Wahabil where we might not be overheard as we spoke in low tones, the breeze masking our whispers with the rustle of palm fronds as I reviewed the last of the matters he must attend to in my absence. In five days I would begin the journey north at last, to Israel.

We were so engrossed that I never noticed the opaque cast of the sky.

"Princess," Yafush said, "you had best look up."

His voice startled me; my Nubian shadow rarely spoke in the presence of others.

I glanced from him to the sun dimming before my eyes and pulled the veil more securely over my face. Once or twice a year the cooler air stirred up the desert, shrouding the plain and foothills in a greenish pall for days.

Beside me, Wahabil squinted, his head tilted as though listening to the strain of a tune he could not place.

And then I heard it: the faint vibration, the distant buzz.

The sky began to fall in winged hail.

Locusts.

That day I stood by the lattice of my window for hours, the palace grounds obscured by a cloud of scissored wings.

By morning the tender shoots of the winter crop were gone as
though the fields had never been planted. They left in their wake a
bare stubble of stalks, skeletal brush, and branches. Some trees had
been left entirely intact but the fields lay bare, the pastures shorn
free of grasses and brush as hungry camels lapped up the wingless
hoppers left to march in pursuit of the swarm.

"What does it mean?" I asked Asm, staring out at the ruin of the
garden.

"They came after good rains. Some enemy threatens your best
interest, my queen. But your interests may also be multiplied. What
is eaten will return more lush," he said.

I found that hard to believe.

The city turned out in droves to collect the insects. The smell of
locusts cooking in sesame oil and coriander filled the palace kitchens. And though Yafush pronounced them especially delicious—
thanks, no doubt, to the rich crop they had all but obliterated—I
could not bring myself to eat them even in retaliation.

I sent riders to survey the devastation, gave orders for the camels to be fed grain from the storehouse and dried fish. They could
not afford to go hungry now!

Tamrin arrived at the palace several days later, his gaze as shifting as the desert dunes, keeping mine with seeming effort. I had
seen the same look in a caged predator, once.

"The locusts came from the north," he said, drinking more palm
wine than I had ever seen him consume at once. "They crossed the
narrow sea into Bakkah and came down from there after eating the
oasis dry. The oases between here and there are barren. There isn't
enough fodder to support a herd of camels, let alone a caravan."

He did not voice what we already knew between us:

No one would journey north that year.

Behind the door of my privy council all my arguments of before unraveled. Even my peaceful advisor Abyada wondered aloud if we were not to journey to Israel and treat with this king but go to him in war.

"Do you not see," Khalkharib hissed, "it is a sign that we must go not as emissaries but like an army of locusts?"

"Are you a priest now that you interpret signs?" I said, peevishly. "The locusts came south, invading our land, not the other way around. And if there is no forage for a caravan from here to Bakkah there is even less for an army. Meanwhile, the king, too, has lost revenue and tariffs. And so as we suffer, he suffers. If anything, the gods show us our need for water routes more than ever. With ships we might trade frankincense for the seed we lost to replanting, because Almaqah knows we cannot sow incense!"

Worse yet, I could send no message north. A few riders might find fodder enough for their number. But bandits would soon be out in droves searching for food and animals to replace those they must now slaughter. Saba's few ships, meant only for hugging coastlines, had already set sail for ports in Hidush and Punt. By the time they returned, the Red Sea winds would have shifted from the northerly flow of winter to the southern current of summer, and we were no Phoenicians able to harness the winds.

What would the king make of my silence after his demand for more words from me? And how weak would Saba appear to have fallen prey to such mundane plague, and how ill-favored by the gods? This, after I claimed that they doted on Saba as no nation on earth!

And what might he make of not only my silence but the absence of my trader in spring? The new Phoenician king had had time by now to renew ties with Israel, and for all I knew Solomon's fleet neared completion and prepared to set out for the ends of the world. And I, unable to leave or send anyone at all!

I had promised so much, fired by vision—not just for me, but for my people.

I had dared to hope, which was my greatest sin of all.

Tell me: Do you think your gods know you as well as I, whose face you have never seen?

That night I fled to the orchards, my feet churning beneath me. Faster, faster, so that even Yafush could not keep up. When I was far beyond sight of the nearest palace guard, I spun back and shouted at the sky.

"What do you want of me?" I raged. "Where are you, that you turn your back like the most faithless of lovers? What blood do you require that I have not given you—what hope of mine have you not seized at whim? What more do you want? Speak! Speak it and let us be done!" But the moon was silent, the naked branches of the fruit trees stark as black lightning before its face.

Those months were the longest of my life. I paced the halls of the palace and then the ruined hedges of the garden by day, standing at the window for long hours at night, the clamor of a hundred letters written and received only in my head.

Spring came with heavy rains, and the farmers double-tilled the fields. I retrieved the scroll I had steadfastly avoided all this while, as though I had not reread it in my mind a thousand times.

How you torture me with your words as with your silence. How you test me. How you delight and anger me at once!

How you keep me waiting . . .

My words to him had been filled with haughty challenge and invitation, and though he claimed both outrage and anger at them, I knew the thing he would not abide: silence. It did not matter that the swelter of summer was a bare month away; this was not a man who would stomach rebuff. He would never excuse that he had humbled himself in asking for word from me and received nothing and I could not afford to let the correspondence by which I had piqued the king grow cold.

I took out parchment and ink and sat down at last. But after so long, and so many conversations within myself as though we had spoken for months, I was out of cleverness.

Lady Riddle says: I devour with a million mouths. I am devoured in a single bite. I have no king but march in rank. Who am I?

I am alone. There is no one to hear these words. That is the woman, speaking to herself.

The queen says to the king: Is it my god who has conspired to hoard Saba's fruits . . . or yours who has jealously closed the corridor between us? Some way or another we must let them treat so that I may send you the emissary with the many words you long for. Speak sweetly to your god then, as to a lover, even as I cannot. Let him soften his immortal heart along with his invidious resolve.

I said, "I will send Saba to you." But the sun will not rise from the south for another year. And so the gods make me a liar unless we decide together that these months are but days, that they pass as a dream so that when you rise from sleep at last, Saba will be within the walls of your city like the moon before the face of the sun. Not like the eclipse that stole Hiram from Phoenicia, but one that heralds the suspension of the world when time forgets herself so that the ibex feeds at night and the lion hunts by day.

You tire of music and gold and feasting. Then we will pretend that there are no feasts, there is no gold. But there must be

music. You play a flute made from a reed and I clap my hands.
You are no king, and I, no queen. There is no palace. There is
only a garden and our heads are adorned with only crowns of
flowers . . .

    Until the day you must take up the mantle of the wise once
more, and I the veil of fire.

    I am Bilqis.

I lowered my head to my arms and wept. After a while, I sealed
the scroll. No clever gifts this time, only these words as simple as a
virgin sheathed in linen.

The fields flourished beneath the hot sun that summer. But I
was distracted and tense, searching the road with rising frequency
for my small band of Desert Wolves, those enigmatic dwellers of the
harsh sands who drifted into my service long enough to earn a camel
or a few pots before disappearing into the dunes again. I had sent
them with my scroll by way of Gabaan, there to be joined by two of
Tamrin's men to guide them.

By the time the harvest proved plentiful—more even than years
past—I had already journeyed north and back again with them in
my mind ten, twelve, twenty times.

"My queen, are you listening?" Wahabil said. He had come to
talk about locusts and the ground burned for the vast repository of
their eggs. "I worry for you, for your distraction over this king who
agitates you so."

Shara had already expressed her own concerns about my waning weight, the color that had left my cheeks. But what else could
happen to me, cooped up inside the palace with reports of crops
and whether the locusts had emerged and in what quantity, and how
many had been seen coupling on the millet stems!

That autumn, Tamrin arrived at the palace.

"My Wolves?" I said.

He rose from his bow, brows lifted. Without the arduous journey that seemed to define the very cords of his arms and neck each time he returned, he seemed a thing more cultivated than ever. But the unrest in his eyes belied him. I, who had thought this year torture—how much more so had it been for him, this nomad among nomads?

"I greet you as my queen, and you say to me 'My Wolves?'" His voice was like warmed honey when he chuckled, though I knew the sound was forced.

"Forgive me. Welcome. And now, have you seen my Wolves?" I smiled sweetly.

"Alas, no." He shook his head, staring toward the windows, the shutters thrown wide in the cool of early evening. He, too, was impatient for word from his men—or from the king himself. "It is too soon for their return. Who knows how long the king might have kept them, or if he even received them at all?"

I had not thought of that possibility. Renewed anxiety surged up inside me.

"I'm surprised you didn't escort them yourself," I said.

He paced away, digging his fingers into the unbound hair at his nape. "How I nearly bolted after them!" he said through gritted teeth. "And I would have, had I no camels to negotiate fodder for, doing business cooped up in the city like one of the queen's ministers!" He went still. "Forgive me."

I waved it away.

I, too, was tired of waiting. I was tired of many things. I had told myself that I would not waste time here, even as the words of Solomon's letters trailed me like the hem of my own gown. How had I allowed a king on the other side of the world such power over my every waking thought? How had he worked such effect over us both?

"Why have you come, if not with news?" I said, squinting at him.

"I don't know why I came," he said quietly. "This last year has dealt all my tribe such a blow, as for all of Saba. I thought that if the queen would receive me that I would at least not stare at the same camels and faces of my foremen and slaves, all looking at me, the same question in their eyes." He shook his head. "But my memory is deficient."

"How so?"

He glanced up. "I forget that when the queen receives me in private, she no longer wears her veil. And that I always leave more distracted than before."

Outside the moon had risen large and orange over the sill of the window.

"Have you no wife, Tamrin?" In all this time, I had never known, and though I had refused a proposal from his tribe, it had not been for him.

"No." He sat down with a rueful smile. "Nor will I. No woman wants to be loved second most."

"Marriage is not about love," I said.

"No. But every woman—even a queen, I think—wants to be loved and loved before all others. I could make a wife content, I think. But I would not make her happy. And I would come to hate her duty, if only because I knew it mirrored my own."

I had never heard him speak with such baldness.

"Your first love is given then—to whom?" I asked.

"Not given, but taken from me."

I looked away.

"Ah," he said softly. "You think I mean my queen, whom yes, I love. But that is not what I meant."

Now I could look at him. "Who has seized this love from you?"

He shook his head as one lost. "The gods of air and sun," he said with a helpless laugh. "Of the road, the sands, oases . . . who chase me away to Israel, Damascus, and Tyre. To the courts of kings and then home again to Gabaan, which I crave to the point of tears, and then despise the moment I return. It is the same with the sands, or the tents of the oases, which I long for and cannot wait to leave. There is no place, but that one in between, where I am at peace."

He lifted his eyes to me then.

"And yet I come back to you, unable to help myself, knowing I will leave. Trusting you will tell me 'go.' Knowing you could command me to stay and that I would obey, but only because you compelled me."

Impossibly, his anguish made those feral eyes even more beautiful.

"Yafush," I said, never looking away from Tamrin.

Without a word, the eunuch left, quietly closing the door behind him.

Tamrin sat very still.

I hesitated a moment, thinking of the king's letters. Of the gravity of them, so like an unbroken spell. And of the king, certainly not lying alone all these nights even as he claimed himself tortured.

"I will not command you stay," I whispered.

In an instant he had crossed the short space between us, a bare arm pulling me to him as his mouth descended on mine.

I had forgotten the scent of skin, the warm musk of it. He smelled of sandalwood and oil.

Tamrin returned to Marib twice more before the autumn rains ended.

And then, the Wolves of the Desert returned.

You send not emissaries, but Wolves, and I opened my gates to them. Such gifts I would have given them for the journey they made beneath the merciless sun had they only the animals to carry them. And so I know now you command the curious hoopoe bird your trader, and the wolves of the very desert, and the jinns to spirit all of them here. But do not think you can command a king.

I hid my tears from them. How do you cut to the heart with a simple tale of a garden and not draw blood? These are not my tears, but yours, for if you are my Riddle, I am your Mirror.

And yet I am the one devoured in a single bite and you are Locust, the plague of Israel's enemies. Are you my enemy, then? Only demons treat with succulent words. Only demons may so distract, using the secret longings of a man against him. How you have swarmed my thoughts, and consumed them.

But even as I say "I will not be confounded" because I find you haughty, you turn gentle and melancholy. And I must be gentle in return even as you bring me to tears for your loneliness, which is my own.

Now you are angry, for I have found you out. Do you delight in my distraction? Of course you do. You are Woman.

Take care, Bilqis—how many times have I whispered your name?—many women have played at the emotions of kings, few to good fortune.

But play at them, even as I command your caution. I beg you. Let me pretend a little longer.

Send your emissary with words like a swarm that I may be devoured.

"Send word to Tamrin," I said to Wahabil later that day. "It's time to leave."

SEVENTEEN

The day we departed, the priests sacrificed a bull in the courtyard of the Marib temple at dawn. It was cold; even wrapped in a heavy woolen shawl I shivered in the pale light. Reading the steaming liver, Asm hesitated before declaring our journey profitable, his forehead drawn.

I drew him aside afterward. "What is it?"

"The return, my queen. It will be . . . more difficult."

It was an omen I could live with.

I took my leave of Wahabil there in the temple and to all eyes it must have appeared as though he brushed noses with a slave girl. I had exchanged my purple gowns and carmine silks for a simple tunic, my head cloth and veil obscuring all but the barest part of my eyes so that I was indistinguishable from Shara or my slaves.

"Care for my kingdom," I whispered.

"I shall do so as though your eyes are upon me always. Return safely next year, my queen. Almaqah speed you. Almaqah grant you favor. Blessings on the camel that carries you."

He had grown precious to me, my stalwart councilor, my friend. I embraced him then and kissed him as a father.

Before I left the temple complex, I stopped at the mausoleum to

stand before the limestone plate of my mother's grave and the alabaster face of the funerary mask set within it. I sighed and touched
the vacant eyes. They were cold.

At twenty-four I was now the same age she had been when she
died. Did she know that I was queen? I stroked her carved cheek.

I lingered a moment more, wishing—hoping—that her voice
might come to me. But there was only the wind and the snarling of
camels in the distance. At last, I drew away and followed the others across the causeway where the men and camels waited. Four
hundred camels. Seven hundred men, including twenty Wolves of
the Desert. Half the caravan, prepared to journey north to Tamrin's
tribal lands where we would meet up with nearly three hundred
camels and as many men more.

As we crossed the oasis through which I had marched just six
years ago, I looked back at the tiny procession of Wahabil and his
slaves wending their way back to the capital. Morning had broken,
infusing the brick buildings of Marib with golden warmth, turning
the alabaster windows of the palace ruddy as fifty new suns. Willing
the sight of them to memory, I turned my face north.

Tamrin had taken pains to hide my presence, and to find excuse to
install Shara and me, and the five girls I had brought with me toward
the front of the caravan where there would be less dust.

"They are not hardy for the ride," I overheard him sigh loudly
to one of his foremen, who shook his head at the litter that carried
two of them. And so we were well within earshot of Niman and
Khalkharib, who had brought with them ten men and fifteen camels
each of their own.

The eunuch was the most difficult aspect to disguise, as it was
well known the Nubian was ever at my side. He wore a head scarf

and Khalkharib claimed he was his slave and took pains to call him Manakhum, though I heard him slip once on the second day of our journey.

We could not keep up the charade forever, but I hoped at least to conceal my departure until the Jawf lay several days behind us. At the palace, Wahabil had taken pains to select a slave my height and secure her in a secluded apartment of the women's quarter. Once every day, she was to walk through the portico covered by one of my veils and wearing one of my gowns. She was even to sit on my throne in the Hall of Judgment, leaning toward Wahabil in conference as he pronounced judgment as though it were my own. It was not a foolproof ploy, but it might at least stave off public knowledge of my absence for a little while.

I had never seen Tamrin's caravan, which was normally three hundred and fifty camels large with nearly as many men. Those first days our sheer size, which was only half of what it would be—astounded me.

Such noise! There was the constant talk of men, of the foremen calling orders to those at the head of each section and riders crooning to their camels in tones as cajoling as a lover. Camels seemed to gurgle and roar day and night, protesting when they were hobbled to forage or coaxed to let down their milk and then when couched at night, and again as they were mounted with pack-saddle and bags.

Nearly one hundred and fifty camels carried gifts of gold, textiles, and spices—all of Saba's usual fare, but in such quantities that even I had never seen. One camel bore an entire load of ivory. Another, ebony. Another, rhinoceros horn and ostrich feathers and delicately packed ostrich eggs painted and adorned with jewels. Another, a pharmaceutical chest of aloe and unguents, salves and balms of myrtle and oliban, and another of kohl and cosmetics. Three more bore jewelry, cups, and gold boxes encrusted with precious stones as well as wool, hemp, and linen fabrics dyed in a variety of colors. Enough gifts for nearly three hundred wives and concubines, if indeed the tales were true.

The litter that carried my girls was in fact my own palanquin, made more lavish than it had been before, but ingeniously so that it could be removed in parts, its gold struts and feathered canopy wrapped in woolen blankets on a camel farther back. My own wardrobe and jewelry chest required five camels, and that of Shara, Yafush, and my girls, eight more.

Twenty camels strung together by a rope carried gold and silver tassels, saddle ornaments and elaborate tack, tents, rugs, blankets, and incense burners. Asm had eight camels for his own use and that of his acolytes, laden with idols and the objects of his mystical office.

Thirty musicians traveled with us, Mazor among them. I had vacillated about bringing him if only because I could not afford to have him inform on the activities of my palace. Just weeks ago, I determined to bring him under sword oath. The musician had wept, creeping forward to kiss the top of my foot when I asked him how he would like to see his homeland again.

"You have made the arduous journey once in coming here. Do you feel fit enough to make it there and back again?"

"And there and back a thousand times, to see Israel again," he said, his cheeks wet with tears, his nose running like a child's. And then such songs he sang that night, well past the time I slept so that by morning I woke to find him still softly playing the lyre.

At the center of our caravan traveled Saja, my prized white camel. And behind her, on another she-camel, the *markab*, wrapped in linen and woolen blankets so that it looked by its shape like only a spare litter. It was unthinkable that I not take it with me—the capture of the acacia ark in my absence would all but constitute a

seizing of the throne. Wahabil had publicly removed it for place-
ment in my private reception chamber over a year ago in the name
of its safekeeping. Today a simple imposter lay in its place, covered
with a gold embroidered cloth.

One other item of my office followed behind the *markab*
wrapped in cloth and strapped to a large bull camel: the duplicate
throne that had stood in my garden the night of my now infamous
banquet. This had not been a part of my original inventory, but a
woman can decide to pack many things in the extra space of a year.

Animals followed in wicker cages: sand cats, songbirds, pea-
cocks, pelicans, and yellow-head parrots. Two camels bore between
them a cage with a hissing black panther, and another two monkeys
from Punt.

Nearly a hundred camels carried flour, dried meat, dates, water,
sesame and other oils, and camel's milk in goatskins where, by day's
end, the frothing cream would contain a lump of butter. Behind
these, seventy more bore emergency fodder.

Armed men rode the length of the train on either side of it,
concentrated at the treasure in its middle and provisions near the
dusty end. Four men dispersed throughout our length bore the ibex
banner of Saba, distinguishable from the royal banner only by the
absence of the silver crescent between the animal's horns.

Two short hours of numbing pain into the journey I remembered how sore I had been the last time I sat a camel saddle, so that
I walked as an old woman the first night I dismounted. Shara and I
had no choice but to wrap our middles tightly with spare head cloths
the second morning, if only so we could bear to ride again.

I had never seen Tamrin in such form. If he had struck me as
obsequious once, he was a wholly different creature now. Gone
was the flattering courtier. This was the Master of the Caravan,
at one moment shouting commands, at another conferring with a

foreman and then riding ahead to scout forage, tasting for himself the water of a nearby well that had had good water two years ago. On occasion he would break out in song to be joined swiftly by his foreman and the next of his men within earshot, all the way down the line.

The first few days of the journey my mind had run like a break-away colt, the frenetic pace of my last preparations finding no outlet in the tedium of the road. This was not the desperate march of a queen for her throne, stealing through valley and foothill and gathering men to her like the wadi waters, but a slow progression across the ground like a shadow lengthening through the course of the day.

I came to understand why the Desert Wolves, who rode kneeling in their saddles, told so many stories and argued vehemently and pettily to pass the time. Barring the accidents of broken girths, lamed animals, or sick companions, there was nothing to break up the monotony of land before and behind without cease.

Even surrounded by the chaos of hundreds, the caravan had an isolating effect; without privacy, one must make noise continuously or retreat into the solitude of thought. In three entire days I never heard a word come out of Yafush's mouth, and even Khalkharib and Niman, though they spoke to one another and to their men, seemed strangely contemplative.

Nearly every day a few people from the nearest settlement came to eat by our fires and ask for news and why there were so many more camels than usual. Was Saba going to war? What god or kingdom threatened, or had the queen finally made promise to marry, may Wadd, Sayin, Shams, and Almaqah make it so?

"Why do you care so much that the queen marries?" I said through my veil one night to an older man wearing only a loincloth who had come to sit by the fire of my feeding family, which consisted of Khalkharib and his "slave," Yafush, my women, Tamrin, and me.

"The spirits of women wander if they are not married," he said in his wizened voice. I could see by light of the fire that his one eye was rheumy. "And then they do not possess themselves but are open to other spirits. As they grow older it makes them insane."

I laughed out loud at this. "Truly, you think this?"

"Of course. There is proof everywhere. They are changeling already because of the moon upon them. No, it is not good for a woman to be unmarried."

"And does it have the same effect on men?"

"Oh no," he said, shaking his head. "Not at all. Being unmarried makes a man ambitious and he may only become violent. But that is if he is young."

"And if he is old?"

"If he is old and has no wife, it means he is hungry." He smiled then, showing only three teeth in his mouth.

Traveling unknown, I could watch, if only from a distance, how the tribesmen of the oases haggled with Tamrin over the price of fodder, the hire of slaves to water so many camels. How they laughed and clapped him on the back once the quibbling was over.

Tamrin was careful all these days to avert his eyes from me, to seem to see me not at all. Only I noticed the way he came to check the girth of the palanquin my girls rode in before leaving in the morning, or sometimes at midday. The way he handed his bowl to one of the girls as though they were indeed the slaves Khalkharib attested they were, but never to me.

At Nashshan, Tamrin's men took a pack of incense and several gold items to the newly built temple. By law, no camel might turn off the road except after it had paid tithe to the oasis temple. These were the same tariffs used to fund Saba's ritual feasts and her public works. The men returned hours later leading a line of goats tied nose to tail. We slaughtered them that night, which seemed to bring guests to our fires in droves—including the seller of the goats himself—where we were obligated to share bread, meat, and the soup cooked in the goat's stomachs buried beneath the fires.

If there was no privacy in a traveling caravan by sunlight there was even less in camp, where it was impossible not to hear intermittent conversations through the night—the continuation of a petty argument, the sudden curse of a scorpion in the blanket, the random memory of a kinsman spoken aloud to the air. Anything to fill the darkness, as though the vastness of the desolate terrain by day became unbearable beneath the endless stars.

I was plagued by the opposite as night after night I lay awake staring up at only the black wool of my tent, pinpricks of the moon on its brightest night like stars in the obsidian weave until I felt the sky would smother me.

When we reached Najran, the farthest north I had ever been in my life, I gave Khalkharib my simple message to send ahead with a company of men:

King of contradictions! You are tortured and commanding.
You beg and then require.
  I delight you. I anger you.
  You say if I am wise I will be cautious. The wise and cautious both speak little and yet you crave my words.
  You say if I am clever I will be simple. And yet you relish riddles.
  You say I must send words in quantities to feed a king, but not by my wisest or cleverest man.

Very well. I grant them all. I shall send no man. As you cast
your bread upon water, I shall cast mine upon the sands.
Prepare a place for me.

The first weeks of the journey I had felt liberated, interested
in every detail, invigorated the day the entire caravan covered
itself against a rolling cloud of sand from the desert and awed by
the mystical shroud that hung over us after. And by even the sand
itself, ever in the ears and hair and food, as messy as bread and
lovemaking.

But now, after dispatching my men, I was restless. I could no
longer fall into the meditative stupor of the saddle, nor be lulled by
the tinkling of the amulets and ornaments dancing from bridles. I
felt worn down by the endless stretch of the world before me. And I
was weary especially of the smell of burning camel dung.

Even the tribespeople who came to sit by our fires failed to fas-
cinate me, one of them most recently raising my hackles when he
pointed at me and asked loudly if I were a gift for Solomon's Egyptian queen. Many of these people, upon seeing the presence of such
good bulls, left quickly and came back leading a she-camel in estrus
to have her serviced. Sometimes it was not camels that were brought
to our caravan, but women, by their seedless husbands or even their
mothers. I never watched to see whose fire they went to, though I
did wonder if Tamrin had serviced such women himself.

The terrain grew dryer, the acacia and junipers more stunted as
we skirted a bizarre landscape of lava fields. By the time we entered
the fertile plain south of Bakkah with its pale, yellow soil, only the
Desert Wolves could ease my stiff ennui. On more than one occasion I watched them break suddenly away from the caravan, disappearing at times for an entire day before returning to their feeding
fire at night with a gazelle. At night, I listened to the peculiar cer-

emony with which they divided the meat among them, drawing lots for each portion as it was served, while in other camps men argued endlessly that they had received far too much until their meat went cold.

"This is for the smelliest man," the lot drawer would say and pluck a reed with a man's mark upon it from his fist. Laughter and shoulder slapping ensued.

"This is for the most virile man." Another lot. "This is for the one with the tented tunic that makes the goats run in fear." The men around their fire howled.

I had never seen the matter resolved so effectively or hilariously.

They always sent a portion to our fire, I assumed because we shared it with Tamrin, whose status here far outweighed that of any noble.

Three nights north of Bakkah one of the Desert Wolves—my favorite of them, a young man named Abgair with an uncanny knack for identifying the tribe of any camel—came to our fire with a clutch of jerboas and sat down to skin them right there.

"That is a fine knife," I said, watching him.

"The king gave it to me," he said, obviously happy with it, but not holding it so sacred that he would not dirty it in practical use.

"Which king?" I said through my veil. At this, he stopped and squinted at me as though I had lost my mind.

"The one you sent me to."

I sighed and unwound my head scarf at last. Across the fire, Shara did the same, with a half smile that I had not seen by light now in nearly two months.

"How did you know it was me?" I said, at which Abgair tilted his head as though to say was I really asking that? I laughed then, the sound ringing out over the fire, grateful at least that he had not given me up—even to myself—until now.

"And do the other Wolves know that I am here?"

"Of course," he said, tossing the first jerboa down onto the sand, carefully setting the tiny hide aside. "But I knew first."

"Of course." I smiled.

That night when Tamrin returned to the fire with a swift second glance at sight of my face, he dropped to his knees, saying clearly, "My queen, you honor my humble caravan!"

This caused a violent ripple through our number. Armed men and foremen flocked to our fire first to stare and then to bow before me, the foremen asking how it was that I had shown up here as though I had walked out of the very lava fields, others asking if they had known—if Tamrin himself had known—that the queen was with them.

The next morning, the bearers replaced the banner of Saba with the royal standard and I changed out of my plain tunic and veil but only for cleaner versions in simple browns and reds.

In Yathrib we were welcomed beneath the date palms by the tribesmen of the oases. I had not, by now, seen a brick house in over a month, nor so many tent dwellers gathered in such number.

"Welcome, welcome a hundred times, in the name of the god that brought you!" the local chieftain, a man named Sabahumu, said. "Please, great queen, come eat by my fire or I will divorce my first wife." I relented only because he would be obligated to do it if I refused and I assumed he might be fond of her.

We stayed in Yathrib five days. On the last day, my men arrived from the north.

"My queen," the captain of the small cohort said, "all that the king said was true! How he taxed us with questions when he read Khalkharib's message, asking how your travel fared even as we explained it was the royal caravan but that you were not among it. Three times he questioned us, and we swore by his god that you were not among us. When the king questioned us a fourth time about the slaves and musicians in our number, and we said that the noble Khalkharib had with him five slave women, the king began to laugh. What fools we have appeared!"

"Be at peace," I said, as he delivered the king's message into my hand. I tried not to clutch the scroll too tightly.

The sun rises under guise of dark, the horizon is her veil.
The sleepless king with no hope of dawn has gathered the light of his lamps. He is as a beggar huddled before their flame against the endless night.
The watchman shouts but none believe him: the light of a thousand flames rises to the south!
My men will go to her, to the very border of our land, to usher in the day.

Twice in the barren days of sparse grazing and silted wells beyond Yathrib, alarm rose at the back of the train. We lost two men, but killed ten bandits and left their heads on poles in the ground, curses carved across their foreheads. At night we circled in unending spiral, a galaxy upon the earth, our fires as stars, the black tent of my women in the center of it all. Bandits managed to coax off two camels as they foraged at dusk, but at least their packs—one with a quantity of gold—had already been removed.

By the time we reached the oasis of Dedan we had been five months on the journey and I wanted nothing but to drink cool water by day and eat hot stew by night—anything but dried meat and pressed date cakes, sandy bread or moldy cheese—and to sleep for a week. After feasting at the tent of the local chieftain and giving gifts of incense and knives for his sons and bangles for his wives, I all but collapsed in my tent, grateful to lie down without fear of viper or jackal, wary only of scorpions and the ever-present spiders that had caused Shara and my girls to scream regularly since the day we left.

Only the Desert Wolves seemed unfazed by these months of hardship—these men who told stories of causing camels to vomit in order to drink the contents of their stomachs or mixing salty camel milk with brackish water to make it drinkable. Whose women washed their hair in the urine of camels, which they claimed was sweet as herbs—and which I could attest smelled nothing of the sort.

The day after we left Dedan, a camel kicked one of Tamrin's foremen, splintering the bone. Tamrin cursed the camel over the man's screams, and then set to the grim business of binding the man's leg once he had passed out. I told his men to put him in the palanquin, where he groaned and fell into delirium for days, aided only by the herbs Asm gave him that made him stare wildly and swat at the air. We had by then seen many injuries and snake bites and cured most of them with salves, aloe and incense. But this . . . there would be no good help for him until we reached Jerusalem, if he survived so long.

A few days later, one of the camels carrying a load of gold went lame. We slaughtered it that night as its owner openly wept. Despite the fact that he knew he would be compensated, the man was inconsolable over the she-camel he called Anemone and carried her harness around his neck for days.

"I have seen this before," Abgair said, shaking his head. "It is very bad."

I grew quiet for days. I could not explain this change in me when Shara asked in a whisper, and Yafush with silent gazes. Something had happened to me along the journey, like the peeling away of veils. I had gone from queen in my own land to queen of a neighboring land, to an exotic queen of a distant land that worshipped the moon by a foreign name. As we emerged from the oases of Hegra and Tabuk, I felt I had molted my skin like a lizard until I looked about me and recognized the faces around me better than my own.

As we entered the final stage of our trek, I searched the sky for the face of Almaqah. But even the moon seemed different, a cousin of the one I knew, whom the tribespeople of the Hisma called Sinn.

On the day that we emerged from the desert into the arms of the Ramm oasis, Saba's mountains seemed a lifetime, a dream away. That evening, strange lightning lit up the sky in white veins, and I belatedly noticed that the nights were no longer as cold. As the first drops of the storm shower fell, I realized that it was spring.

That night I witnessed a miracle. One of the families that came to our fire had a young girl with them whom they called "Heaven" in their language. I had never heard a name like this and thought how beautiful it was with a wistful longing that I had been given such a name, or might have given it to a daughter had I not been barren.

When Heaven came into our midst, one of my musicians took out his drum and began to beat it. And then I noticed that the little girl—she must have been three or four years old—was dancing by the fire.

She was oblivious to all of us, who fell off in our conversation to watch, caught up in an ecstasy without aid of datura or wine or the things that remind us how to be as children again. She swayed and stomped and leapt to the drum—to instruments, I imagined, unheard to us, our ears too long closed to the celestial realm from which children come and some remember even to that age.

I had seen so much of fear in its many guises: prevention,

caution, safeguarding, self-consciousness. Heaven was the antithesis of them all. Dancing with closed eyes, she was seductive in her innocence, looking neither to god or tribesman or moon or air. How I envied her!

We stayed in the oasis for three nights. And though I looked for Heaven each evening, I never saw her again. The last night, it stormed again, and I went out and turned my face up into the rain.

"My queen!" Niman said, but his voice was as distant to me as Saba itself. There was only the sand beneath my feet, the rain falling on my face in spattering baptism, the rivulets of water running along my scalp and plastering the linen of my tunic to my body as it washed away the dust of nearly six months.

That night, I was neither queen, nor Bilqis, nor Makeda, nor lover, nor High Priestess of the Moon but something more and less at once.

I entered Edom in a new state, Heaven in mind.

I was ready to meet this king.

EIGHTEEN

I had forgotten the glimmer of gold and gleam of silver, the brittle color of gems. They had become paltry to me in our passage through the sands, trifles that could not be eaten or used for shelter or healing.

But they could be traded for ships and ports to sustain a nation.

My girls dressed my hair. They took out the beaded gowns. Shara burned incense down to ashes and, after mixing them with oil, lined my eyes. The night before she had decorated my hands with henna, my feet in ornate lacework to my calves.

My armed men donned jewel-encrusted scabbards, my bare-chested eunuch enough gold to put a prince to shame. My musicians transformed once again into the celestial spirits they had been the night of my banquet.

Had I ever seen a more majestic sight? Nobles in their tribal finery, girls dripping gold as carelessly as rain, priests in their somber robes and silver collars, the handles of their sickled knives glowing in the faint morning light. Even the camels had been fitted in cabochon halters, tassels swinging from their saddles.

Tamrin had warned me against the ibex headpiece, saying such images were repugnant to the Israelites, as was any idol's image. He did not know I had already chosen the crescent crown, the sun disc eclipsed by the slivered moon. I said it told the story of the tribal goddess Shams eclipsed by Almaqah, over all. But the king alone would know it as a riddle, a secret disguised in full sight.

Shara laid the heavy crescent collar I had commissioned for this occasion on my shoulders. It shimmered with a waterfall of quartz to my waist—the moon and its cascading beams. She belted my gold girdle over my gown, fastened my veil and kissed me through it.

"You are the queen of queens, the queen of kings. Truly, you are the Daughter of the Moon," she said, bowing low before me then.

Khalkharib himself assisted me to my palanquin as the censers were lit and white smoke began to waft into the air.

In plain sight for the first time since leaving Saba, was the *markab*, its acacia wood covered in fresh gold leaf. Only my palanquin rivaled it, with its inlaid posters and golden finials, one for each phase of the moon: waxing, full, waning, and dark, the last an obsidian disc. I had never seen Saja, my she-camel, so beautiful, silver tassels swaying from her sides, her harness sparkling with jasper.

The stars paled with the first tinge of peach. The moment the sun breached the horizon, its rays shot out across the sky, a hot, glowing disc incinerating the east.

We had entered Israel yesterday and traveled in the dark to a shallow valley near a town called Etam, directly south of Jerusalem. The small party of men who met us near Hebron said this place was the source of water for the king's pleasure-grounds and gardens. I could not think of a more fitting site to appear with the morning.

Tamrin whistled and threw his arm forward. Twelve men surrounded my palanquin as the caravan began its slow undulation forward, emerging from the shaded eastern slope into the light. I looked back and shielded my eyes against the gilded serpent unfurling behind me, knowing I would never see this sight again.

We rose up from the valley, the sun growing more intense on our every gleaming surface. I was grateful for the spatter of last night's rain; today the only thing to rise in our wake would be a plume of incense where the column of mortal dust had marked our progress the months before. Lyre and oud broke the stillness of early morning. A beautiful voice soared over it all, singing praise to a god who had no name. Mazor.

In the distance before us I could just make out a large escort of what looked like a hundred men come out to meet us on as many horses—and then the rise of the capital beyond, which had been nothing but the starry flicker of lanterns against the northern sky as we arrived last night.

"That is Benaiah, the king's commander . . . and his axe-man," Tamrin said, riding alongside me. Color was high in his cheeks, light glinting in his eyes. He was enjoying this.

"Why does he not come to greet me?" I said as the escort turned to lead us into the city.

"The king has ordered that he be the first to greet you. And in so doing, all must embrace you."

"You say it as though there are those who would not," I said, leaning back onto my elbow with the swaying of the palanquin.

"The Israelites are accustomed to foreigners in their courts," he said with a shrug, but I sensed he chose his words carefully. "They have seen many foreign women enter Jerusalem's walls, never to leave. But never a queen like you . . . and never an entrance like this."

There could not have been a more perfect day for my arrival in Jerusalem. The sun rose into a pocket of cloud for nearly an hour, sparing us the heat. But then, just before we descended through the valley to the city gate, it broke, the full force of its glare blazing off gemstones, tack and tassel, and every polished surface in my company.

The king's capital sprawled from the mount, surrounded to the south and east by valleys filled with olive trees and cultivated plants green with the new rain and trickle of gutters from the city walls.

From here I had a clear view of the palace rising to the northeast, the verdant rooftop gardens. And above even them, a paved courtyard like a platform to the heavens, the temple thrust up to the sky behind a veil of smoke. Did my eyes play me, or had a purple-clad figure just moved on the roof of that palace?

A large crowd had gathered along the road, the curious coming as close as they dared to my guards, the poorest with hands outstretched. They received the last of our date cakes and bread as children darted from the protective arms of parents to grab sweets from the hands of my girls.

Another company of men waited just before the city gates, clad in leather armor and linen. Tamrin barked an order and my noble company broke forward from the rest of the caravan, fragrant white smoke rising from the censers as Mazor's voice rang out over his lyre with a beautiful, bell-like clarity I had not heard from him before. Fifty of Tamrin's men followed, bearing wooden chests and the cages of animals between them on poles.

We passed through the double gate behind this smaller escort and filled the narrow street. All of Jerusalem could easily fit within Marib's walls, I noted with some satisfaction. But I had not expected the crowding of the houses, the people gathered on the rooftops. The palace complex, larger than my own. I had not expected a temple within the walls of the city, clad in so much gold it glittered in the sun. Even from here I could see the quality of the dressed stone, and envied it. The Phoenicians had served Solomon well.

Men greeted Tamrin as we traveled through the upper city. I realized fully now the kind of alliances he had made here as their faces lit up at sight of him, their eyes shifting invariably back to my men and to me.

I had been curiously observant all this while, listening for words I knew in the language I had practiced with Mazor, wondering where the girls with their earthen jars went to draw their water. But as we entered the royal complex, my heart began to batter my ribs.

Fearless or reckless . . .

In the outer court, palace slaves rushed to couch our camels. I waited as my men shouldered the poles on either side of my palanquin, and Tamrin himself unfastened the mighty girths that attached the litter to Saja's custom saddle. The palanquin lurched and I clutched its edges—oh, wouldn't it be fine if Saba's queen spilled to the ground before she reached the palace steps!

An instant later the entire litter lifted up and I was carried forward. Now I noticed the columns all around the open yard, the fruit trees ready to bloom, the peacock that watched our commotion from between two flowering shrubs. I glanced up at the terraces raining down tendrils of greenery over the walls. Truly, the king had built for himself a paradise, though now I could see where it was unfinished, the western portion farthest from the temple falling off in a ziggurat of stone.

A man more finely dressed than the others came to greet us and, after brief words with Tamrin, led our procession through the inner gate. We filled the stone archway with music, Mazor singing hymns to his god, and entered the palace with incense.

The outer chamber was full of people gathered in knots—rough peasants and well-dressed merchants, scribes and robed priests. All around us, conversations drifted to silence. Ahead of me, the great doors to the king's hall lay open. Was it there that he had proclaimed the famous judgment over the prostitutes—who were, I was certain, not prostitutes at all, but unmarried women? Countless nights on our journey I had bade Mazor speak of his people's stories, rituals, and exacting laws, and Tamrin had warned me to never be seen alone in the company of a man—including him. I did not understand this people's ways, but neither would I give offense.

I had barely registered the open curiosity and widened eyes of those in the outer chamber, hardly begun to assess the Israelite from the foreigner—to determine if here, so close to me, were the astronomers and engineers I so coveted—before we passed through the great doorway.

The hall bloomed to life before me. It was filled with a forest of great cedar pillars. Lamps and incense burners as tall as men stood sentry between them. The floor was inlaid in a zodiac of sunbursts, flowers, and date palms. Perhaps a hundred courtiers crowded the gallery. Military men. Finely dressed nobles. Scholars. I knew the look of a scholar anywhere if only by the frayed hems of his tunic and eyes squinted from too many hours spent peering at scrolls. They all leaned this way and that, craning to see our procession emerging into the hall.

I took this all in with a cursory glance, aware of every opulence, but my eye was fixed at the hall's apex. There, six broad steps flanked on either side by sentinel lions ascended toward a throne with high, rounded back not unlike the sun disc that had adorned my father's before he had it changed to the silver moon. And there, seated unmistakably upon it: the man himself.

How strange to lay eyes on him at last!

Perhaps ten years my senior, he wore the same neatly trimmed beard as my musician, Mazor. His eyes glittered from beneath well-formed brows. He was wide across the shoulder, a warrior's son indeed, and many rings were on his fingers.

The men lowered my palanquin.

Khalkharib and Niman went before me, but only a little ways—why did they not walk directly to the dais? They bowed low, and when they straightened, Niman said, "Solomon, King of Israel, we greet you in the name of your god. We have heard tales of your greatness and have come from the edge of the world to see with our own eyes."

The king rose. From what I could make out from this vantage, he was tall. His voice, when he spoke, carried easily. "Welcome to Israel, and to Jerusalem, the holy city. In the name of Yaweh, the One That Is, we greet you in peace. Our eyes are glad."

His voice surprised me. It was not the booming baritone I had expected, but a voice for singing, much like Mazor's, smooth in timbre.

"I stood atop the roof of my palace this morning," he said, looking now to his right and then to his left. "And what a marvel I saw! For the first time since the beginning of the world, the sun rose not in the east, but from the south." He descended a step. "But then I looked again, and it was not the sun, but the moon, risen in the day. I have not in my life seen such a marvel. But tell me, Niman of Sheba, what is the treasure borne on this litter that so graces my hall?"

My heart thrashed in my chest.

Niman bowed low again. "I present to you my kinswoman, the queen and jewel of Saba and the glory of Punt. Bilqis, Daughter of the Moon."

We had agreed that he would not announce me as the Daughter or High Priestess of Almaqah. We must be politic. Nor was I certain Almaqah had followed me all this way, if he had ever looked upon me at all, though of course I had not said this to Niman.

The king descended the dais. But when he came no farther, Niman hesitated. For a long, awful moment, I waited. Why did the king not come forward to greet me, to extend his hand? But he stood fixed upon the last step of the dais. Though it was cool within the stone court, sweat snaked between my breasts. For once, I praised whoever had first drawn the veil across the face of woman.

A queen adept at pronouncing judgment must be expert at many things, but foremost among them is swift appraisal of any man. I noticed immediately how every face in the hall, which was larger than the Hall of Judgment at Marib, returned to Solomon if only to see what he would do next. In what thrall he held them! In an instant I understood why Tamrin had been devastated to the point of gauntness when the king would not receive him.

Niman finally moved as though having waited precisely for this moment. He came around to the side of the litter where Shara stood frozen. She fairly skittered aside as he held out his hand to assist me. Stepping out, I ducked below the canopy and slowly straightened, the crystals on my chest making music like the trickle of water. Niman moved aside, and as he did I noticed two things at once. The first was that the floor directly before the king, different from the mosaicked rest, was not polished marble as I had thought, but a shallow, square pool filled with water.

The second was that several broad steps down from the king's throne perched a second, simpler seat. In it sat a woman so quiet and unmoving as to appear a painted statue. She wore linen white to rival my own, and on her head an elaborate black wig.

The Pharaoh's daughter. His queen.

I stepped forward and the court bowed low, and in the moment that their eyes were not upon me—but the king's undoubtedly were—I confronted the shallow pool. Such an unfamiliar position, to approach a dais like a supplicant, and not the one seated on the throne!

I thought of Heaven, dancing by light of the fire. I lifted my hems. I heard behind me the swift intake of breath from one of my girls.

The king's eyes dropped to my toes as I slid out of my slippers. On silent feet I walked forward, the marble floor cool beneath them. Without hesitation, I stepped into the pool. Water engulfed my ankles. My hems trailed, sodden behind me. I never took my eyes off the king even as I noted the quirk at the corner of his mouth, the way his eyes, so carefully fixed upon me for the sake of the others, began to dance. Ten steps. Fifteen.

I stepped from the pool onto the floor directly before the king, my hems trailing me into the water.

He was nearly a head taller than I. His lips, which were generous, turned up in a smile.

"Welcome, Lady Riddle," he said quietly, for me alone. "The moon and the sun share the sky at last."

NINETEEN

I praised the luxurious apartment appointed for my use to the king's steward, Ahishar—how strange these names were to me!—but not overly much. I thanked him for the pitchers of wine and Nubian millet beer, the platters of bread and olives, cheese and boiled eggs of all sizes and colors, the bowl of figs, pomegranates, winter melons, and grapes, thankful to see not a date among them. How tired I was of dates!

I nodded in silent appreciation at the roses on the terrace, the tapestries, and imported linens. I discussed quantities of flour and oil, portions of oxen, goat, honey, wine, and fowl to be delivered to the enormous camp of my caravan outside the city walls. I inquired about the comfort of my nobles and was assured that their apartments were nearby, and was shown which corridors might take me there, and which colonnades led to the hall, the kitchens, and the office of the steward himself.

I instructed Ahishar to speak with Tamrin on the delivery of my gifts for the king's wives, and the others for his concubines.

"Your door is well guarded, my queen. You must fear no harm while you are here," he said, glancing at Yafush.

"Thank you. And my eunuch," I said, emphasizing the word, "will guard me also, as he always does. Meanwhile, a man in my company is in swift need of a physician." The steward said Tamrin had spoken to him already about his man with the crushed leg and that the physician was with him now.

When at last the arrangements were done and Ahishar left, I gestured for Shara to send the Israelite slaves away.

Outside my apartment, the sounds of Jerusalem wafted up to the terrace: a market in the lower city, dogs barking in the distance, the grinding of a press. The smell of baking bread mingled with roses as the drapes billowed in with the breeze, their hems brushing soundlessly over fine, woolen rugs.

I threw myself down on a sofa, already exhausted though my mission had only just begun.

The girls flitted about the chamber, touching everything, exclaiming over the furs across the bed and the couches, the pillows and silk cushions, the lanterns with their many wicks as though they had never seen such a thing as a lantern before, the ninnies.

Meanwhile, my thoughts were stirred to a froth.

I recalled the ceremony of the hall, the brief procession as the king and I walked together around the pool to sample my gifts. As I stated the full quantity to be transported to his treasury, cellars, kitchens, and temple or into the keeping of his steward, I had treated each as a trifle. And I had taken pleasure in the way Solomon had repeated, as though I had erred, the amount of gold I had brought with me. The way he crouched down in front of the panther to see it like a boy, accepting the dried meat from its tender—ah, that was clever of Tamrin—to feed it to him, and then nuts for the fickle monkeys. One of them was famous for flinging scat throughout our journey. Luckily that did not happen.

In fact, nothing happened. There was no indication other than the king's quiet words to me that here stood the same man of the letters I had read so many times. I had expected strange tension between us—of shared secret and unsettled dispute written these years with such poetic wrath. But no. We were two sovereigns surveying the goods of the world, one of us on a diplomatic mission, the other diplomatically receiving his guest. And then he had said that surely after such a journey we must have time to recover and enjoy the best his kingdom had to offer.

"You have come on the perfect day. Tomorrow at sundown the Sabbath begins, a time of contemplation and rest commanded by the I Am, Yaweh. We will see your camp well provisioned and your servants given all that they require to tend you. And we will meet again soon."

I refused to be so summarily dismissed before his court.

"We require a full five days to tend matters of our own," I said, "and make sacrifice to our god for our safe journey. I assume there is a place my priest may set up the house of the moon outside your city."

And so it had begun.

My demand was simple hauteur, though part of it was true; the dark moon would arrive in three days, during which Asm must make his sacrifice for its renewal. Almaqah required it, the fields of the earth required it, and Asm was nothing if not pious.

I told myself five days was nothing; I had six months to win the matter of ships, ports, and terms as well as to prepare and provision the return trip south.

Still, I brooded.

I left my girls to shake out my clothing and went to the terrace bathed in setting sun.

Below, large houses—administrators' homes, I guessed—packed the space to the very wall of the incomplete palace. To the north smoke rose high over the temple. Had it even stopped? I watched the worshippers coming and going from that outer gate, the procession

of linen-robed men I assumed to be priests. I could smell it from
here, the burning of meat. What was the day's significance—and this
not even the waxing moon?

In Marib, I knew the sound of my emissary's camels on the road.
I knew the faces of the slaves, the name of each gardener. I knew
the corridors through which I might pass if I did not want to be
seen, and the temperament of each of my advisors. Here, I knew
nothing.

I realized then what was bothering me. It was the king's utter
self-possession. This was not, in the flesh, the same man who had
shown himself capriciously arrogant one moment and lost the next
in his script.

In truth, I knew this king not at all. And now, while I was in
his palace, he had every opportunity to observe me and my people
while he kept to any shadow he wished.

I went inside and called Yafush, Shara, and my girls to me.

"Listen to me," I said, looking each of them in the eye—my
girls, the oldest of which was no more than eighteen, especially.
"You are not in the court of a benevolent king and these people are
not our allies. You will veil yourselves at all times. You will wear
fine clothes and jewelry and perfume at all times. These Israelites
are fond of washing. You will send for water to wash daily. Your
hands will never be dirty, or your feet. You will not publicly be
seen speaking to any man, let alone touching one. Your actions
will be beyond reproach. You will report anything you hear from
the servants or the guards to me. You will entrust nothing to these
foreign servants but undertake all yourself, even the emptying of
the night-pots, and so learn the corridors and back ways of this
palace. If you are abused in even the slightest way, you will report
it immediately to me.

"You will speak nothing about our journey, or me, or the work-

ings of the palace at home to anyone, or in the presence of any servant, slave, kitchen boy, or wife of the king should you find yourself
in such company. If you are asked, you will say only that Saba smells
of perfume day and night, that her palace glimmers with alabaster—
this kind of thing. You will not speak of Hagarlat—" Here, I looked
at Shara and Yafush. Did I imagine it, or did Shara wince? "Or of my
king father unless asked and you will say only that Saba's enemies
met grisly ends. Do I need to explain all of this? You know as well as
I that every servant is a spy, and every slave has ten ears and twice
as many mouths."

I leaned forward. "Every court has its intrigues, lies, and alliances woven together like a net. Do not be snared, but notice everything. You are my eyes, my ears. Be alert, and wise."

They nodded. "Tell me aloud you understand me."

"Yes, my queen," the girls said. Yafush did not need to answer.

I sent for Khalkharib and Niman, who arrived a short time later
in fresh clothing, looking not at all rested and in fact perplexed—and
more so as they looked around the outer chamber of my apartment.

"I do not trust this king. He says that their god calls for rest
beginning tomorrow—where is the feast with which to welcome us?
He all but dismissed you before his entire court!" Khalkharib said.

"Listen to me now," I said firmly. "You must order that the camp
burn incense at all hours. The animals must wear gold and silver.
Every man down to the last slave will wear clean linen or the best
that he has. As long as we are here, that camp is Saba. There must
not be a single hole or tear in even the corner of a tent."

I turned to Niman. "I want ten of my armed men in the palace
at all times, four of them directly outside my door. Any one of my
men who displays drunkenness or looks even askance at a woman,
I will have delivered to the king for whatever punishment he sees
fit while we are here, and then I will have him bound and stoned

on the journey home. He will never see Saba again. The priests are to set up an altar within our camp. Asm and his acolytes are not to neglect any aspect of our people's worship. They must buy animals for sacrifice."

Khalkharib jutted his chin toward the terrace. "That is the second sacrifice these Israelites have burned today. Their animals are marked for the eternal fire of their god."

"Nonsense. Did you not see the shrines and high places on the eastern hill as we passed through the gates? Those are the gods of his wives. Neither will we neglect our ways. Meanwhile, do not for a moment drop your guard. This king is clever. But if we are wise, and if we are careful, we will have all that we want from him."

I started to turn away but then added, "Make sure the Desert Wolves wear tunics."

As they left for the camp with my orders, a wave of anxiety welled up within me at the thought of the coming five days. They would not be filled with rest, but of questioning myself a hundred times and going mad in general in my self-imposed seclusion.

But that is not what happened.

I was bathing late the next afternoon in the inner chamber of my apartment, seated upon a stool within a shallow bronze basin.

Music drifted to the terrace with the ubiquitous smell of burning meat. "They say this is a day of rest, but it seems the priests are hard at work," I said as Shara squeezed water over my back and shoulders.

I wondered where Tamrin was, how my men fared in the camp. Wondered, too, what business the king tended on this day of repose. I knew better than to think a sovereign had any such luxury.

One of my girls slipped into the chamber. I was about to compliment the citron of her dress when I saw the thing in her hand.

"My queen," she said. "One of the king's men delivered this for
you."

"Which man?" I said, gesturing for her to come closer.

"I don't know, but he was dressed very fine."

I dried my hands, took the small scroll, and turned it over.
The king's seal.

I broke it open and read the short message:

*Do you know what sweetness is? Knowing you are within my
palace.*

*Do you know what torture is? That I cannot lay eyes on you.
If the months of the last year were as days, these days are as
years.*

*How fair your hands are! How beautiful your feet! Your form
is that of a gazelle. Your cheek is lovely with the ornaments of
your veil, your neck with strings of jewels. Your eyes are those
of an adder—they mesmerize before they strike. Will you poison
me, Lady Riddle? Your brows are doves. Will they fly away?*

*Down the corridor from your chamber there is a small
passage. It is always guarded. It is the stair to my garden, open
to no one but me, and now to you. But only you.*

I lifted my gaze and stared at nothing.

"Bilqis . . . ?" Shara was watching me carefully. She could not
read. Even so, I held the note close.

So. He was intent on seduction. Would he summon me like a
common woman, or did he mean to convince me to marry? All day
I had been looking forward to waging the silent battle of gravities
that I had not felt yesterday upon my arrival. But not this. This was

insult. Did he think he would host me, bed me, exchange pretty gifts, and be held to no account?

"It is nothing," I said to Shara, and meant it. I got up from the tub, went to the incense brazier, and, holding the corner of the parchment to the ember, set it afire. I tossed the remains inside and then returned to the stool. "Send for more water," I said. "I want to bathe again."

A few hours later, the first gift arrived: delicate carob cakes from the kitchens. A short time later, a servant delivered goat's milk and a strange dish of pancakes that the servant called ashishot.

"Some kind of bean or lentils . . . honey . . ." Shara said, taking little nibbles.

"Cinnamon . . ." one of the girls added.

"And oil," Shara concluded, eating the second half in a single bite.

The next time my girl responded to the door, Shara said, "What now?" But this time the girl returned empty-handed.

"My queen, there is a servant waiting outside. An Egyptian girl."

I sat up, wrapped the linen sheet around me, and said, "Bring her here."

She returned with a small nymph of a girl I estimated to be about thirteen. The linen she wore was better than that of the women I had seen serving in other parts of the palace. A wide faience collar sat around her neck nearly to her shoulders and her eyes were rimmed with kohl. When she saw that I wore nothing but a linen sheet, she smiled and took off her head cloth to reveal a simple black wig.

She bowed low and said in accented Aramaic, "My mistress the queen has sent me." I gestured her closer and one of my girls offered her the ashishot. She slid one of the small cakes off the platter with a shy smile and took a bite.

"She has said—" She caught at the crumbs of the cake, poking them back into her mouth in a way that made me stifle a laugh. "'—welcome, in the name of Israel, and of Egypt.' She says also that sundown begins the Sabbath. 'But these customs are not our customs, you and I . . .'" She paused and added, "She said that, not me."

I nodded, straight-faced.

"And she invites you to dine with her, a simple meal, but a simple meal is made pleasurable by exotic company. And so she hopes you will come to her temporary palace—hers is being built—you and your servants and the Nubian, whom she has heard is with you."

I sat back and regarded the girl as she glanced at the cake in her hand and surreptitiously took another bite. I thought of the king's plea, which by now only angered me more.

"I will be honored to do so," I said.

The Pharaoh's daughter—I had a hard time considering her a true queen—sent her litter two hours later. I went out with my women and Yafush, accompanied by four of my armed men, and stepped into the litter without even bothering to close the drape.

Of course this was laughable—the litter carried me across the inner court to the other end of the palace and down a fine colonnade that ended in a great double door. All of this, as though after having traveled from the end of the world I could not walk so far.

Ah, Egyptians.

Outside the double doors a black-skinned guard in a fine linen tunic bowed low as the litter was set down on a carved block that appeared specifically placed here for this purpose.

A horn sounded from the direction of the temple—I assumed to mark the sundown, as though no one could see the orange spill of that yolk for themselves.

The doors opened on the queen's chambers seemingly of their own accord, and I nearly gasped.

The painted palace walls, which had been beautiful to me before, paled in comparison to the sight within.

Great columns opened as trumpets to the ceiling, painted like giant palms, and a fresco of green reeds and lotus flowers adorned the wide walls. Bronze bowl lamps flickered throughout the room gilding it all against the settling dusk. Overhead, an opening in the ceiling spilled an indigo and purple sunset more vivid than any painting over a small courtyard. Everywhere there were the colors of Egypt, from the mosaics on the floor to the inlaid tables, great statues of Ra and Seth standing sentinel in the corners. Something uncoiled from behind the idol of Seth and slunk away—an Egyptian cat.

At the far end of the chamber lay a blue-green pool. Fish moved like shadows between floating lilies. I realized belatedly that music was coming from somewhere in the apartment.

Truly, I wasn't certain that my own chambers in Saba were any more opulent.

Two slaves stepped out from behind the doors and brought us to a side chamber populated with carved, short chairs, an ivory table, and a great, reclining sofa with gilded wings of Isis spread out in either direction from the center of its back.

The woman I had seen in the throne room emerged at the other end of the chamber and spread her hands as she came to us in greeting. She was taller than I had thought, this figure who seemed so diminutive next to Solomon's throne.

"Welcome, Saba," she said, smiling and inclining her head. I mirrored her posture, if not quite as low.

"We thank you."

I had thought her beautiful at first glance and my estimation had not been completely wrong. Her face was round and slightly flat. The green malachite of her lids extended beyond the corner of her eyes beneath prominent, arched brows. The red ocher of Egypt was on her lips and cheeks, a woman as painted as one of her walls. Over her forehead and wig sprawled a golden headpiece—the wings of Isis, crowning her face down past her ears. The entire effect was breathtaking.

"I am Tashere. Do you mind if I call you Makeda? We are the closest thing to sisters in this city now," she said, drawing me toward the sofa. "You, raised in Punt, and I in Egypt. How is it that we come to find ourselves in this faraway barbarian land?" She smiled then, the expression knowing and girlish at once. I could see now the lines at the corners of her mouth. But of course, she had to be several years older than I.

She sent her slave for beer, then turned back to me.

"I have been looking forward to setting eyes on you since the king first told me of your coming."

"And I as well." I smiled. I reached toward Shara, who handed me the small chest she had carried with us. "I have brought these gifts for you."

She exclaimed over the bracelets and the headpieces, the long girdle of hammered gold set with gemstones. And then she handed the chest to a slave as another brought forward an ivory box.

Inside I discovered the idols of Seshat, the Egyptian goddess of wisdom, and her male counterpart, Thoth. Between them lay a scroll. I glanced at her and lifted it from the box and then, despite myself, unrolled it a little ways with an intake of breath.

"These are the writings of Ptahhotep!" I said with true surprise.

She leaned to look over my shoulder. "Translated into Aramaic by the king's own scribe. I have heard from the king that you are a lover of wisdom."

I wondered what else the king had said about me.

"Thank you," I said and meant it. I had read the maxims before, though never in their entirety. "These writings are at least a thousand years old."

"One thousand four hundred." She smiled. "But who's keeping count?"

I almost asked how the king came by a copy of the maxims, but of course that was a foolish question. The queen's father had given him a city—what was a single scroll to that?

"The king reads these writings often. As for me . . ." She sighed. "I find them a bit commonsense. 'Love your life with passion.' Well, of course! Perhaps you discern in them far more than I do. But now, I hope you are hungry."

I lied that we were.

I took down the side of my veil in this company of women. Tashere sat back and openly stared.

"I had not thought the tales were true! Every courtier exaggerates a queen's charms. But in fact, you are a beauty! Let me look at you."

I was not accustomed to flattery from other women. All my life I had watched them glance at me from the corner of their eyes, saying nothing until I was gone, hearing only later that they had been unkind. That day, I did not warm to Tashere's flattery, but to her frankness.

"The king's own mother was a beauty like you."

"And you knew her?"

"For a few years, yes." Her silence after that spoke of something either unfinished or bitter. I wasn't certain which.

We ate chickpeas, lentils, and onion stew—"the only things I find agreeable here," she said—reclining on the overlarge sofa together.

"This is made in my own kitchens. The Israelites won't light a fire to cook on the Sabbath."

"Who serves the king's meals on such a day then?" I asked, at which Tashere waved a hand as though to say not to start her on the subject.

When we had finished, she invited her girl to show Shara and my women her private garden. And then she smiled at Yafush and spoke to him in a language I had not heard except a few times in my life and, to my shame, had not learned. His face lit up strangely at that, and with a nod to me, he went after them. But I knew better than to think I would be completely out of sight.

"My eunuch is Nubian also. All the best ones are. He's been with me since I was ten." She settled back. "Now I can finally tell you not to be offended if the king is seldom seen these first few days of your visit. He's recently taken a new wife and there are . . . the obligations."

I hesitated. And yet he had told me to come to his garden! I wondered what she would say if I told her that?

"How many wives does he have now?"

"Nearly four hundred," she said, seeming unfazed by this.

"Four . . . hundred."

"Yes. I know. But he is a king. Every marriage treaty he makes gains his kingdom some prize. A queen cannot afford to be jealous—and why would I? Which of them will have her own palace?" She laughed, her chin tilted toward her shoulder.

"I have seen it in progress. Fine construction," I said. "I have seen no better."

"Though certainly larger—ah!" She sat up at the appearance of a figure I at first mistook for a servant. "Here he is, my darling." She got up and kissed the boy, who looked embarrassed, and brought him around to face me.

"This is my son, Itiel," she said, her hand on his chest as she smiled. "Itiel, this is the great queen of Saba." She said it with a pause between each word, breathlessly patting his chest with each one: Great. Queen. Of Saba.

I smiled at the boy, who was not so much a boy after all, as I estimated him to be about twelve, already showing the lankiness of early puberty. He bowed his head and murmured something polite before going away, obviously relieved to be done with state matters for the day.

"He is my joy," she said, beaming.

"And the king's heir?"

She sighed and sat down. "That is for the king to decree. But the king is very Egyptian in his ways."

"Is he?"

"How do you think all of his cedars are cut down in Lebanon, or the quarries dug out or the temple and palace built?"

"The corvée," I said. The Egyptian levy.

"Yes, the labor is conscripted. Mostly from the north, which they deserve. Always opposing him—one can't afford to have them all conspiring at once. Even the king's administration is run in the Egyptian way."

I was surprised at her knowledge of the king's government. This was not my impression of treaty wives at all.

"And yet Egypt rejects the idea of a single god and the king embraces it."

"That, yes. But look to the mount just east of the king's temple. There you will find high places to Chemosh, the grim god of Moab. And Molech and Asherah and Au and a half dozen others. The place is populated with their altars, carved pillars, and priests."

"I did notice. But the tales I had heard of the jealousy of this god . . ."

"We women are difficult to please. And a truly wise man keeps his wives happy. The midwives say they conceive better in sweetness than in bitterness," she said and laughed then. "At any rate, Israel is inexorably tied to Egypt. But you, Makeda. Do you have sons?"

"No. Much to the chagrin of my chief minister."

"Ah, the pity. You must soon rectify that. But you are not married, either, I hear. Why do you not marry?" She asked it lightly, a date in her hand.

"Whom should I marry?" I said with a smile.

"Why, a king, of course. My husband."

I choked out a chuckle. "My kingdom is far away. I do not think I would get many sons that way."

"You want to know how any woman gets sons here. How I call him 'husband' at all when he has so many wives—and that is not counting the nondowered peace wives, the concubines."

"I had wondered that," I admitted.

"They don't all live here. How could they? Some of them have spent only a single night with the king." She paused, her gaze drifting off. "It isn't the marriage brides dream of, is it? But you and I know the serenity of nations takes precedence over a woman's dreams. Even a queen's. But those who leave are wives of a king and receive many gifts and status in their homelands. And those who live here are safe and comfortable and want for nothing." She smiled a quiet smile. "But you . . . you may have any man. Saba's ways are not Israel's ways—or Egypt's. Who is to tell you to stay or go? But you should consider the proposal of the king. He is building a fleet of ships and you would not have to make this terrible overland journey to return to his house—or mine."

"Truly, it is not a consideration. There is no proposal."

Tashere lifted the date to her lips, forming a perfect O around it as she bit it in half. "I can only guess at the negotiations between your kingdoms, but I know my husband very well. The proposal will come. If not for Saba's wealth, then for the beauty in your exquisite face should you ever let him see it."

I thought again of the invitation to the garden.

She smiled. "But enough of that. Have you tried the king's wine?"

The night the Sabbath ended I went out to my camp to preside over the sacrifice of the dark moon. I did not do this every month even in Saba—had, in fact, less and less of late—but I had made it my excuse and so must be seen going out of the city.

I stayed within my own tent that night, which had been erected in the center of camp with my standards. It was far less comfortable than my apartment in the palace but lying on my blanket that night, I felt more myself than I had since our arrival.

The next morning as the smoke rose over the temple, I sent for Tamrin but was told he had gone on to another city on business.

Short hours after my return to the city, new gifts arrived at my apartment: delicate sesame cakes, brined capers and fresh goat milk for my bath.

The next day I received the softest leather I had ever touched, with a promise that the sandal maker would attend me at my leisure. Again, with the compliments of the king and accepted by me without a word. Later, two of the king's wives arrived at my apartment—one from Edom and another from Hamath. I received them with food and welcomed them as guests, though it was obvious they had been sent to attend me.

The day after that, Tashere sent the Egyptian girl who had come to me before as a gift for the duration of my stay. I welcomed the girl, who brought with her an ebony and ivory Senet game set that stood on carved legs like an animal with the tokens stored in a drawer of the body.

The next day, the king's Ammonite wife, Naamah, sent one of her servants to tend me as well.

Now I knew Tashere's chief rival among the women.

The gifts continued: wine from the northern mountains. Olive oil and oil of mint. Cucumber and citron, rings for my toes and fingers, wool rugs woven in elaborate patterns. Rose oil for the baths that I seemed to enjoy so much. Finely carved instruments for my musicians, who came to play on my terrace in the afternoon.

This went on until the fifth day. The morning of the sixth, I put on my purple robe and jewels, ready to begin negotiations. I waited all day for the summons to meet.

None came.

Three more days came and went after that.

TWENTY

I was by now livid. I sent for Niman and Khalkharib, whom I assumed had been wasting in a state of impatient and divine boredom as much as I. But instead of my advisors, one of the steward's men arrived at my apartment to say they had gone with the king's brother Nathan to tour the city of Gezer.

"Without taking leave of me?" I demanded.

"The king assured them that you were occupied with matters in the city, and that they must go on your behalf and report all that they saw with their own eyes to you," the man said. This, from not even the king's steward himself!

The moment he was gone I stormed out to the terrace. The girls played endlessly at Senet, obsessed with the morbid game about the journey of the dead. The Egyptian girl, whose name was Nebt, seemed to put near-religious faith in the game as a practical indicator of the gods' favor—and apparently they favored Shara, who won consistently as soon as she had learned it. Yafush, who knew how to play, would not take part as he stood with crossed arms, though he was not beyond raising a brow or pursing his lips when one of the girls looked to him for direction.

"Ah, the House of Three Truths!" Nebt cried after throwing the sticks.

I knew three truths, I thought sourly. One, that the king was trying to shun or aggravate me into meeting him in the most compromising manner. Two, that my trusted advisors were conveniently gone, having ridden off like boys at first mention of forts and horses. Even Asm had said that he intended to seek out the priests of Asherah, whom he said some regarded as the consort of the Israelite god. Apparently he had become a scholar since our arrival, set upon studying the divining methods of others.

Three, that I would not be outwitted.

I looked out on the city's myriad rooftops, comparing options like the houses around me. I could confide in Tashere. But even though I liked her and she had proclaimed as I left that she knew we had been destined to be friends—"perhaps even sisters"—I knew that any court was like the ocean: smooth and blue on the surface, its depths filled with monsters conspiring to devour one another.

I could try to befriend one of the king's advisors and enlist his advocacy. But who was I to them but one more queen within the king's walls with foreign gods outside it?

I could send for Namaanh, Tashere's rival. Nebt had openly confirmed that Namaanh had a son a year younger than Tashere's, favored by the king. I found that interesting—wasn't the dread child eater Molech Namaanh's god? But I was not eager to be drawn into their schemes against one another. Nor could I afford to lower myself to it.

Behind me, Shara groaned as she lost a pawn. A stick throw later, she had won.

I was left with only one option.

Below on the street just then, a man in mean clothing stopped beneath the terrace. Looking up at me, he shouted, "Foreign queens! Foreign gods! In the holy city of the anointed one!"

I drew back, astounded at this. Had the man just threatened

me? Even when I fell out of sight I could hear him ranting as one
mad.

I leaned out over the balcony again to find the man staring
directly up at me. Our gazes locked, his filled with righteous fury.
And then he began to mutter again and went on toward the temple.
I watched him go all the way to the gate and turn around. This time
when he passed beneath my terrace, he seemed to have forgotten
me. But neither did he go back down the street the way he had
come, but disappeared, ostensibly, into the palace below.

"Shara," I said, summoning her to the terrace.

She got up reluctantly, Nebt having already called for a rematch.

"Make me beautiful," I said.

TWENTY-ONE

I would be a liar if I said I hadn't paid attention to the corridors as I had traveled the laughable distance to Tashere's apartment. I had seen the guards standing at the foot of the narrow back passage. It had haunted me every day since.

I brushed past the guards outside my chamber, Yafush in my wake, and walked down the corridor as one entitled. And why not? I was the queen of Saba.

And yet it felt like a shame-filled walk, as though I skulked through shadows. I fastened my veil more tightly.

When I came to the narrow passage I stopped before the two guards. They looked past me as though not seeing me. I stepped beyond them and looked back. They did not acknowledge, let alone challenge, me.

"Do you know who I am?" I said, moving back to confront one of them.

The man looked away.

"Do you know who I am?" I said again.

The guard blinked, looking somewhere over my head.

"The sun is in my eyes," he said. "And at night, the moon."

"And so you do not see me. How clever. Did your master bid you say so?"

"The sun is in my eyes," he said again. "And at night, the moon."
And then he looked at me. "The queen goes where she will. She is
a ghost. Or I am."

I pitied him then. I did not know the penalty for armed men who
disobeyed in this land but suspected it was quite universal. I slipped
a ring from my finger—the smallest one, a thing of the tiniest conse-
quence—and gave it to him.

"You are right," I said.

I laid a hand against Yafush's arm then.

"You cannot follow me," I said softly.

He frowned. "Say that only when you are prepared to cross into
the afterlife, Princess."

I leaned over and touched my cheek to his.

And then I confronted the stair.

I took them slowly, pretending for the sake of the guards to be
weighted down with the train of my gown. In truth, the last eight days
had been longer to me than the six months it took to get here. I glanced
back once at Yafush standing broadly across the bottom stair, all but
blocking it, his eyes on me.

Earlier this afternoon when Shara brought out my gowns, I had
chosen one the color of rubies. The fabric had come with the ships
from Hidush just last year. Ruby. A hard and unyielding stone, my
mother said once.

I needed ports. A share in the ships. I donned the gown.

But I would not sell myself for them even though I had ascended
the stair behind me, alone and as furtive as a harlot.

Fearless or reckless . . .

Almaqah, I was certain, had long abandoned me—the moment I
left Saba's borders, if not in Saba itself. But any god must recognize
me if he were a god at all. And so I prayed silently to the gods of this
place, including the Nameless One.

I expelled a breath and turned the latch. It moved easily. I pushed open the door.

The sun was setting, bloody against the west. Almond blossom and rose filled my nostrils.

I strode out onto the terrace and a vista of verdant green unfolded before me—a high garden before an apartment perhaps three times larger than my own. Lamplight glowed through carved limestone window screens. Sheer drapes, illuminated from within, billowed softly with the wind in its open double doors.

There was no sound. Nothing but the hiss and sputter of torches in the late twilight of encroaching summer.

Was the king within? It didn't matter; I would not risk the scene I might come upon there or be discovered waiting in his chamber like a wanton.

I angrily turned to leave.

"Wait."

The voice startled me—I had not seen any figure. And because it was not the voice of a king.

It was *his* voice. But there was nothing of the king in it.

I turned back slowly in time to see the figure rising from the shadows in the farthest corner of the garden.

"What game do you play with me?" I called out, chin lifted. "How will this appear to your courtiers, should they come to your apartment? To your new wife, to anyone who sees my eunuch on the stair?" My anger, contained all this time, came out at last.

He moved toward me and I could see now that he wore none of the finery he had the first time—the only time—I had set eyes on him. Only a simple linen tunic and mantle, and a gold ring upon his finger.

Now I knew who had inspired Tamrin in his tastes. And so this king influenced everyone around him in even the littlest matters.

"Call for your eunuch," he said quietly.

"You said I was to come alone."

He came within an arm's length of me.

"Woman of mystery," he whispered. "You filled my hall the moment you entered it. You towered over the shallow pool. And yet I find you are a tiny thing. Will you let me touch your hand before you call for him?" With a slight smile, he said, "He seems a formidable fellow."

"It doesn't seem the custom for your men to touch women except for their wives," I said. "Why do you make these unseemly requests?"

"It is unseemly before the eyes of others. A custom to give no scandal to the one who sees it. But we are not seen. I would only touch the hand that penned such words to me. The hand of the Riddle. I would count it greater than any gift you carried here across the sands."

"Is it not enough that I came from the edge of the world? That I stand here alone on your terrace, against all judgment, after you have keep me waiting all these days?"

He looked down.

"I thought . . ." He shook his head. "I'm foolish."

"You thought what?"

"I thought you would return a message to me. Anything—even a note of thanks for my gifts. I waited."

"Why, when I am here? For what have I come if not to speak face-to-face?"

When he lifted his head, his eyes were stark. "Do you truly not know how your words have brought me to life? How they have revived me—yes, with the echo of my own? Or are you so fresh upon the throne and to the rigors of kingship that you know nothing of loneliness?"

I looked away.

"Ah." He came a step closer. "Why do you think I commanded you to send your emissary? You, who rebuff kings with silence?"

"Because against all logic, provocation wins more regard than flattery."

He laughed softly. "So you see, I am a boy, tugging your hair. And in return you slashed me. Hauteur, flattery, flirtation—any one of these I would have tossed aside. Instead, you slay me with a story of a garden."

I dare not say that writing those words had nearly broken me. After a long moment I lifted my hand between us.

A soft sigh escaped his lips as he took it by the fingertips—carefully, as though it were a bird that might, at any moment, fly away.

He touched the hennaed nail of one finger with his thumb, seemed to read the design on the back of my wrist. He brushed his thumb over these, too, as though he had never seen such a thing before.

I drew my hand away and he stood staring at his, empty, where it had been. At last he dropped his arms to his sides and said, "Call your eunuch, if it will put you at ease."

I went back to the stairwell and pulled open the door to find Yafush standing exactly as he had been. At sight of me he took the stair with swift, great strides.

"Peace," I said. "All is well."

I returned to the garden, not wanting to admit even to myself that I felt more settled as Yafush closed the door behind him.

The king walked a little ways away, and I followed with him. When he did not speak, I said, "What were you doing here, sitting in silence?"

He placed his hands on the terrace wall and looked out over it. "I have come here every night since your arrival. I told you, I was waiting."

"What does your newest bride think of that?"

"She is, I am certain, glad to be relieved of my company."

I almost asked if he was so bad at the bed arts as that, but bit it back.

"Why have you sent my nobles away without a word?"

"Because," he said sighing, not looking at me. "Because I know what you have come for."

He came to me then and it seemed he would reach for my hand again, but he stopped himself.

"I want to show you my kingdom," he said earnestly as a boy.

"As you are showing my nobles your prize city of Gezer?"

He waved this away.

"Your man, Khalkharib, is loyal but shortsighted. Your kinsman Niman is ambitious. I see it very well. I have no use for them. But you, Lady Riddle . . . you remain a mystery to me."

"To the great wise king? I am no mystery. I am Saba, and your new fleet threatens my future and my caravans. But if we could negotiate together, for the building of p—"

He lifted his palm.

"Time enough for that. There are things I want to know of you."

"In my country that is the posture of petition."

"Then I petition you," he said with soft urgency. "There are things I want you to understand. Tomorrow I want to show you my city. And the night after, I will throw a banquet for you and your retinue."

"I wasn't informed of this banquet," I said, feeling my irritation rise again, realizing that each time it did, it was more out of a sense of helplessness than true anger. I was accustomed to deciding the timing of everything I engaged in. But with this king, I felt as though I butted up against a wall.

"I've just decided it."

"I will go with you into your city," I said. "But you must do one thing for me."

"Yes?"

"Do not think to lead me by the nose or continue to insult me by asking me to come to you like this."

"You think I insult you?" His brows lifted, and I couldn't tell if his surprise was genuine or manufactured. "I have no privacy anywhere else!"

"You are a man in a man's kingdom. Were I Baal-eser of Phoenicia, we would not be having this discussion. Surely I do not need to explain this to you."

"Were you Baal-eser, I would not have invited you to my garden."

"Exactly."

"I am not a molester of women."

"I didn't suggest it."

"And yet you are more brave with your eunuch nearby."

"Would you have kept Baal-eser's advisors from him? And he from your council chamber?"

"Do you not see? I am weary of treaty! Of negotiation. And so are you, I can see it."

And to think it only took four hundred wives for him to tire, I thought sardonically.

"What have I come for, if not that?" I said. "You demand my emissaries and threaten the future of my kingdom. Well, I have given you better than an emissary. But do not think I came to sample delicacies."

His expression changed and for an instant he appeared injured.

"We are two of a kind, you and I. But if treaty is all you have come for, then my answer is no."

I blinked.

"You cannot mean that."

"And yet I do. It is no. You may try to move me, but I promise you it will take a great deal of persuasion on your part. Persuasion I am not certain you are capable of, even if you are willing."

My mouth opened beneath my veil.

"Now that that is done and there is no gain to be had, either way, will you see my city with me tomorrow?"

"Your temple will have no incense to burn! Is it not a command of your god that you do so? And how will he exact his revenge on you if you do not?"

"Do you think I cannot find incense anywhere else in this world?"

"You will have none of Saba's gold—"

He spread his hands out toward the palace and in the direction of the temple. "What need have I for gold?"

"You cannot mean to have another wife!"

He laughed at this.

"Of all things, what need have I for another wife!"

"Then for what did I make this journey?" I demanded.

"I had thought you wise," he said, turning away.

"I cannot go back empty-handed. You know this as well as I. My council will cry for war."

He waved his hand. "I will send gifts to astound your court. And there are other routes for your caravans. East, toward the great gulf, between the two rivers—"

I forced down panic, searching for even the smallest lever to turn his capricious mind. I had prepared for so many contingencies. But I had not prepared for this.

I imagined the Senet board between us, the pawn sacrificed upon the square. I laid my hands on the wall. "As you are tired of treaties and negotiations, I am tired of gifts. And so it seems we are at an impasse," I said simply, trying to quell the rising sense that I might be ill.

"So it seems," he whispered.

Somewhere in the dusk a bird trilled its night-song and a mother called her children into the house.

"I cannot leave until late autumn. And so we might as well take in the city and feast as though we die."

I felt, more than saw, him look over his shoulder at me.

"Until tomorrow, King Solomon," I said, taking my leave.

Let him think he had won.

That night after I returned to my apartment, I closed myself into the inner chamber and fell back against the door, pinching my forehead.

A moment later I pulled my veil free and promptly vomited in the night-pot.

TWENTY-TWO

I had been fearless. I had been reckless.

Now I must be wise.

Egypt was weak. Baal-eser was newly on the throne. The ships were not finished. And I, I was certain, would never make this journey again.

How was it possible that after a single conversation I had less than when I had first arrived—than if I had never made the journey at all?

I had six months. Six months to change an enigmatic king's mind. To secure Saba's future.

But as I lay awake that night, I found no purchase. He would not be moved for incense or gold. He tired of treaty. He disdained flattery. I wondered how many women had repelled him in attempting the usual wiles.

He was eager to show me his city. But not for my praise, surely—he had, no doubt, plenty of that.

He had studied my hand as though it were a marvel.

So he wanted something to worship.

But he himself claimed his god above all others.

He tired of gold and wealth, and yet he pursued it as one addicted.

So then he wanted worth. But that, he had.

I pulled at my hair and went out on the terrace to gaze up at the impassive moon. What might move a king for whom the luster of conquest had dulled?

I sighed and drew back, about to go in when I noticed movement on one of the rooftops below. A man, pacing to its edge, looking up at the sky as I had just a moment ago.

Who was he, I wondered. A merchant? A scribe? What thoughts did he ponder at this late hour, what thing nagged at his soul? A shipment of olive oil? An unfinished work as dawn threatened the eastern sky?

All the while the moon shone on us both, queen and commoner alike.

Did the king pace upon his terrace as I did even now? What kept him from his rest? Not an invading army. Not lack of women to warm his bed. Almaqah knew he could have one every night and not have them all in a year.

Lady Riddle, he called me. Yet I was the one stymied.

There are things I want to know of you, he had said. *Things I want you to understand.*

I looked out at the rooftop again, but the man was gone. I wondered if he would turn on his bed as fitfully as this queen a stone's throw away.

The next day I went out with the king and a small retinue of servants—his, and my own. Shara had spent the morning fretting about the bags beneath my eyes, patting them with milk, drawing the kohl around them thicker than usual. My fatigue fell away at first sight of the king, waiting in the palace garden as though he had never spoken a word to me in private, let alone asked like a boy to touch my hand.

He who listens becomes the master of what is profitable. So, at least, said the ancient sage Ptahhotep, whose words I had read unceasingly these last aggravating days.

I had come intent on being heard. I would correct that error. Now. Today. And every tomorrow until I turned south, ships in hand.

We went down to the lower city. I had not allowed the servants to fetch my palanquin, and it felt good to stretch my legs.

I tilted my head politely as he pointed out the original city of his father. The terraced Millo, the old palace, which housed many of his advisors and captains today. The tower that protected the Gihon Spring, from which the city drew its water.

"All of this, from the palace up to the temple on the mount, I have built," he said, with a sweep of his arm.

"Where was your temple before?" I said.

"Our temple was a tent. Our people were much like yours of old—tent dwellers. As was our god."

"Your father built the city. Why did he not build the temple, too?"

"My father was a warrior, a killer of many men. It was not for him to build the house of Yaweh."

"And your hands are free of blood?"

"Is any sovereign's hand free of blood? If not the right one, then the left? Are yours?"

Of course, I did not need to answer.

"The temple stands on the place where my father built his altar, over the same site where Abraham was told to sacrifice his son."

How long could I banter like this, as though I had come only to stroll through his city and praise his Phoenician workmanship?

"I have heard this story," I said. "Do you think your Abraham would have made the sacrifice?"

He shook his head, not looking at me. "Who knows what a man may do in the name of any god?"

"Is that because of the god's power over men, or because of men's belief in the god?"

He shrugged. "Is there a difference?"

We made our way through the market, which caused an immediate commotion. Merchants and housewives and peasants alike fell back like oil and bowed low. Solomon seemed to delight in stopping at each stall, smelling apricots and pomegranates as simply as any country boy. And of course each merchant protested he must take whatever he wished—no doubt so he could boast in perpetuity that the king had admired his produce. I had not come to bite into apricots or nibble sweet cakes and goat cheese—all of which I did as he pressed each one upon me, beneath the edge of my veil.

"The queen loves it!" he said jubilantly.

We went up the hill again, toward the palace.

"Are other gods not jealous that you have built such a grand temple for Yaweh and not for them?"

"I have financed high places for my wives."

"Is your god not jealous?"

"I have no god before mine. And as you see, his is the only temple within my city."

"How do you expect good harvest, good trade? Fertility of field and womb—or is your god the god of all of that, and thunder as well as hospitality?"

"He is the god of every created thing."

"The worship of one god failed utterly in Egypt. Do you truly think such a cult can survive?"

"If one worships the right god."

"Among so many! And if you have chosen wrongly, do you not worry that your record will be erased in retaliation, as Akhenaten's?"

"No," he said softly. "Because in truth, my god chose me."

I paused.

I could not help but think back on that day I had been appointed High Priestess. On every ritual I had presided over. The night I first offered the only precious thing I owned to a god I had never worshipped until then.

I had chosen Almaqah. Had Almaqah ever chosen me?

I noticed Solomon studying me from the corner of my eye.

"How do you know for certain the god chose you?" I said lightly. "Because he came to you in a dream? I dreamed of a three-headed goat once."

He picked a stone off the street and tossed it aside. "Because I have never needed to ask myself that."

I fell silent.

"Your brow furrows, Queen Bilqis."

"I was simply wondering if it was true that no hammer was ever heard dressing any stone as your temple was constructed," I said.

"That is true."

"Ah, and I also heard from the hoopoe bird that flies to my sill that jinns built the temple in the dead of night."

Solomon smiled and said, "That hoopoe bird has been known to spin many tales." He considered me again. "Though I find there is always some truth at the core of them."

"And so your father was as my grandfather," I said, pretending interest in something on one of the rooftops. "The federator of his people. We have a name for that—the *mukarrib*."

Now the king turned to me with a dramatic gasp. "Why, lady queen, are you likening me to your father?" And then, to our company: "I believe the queen has called me old!"

How easily he made light, this king who claimed to be slayed by a story just the night before, who even now held my kingdom's interest hostage!

"We do have a saying in Saba, that the juice from the frankincense sapling is whiter, but an older tree has more scent."

The courtiers laughed, a few of them politely applauding as we made our way past the palace.

"And so you have come from nomadic blood, as have I."

"As have we all."

"But you, much more recently," I said pointedly. "How do your people fare in cities—are they at peace, or do they long for their tents still?"

Solomon sighed. "Every man remembers his tribal blood."

I had said the same once, myself.

"And your tribal laws—they are given by Yaweh, are they not? How do they apply now that you dwell in cities?"

"They teach us how to dwell in community."

"I have heard these laws. They are rigorous. Your god is exacting. Do your people not live in constant fear of punishment—if not by priest or king, then by your god himself? Does your god wish only to be feared and not revered?"

"He wishes to be loved."

I thought back to my conversation with Asm years, a lifetime ago.

"How can you, even as a king, know the mind of your god?"

"Because it is said to us, 'You will love the Lord your God with all your heart and with all your soul and with all your strength.'"

"And yet you buy his favor with the keeping of laws, and with sacrifice, as do we all. Is that love?"

He stopped then, seeming to forgot the others. "How does one love any god? With fear. And then with friendship. My own father was a friend to Yaweh."

I squinted at him. *Friend to a god?*

"My god is different in this way," he added. "As our laws are different."

"How is one statute against murder or rape or theft different from any other?" I said, though my mind had careened into a hundred different questions.

"They are different in that they come from a god who says we are to show honor of him by honoring others. And so as we feed our hungry neighbor and do not steal from him we honor not our neighbor, but the image of the One who fashioned him. You say our god has no face. This is not true. Yaweh's face is before us in every person we see, as we are made in his image. Living people who require more kindness and adoration than any idol."

The courtiers walking a few steps ahead of us had stopped and turned back to listen.

"It is easy to love a statue that is fearsome or beautiful," he said. "But our love is proved when we love those who are not beautiful, who wound with word or deed. When we love not out of pity, or even for their sakes, but for our own. And here is the secret: they do not wound us, as Yaweh does not wound us. We wound ourselves by allowing the offense. And so Yaweh commands forgiveness for our own healing. Because in honoring ourselves—and others as ourselves—we please and honor Yaweh, who looks not on what a person does, but on the heart."

I had never heard anything like this—so deviant from the school of merit and favor, the cult of blessing and curse. It defied logic.

He gave a soft laugh, his expression strangely bemused. "You prove me with hard questions, lady."

"You answer deftly, sir."

"He is philosophizing," a man who had been introduced to me as Jeroboam said loudly enough for the king to hear. "We will never make it to the temple at this rate."

"He's come from the north to report on labor. I keep wondering when he will go back," the king said loudly, as though to me. The man laughed and walked on.

I glanced sidelong at the king as we made our way to the temple gate.

He enjoys this.

When we entered the courtyard, I stopped. How different the temple seemed now as I stood before it! I took in the enormous altar, the horns at each of its four corners. The gigantic cauldron opposite it, taller than a man, on the backs of twelve bronze oxen—one for each tribe of Israel, the king explained, poured in the clay in the plain of the Jordan. He gestured to the sides of the court, explaining its length and height as one who has had to do this many times, as I supposed he had.

The smell of roasting meat pervaded everything. Somewhere—on the balcony—there was music and singing.

I gestured to the temple building itself, where two giant bronze pillars like date palms stood sentry on either side of the gold folding doors. "May we go in?"

"We dare not, for you are priestess of another god." The king began to describe the giant cherubim within the sanctuary, the gold and palm trees and flowers upon its walls, which I assumed resembled those on the folding doors, the room behind the curtained back where a gold ark resided—a *markab*, over which the god hovered invisibly like a ghost.

"The day that the ark was brought to the temple and Yaweh came to live in it, the sacrifices had to be spread across this entire court as the altar could not contain them all. Twenty-two thousand oxen. One hundred and twenty thousand sheep."

I had seen a thousand animals sacrificed. But twenty-two thousand? One hundred and twenty thousand? I had seen and presided over countless sacrifices. But even I could not imagine so much blood.

I suddenly wished I had eaten this morning. The smell of the meat was overpowering, the song of the priests eerie in my ears. I glanced again at the oxen beneath the cauldron—three pointing each to the north, south, east, and west. It seemed to me that one of them wavered.

Look, I thought. *They are breaking apart in separate directions. The cauldron will fall and spill!* I lifted my hands in alarm, against that thundering crash. Someone steadied me. The king.

"My queen, are you well?"

I glanced swiftly at the cauldron. But no, the oxen were in place, unmoving as the statues they were.

"It is magnificent," I stammered, hoping I would not faint here, in the temple yard. "It is twice the tale that I heard, and that one I did not believe."

I said this in part because it was true, and in part because I could see how much he craved to hear it. And also because I dare not stand like this anymore; already my ears were ringing.

"I would like to arrange the gift of animals for sacrifice here," I heard myself say, "by one of your agents if I cannot by mine. You said there is an ark within . . ."

Our company turned to leave. Thankfully, my vision began to clear.

"Yes, of the covenant between my god and my people, and ten laws on their stone tablets are within it."

"Such an ark is the very emblem of my office. You have seen it, the day I entered the city."

"And in Egypt, too, there are such boxes," he said. "But none like this."

Of course.

"Because it is the very seat not of a sovereign," he said, "but of the sovereign god. And so the god resides here, in the temple, and not even the priests may enter that most holy room except once a year, and then with trembling in a cloud of incense, as no one may look upon the One."

"Have you no priestesses in the temple?" I asked queerly.

Solomon shook his head. "It is not permitted."

No wonder his wives worshipped other gods.

We returned to the palace, to tour the portion in progress, the king pointing out the three tiers of stone and the cedar beams placed before the fourth, filled in with gravel—a Phoenician ingenuity designed to withstand earthquakes.

I took interest in each of these things, but grinding, always, like a mill within me was the question of what the king wanted, and how I must wage this war of intellects.

The king prized conundrum. He disputed logic, craved praise, and revered the touch of my hands. He was a puzzle—one I must swiftly assemble.

The next night I attended the banquet within his hall. My advisors and trader were still conveniently gone from the city, but the young up-and-comer he had joked with earlier in the day, Jeroboam, who served beneath the chief of labor, as well as the son of his brother Nathan and the sons of Tashere and Namaanh, were all present. I noticed the two wives did not sit together.

"This young man," Solomon said, laying his hand on Jeroboam's nape, "is like a son to me. My pride, if not one to add to my joy," he said with a chuckle.

Jeroboam opened his mouth in mock offense.

"He is overly pious and listens too well to the ranting of my prophet, and takes me often to task over many matters. He has not learned that it is not healthy to challenge a king, but he is young and

I will win him in the end! He keeps me sharp, this one." He pat-
ted him on the shoulder. Despite his words, the king's fondness was
obvious.

"The king prizes his prophet, if only because he disagrees with
him," Jeroboam said.

"Indeed." The king nodded. "Anyone who agrees too readily is
never telling the truth."

I did not say that in my court open dissenters risked strangula-
tion.

I publicly admired the dancers of his court, his musicians. But
the king, I noticed, grew withdrawn and quiet.

We lounged after, complaining of our full bellies and, in so
doing, complimented his kitchens and the exotic foods of his table.
And then his chief scribe, Elihoreph, came to entertain with tales of
Jacob and other patriarchs of Yaweh's cult.

"I had not known that scribes could be so animated, being lovers of the spoken word as well as the written letter," I exclaimed. Of
course, this was only half true; in my father's household the scribe I
used to bribe for access to his library of tablets and scrolls had been
a great storyteller, even if I had been his only audience.

I found the king gazing at the fabric of my veil as though trying to assemble my face, much as one does a mosaic with missing
tiles.

"The stories are alive to them in ways lost on us," the king said.
"I find great worth in stories. They are the mortar of our identity.
They remind us of our coalescing into a nation. And so I encourage
all art, music, poetry . . . as you well know. How else may we chase
the mind of the divine . . . or the demons that taunt us?" His gaze
drifted to my eyes, and then again to my veil.

With a flash of clarity I realized that the mystery of my face
intrigued him more than the reality of it ever could.

How you torture and delight me . . .

He was not a man who wanted plain negotiations. Or a god with a graven image or a woman without mystery.

Now I began to understand.

Late that evening after I had begged off on behalf of my party that we were full to drowsing where we reclined—"See, my girls are all but asleep," I said—I slipped out of the apartment with Yafush and ascended again the garden stair.

The king was waiting and I did not mistake the relief that washed over his face at the sight of me.

"I thought never to see you in this garden again," he said, coming toward me. "I was melancholy all throughout dinner, thinking it."

"And yet, here I am," I said. "As you say, there is no privacy elsewhere. Forgive me my perceived insult."

"You were not well yesterday," he said, his head bent slightly as he looked into my eyes.

"You are not so all-wise as to know that."

"Did you forget I grew up in the harem? I understand the silent language of women far better than most men. Better than some women, I daresay."

"Almaqah knows you've wives enough to speak it fluently."

He laughed, and the sound rolled out through the garden like a breeze.

"And you feign interest well in my building projects."

"I did not feign it. Or do you forget that mine is the country of the great dam, and not one, but many temples?"

"I did not forget."

We sat down. Where there had been one seat the first night I had come here, there were now two—not facing one another adversarially or side by side, as intimates, but at an angle to one another. Clever.

"Tell me, at which temple does your god reside?" Solomon said.

"Why, in all of them," I said with some surprise. "Anyplace the moon touches, there the god is, as with the sun. It is why the sanctum is open to the air."

"And without your sacrifices to the moon god your father, he will not return renewed?"

I sighed and sat back. "Of course he will. You know as well as I that we make sacrifice not for the sake of the god, but for ourselves. What need have the gods for meat or blood or gold? We make gods in our image as much as you say Yaweh made you in his."

I felt his eyes upon me, but I had drifted back to my conversation with Asm in the early days of my queenship.

"In that way I see the wisdom of your unseen Yaweh," I said, "who defies graven image or name and will only be the 'I Am' of your stories. A god who must be seen in the faces of others. I have thought on that all day."

His face had changed in the flickering of the torch, the melancholy of moments ago gone, having fallen away like a cocoon.

"I have heard the story of you," he said quietly. "And of the ark you call the *markab*. Is it true?"

"It depends what story you heard."

"That you leapt into the acacia ship and shouted your men to victory. I admit, I half expected a wild woman of the hills with a painted face when you came to Jerusalem. By the light, you did not lie when you said the sun would rise to the south! The people in the city say that your caravan glowed like a trail of sunfire—and then they said it was more like a serpent. Because of course, you are unwashed."

"Of course."

"Yet, as I stood here in the garden, I could smell the perfume of your coming."

"And that must make me a demon of some sort, I suppose."

He waved his hand. "That myth is long dispelled. You showed your feet, which were rumored to be those of a goat."

"Did you have the pool installed only for that?" I blanched.

"I did. It was unfinished until the day before you arrived. I wanted to refute that story of you."

"How did you know it was not true?"

He gave me a droll look.

I chuckled.

"Why did you not walk around it?"

"Because. After such a long journey through the sands, I thought it would be the most delicious feeling."

He laughed then.

I did not add what I had wanted to say: to show that nothing could stop me.

"If your people thought that I was a demon with goat feet, did they also realize your patriarch Moses was a magician? Did he not turn a staff into a snake and produce water from a rock and all manner of wonders in Egypt—even as an Egyptian magician?"

We laughed together, and he asked me many questions about my father, and of my mother, and how it was that they had come from the same tribe.

"I was the product of love," I said simply.

"As was I." Something like sadness crossed his face. "I am not even the first son of my father. Or the second or third . . . or the fifth, but the tenth. But I was the one who was to be king. Who dreamed the dream of my god."

Something niggled at the back of my mind. And again, there was the image of the bulls, pulling away from one another. Why did it not leave me in peace?

"Are your wives not angry that you are not with one of them tonight?" I said after a time.

He shrugged.

"Surely they keep track in the harem of the women who go and come back. Surely Tashere and Naamah keep count."

He sighed and rubbed at his face. "Yes, and they come to ply me for favors with their fingers and the softness of their lips."

So. Every moment I asked for nothing was a moment he would cherish with me. But how was I to accomplish that? Again I found myself in the impossible situation of negotiating without negotiating, of asking without saying so!

"Of course they do. It is the only audience they may have with their husband, if not their king, for a long while."

I reclined against the cushion. "In Saba, my palace is covered in ivory and gemstones. High alabaster discs let in the light like moons. There is gold everywhere. And eyes, everywhere. And courtiers . . . everywhere. I am petitioned by the day by one tribe or another wanting treaty with me . . . I told my priest, Asm, that I thought I knew what it must be to be a god—not out of arrogance, but if only because it is hard to know when one is loved, or when one is merely the bestower of favors."

He gazed at me in silence.

"Surely any king would say the same," I went on. "But—I have spoken this to no one—I have begun to despair that even love is like this. That it is all and only the transaction of agreement. 'I will love you if you please me.' 'I will love you if you desire no other.' 'I will love you if . . .' and so on and so on."

I said it, because it was true. And because it seemed to be the kind of conversation he craved. But also because I knew he would understand. Perhaps I hoped he would shed the insight that had so confounded me yesterday on it like a lamp. But instead, he lowered his head and covered his face.

He sat like that for a very long time.

"How you cut me," he said, his voice thick. "How you wound me, to speak these words."

"How do I wound? These are only vain musings. Forget them if they injure you."

"I cannot forget them. Because I know them to be true. And here we sit, the product of love, with such grim thoughts! Have you ever known a love that was not this way?"

"My mother's."

"Other than that."

"Shara, my woman."

"Of a man."

I sat very still.

"Ah," he said softly. "Then you are to be envied, to possess something few sovereigns do."

"I possess it no more," I said, then got up to take my leave.

He caught at my hand.

"Do not go. Not yet."

"I will stay if you answer my question."

"What question is that?"

"What is the thing you want more than love?"

He released me then.

"Pray rest well, Sheba."

That night after I returned to my chambers, long after the rest of my household had gone to sleep, I sat up scouring his letters by

light of the lamp and reconstructing my own, line by line, written
to him.

I landed, just before dawn, on a single line.

Even the gods wish to be known.

The words that had moved him from the start, penned in a raw
moment by me.

TWENTY-THREE

Sweat ran in rivulets inside my gown, and even beneath the canopy of the king's litter I felt that all I did was swat at flies. It had been like this all the way to Gezer until, after trekking to the city's ancient standing stones, a breeze off the western sea relieved us at last.

There, in Gezer, we met up with Khalkharib and Niman, Solomon laughing at the surprise on their faces when we seemed to magically appear at the table of the king's hall that night.

It was the Israelite month of Tammuz. Except for the Feast of Weeks—during which I paced the halls of the palace and then the Sabaean camp for seven restless days—and the two occasions of the dark moon since my arrival, the king and I had spent time together every day. We went out of the city to survey olive trees and into the hills to play with the year's new lambs. We snuck out the cellars and into the myriad tunnels beneath the city like children, Yafush and his bodyguards following after us with torches, ducked low in the dank darkness.

I had agreed to every outing, banquet, state function, and errant adventure to date, after which we invariably continued the debates or discussions of dinner alone in his rooftop garden.

All the while, I felt the passing of days since my arrival with growing alarm. I was no closer to an agreement—to even broaching the conversation again—than the day I first arrived.

Even as I admitted this I forced myself to push the thought aside. That was not the way with this king who had already denied me once. It was only summer. There was time.

The king had by now neglected his harem to the point that the second time Tashere feasted me she made mention of it with a suggestive lift of her brows.

Well, there was nothing I could do for that, or for the rumors that were no doubt circulating within those harem chambers.

Khalkharib talked enthusiastically about Gezer's new fortifications and chambered gates the evening we joined them, seemingly reanimated by all he had seen.

"And you, my queen, how do you fare?" he said with double meaning when we had a moment alone in the corridor.

That was indeed the question, wasn't it?

"Well enough." I did not tell him or Niman about the war I waged privately, this challenge of wits and agendas.

"I think . . . " Khalkharib pursed his lips, this most stoic and gruff of my councilmen so obviously choosing his words carefully for the first time in my memory. "Saba would do well to ally with this king now that I see for myself the traffic that flows upon his roads. He seems a man given to new venture."

This, from my councilman so bent on war! "Who is this man wearing the face of Khalkharib?" I said, with only some mock amazement.

For a moment, I found myself actually disappointed in Khalkharib. Was there no one immune to the growing influence of this young kingdom—and the persuasive holdings of its king? Niman had frowned, and I recalled what the king had said upon his first appraisal of him. *He is ambitious.*

"I would speak to the king on your behalf of this, cousin," Niman said.

But of course he would; what ambitious man would not want to call the king "kin"? And with such a marriage unlikely to result in any heirs, no doubt Niman hoped I might name him yet.

"I will consider it," I said, though I had no such intention.

In Megiddo, that important juncture along the coastal road and the king's administrative center in the north, I toured the markets, giving opinions when the king solicited them as though there were no question of our future commercial dealings.

We visited the ruins of an ancient temple complex and then the king's famous stables, of which I had heard so much. I had never seen so many horses as I did in the Jerusalem stables, but the sheer number of those in Megiddo overwhelmed me.

How sleek and beautiful these animals! I did not say that I saw these creatures as the future of Saba and was jealous for stock. Though the king played middleman in the Egyptian horse trade, there would be time enough for that—after the ships, which might bring them to us, had been acquired.

"I have a gift for each of you," Solomon said with obvious delight. "Pick any horse, and it is yours. But let me show you the ones you should choose."

"It is too much," I demurred.

He led us to three stalls, all the while talking bloodlines and sires. I exclaimed over the black mare and proclaimed her beautiful, stroking the broad space between her eyes, and did not miss the swift glance my councilmen exchanged when they thought I wasn't looking.

Wahabil would not have been bought so cheaply.

We toured the newly fortified walls and then the storeroom of chariots—thousands of them—that Niman took in with an all-too-

greedy eye, seeming to forget that such war machines weren't practical for the terrain of Saba.

Twice the second morning after our arrival the king's officers
urgently called him away. He returned to me later with tightened jaw.

"Tell the story," he said, as we lounged beneath a canopy in the
palace garden the third day, "of the garden. I beg you."

"I will do better," I said, going to pluck several stems of flowers. I
twined them together, fastening their ends. He bowed as I laid them
on his head.

"Ah," he said, and for a moment his face was rapt.

"The flowers appear on the earth, and the time of singing has
come," I said, then crooned one of Shara's songs as he gazed, radi-
ant, into my face.

"Though you wear a crown, you are not a king," I said softly.
"But a boy, gone down to the gardens to gather lilies."

"You are a lily among brambles," he whispered. But he was no
longer smiling.

"What is it?" I said, when he fell silent.

"Who are you, lady, who are you really?" he whispered.

"Why," I said, forcing levity into my voice, "a shepherdess. What
else?"

"Turn away your eyes from me. They overwhelm me. But I beg
you, let me see your face."

I stood unmoving, even as one of his men came running toward
us.

"My king!"

Even then it took a moment for him to break that gaze.

"My king—a messenger from Zemaraim. A skirmish has broken
out."

And then he was gone, striding away from me on legs as lean as
a gazelle's, the crown of flowers still on his head.

He had included me in many aspects of court life until that point, asking me to rule on several matters of lesser import as a visiting sovereign. But that day he went off with his advisors for hours. I instructed Shara to ready our things, expecting our hasty return to Jerusalem.

I had been well aware of the escalating tensions between Damascus and Israel, and the northern and southern tribes. Of the tension, too, between the wives' foreign priests and the priests of Yaweh—including the madman of the street who I now knew to be the prophet Ahijah, a man the king actually valued if only because he had the courage to disagree with him. Tension, too, between the scholars and laborers, and the foreign and native Canaanite populations of Israel. Kingdom of conflicts!

And over them all, a king of contradictions. I knew the king now for a poet and merchant, philosopher and businessman. An Israelite who commemorated the exodus of his people from Egyptian forced labor . . . and conscripted his own tribesmen in turn. A king of nomadic blood who urbanized his people and built a house for his tent-dwelling god, who collected the wisdom of the world, then debunked it all with infallible logic. The wise man who pursued the sublime in luxury and craved mystery to match that which was known.

We did not return to Jerusalem that day, though I later learned he had dispatched one of his generals with a company of men.

We dined that night surrounded by courtiers who paid rapt attention to the questions he posed with the arrival of each dish. Some of them riddles. Some of them the seed of some philosophical debate. Every one intended to incite, amuse, or provoke.

Time and again he inverted the reason of his most vocal opposition, inflecting their every argument until they could do nothing but agree with him.

Only I saw the thing like desperation in his eye, as though he exorcised some demon in himself with every rebuttal.

"Tell me we will continue our story," he said, as he bid me good night. "I command you. I beg you."

"We will continue," I said, lifting my hand to his head in blessing.

The next day Niman stopped me in the corridor.

"Let me speak to him," he said urgently. "Let me approach him as your kinsman."

"You will not," I said. First my trader, turned jury against me at the king's suggestion three years ago, and now my own councilmen, swayed to the king's best interest in the name of Saba's own! Niman no doubt imagined he had everything to gain were I to marry for ports, ships—even the horses I coveted. I had been right not to leave him in Saba in my absence but now I wished he had returned to camp.

"What have we come for if not for this? My queen, he will give you all that you ask!"

"No he won't. Not yet."

"My queen. Kinswoman. Do you not see the way he looks to you? As a man looks on the very idols he argued for and then against with equal veracity last night! His own men say he's a man inspired since your arrival. Did you know you are the very reason he would not ride out to the skirmish, even though he sent two thousand men?"

I had no idea. Why did the thought warm and alarm me at once?

"There are too many ears in this place," I hissed. "We will talk when we return to Jerusalem."

"Why do you not marry, Bilqis?" Solomon asked me the night after we returned to Jerusalem.

Did the very air have ears?

I gazed out over the low wall of the terrace toward the eastern mount. Fires glowed from several altars and I thought I heard even from here the perceptible beat of a drum. "How is it that you married a Moabite, when your god has decreed against it?" I countered. "And not just a Moabite, but an Egyptian, a Sidonite, an Edomite, and I know not how many others restricted to you by your god?"

"My god declared against it not because of the women—and not even because of the gods they worship—but because there is no limit to what a man who loves a woman will do. My own father venerated my mother as though she were the queen of heaven herself. How much less is it for a man to worship his wife's god with her when she plies him with soft promises?"

"I see. And so woman becomes the temptress of a man's downfall?"

I could feel his gaze on me from the seat adjacent, considering me beneath the stars. "A weak man declares a woman a temptress and orders her to cover herself. A strong man covers himself and says nothing. I must have peace with my wives' people though I do not worship their gods."

"You must also have peace with your wives, and so you have built them high places to their gods."

"My god does not call them to worship him. He knows that I am his."

I did not say the thing I wanted to, which was: "And if your wife goes to the bed of another man, will you still know her heart is yours?"

Instead, I said, "Such a man who bends the law to his will is dangerous indeed."

Solomon paused and finally said, "I do not bend the law. I understand it. It is far more dangerous to obey a law without understanding.

Do we wish our children to do as they are told forever, simply because we told them what they should do, or because they fear punishment? Or do we hope that they grow in understanding to discern for themselves and freely choose right? We are not children and neither can we afford to think like them. One day we allow a man to live in our kingdom. The next, we dare not. And so even though we spared him one day, we must call for his death the next, even though every law in the world says 'Do not murder.'"

Always a clever answer with him. Always an answer that chipped away at the very idea of certainty in me.

Solomon fell silent after that, and captured my hand in his. This had grown common between us, the king taking my hand as though we were children, holding it sometimes tightly, sometimes reverently as he had that first night, like a thing that might take flight.

I waited for him to make his demand—for more of our garden story, to see my face, to escape the palace, for whatever unpredictable thing he would ask of me next.

"Who is this," he said softly, touching one of my rings, "who looks down like the dawn, beautiful as the moon, bright as the sun?" He glanced up and lifted his fingers to my face. But when I thought he might tug at my veil, he only traced the line of my cheek through it with a fingertip.

"You run when I pursue," he whispered. "I grow cold and you come near. And what you ask of me is not the thing you truly want."

My breath was stifling beneath the fall of silk.

"Yes it is."

I took my leave a moment later.

I had not seen Tamrin except a handful of times since our arrival two months prior. How much a lifetime ago those nights together in my palace seemed. But then, even my palace felt like a thing half remembered, as though from a dream.

He bowed low the day I saw him in the camp outside Jerusalem, the courtier in the body of the caravan master, at last.

"Tamrin! All this time I thought you beyond Damascus."

"My queen is indeed an oracle," he said. "I leave tomorrow."

"And so your heart calls you on," I said.

I had thought his gaze feral once. But now, even as he smiled, I saw it was merely tormented. "I suppose it does. But do not fear; I will return in time for winter."

Winter.

"Ah, the life of the trader," I murmured.

"How go my queen's negotiations?"

"Let us not speak of them."

"The king is a fool if he denies you anything," Tamrin said quietly.

I looked away a moment, then said with a forced smile, "Will you come to the palace to dine on your return?"

"I will be famished for decent food and gentle manners even before I return," he said, but his gaze had already drifted beyond camp. "Ah, but there is my foreman. I beg your leave and your blessing, lady."

I gave both and watched him walk away.

That night in the rooftop garden, the king gazed out toward the lower city. We were alone, as I had begun to send Yafush away early days ago.

"What will you give me?" he said finally, not looking at me.

"For what?"

"For what you want of me."

He turned toward me then. I knew the astute face of that businessman well.

"I haven't even said what I want of you."

"You need my ships to stop in your ports. Your ports cannot accommodate them. My men have questioned yours at length about the architecture of your cities, your roads, your shores. You need men to expand your ports, and me to bolster your trade by sea."

"As you say."

"And so what will you give me?"

"What do you want?"

It was the wrong question, and I knew it the moment it left my lips.

"I will negotiate engineers for your ports and even labor if you will raise half the labor yourself. We will chart together the Red Sea route, and I will give you favorable terms. I have far designs for my ships, and you will share in them."

"I will see that you have gold from Punt—enough to finish your palace and three more besides, and incense for your temple until the end of the age."

He said, as though he had not heard me, "Egypt, Edom, and Damascus would like nothing more than to ally with Saba. Phoenicia, too, though they dare not go around me." This was news to me.

"It would be in my best interest to keep that from happening," Solomon said. "And the way to do it is to ally with you myself."

"I agree. As allies, Egypt will never control interest over either one of us. They will not over me, in any case."

"You don't know that. The Pharaoh will not live forever, and the Libyans hold power already. There is something else you want, though," he said.

Why had his demeanor turned so chilly in the stifling evening?

And why did I feel no joy in this negotiation, now that he had brought it before me at last?

"Yes. I want scholars and astronomers and mathematicians and priests at my court. The sages and scribes who congregate now in yours—I want a twin capital of learning in Saba."

"I will treat with you on all of these things. But I have one condition."

"What is that?"

"Marriage."

I felt the word like a slap.

"You yourself said you wanted no more wives!"

"I said, what need did I have for another wife."

"All the same!"

"And yet that is my condition."

"I am a queen, not a princess to be given in treaty," I snapped. "And the Sabaeans will never accept a foreign king."

"You are the queen. They will accept that which you tell them makes sense."

"It does not make sense to me!"

"Bilqis." He came to me and seized my hand. "Do you think me a conqueror? I, who have never even seen your face!"

"What else should I think? You expect me to take a husband who will share my bed but once? Or would you simply add me to your collection like a doll?"

"I will give you an heir."

I could not help the bitter laugh that escaped me then. I did not tell him that no man—let alone a circumcised king—could do that.

"I will not be one of four hundred. And make no mistake: I will not spend my life sleeping alone."

"Have I seen even one of my wives in the last month since spending all these days and nights at your side?"

"I don't know. Have you? I certainly haven't asked it of you."

"No! Though they send messages and entreaties and though I know they are angry. Do you not think I am well aware that they are jealous? And I forsake them all to spend time with you!"

"How generous you are!" I pulled my hand away. "And what will your mad prophet say of that? Already he says your god is angry with you. Every day he parades through the streets and renounces your wives as worshippers of demons. Already your people look to me with suspicion, except those whom you receive to your table and hall, forced to pay obeisance. Do you think marriage to me will endear you to them? No."

"I see," he said coldly. "You say you will not be just another woman to me, but I see I am just another king to you."

I sighed. "And now you require reassurances from me?"

"Do you think any other king will offer you what I do? Saba's future is lost without alliance to me. Are you so selfish that you will not marry for the sake of your people?"

"And you are so selfless that you marry again and again and again!"

"Yes!" he roared. "I dole myself out in pieces for the sake of the kingdom—this unified and spiritual kingdom—for the sake of peace and for my god!"

"Well, you are not the only sovereign of a unified and spiritual kingdom. And yet somehow I manage to do it without selling pieces of myself away!" I hissed.

What was I doing? But now the floodgates, once opened, would not staunch their tide. All the tension of the last weeks and months of this limbo, this two-sided dance, flooded my veins at once, bringing me to my feet.

"You say your god is supreme over all. And yet my god is far more forgiving than yours! Yaweh would not approve of your marriage to me, High Priestess of another god. Mine gives me free rein to marry or not, to lie with any man I wish. You, though, must marry again and again to legitimize your unending lust for wealth. But even then, the divine author of your laws does not condone it. And so you explain it away. You think you expand your kingdom, but you are like an animal in a trap, unable to turn one way or the other without some retribution, divine or otherwise. Your prophet treats your wives as harlots. Well, who is the harlot here?"

For a moment, I actually thought he might strike me, he trembled so violently. The look on his face was terrible.

"I thought you wise. I see now that I was wrong," he said and walked inside.

He left me there, standing on the roof.

It was ruined. Saba was ruined. And I had been her undoing.

TWENTY-FOUR

I had failed. I had lost, all.

On the second day after I roused myself from my torpor, I sent the women given to me out on contrived errands—one to the kitchens with instructions for a Sabaean dish I claimed to crave, one for fresh flowers for the apartment, and the rest to the market for news.

"The wives are jealous," my eldest girl said, when they were gone and I was alone with her and Shara. "None of them have spent a night with the king in well over a month, except at the dark moon. I heard the Edomite and the wife from Hamath talking. But Naamah and the Pharaoh's daughter are not worried for that—only for the favor he shows you. If you are to marry him, they worry that any son by you will have more favor than their own. Twice now, Naamah's girl has asked when we are leaving. She does it under the pretense of wanting to stay with us for as long as she can. But we know the question comes from her mistress, who calls her back under the guise of sending gifts for us and for you."

"Well, of course, what did you think?" I said.

"I'm afraid, my queen," Shara said to me when we were alone. "Nebt says that it is not unknown for one of the new favorites to turn ill from poison, and to expel a child before it has come to term."

"Well, there is no chance of that," I said. Nonetheless, I had requested my own food taster some time ago.

Now I must decide what to do. I had been rash—reckless. I had been clever, but not clever enough.

I could make my peace with Solomon. But I did not think I could bring myself to ascend that garden stair now even if it wasn't barred against me already. Nor did I know if he would even receive me.

I could leave. But to do so now and have it come out later that I had failed utterly after all my promises . . . I couldn't stomach the thought. Not yet, while there was still time.

Neither could I bear these few months until winter dwindling to days.

Worst of all: I missed the king. No, not the king, but the man who captured and revered my hands. The poet who begged for the story of the garden, of the shepherd and shepherdess. The boy who took me stealing from the palace. The soul who drifted inexorably closer the more I shed the mantle of queen to expose the raw vein of my own loneliness.

Yes. He was a mirror. And I was his.

I told myself I could begin again and ply him with the stories and riddles he so craved . . . but my riddles were exhausted, and the words I had spoken could not be undone.

Or I could consent to his terms.

"I think that I have lost," I said faintly, when Shara and I were alone. "Even though he offered me everything I wanted. He proposed marriage. And I wanted to accept."

Despite all that I had said.

I laid my arm around Shara's shoulders and wondered why I had not confided in her more. I had done her a disservice in protecting her that way, leaving her only to comfort me in silence.

"It is a difficult thing, to keep the favor of a king," she said, in a stilted whisper.

"No. Only to keep it without losing all." I sighed, and got to my feet.

Shara sat like a stone, staring at her hands. Her breath began to come in short gasps and she threw her arm out to the edge of a nearby table.

"Shara! What's this?" I took her by the shoulders.

I had never seen Shara so concerned about any matter of state. What made her panic now?

"This is the business of kings and queens, that is all." I pulled her against me, looking for my girl to bring wine. "Soon, we will go home."

"At least you choose and were chosen." Her hands went to her face and her voice tightened and rose in pitch. "And were never given."

She trembled violently in the circle of my arms.

"Shara. Shara! What ails you?" I pulled her hands away.

But she would not answer with anything but the pleading in her eyes, some awful need. The look of a person who cannot speak, but must have it spoken for her—or of a woman who has carried a secret one day too long.

Something niggled, a memory of years.

The night of the banquet, when I announced she must not be invisible, and dressed her in my own gown. *You will not give me away.* And I had sworn that I would not.

Chosen and not given. Given to whom?

All those days of plain dress. Her hatred of Hagarlat, who ingratiated herself to my father and his fruitless spiritual pursuits . . . who never begrudged him even his concubines if only to placate him for the securing of favors. Hagarlat, who did not flinch at the ruin of others if it furthered her own purposes . . . who first turned, I knew in my heart, the eyes of her degenerate brother my way.

"You cannot mean Sadiq . . ."

She shook her head, near to hyperventilating. "Forgive me. Forgive me."

If not Sadiq, then for whom did she ask forgiveness? The only other man in my life at all had been my father.

My arms fell away.

Shara slid from the sofa and fell at my feet. She clutched my hems with a terrible wail. My stomach turned and threatened to empty.

My own milk sister . . .

My father's *concubine*?

But even I had not known or heard the names of those women—either in Saba or across the sea. Hagarlat was far too proud, far too ambitious to share the king's favor, especially after a queen who shared it not at all. But Shara was not one to make herself seen. And Hagarlat knew it.

"All this time," I whispered. "Why did you not tell me!"

"How was I to tell you?" She hitched a breath. "Every day I have known—the hour would come when you would despise me. Every morning . . . I wake and wonder if this is the one and how I will bear it one hour more. Do not hate me—Bilqis, my sister, my queen, whom I love! I dared not tell you—how could I tell you, knowing you would cast me away?"

Her words jarred me from revulsion.

I knew that feeling. I knew it well.

How long had I carried the secret of Sadiq, speaking it to not a single soul . . . wondering every night as I lay with Maqar how he might recoil from me if he knew, and wanting only to be known—and loved—in full?

I grabbed her fiercely then, not knowing until that moment that I would. I clasped her to me and she fell into my arms.

I was horrified, overwhelmed with I knew not what—aversion. Compassion. The urge to protect her against another, years dead, and a past I could never erase even as she shuddered in my arms.

Shara, too, longed to be fully known.

She was laboring to breathe, her lungs refusing to expand. "She gave me to him to spite you. And I—what could I do but take my life, and I—without the courage even for that!"

Her eyes rolled back and I shouted for my girl as she slumped in my arms.

I sat out on my terrace that evening, listening to the night sounds of the city. The bark of a dog. The cry of a child. A group of men singing as they ambled down the street. I closed my eyes and tried to remember the gardens of Saba as they had been before the locusts came. They would be lush again by now if there had been a good spring rain, the mimosa trees sending yellow stems of flowers to the ground. Overhead, the moon drifted against an inky sky, a waning crescent hung by invisible threads.

Had Shara gone willingly, I wondered? Had a small part of her hoped to find favor, to elevate herself above her station—to get back at Hagarlat, perhaps, or to steal something from her for herself or even in retaliation for her cruelty to me? Had my father been cruel to her to make her cringe the way she did, or kind enough to drown her in guilt all these years?

I had thought to ask every question. Later. Tomorrow. On the journey home, perhaps, if only so that I could reconcile it all—if indeed I could. But as I stood on my terrace that night, I realized that Shara's answers would change nothing.

She was not my enemy. She was not my competitor. She was not mine . . . to give or take. If anything, she had suffered for her loyalty to me. When she woke, I would shower her with love. I would erase the face of Hagarlat—and even that of my father—from my mind, and in so doing, abolish it from hers.

A step sounded behind me.

"Yafush."

"I am here, Princess."

I exhaled an exhausted sigh and found myself sagging where I sat.

"I think . . . it is time to return home," I said. I knew no other course. The gods must do as they would.

"This is not the princess I know," he said. I lifted my eyes to find him standing off to my side, gazing up at the stars.

"Who is the princess you know?"

"She is strong. As strong as a man. Stronger."

I shook my head.

"I don't know where that woman has gone."

"I do not think she is gone. She has only forgotten who she is."

I dropped my head against the chair's curved back. "Yafush, what is the thing you want most?"

"I want to see the face of God."

I smiled just a little. "And which god would you like to see? There is a small shelf of them inside. I can fetch one for you . . ."

"I do not think God is in those statues, Princess."

"Neither do I," I said quietly. "But do not tell me now that you are a monotheist . . ."

"I think God must have many faces."

"One for the sun, one for the moon?"

"Yes. I think it must be so. And many more."

"And where does this god live?"

"I think God is there," he said, pointing at the stars. "And here." He tapped his chest. How beautiful he seemed to me, the moonlight drifting over the dark curves of his face. I looked from him to the stars.

So wise, my Yafush.

"Yafush . . . why was it done to you?" I had never asked him.

"There were some men. They did these things."

I closed my eyes.

"I was a boy. My family sold me to those men."

I opened my mouth but didn't know what to say. "I'm sorry, Yafush."

"I am not."

How did a man mutilated by his family say such a thing?

I took his hand, twined it with mine, and then lifted it to my lips. I thought of what Solomon had said, of how we injured one another and so aggrieved his god—the god whose image we violated, offending ourselves in the end. *Yes*, I thought. *I see*. So many hurts. So many hurting. Shara, Yafush, Solomon himself. I wondered what secret wound required the poultice of never-ending acquisition.

"Yafush, do you want to return to Nubia?"

He was quiet for a moment before he said, "I do not think I will go there."

"When we return to Saba, you will be free," I said. It hurt to say it. It hurt and was beautiful at once.

"I already am, Princess."

I stared at the sky for a long time after he went back inside.

TWENTY-FIVE

After three days, I wrote simply:

Let us talk. Face . . . to face.

But the messenger returned and said that the king could not be disturbed, that he had gone to visit his Egyptian wife.

I went down that evening to the Sabaean camp with Shara and Yafush, clothed so simply that no one would have mistaken me for the same queen who had traveled these streets innumerable times before.

Within my tent, I felt at least that I could breathe once more. Perhaps there was still some nomad left in me as well.

That night I took a simple meal with Asm.

"How do you find your time in Jerusalem, my friend?" I said. He had changed, I could see that, though I couldn't discern how.

Something had happened to me, too, in the space of the last day. I had failed. But in failing, I felt as though a great burden had rolled from my shoulders.

"I am troubled. There is something I must tell you."

"And what is that?" I did not think I could bear the weight of another confession.

"I have met with the priests of the gods of Molech, Asherah, Baal, and Chemosh . . . and I have met with these Israelite priests."

"And? Have you new wisdom to share with me?"

"The priests of the high places are glad for your presence, and the presence of the god that is with your camp. But the priests of Yaweh . . . are eager to see you gone, my queen."

For some reason this surprised me.

"They are fearful of your influence over the king."

"Well." I laughed. "They need not worry about that now. What else did you learn from the priests?"

I listened to him talk at length about omens and ritual, of sacrifice and oracle.

"None of them, my queen, has known an oracle such as you."

I lowered my gaze.

"They confide in me that they often recast their runes, that they often guess when they read livers, and that they doubt or do not understand their visions. These, the priests of gods older than Almaqah, whom I have revered from a great distance all my life! How it has shaken me to my core to hear this from them!"

Great compassion for him welled up within me.

"Tell me, Asm, have they described what it is to have a vision—a true vision?"

"No, my queen, they have not. Only that they dream strange dreams, or that they may think they see something and realize it is not there or that their eyes seem to have erred."

I thought back to my day at the temple, the apparition of the cauldron spilling to the ground. Of how my vision had clouded and I thought I might faint, but not before the great bronze bulls seemed to strain in the wavering air before breaking apart from their invisible yoke.

"I have had a vision here."

Asm leaned forward as though he would peer into the wells of my eyes, as though I were not a woman but a golden bowl. "Speak it, Daughter of Almaqah!"

"It is for the king's ears only, because it came from the god of this place."

His brows drew together. "Are you certain? Almaqah takes many guises."

"I am. Do you remember our conversation my first months as queen?"

"I do," he said, looking troubled.

"You said that if Almaqah did not speak to me, whom would he speak to?"

"I did. But he does speak to you, and fortunate is Saba because of it."

"Asm." I didn't know whether it was that I had already lost all for Saba that made me want to set aside this, too, or if in seeing Shara's face this morning, renewed, I also longed to be free. Perhaps I was only tired. So very tired. "When we return to Saba, I will relinquish my office as High Priestess."

"My queen! *Why?*"

"A god saved me when I was young. But I do not know what god it was." I had never spoken of Sadiq to him and did not expect him to know what I referred to now. "I called upon Almaqah but I know now Almaqah did not call to me. I called to him, I dedicated myself to him, and he was silent. He has never spoken to me, I think because he does not recognize me. I was made in another image."

Who are you really? Solomon had asked me. I knew my titles. I knew my positions. But I had not known the answer to his question.

I thought back to the night I had stood beneath the rain—crown, title, position forgotten, Heaven so vivid in my mind. Of Yafush whom I knew no better way to keep than to free. Of Shara, whom I knew no better way to love than to take her hurt into myself.

"But which god do you speak of? There are many gods in this place—here, and on the eastern mount—old gods of this place, and those that journeyed here," Asm said, visibly confounded.

"The mysterious one."

For that much, at least, I could thank Solomon.

The next day I sent my message to the king again. And again, the messenger returned, saying that he was with his Moabite wife.

And again the next night, and again he was with one of his wives.

This time I laughed. Yes, how very loudly I received his message even if he did not receive mine! And then I slumped against the door after closing it and covered my face.

"Show me a way," I whispered, I knew not to whom.

The night after the rite of the dark moon I prepared to return to my apartment in the palace. But before I left, I received Abgair—surprised and relieved to see that he had gained weight in the time since our arrival.

"I wish that we would be going soon," he said with a smile.

"Are you not happy in your time here?"

"These people beat their camels."

"Soon enough, we will go."

"I wish that I would see this king again before we go."

"I will see what I can do about that. But why do you want to see him?"

"I want to see the face of the man with so many enemies."

I blinked my surprise. "Why do you say he has many enemies?"

"People talk when they do not think others can understand them. I am just a wolf at the well. But I have learned this language."

"Who are these people, Abgair?"

"There is a man in the king's house. An important man. I have seen the tracks of their animals with his. Twice this month he has gone and come back from the north with workers."

I squinted. "The conscripted workers?"

"The ones who complain so much. They say they are gone from their homes for a month, that the king does not treat them well. But this man says soon this will all change. That his god has said so, and he will be king."

"To the north and back—are you certain?"

He gave me a look.

I searched back through the myriad days, the dinners, the faces at court in Jerusalem, Gezer, Megiddo. What name, what face—a young man, with whom he joked. The promising young man over the corvée workers, in whom Solomon showed such pride.

Jeroboam.

I returned swiftly to the palace.

"Deliver this to the king and to no other," I said to the steward's man, pressing a message in his hand. It said merely, *Jeroboam means to betray you.*

Three days passed. On the fourth, a messenger delivered the simple note:

Come to the garden.

I left immediately, leaving Yafush behind as I ascended the narrow stair.

I closed the door at the top, looking swiftly around me. When I did not see him, I went boldly into the king's apartment. For all I knew, I'd walk in on one of his wives, or worse, the two of them together. But the moment I entered, there he was, standing in the center of it.

His hair was disheveled, his clothes rumpled. I saw that a wine jug and cup sat on the edge of the carved table.

"Jeroboam has fled," he said, not moving.

I knew he was fond of the young man, but I was surprised at the measure of his distress. And then I understood: For all of his children, Solomon had loved this one as a son.

"My own prophet . . . has had a vision. My kingdom will break. My own prophet, Ahijah! Who did not come to me, but went to a boy with visions of my kingdom breaking apart. He told the boy he would be king!" His arm swept out and dashed the wine jug from the table, sending a spray of crimson across the floor. And then he was throwing over the chair, and then the table, until he staggered and slumped against the wall.

I crossed the floor swiftly and clasped him by the arms. He stared me in the face like a wild man.

"No vision is static, the stars are not so set. You are the king. Whatever tomorrow brings, you are king today."

He shook his head. His eyes were swollen. "Do you know . . ." he whispered, "that you have ruined me?"

I let go of him. Surely he did not blame me for the actions of this boy?

"You have ruined me," he said again, his expression desolate. "They say my kingdom will break apart. But I will not let it. I will not allow it! But I am the one ruined."

"Then I will leave—"

"No!" He seized me by the shoulders. "Don't you see? I cannot let you, even as I must! My kingdom will break, the prophet has seen it, and I must not let it! And yet every hour of these days, I have wanted nothing but you by my side. To rage at you, to consult with you. To weep upon your knee like a boy. Do you not see? You have conquered me! I, the lion of Judah!"

I was trembling, my heart living and dying with each beat in my chest—ships, ports, Saba forgotten.

He took my face between his hands. "I cannot eat. I cannot sleep . . ."

"Because you have been with your wives," I said, faintly. But he would not let me pull away.

"Have I? I went to see Tashere, though I was not present even as I ate at her table, and she is angry with me. I sent for my wives . . . But I cannot talk of my heartbreak over Jeroboam to them—he, whom I must put to the sword if I ever lay eyes on him again! I cannot be other than a king to my wives and I cannot weep in the company of my council or brothers.

"I was given discernment. I have spent it like gold. But you . . . you have chased it. And you spend it wisely, as the son born not to the rich man but the poor, who earns his wealth. I am the son of a rich man. But you are the one who has entreated the gods. How can that be? You who worship the moon! And now you will leave me, too. And I will give you all that you desire. And what will I have in return? I pursued you, and you kept your face hidden from me. I have come at you with arguments, and now I am the one to lose."

"You do not lose," I whispered. "But gain the thing you cannot get from a treaty wife, or a vassal, or anyone who calls you 'King.' You seek me because I am none of these. You ask me about love. I have been loved—beautifully. Mightily. Selflessly. But what is love to one who wants, more than anything . . . to be known?"

He covered his face.

"How can I let you return to Saba?" he cried. "I have driven you away with my demands. With every argument to hold you to me. You, who have ruined me . . ."

"I, who love you." Imperfectly, selfishly and selflessly.

He took my hand and clasping it, said, "Then do not leave. Not yet. Stay." He drew me to a chair and sank to a knee in front of me. "Stay, and I will give you everything I am. If only you will allow me to serve you. "

"I will stay," I said. "Until winter."

He lowered his head to my knees.

We stayed like that for a very long time. When he lifted his gaze at last, I reached for my veil and let it fall.

He pulled me to the floor with trembling hands, fingers like the flutter of a bird's wing against my cheek and over my lips, parting them gently. He traced the line of my jaw for an hour, the side of my neck, the curve of my shoulder. He hesitated and when I did not rebuff him, he touched me softly, as hesitant as a boy and then with the liberty of a lover, caressing me through my gown. His arm wound around my waist, my fingers all the while grazing the stubble of his beard, the arch of his brow, until I laid my lips against his. He sighed and I inhaled the soft sound of revelation.

I left a short time after, broken and remade, a shattered king in my wake.

The next day I sent only one message:

> *I have slaughtered my animals. I have mixed my wine. I have set my table and sent out my servant girl.*

They were not my words, but his, lifted directly from his writings of Lady Wisdom.

I sent my girls to the camp to observe the sacrifice. They took with them all of the women of my household; only Shara and Yafush remained behind.

The king came late that night.

He entered my apartment with a glance around as though it dwelled not in his palace, but in that of another, foreign world. The carpets of my tent and those he had gifted me were laid across the floor of the outer chamber, the most opulent of them beneath the replica of my throne, which was covered with the leopard skin I sat upon in my palace. Beside my throne on a broad stand sat my *markab*, symbol of my office.

The king paused before the ark and then reached out to touch it.

"This is the *markab* you rode into the battle for your throne," he said with wonder, fingers brushing over gold leaf, the fringed end of an ostrich plume, much as mine had the first time I saw it.

"The very one." I had not worn my veil, or even all of my jewelry. Such weapons lay forgotten.

"You told me earlier that your departure was secret. Have your advisors not noticed your ark missing?"

"There is one similar to it held in my privy chamber, while the true one has traveled with me."

He considered this somberly as his hand twined with mine and his gaze drifted to my throne. I had received several visitors and resolved several arguments seated upon it—including that between the injured foreman and the owner of the camel that had kicked him. The foreman would limp forever, but Solomon's physicians had proved adept; the man had neither died nor lost the leg.

He guided me toward the alabaster seat. "I want to know what it is like, when you ascend your throne in Saba. I want to see it with my own eyes."

I gave a musing smile and walked past him to sit down, straight-backed, my arms on the rests. "The throne in my hall is larger than this one. There is a great silver moon behind it and three steps to the dais before it." I gestured to the walls with a sweep of my arms. "There are twenty-eight alabaster discs set high into the walls. They shine white as a moon at night . . . and gold as the sun by day, morning to sunset."

He stepped back, and then, to my great surprise, knelt. He did not speak, but slowly leaned forward to kiss my toes, to chase the intricate flourish of henna to my ankles. I closed my eyes as his fingers slid inside my sandal to caress that sensitive arch.

A little later we walked together past the idols of Almaqah, Asherah, Thoth, and Neith to the inner chamber. He paused inside, taking in the sofas with their silk throws and cushions, the ibex incense stand.

"Where do you sit when you recline?" he said. "Here?" He went to one of two low sofas.

"Yes. There."

"Then I will lay here."

"No," I said. "Lay beside me."

We drank wine, his fingers roaming the slope of my shoulder like a gazelle. We sampled a parade of dishes that arrived from the kitchens with the food taster, Solomon eating from my hand, I from his.

"And now I forget the rest of the world," the king murmured, his face turned against my hair, inhaling the perfume of it. "Day becomes night. The ibex and lion feed together."

"There are no feasts, there is no gold . . . There is only a garden," I said.

"I am a shepherd, as my father was." He tilted up my chin and kissed my ear.

"And I a shepherdess."

"And your dark-skinned people come not from a world away," he whispered, "but the Valley of Shunem. Do you know I have imagined your face for years, both wanting and not wanting to see it, in the case that it was not as I envisioned?"

"And here I am. And my face is as it is."

He traced my cheek. "It is more lovely even than I imagined, and I feel I have known it always . . . and that it knows me."

He heaved a great sigh and lowered his head to my neck.

He wept that night in my arms, and I, later as he slept.

TWENTY-SIX

This was my world: the smolder of those eyes, turned in my direction. Perfumed sheets, laid fresh upon my bed. The roses of that garden wafting to my window, saying, *come*.

I no longer noticed the ever-present smell of burning meat; it was lost on me altogether as flowers flooded my chamber.

By mid-morning, his latest poem was delivered to my door.

You have captivated my heart with one glance
    of your eyes,
With one jewel of your necklace.
How much better is your love than wine,
    and the fragrance of your oils than any spice.

Mine flew back to him in return:

While the king was on his couch, my fragrance
    was nard.
My beloved is to me a sachet of myrrh that lies
    between my breasts.
My beloved is to me a cluster of henna blossoms.

I sat beside him in his hall, where my throne had been transferred. I took dinner with his advisors, all of whom glanced between us, the king saying often in their presence, "But what does Sheba think of such-and-such a matter?" until the eyes of the most astute—and most careful—councilors began to look of their own accord to me.

We sat as kings in his privy chamber and heard the case of Jeroboam, condemning the noxious fruit of rebellion's seed. I was there when the boy's poor mother, a widow, was brought before the king for questioning.

We denounced Egypt together for the housing of his enemies—Jeroboam, and before that, Hadad, who reigned now in Aram and with whom Solomon had made peace by marrying his daughter.

New reports arrived from Hazor about another skirmish, this time on the northern border with Rezon of Damascus. We debated what was to be done.

But at night, we forgot it all.

He came to my bed as supplicant. I came bearing tribute. He demanded and I pulled away. He whispered and I went into his arms.

"My mother was a conqueror of kings. I disdained him for that, years after he was gone. But no more."

We spoke of gods and crops, of sea routes that would take a year and a half in the going out and again in the coming in. The conversations he would have with Baal-eser on my behalf. The ships that would sail to my ports. The way we would shape the world.

I sang the songs of my mother, and he, the hymns of his father. He whispered stories of his eldest brother, whom he worshiped as a boy—Adonijah, whom he had been forced to kill.

And for the first time in nearly five years, I spoke the name of Maqar, and wept.

"I, too, love this Maqar, though I never knew him," he said. "He died for my queen, and because of him, I am with her now. We will send a sacrifice to both our gods, in gratitude." We sent agents to the market to buy animals the next day, and the smoke of them went up on our altars. And I could be grateful at last for something bitter in my mouth turned sweet after so long.

I passed the afternoons in the heady languor of sleepiness, napping as larks sang outside my window, bathing as the sun canted toward the west.

At night, I ascended the stair to the terrace or sent for him to come to the bower of my apartment. *Come to my garden and eat its choicest fruits.*

We were shameless as children, brazen as we dared. We bathed in the middle of the night on his terrace. We sent secret glances across the table at state dinners. We stole through the tunnels and out of the city to lay like divine consorts of antiquity.

He came down to my camp on the next dark moon, bringing animals with the servants in his company. There he observed the ritual of Almaqah as a still-troubled Asm and I presided over it both. It would be my last ritual to the silent god.

"How terrible and beautiful and magnificent you are," he whispered in my tent that night, long after the drums had ceased. "And how you have enchanted me. What power do you wield, Daughter of the Moon?"

"The power of wish," I said.

"Do you believe in such things?"

"What is a wish, but a prayer? A man stole into my chamber when I was twelve. He took me by force. And again, on another occasion. And another." He leaned up, face stark. "I prayed for deliverance.

And the wadi flooded and washed him away. I dedicated myself to the god in gratitude. But I think I am barren."

He clasped me more tightly then than he ever had. "My poor love! Were that man alive, I would see him suffer. And to think I bid you come to me that first night alone. I curse myself that I ever dealt harshly with you. Forgive me. Forgive me," he said, holding me to his chest.

"You never laid a hand on me."

"I should have been gentle with you from the first pen stroke."

"I would never have responded."

"No, I suppose not."

"So you see, I do believe. I prayed to the moon to deliver me. I prayed for freedom, and my father sent me to Punt. I was happy for years. I lived in love. But I wonder if a part of me prayed to be queen. I wonder now, if our souls are all-seeing, and if mine saw that I would come here. And if it knew I would not come if Maqar still lived . . ." I drew away to look at him in the lamplight. "The first time I wrote to you, a part of me wished for you. And the first time I set eyes on you, I wanted you. And here you are. But the god I dedicated myself to did not dedicate himself to me. So which god is it that has given you to me . . . and will soon make us part?"

"The same that will make us whole again," he said softly. "We worship the same god, after all," he said.

"Which god is that?"

"His name is love."

Solomon, my poet.

After a time, I quit summoning him to my apartment, where my girls and the two lesser wives were, and had my things sent up to his.

We lolled in bed late into the morning. He kissed my navel and

I compared him to the smooth alabaster of a fertility statue. He laughed at that and pretended to dress in shame.

And then we went away for a few hours to be king and queen, composing poetry in our heads.

We did not talk about the coming winter, even as our days took on a frenetic pace and summer careened toward fall.

TWENTY-SEVEN

Khalkharib and Niman paid me a visit during the festival of trumpets, for which pilgrims had been swarming the city for days. The king had gone to the temple; I would not see him until tonight. The ram's horns had sounded every morning by then for a month, jarring me awake from the king's arms more than once, but having no such effect on the king, who snored softly through the loudest of them as the smell of baking bread wafted from every oven in the city.

I received them in my apartment, the table set with quince and honey from the king's kitchens. It was the first time I had been in the apartment in days, and the first time I had sat in council with them in many more.

"My queen, we are troubled," Niman said.

"Why should you be?" I said lightly. But I had expected their censure and received them with reservation. I had attended the king's hall and privy chamber for weeks. Obviously the king had agreed to the treaty. With ships in hand, there was no reason to loiter here. The tribesmen of the camp were restless, and still I commanded we stay.

"There are . . . unkind rumors circulating about you and the king—circulating repeatedly and more fiercely among the pilgrims, who increase by the day."

"There are always rumors. There are rumors about me in Saba as well."

Niman shook his head. "My queen, this is a different place from Saba. Our ways are not their ways."

"I am well aware of that," I snapped. "Is this what you have come to tell me?" I glanced at Khalkharib, who stared grimly at the place where my throne had stood before it was moved.

"The king has many wives, who have many servants—servants who talk and spread their mistresses' jealous gossip. And there are many priests and members of council who chafe at the presence of a foreign sovereign with more influence over the king than they. This is not a country given to foreign authority—least of all a queen's. You have become the favorite target of threatening conversations. Though they may nod and smile in the council chamber, you have no friends in those chambers but the king himself."

"How would you know? You are not privy to the king's council."

"We have gone into the city under guise and have heard it for ourselves," Khalkharib said finally. "The people in the market speak against the Sabaean harlot, and call your guard 'the whore's men' in the streets."

My face flushed even as cold prickled down my back.

"They dare!"

I got to my feet and paced away, smoothing back my hair. "Cowards will always speak crudely against women of power. Do you think this is the first time mouths have rattled about me? Do you think I give two nits what they say? They are not satisfied with the king's marriages, though they receive every benefit of them. These are a people used to scandal, who seek it out and make morality tales of even the union that produced their beloved king, appointed by their god," I said angrily. "Imbued, even, by their god with the wisdom of Yaweh!"

"These people fear that same god will visit retribution on them for the actions of their king," Niman pressed.

"My queen, I am not certain that he is as well loved as you may hear from the sycophants in the palace," Khalkharib said.

"They dare not speak against him."

"Not publicly. But they grow bolder after Jeroboam."

"My queen, it is clear he favors you," Niman said. "And Saba is the benefactor of such favor. He is obviously charmed by you. But of course he is—Saba is the richest nation in the world."

I laughed. "Just weeks ago neither one of you could say enough of this king. I saw the way you devoured with greedy eye the gift of his horses, and you, Niman, the gold of his chariots. Are you not the same kinsman who begged to arrange my marriage to this same king, who saw in him every opportunity?"

"My queen, if you would marry him, then marry him," Khalkharib said. "But you must silence this scandal. Not only for Saba's sake, but for the safety of those in our camp."

I wheeled back. "What are you talking about?"

"Rocks and garbage have been thrown at the camp under cover of dark for weeks now. And just last night a group of northern tribesmen tried to rouse our guard into a scuffle. They injured three of Tamrin's men."

"*What?*"

"If you would not marry him, then let us leave soon. Clearly you have in hand, or at least on promise, that for which we have come!"

I had been avoiding thought of the coming rains, the days as they grew shorter, telling myself that the night merely came sooner with more hours to spend with the king. Of course it was a lie.

"We will not leave until winter. There is business to be finished yet," I said, chewing a nail.

"There is talk that you have all but moved yourself to his rooms," Khalkharib said. "And the entire court knows you sit beside him in his hall—not as though you are a visiting sovereign, but as though you were his queen!"

I wanted to shout "I am!"

I was more queen to him than any of his treaty wives! Without marriage, without dowry, without the uniting of nations. More than any woman who had ever borne him a son, if only because I had not done any of these things.

What would they think if they knew how we conspired late at night to shape the world? How we would draw Hidush and Babylonia to us in treaty even as we staked out our share of the road that winds to the far silk lands? How we would hamstring Edom between us for the sake of my caravans and his ships moored in the gulf . . .

"Where have you been as I have been sitting in the king's hall in negotiations and in council? And what care is it to you what transpires in these hallways? I make no account to you. I said we would come for ports and ships. And I accomplish so much more. You dare censure me?"

"That is not all," Niman said. "There is talk, too, that you have denounced Egypt together for harboring the king's enemies."

"Of course!"

"Do you know that the Egyptian queen has started a campaign of vile whispers against you in retaliation?"

This startled me.

"Since when do you harken—or stoop—to women's gossip?" I said. "Or even market gossip for that matter? No doubt much the same is said of me in the markets of my own capital, and among my own nobles' wives." I looked pointedly at each of them. "Winter will

come soon enough. Concern yourselves with provisioning the caravan, because it will be a long journey south."

I sent word to the king's steward the moment I sent them away. I
was shaken, worried for the safety of my camp, anxious at Solomon's
absence, and unwilling that the world enter these privy walls. For
the moon to set or the sun to rise on another fleeting day.

Within hours, additional guards had been posted outside the
Sabaean camp. I was consoled, for the moment—until I arrived in
the king's apartment. He caught me up in his arms, but his expression was torn.

"I cannot stay here tonight," he said.

"Then I will go where you go."

"I have not gone to Tashere in weeks. She is angry, and jealous."

Then it was true. I pulled away.

"I thought her too practical a wife for that."

"It is no secret that you reside here with me. That your throne
is on my dais. She has conceded much. But she is desperate to conceive another son, and she will not concede that."

Jealousy flared up within me, hot and incendiary.

"Well, then. I will call another man to my chamber!"

He tore at his hair. "No. Do not. I beg you. Let me go as is my duty."

"Duty? You are the king."

"She is the Pharaoh's daughter!" he said.

"Yes! And how many times have we said that Egypt is weak? It is
the house of your enemies—we said so publicly. What duty do you
owe her now?"

And then I realized: he loved her.

I felt it like an icy stab.

How many times had he written her poetry before he first
penned words to me? How many letters had he sent, how many
gifts?

He took my hands. "My love, please. Stay. Wait for me. I will return with the morning. Sleep late, and I will join you."

"Fresh from another woman's bed," I said bitterly.

"And you, from another man's before you came to mine."

I gave a sharp laugh. "And you from hundreds. I make no pretense at virginity. Or will you call me 'whore' as your people do in your markets? If I am, their king makes me so!"

"Do you not see what I risk to be with you?" he said, as though at wit's end.

"What *you* risk?"

"Yes! They call you 'whore'—any woman not wedded to a man will be called that. But you know this better than I. Do you not see that I risk the disapproval of my priests, who say even now this is the very reason the north and Damascus and Jeroboam and a host of others conspire against me?"

"Do you not see how they point the finger at the women nearest at hand whenever a nation struggles—the same women who have had no power in it?" I said. "Even your Eve did not chew the fruit and spit it in your Adam's mouth but he took and ate it himself. I have read your priests' stories! Do they not see that they are painting the very portrait of their own weakness?"

"It is not just the priests, but my men, my people—and yet I lift you up before them. I put you in judgment over them. I risk scandal, I risk my kingdom, for you!"

"The priests you choose, the men you choose. Then choose others. You risk your kingdom by taking a nation as rich as Saba to your bed? By letting the world know our kingdoms must be dealt with as one great power? How is this any risk to you, O king? You who call yourself dangerous and then run at the beckon of your wife?"

"What do you want of me?" he said, and I laughed. Weeks ago I had asked that very thing.

"Shall I say as you did that my condition is marriage?"

"You have never wanted marriage."

"I am a queen. I have seen you change your mind a dozen times. Am I not entitled to do the same?"

"I have married you in my heart, in body—"

"Your heart will not appease your people, who condemn me in the street. Or your mad prophet who stirs up your enemies against you. You marry the daughters of nations your god prohibits, but your god has said nothing of marriage to Saba—and you will not marry me?"

"We will talk. I will return. The night is short—"

"It is not short. It is growing longer! Have you looked out your window—do you not see the fading sun? It is autumn, and the time before us may be measured in hours. Spend a month with Tashere when I am gone. Never emerge from her bed if you like. But stay with me now."

"Bilqis," he said, his expression worn. "You do not know what it is to be husband to an angry wife, let alone many of them. You are my peace. Let me do what I must and return gratefully to you."

There was nothing I could do. Throwing my anger about would not gain me a thing. What had I expected of a king with so many wives—of a king at all?

"Go then. Perhaps I shall be here when you return. Or not."

He sighed, bent over my hands, and went out.

I woke late the next morning, alone. But the king did not arrive that morning. Nor in the afternoon after I sent for Shara to dine with me. We looked out at the streets filled with pilgrims. The rooftops were covered in bowers thatched with palm fronds; last night I had seen the lamps of their guests gleaming like a constellation of stars. All through the day pilgrims came in and out of the city as the hawkers' cries soared from the markets to the palace.

The smell of the public ovens hung like a yeasty pall over the city, causing my stomach to grumble and me to eat off and on throughout the day. Shara did not seem to notice; she had brought the Senet set with her and soundly trounced me three times in a row.

Shara was a different woman. Her shoulders tilted back where they had canted forward all these years. Always so still, so timid in the past, she moved today as one who breathed. Even her movements were more expansive than before, no longer apologizing for the space her slender frame occupied, no longer bound by the past.

Right before dusk, a great wail tore through the palace.

I got to my feet, bumping the game board and sending pieces skittering to the floor as I strode through the king's chamber to the door, Shara at my heels. Yafush put out an arm, staying me, and then stepped out into the corridor first.

There was a slamming of doors from the direction of Tashere's apartment, raised voices—one, a woman's, in an angry shriek. The other, a man's. The king's.

I questioned my guard in low tones but did not send for the steward. It would not do to lower myself to some marital dispute.

Late that night the king's brother, Nathan, arrived at the king's chamber, just as Shara and I prepared for bed. I saw the way he regarded me, his eyes veiled, the set of his mouth grim.

"A rider came early this morning," he said. "The Egyptian Pharaoh is dead."

TWENTY-EIGHT

The king was shut up in council all the next day. When I sent for him, I was told only that he would come to me as soon as he could.

I was not invited this time to sit at his side.

I paced my apartment in agitation and finally sent for Asm, brought up from the camp with an armed escort of king's men for his safety.

After he ate only a token amount of the food I had set before him, I said, "The Pharaoh has died. Have you received any omen?" But I knew what the answer would be.

"None. I have seen no portent or sign." Did I imagine it, or had his face grown gaunt in a mere matter of weeks as though he had neither eaten nor slept?

"I want to know what you saw the day we left," I said. I had forgotten about it all these months, but it had come back to me this morning before dawn, foreboding as the moon-dark sky.

He shook his head. "Only that the return was obscured."

"What does that mean?"

"I don't know. It may mean that the return will be difficult—"

"The journey here was difficult enough!"

"It may mean we will take a different route back, in the least."

"And at worst?"

He hesitated. "That you or someone else will not return."

At that I sat very still.

"Yes, well," I said eventually, "omens have been wrong before."

Every time I claimed Almaqah had spoken, he had not. Every time I thought he had shown me some favor, disaster ensued. It was the reason I dared not think Abgair's revelation of Jeroboam—the one that broke the king but mended all between us—a sign of our future, lest some calamity descend on us now.

Sometime that afternoon, cries flew up from the city below and a company of guards was dispatched from the palace. I watched from my terrace as the streets cleared before them, their breast-plates catching the sun. A commotion of some kind had broken out near the market, though I could see only a portion of the flurry—people rushing from the direction of the pavilions, shouts punctuating the air.

It made me nervous, this city so overfilled with pilgrims. They spilled out into the valley as far as the market mount so that I had requested more guards for the perimeter of my camp and our own men had doubled their watch. Even in Saba, conflicts and old rivalries exploded like dry tinder in summer with the spark of swift words and wine. I kept my girls and Shara close, forbidding them to go out in the city, appeasing them with delicacies ordered from the king's kitchens and a surprise visit from Tamrin, whom they immediately taught to play Senet.

Solomon returned late that night.

"The Pharaoh is dead," he said.

"I have heard." I poured him wine.

"Shishak the Libyan has taken power in Egypt. And so Egypt goes from weak to strong, overnight." I had not seen him look so haggard.

"Surely that is exaggeration," I said. He shook his head.

"He has commanded the Pharaoh's army for years. Egypt will be a military power again. And he will want Gezer back for Egypt."

"Your first wife is Egyptian!"

"Does it matter to mercenary stock? These are not Egyptians, but Libyans who have taken over Egypt and will turn their eyes beyond their own borders. They already play host to Jeroboam, whom my prophet"—at this, his lips thinned—"has said will rule the northern tribes of Israel. And so he thinks he has in his grasp a future king. No. He will want Gezer. One day, if not today. And a share in the new fleet."

"Well he can't have it!"

"He can."

"How is that possible?"

"Egypt provides men for the garrisons of Kadesh-barnea, Beer-sheba, and Gezer. Men who protect my interests there but are loyal to Egypt. There is something else."

"What more?" I said, incredulous.

"He knows you are here. Jeroboam has told him exaggerated stories of our . . . friendship."

Why did that simple statement drain the warmth from my fingers? Days ago I had claimed to my councilmen that I did not care what others said. But somehow, hearing that stories of my "friendship" with Solomon had reached Egypt, I felt as though the world itself suddenly peered into my bedchamber. More so, because such stories were not exaggeration.

"I must deal carefully with him," Solomon was saying. "Egypt is friend to my old enemy, Hadad, as well. Do you see now what a predicament I am in? And so I must treat with him for both our interests. For as much as he may turn his sights to Gezer, he may also turn them south, to Punt."

I blinked.

"But I will do all in my power," he said. "Do you trust me?"

"I do." I could think of no one I would put more faith in in any negotiation, ever. But to see him so grim, to hear from him only "I will do all in my power" when before I had heard him say "Watch this—I will win him," shook me.

Hadad in Aram. Rezon in Damascus. Jeroboam in Egypt. His own tribes to the north, threatening to turn against him. The prophet of his god. His jealous wives.

Was this a man favored by God? The man they told stories of, given so much wisdom that he made such enemies of others? This man who must secure the tribes his militant father knit together, not with force this time, but with cunning and marriage—the very things that the priests felt threatened their nation's cohesive identity?

I felt Solomon looking at me.

"What is it?"

"There is one thing more."

"What now?" I cried.

"Shishak is related to Tashere by marriage."

I turned away.

So then all of Egypt had been strengthened. There, and here.

"You dare not marry me now," I said.

"I would not have," he said quietly. "I would not make you one of hundreds, as you said, or set any wife over you in rank. It would never be fitting. You are a queen. My queen. And first in my heart."

I sighed as he came to me and laid my head on his shoulder.

"Tashere must be pleased."

"She lost a father."

I thought of my own father, and the tears I had never shed for him. She had been here well over a decade. Did she shed any for him?

"I will go to her tomorrow," he said quietly. "I know you will be angry. But I will."

What could I do?

"I am leaving soon," I said.

"I know."

"And still you go."

He laid his head over mine. "Tashere has threatened to send word to Egypt that she is unhappy and ill-treated if I do not come to her. If I do not openly show before the people my preference."

I laughed, a short, stunted sound.

"I didn't know she had the gall to command a king."

"Shishak will look for any opportunity against me. Jeroboam is in his debt and will be made more so if he is set up here as king. A boy who is barely a man is far easier to control than a king years on the throne."

"What will we do?"

"I will send my emissary with gifts. As it is always done. And I will win my way with him." But instead of sounding confident, he sounded only tired. Where was the brash author of the letters now?

If Solomon's kingdom failed, there would be no fleet of ships. Or the fleet would belong to another. And then what would I do? Whom must I journey to meet with next, and how much of this journey would have been in vain?

No. Not in vain.

"Of course you will," I said.

The next day Tashere recalled Nebt from my service. The girl went with a tearful hug and then, head down, left my apartment forever, leaving the Senet set behind.

I had come to dread the day Tashere would confront me, to crow her fortified position in the king's palace and bedchamber at me, as she surely would. But it was not Tashere who came to my apartment three days later, but Naamah.

She was a plain woman beside Tashere's carefully staged beauty. Austere as a peasant and large-boned, her thick frame spoke the common language of childbearing, though I did not ask how many sons or daughters she had.

She ate only enough to appease custom before she sat forward.

"Tashere is threatened by you and has become your enemy. And so you are my friend," she said. "She believes she has won because she is related to the new Pharaoh by marriage and has publicly taken up worship of Bast, the cat god, whom his priests favor. But Tashere is not the wisest woman. Shishak is a raider, not a conqueror, or a federator as my husband is and as I hear you are, and he is greedy to take back what was given. With a threat on the Egyptian throne, Solomon will never choose the son of an Egyptian princess to succeed him."

"Which son will he favor?" I said.

"My son Rehoboam is a man after his father's heart. A man who has studied his ways. He is too fervent in his blind belief in his father, perhaps, and less tolerant of the north. But Solomon will choose him. Unless, of course, you bear him a son and bring him here."

"And so you ask me to go."

"All the wives want you gone," she said simply, and without malice. If I had thought Tashere frank, Naamah was nothing but stark!

"You need not worry about a son from me."

"So say many new women the king turns his eye to who think only of love. And he has turned his eye toward many. He has loved many. You are not the first. You will not be the last. But I think he has loved you perhaps the best. And so you are in danger. The harem is full of more wars than men have ever waged. The Israelite wives look down on the foreign wives. The foreign

wives think the Israelite wives coarse. The north feels misused
by the south. The south scorns the north as less noble. And they
vie for the attention of a king whom many of them resent in their
hearts."

"And you? Do you resent him?" I asked, as plainly as she.

"Yes. At times."

Perhaps that, too, I understood.

"They are united in one thing: their jealousy of any new woman
who captures the king's interest—politically or romantically. But
none wants you gone more than Tashere. Be wary, Sheba. She is
not without her spies and lackeys. Keep your food taster close.
Though her war is not with you, you are the one at which she will
direct her arrows. You came for treaty. The king will give you the
ports you want. But you will not be safe until you turn your face
south."

I had not realized she was privy to so much and regretted that I
did not invite her to my apartment those first days.

"I understand," I said, and thanked her.

"Israel is wealthy. But you have wealth. If you want peace, you
will not find it here."

She got up to go, but paused. "My girl has enjoyed your service.
She will weep the day your woman, Shara, and the others go from
her. I would consider it a kindness if you would take her with you.
She has never been happy here. If you do, she will be my token of
friendship. We will one day be mothers to the rulers of our nations.
It is good that we should be friends."

I unexpectedly found myself embracing her, this woman of
severe but appreciated truth.

That day, my camp relocated south of Jerusalem halfway to the
port of Ezion-geber and away from the increasingly volatile city. I
bid farewell to my girls, keeping only Shara and Yafush with me, and

said I would see them in a few weeks' time when festival season was over.

I did not miss the unmistakable cheer that went up from the streets as my throne and *markab* were transported under armed guard out of the city. Nor the one that followed, sweeping all the way up to the palace: "Leave, Sheba!"

I spent the evening alone on my terrace and felt the first chill of winter.

TWENTY-NINE

The next night, Solomon and I dressed in plain clothing and, accompanied by a few of his men in simple garb, went out into the crowded city. I had been wary at first, fearful of these streets for my own people and tonight for myself even in the presence of the king, the echo of that refrain with me by the hour: *Leave, Sheba!* But I had been cooped up too long in a palace swirling with as much intrigue within its walls as without, and I would not be cowed.

We walked together as any man and his wife might. Even at this hour the streets were filled with people, making me miss the market and pilgrimage season at home in Saba. But I had never experienced it with the liberation of obscurity.

Somewhere near the old city, Solomon snuck over the low wall of a baker's house and filched two cakes cooling in the courtyard. A dog began to bark and the man came out running, shouting curses at us as we disappeared down a crowded street.

"What were you thinking?" I said, several streets over, panting and laughing despite myself. Somewhere nearby a group of men were singing hymns.

He handed me a cake. "That I judge myself leniently. I am in love. I am capable of anything!"

Throughout the upper city, I had seen curious little structures built against the sides of houses, in courtyards and even on some roofs—three- and four-sided decorated booths covered with fronds and colorful fabric housing guests in their tiny enclosures. Solomon pulled me inside an empty one to explain that they were built to remember the huts his people had lived in for forty years in the wilderness after their journey from Egypt.

Just then a passing fruit cart overturned on the way to the night market, sending pomegranate and citrus rolling into the street. A gang of youngsters and several men came scrambling for them. The king whisked me from the little tabernacle before the onslaught, his men closed tight around us. I looked back, breathlessly, in time to see the booth go down in the jostle.

"Disaster follows in our wake," the king said grimly.

I wished he had not said it, if only because we do not know when we prophesy.

"When will you take me to see our ships?" I said after closing off the streets outside with the shutters, alone at last. We had talked several times about going to survey them, but I said it tonight in a show of faith.

"On the day that I escort you to your camp, we will go down to Ezion-geber together, and you will see your ships. I promise. And you will know the way you may return to me one day."

I could not smile. The day he escorted me to my camp would be the day I left Israel, and him.

Tashere required Solomon two days later for the birthday of their son. And then, three days after that, to observe a banquet in celebration of the new Pharaoh's coronation. Music and laughter issued through the corridors as a steady parade of dancers and musicians came and went from her apartment all evening. It was morning before Solomon returned and threw himself on the bed to sleep until sunset.

The day after that was the Israelite Day of Atonement, for which the king must fast and purify himself in preparation for his duties at the temple. The city had by now swelled beyond what I had thought was possible, so that I wondered how they did not fall from the very rooftops at night. "Forgive me, my queen," he said and kissed me before he left me again.

I walked the garden of his terrace alone, looking out over the city but only from such vantage that I could not be seen from below. Even from here I could see the commotion of the market mount outside the city, the shelters of pilgrims filling the valley in between. Gone, the black tents of my camp, replaced with brightly colored mosaic. Music wafted up from the streets and rooftops, nearly drowning out the singing of the Levite priests whose songs I had been so conscious of those first days, and was so accustomed to now that I hardly noticed it except when it broke through the din.

I played Senet with Shara and Naamah's servant, moving my pawn from the House of Happiness to the House of Water.

How like a board game a sovereign's court was, the fortunes of nations hinging on the toss of a pair of sticks behind closed doors. Loyalties measured against one another, attractions shared in secret. How the bat of an eye or the slightest snub might bring one nation to its knees and raise up another!

Solomon returned to me at night, kissing my hands, and lay with me on the sofa.

"You have captivated my heart with one glance of your eyes. With one jewel of your necklace," he said.

"Gather your lilies," I said in return, as he pulled me into his arms.

I did not ask why he came so late from the dinners or parties Tashere found occasion to throw nearly every week now. What would it have won me? I left it all in peace as we frenetically chased the idyll of those autumn days, drinking in one other as though I were a ewer of sweet water, and he an amphora of wine. Neither one inexhaustible, nor meant to be.

The nights came earlier and began to turn chill.

"Come. I want to show you something," he said one evening when it was too chilly to linger on the terrace and the streets so full we dare not venture out. It was the month of Tisri, and the third feast this month, Tabernacles, was to begin in days.

"And what is that?"

He laid his woolen mantle over my shoulders. "My greatest secret." He disappeared into the back room and I heard a lock turn and the opening of a chest. He returned with a ring of keys.

He led me down to an underground room deep below the palace, his torch held high above us. From these subterranean chambers we had snuck into the tunnels and beneath Jerusalem's walls on more than one occasion. Surely he didn't mean to leave the city; the surrounding valley was carpeted with pilgrims!

But this time he led me to a passage opposite the treasury, beyond the storeroom and cellars. At the end of the passage, we came to a locked and unmarked door.

"Through that tunnel, I can enter the temple," he said, gesturing to the dark hole that yawned opposite us. Did I imagine it, or did I smell the faint waft of incense?

"To appear as a magician in time to oversee your rites?"

He chuckled, the sound echoing in the dank underground. I held the mantle closer around me, the cold here below nearly matching that of outdoors.

He unlocked the door after some difficulty, cursing the key and then the lock and finally the smith who had fashioned them both as I laughed, holding the torch above him.

"You asked me once what was in the temple."

"You said you could not show me."

"I cannot. But I can show you this."

He took the torch from me and led me into the chamber. Shadows leapt out at us from the walls, dancing over a collection of hefty items: footed lamps, golden cauldrons, incense burners nearly as tall as I, and what appeared to be a lion exactly like the gold ones on either side of the steps to his throne. Several chests inlaid with ivory and precious stones lined the side wall covered with what I assumed to be bolts of fabric wrapped tightly in dusty linen. He handed the torch to me again as we came to a covered object of strange shape along the farthest side of the room, which was truly no more than a man-made cave.

"You ask me often about the gods. About Yaweh, the unspeakable name." He gathered the edges of the woolen coverlet and dragged it slowly to the floor.

I stepped back with a soft gasp.

Two gold cherubim, broad wings nearly touching over their bowed heads, knelt on a golden chest with fine filigree all along its top edge. With the cherubim atop it and their broad, spread wings, the entire thing was practically the same height as my own ark, if not as broad. I crouched down to study the faces of the cherubim, noting the design of the front panel, the chest's tapered feet.

"What is it made of?"

The lines at the corners of his eyes crinkled. "Acacia wood."

I let out a short breath. "As my *markab*."

"We, too, carry the ark into battle."

Lying beside it were two long poles and I could see from this vantage where they fit inside the casings on either side of the box—not unlike my own palanquin.

"Is this not supposed to be in the temple?" I said, glancing at him.

"It is . . . and it isn't," he said with an enigmatic smile. "During the building of the temple I had a copy of the ark constructed in secret. In case that day ever came that the ark need be protected. It has been taken from us before, by the Philistines," he said quietly.

I studied it again, understanding only from its *markab* counterpart the notion of its significance. But while the *markab* was the symbol of my office and the ruling tribe that possessed it, here was the throne of Yaweh and identity of a people. God and nation, in one cultic seat.

"My own ark is a copy of the one lost after my grandfather's campaigns. But how are you certain that this is the counterfeit?"

Solomon had been studying it over my shoulder and now he pointed.

"They are exact replicas except in one thing. Here, the workman made an error." He pointed out a slight aberration in the gold near the corner. "But I did not require him to fix it so that I would always know the difference."

My fingers found the place. Did my eyes deceive me, or did he flinch the moment I touched it? I drew back.

"You would not do that and live," he said, "were this the true ark and you were found unworthy."

I straightened. "No one touches it? Then how is it moved?"

"Only the Levites, whom you hear singing in the temple, transport the ark."

"Are the other priests not jealous?"

He shook his head, his gaze seeming to trail over the wide wings of the cherubim. "No. They fear it. All Israel and those beyond who understand what the ark is and know its history part before it like a sea and do not even look at it."

"Truly, that is an ark to be borne into battle, then," I said with a soft exhale.

"Now you have seen my greatest secret. Not one of my wives has laid eyes on this. And none will," he said, looking at me.

"Thank you," I said, and meant it—not only because of that, but because it was the closest I had come to any god. I understood, too, that if I stayed, I would never have laid eyes on it at all. This was a secret that could not be known, anywhere, but least of all within the boundaries of this nation.

Later that night, he was very still as we lay within the light of a single lantern. Outside, the sounds of the city had died to a quiet commotion of barking dogs and crying infants, the buzz of low voices in sleepless rooftop conversation.

"You are very quiet," I said at last.

"I do not think I have ever been so at peace and so much in turmoil at once," he whispered. "My kingdom threatens to break apart. Today I was all but taken to task by two of my brothers before my council."

"Over what?"

"The north. You. The fact that Assyria is gaining in strength as, they say, mine wanes. The lack of rain. The moon and very stars." He gave a soft laugh that was more a weary sigh.

I realized it was the dark moon. I had not even thought of it until now. Every month since my arrival, the drums of Almaqah's ritual had pulsed outside its wall. I thought of my camp halfway to the Red Sea port and half expected to hear them.

"They say that I am losing the faith of my people, that I have not honored my pact with Yaweh." He closed his eyes and I laid my arm around him.

"I was enraptured with Yaweh those first years, enflamed with holy fire. I barely slept, I was so possessed—such vision I had for this kingdom! For the legacy of my father. But more than that, for the approval of the god who set me on the throne, as though he were more father to me than the one who lay with my mother."

"You must remember what it was to feel that," I said. But even as I said it I knew duty would never do for this king who thrived in the first flush of infatuation. This man left wanting when mystery ebbed from the world, leaving nothing so profound as the mundane.

"Ah, from the woman who pursues the very gods. How you remind me of those first days. And I think a part of me would let my kingdom crumble to the ground rather than lose that. You."

As would I.

How well we had pretended that we could run through the city streets and take to the gardens and the underground tunnels forever, even as we did it with a fervor that would never exist were our time not short. But I could not replace his god. And even I knew Yaweh would never stand to be loved second.

For that reason, too, I must leave. But even as I said, "I leave in three weeks," I wanted to hear him protest, to say that he forbade it, that I must not go.

But neither did I want to become as Naamah, who had surely had roses in her cheeks once, until she grew austere and the light came only to her eyes when she spoke of her son. Or Tashere, with her elaborate and desperate banquets—any excuse to hold the attention of her king husband for even a few hours, because not to hold it meant to lose her place in this world. Was I any different?

Who am I?

Daughter, princess, victim, exile, lover, queen, priestess . . . all identities in relation to someone else—until that other person was gone.

And Solomon, the voracious prince . . . I knew, had perhaps known all along, that I could never satisfy him. Not wholly, this man missing the first blush of his romance with God, who chased it with the concubines of wealth, wives, and treaty.

He was weeping now and I held him, this man as strong as the Lebanon cedars he prized . . . and as fragile as words.

"Sometimes I think my god will leave me. Moses saw Yaweh but never entered this land. And I, who have everything in this land, have not heard Yaweh's voice in years. And if he has not abandoned me, how long will he dwell in this temple when I am gone? My prophet has seen that Israel will break apart. And what will become of us then?"

He shook his head, as one who has wrestled for far too long with questions.

"Are you not a friend of your god as your father was? Have you not loved him?"

"What is love?" he said, helplessly. "Contract? Poetry? I thought I loved you and tried to possess you. I love you now, and I let you go. But I am not happy to do it. I know only that the god of Abraham and of Isaac falls in love with certain people. My father was such a one. And my kingdom will stand as long as I am faithful. But I cannot protect it and expand its security without doing the thing my prophet condemns me for doing. Perhaps I have held it too tightly, as you say. Perhaps I consume, as I would have consumed you, and I do not love it well. You were right," he cried, "when you said I found myself in a trap!"

I was very quiet.

"Do you sleep, my queen?" he said softly after a time.

"I am going to tell you something," I said. "And perhaps you will come to hate me. But I tell you, because I feel compelled to it, though I would not have chosen to speak otherwise. There is a time to keep silent, and a time to speak. And this is the latter."

He lifted his head.

"I know something of the tribal heart. My claim to the throne was the birthright of my blood, through mother and father both. Pure. Your children are born to foreign mothers. It is our stories that bind us, you said yourself. Every god of my youth is a story passed down by my forefathers to keep our blood pure. But yours will be poured in two directions. The day in the temple, I saw the twelve bulls of your tribe break away, and the cauldron spill to the ground." At this, his eyes widened. "And so this is my gift to you, that I tell you: choose the successor of your blood carefully if you would keep the favor of your god. Because you have broken fidelity with Yaweh more than with your first wife."

He closed his eyes. "Then I will lose everything."

"Every time I have found that I have nothing left to lose . . . I have been free. There is a time to keep, but then there is a time to let go. And it always goes in that order. But if you cannot, if you will not . . . if the thing that drives you to hold tightly will possess you until you die, then drink your wine and make your poetry. Because perhaps that is, or will be, all that there is."

He tore at his hair. "How ill-timed your words! Only today Tashere encouraged me to take an Egyptian peace bride. A sister of Shishak."

Of course she did.

"And I can see no other way around it, but that I must for the sake of my kingdom! How then am I supposed to do as you say, when the Libyans are practically at my door? And you and I—what of us, not knowing if we will see one another again? How can we live with that, knowing what was lost?"

I shook my head faintly. I didn't know. My heart was already breaking. "I tell myself the story that I have always found a way. But this is a lie. Always the way has been laid before me the moment I surrendered the one thing I held precious. And there is something more precious right now to you than even me."

"I cannot surrender my kingdom," he said, tortured.

"Then," I said softly, "I believe you will lose it. And so the Sumerian sages will be right when they say that all is in vain."

"What am I to do?" he cried. And I had no answer for him.

I held him then, and wept for him and for us both. Because we do not know when we prophesy, but this time I knew that I did.

THIRTY

The next day Solomon rose early before dawn.

"Where are you going?" I said, still tired, the melancholy air that had settled about the chamber lingering like a shade.

"Many of my tribesmen have come in early from the north to meet before the feast," he said, dressing. "They are concerned about unrest within the city. There was a riot in the lower city already this morning, and another outside the city walls."

I pushed up. "What?"

I slept so soundly I had not even heard anyone come to the door.

He came to the bed. "I love you. I love you. Wait for me." He kissed my head, my eyes, my mouth. And then he was gone.

I lay back and dropped my arm over my eyes, listening to the sounds of Jerusalem swelled to three times its population—so loud at this hour! How had I slept through that? I could hear their hymns through the shuttered windows, the strains echoing up through the houses stacked one against the other from the streets below. I imagined I smelled the incessant bread mingled with reek of urine, the animal market as far as the olive mount.

Nine more days, the king had said, and the pilgrims would filter from the city.

Ten more after that, I would go down to my camp, there to turn my face south, to the ports, and then home.

So few, precious days. Why, last night, had I been so dire—compelled as I had never been over the crimson bowl?

Tonight I would tell only lovely stories. Our story, of the garden. Tomorrow. The day after. Every precious night until I left.

I got up but then sat back.

How could I leave this man for whom I had forgotten, if just for this while, this lifetime of a season, my entire kingdom?

I closed my eyes in the solitude of the chamber and clasped the sheets in tight fistfuls to my face. They smelled of him.

How right he had been, this man of obsessions. I had not come for ships or ports. Not truly.

I stayed like that for a long time, telling myself I would secure his promise that I would return—not by caravan next time, but by ship. That one day, perhaps, he would journey to Marib and walk through my palace as he had the day in my apartment when he first asked to see me on my throne. Someday, when his kingdom was stable enough.

Yes. That would be the last story I told him before I left.

Eventually I put on my dressing gown and moved on numb feet into the outer room.

A servant had brought in a ewer and I washed my face. There, too, was a pitcher of honeyed water, which I poured and took out to the garden. Beyond the gates I could see the pilgrims' tents in vivid array from one horizon to the next. Even the trash outside the city seemed to burn more vigorously than ever, so that when I lifted the cup to my lips I drank only a little before the smell wafted up on the wind, sickening me.

I spent the day in my own apartment, sleeping restlessly, the sounds of the city rising up so loudly to the terrace that I cried out for Shara to shut the doors.

I dreamed strange dreams. The temple, in its early building, a mere pile of stone. But then I realized it was not the temple in progress at all, but that it had fallen in. And I could see that the edges of the stones were singed, some of the limestone burned completely away. And that the palace, when I glanced back at it, was no more even as bells, their timbre high and tinny, sounded in the distance.

I woke some time later, dying of thirst. Someone had opened the doors to the terrace and the air smelled of rain. A short time later it came, the patter of it like so many stomping feet. Like an army in the streets. I slept again to the sound of marching, my head clouded as the sky.

I woke later to a mighty shaking, to someone calling my name. "You have slept the entire day!" Shara said. "You are unwell. My queen, we are afraid!"

"The king—"

"Is with the captain of his guard. There has been mayhem every-where, and fighting in the streets all day!" I got up but the room spun and I immediately retched into the chamber pot. But there was nothing in my stomach to vomit.

"I tried to send Naamah's girl for the physician but there are guards outside the door who will neither leave their posts nor allow anyone to pass," Shara cried, clutching me. I looked up, not com-prehending.

"Where is Yafush?"

"In the outer chamber. I have never seen him pray before. How afraid we have been for you, Bilqis—for us all!"

I squinted at her, finally hearing the bells of my dream in the clang of swords.

I closed my eyes and willed my leaden limbs to move.

"Dress me," I said.

A ruckus sounded from the street directly below the palace. But these were not the hymns of pilgrims, or of drunken men. It was shouting, loud and furious, and the clash of weapons again. The city in riot.

I walked on uncertain legs toward the terrace, but Shara grabbed me back, shouting over the sounds below that we must stay out of sight. A projectile hit the outer wall of my apartment and landed near my feet: a large, burnt stone.

I stumbled toward the outer chamber, Yafush instantly at my side. I wrenched open the door to the apartment.

No fewer than ten palace guards barred the way.

"Take me to the king," I said. My own guard was nowhere to be seen.

"My queen," one of them said, "you cannot leave."

"What is this, some sort of arrest? Send for him or allow me to pass. Now."

"I dare not, for your own protection, by the king's orders."

"Is there not a contingent of guards stationed outside the palace?" I fairly shouted in his face. I was rewarded with a roll of light-headedness.

Yafush seized my arm.

"They will not protect you from those within it."

"What do you mean?"

"There's been a murder. A servant was found dead in the king's apartment. You must stay here."

I opened my mouth, having been about to say that I was there just this morning. But I stopped in an immediate wave of dread.

"Dead of what?" I said very quietly, as tremors began to shake their way up my shoulders.

A booming ruckus sounded from somewhere within the palace courtyard, followed by shouts.

I turned in shock toward Yafush. I touched my fingers to my lips.

I, sleeping and dreaming as one drugged, the entire day.

"I think," I whispered, "that someone has tried to kill me."

Shara stared at me, white-faced, and then grabbed my hands.

"What have you eaten? What did you drink, what did you touch?" she cried.

I started to reply but the chamber went dark around me. The last thing I remembered was Yafush, charging through the guards.

I die, I thought.

THIRTY-ONE

We never know the last time we will see someone. My mother, kissing me. Maqar, on the field. His face was before me, as it had not been since that day. He was squinting in the sun. Why had I not taken his face between my hands our last night in camp?

Solomon, leaning over me. He was weeping again.

Ah, my Solomon.

Why hadn't I stayed awake all night, memorizing his eyes? Why hadn't we gone into the city and left our kingdoms behind? Why hadn't we passed out through the gate, hand in hand, and never returned?

Bilqis.

How beautiful it was to hear him say my name.

"My queen. Bilqis!"

My mother and Maqar both vanished before me.

Someone slapped at my cheek. Impossibly, I opened my eyes on the only one remaining: Solomon's.

Shofar horns in the distance. Hard blasts, crude to the ear and splintering to the brain. Shouts, rising in waves to the palace.

"What did the physician say?" he said urgently to Shara.

"That she survived the day, and will live. He gave her a draught."

"She will not die?" he demanded.

"No, my lord. She is strong." She hesitated. "As is the child within her."

The king turned astonished eyes to me and then clasped me hard against him. "A ruler of both our blood," he whispered, fervent in my ear. "It will be a son. A son to rule and unite kingdoms. The ruler I never was." He stroked my hair, my cheek, rocking back and forth. "How do I let you go?"

"It is not time," I whispered. No. Not yet. We were to have days . . .

Another form filled the door and the king looked up. "My king, the way is clear."

The king lifted me to my feet and the floor threatened to give out beneath me. Swiftly, he took me in his arms. And then we were rushing through the corridors, the king's guard before us, to the lower part of the palace. Down, to the subterranean hive of cellars and chambers. I had been this way before. There, the plain tunnel across from the vaulted treasury to the unmarked room. This time, the door was not locked but thrown open. Something gleamed in the passage.

A golden chest, the poles in place, cherubim seeming to hover in flight.

We were not alone. A host of robed figures stood aligned in the passage behind it illuminated by a single torch. Eight—no, ten— priests. I had seen the men in these garments, singing the day I visited the temple court. No, not priests. Broad-shouldered Levites.

Eight of them surrounded the ark, two to a corner at the long poles. They bent and, at a quick command between them, hoisted the poles, faces straining, to their shoulders. Like the palanquin of God, I thought abstractly.

I looked around me for Yafush, a shadow in the darkness. Shara, with ashen face.

The Levites disappeared into the tunnel, the glow of torchlight in their wake. Solomon caught me up more tightly in his arms and we entered the hewn rock behind them.

Hard jostle of every step. Echoed whispers.

Where we were going?

"Yafush—" I said, the sound too soft and loud at once.

"He's behind, with the king's guard," Shara said, breathlessly.

Dank cold of bedrock, the rough incline. Once, Solomon stumbled, but bore up and surged forward.

"Let me walk," I said with growing difficulty, fighting the draught.

"You cannot. I must do this. To save you. You, and our son. Let me save one nation."

I thought distantly: *Why do men always think it is a son?*

It seemed that we passed an eternity in darkness, chill creeping over my skin like damp on stone, the king's breath ragged in my ear, his arms iron around me. I thought I could hear his heart beating wildly in his chest—or was it my own?

Shara fell forward with a cry, gasped as arms helped her up again.

We began to ascend, the Levites ahead bending low in the tightening passage. The king grimaced, a sheen across his face.

The realization came slowly as I fought to keep the numbing fog at bay, unable to escape its sticky tendrils completely.

The temple.

We emerged into a chamber filled with gold cauldrons and braziers, figures blocking the light beyond as they reached for us with arms on all sides. The damp echo of the tunnels that had amplified every breath was replaced almost immediately by the roar of full riot from the city below.

We had come out of one of the side buildings into the inner court. Through the gate I could see a large company of mounted and foot soldiers assembled in the outer yard.

"It is ready?" the king said.

"It is ready."

I strained to look around me in sudden panic. Shara and Yafush had not emerged with us.

"They've gone another way with my men," Solomon said. "They are less recognizable and will meet us south of the city. But there is no way to take you out through the valley in safety. They riot even beyond the gates."

I had never been without Yafush since I was a girl of twelve.

Four Levites had surrounded the ark and, after what seemed a moment's hesitation, hefted the lid away.

Solomon held me tight against him, his cheek pressed fiercely to mine. "Now, my love," he whispered. "You entered Jerusalem as the rising sun, in majesty. You will not leave it without the finery of gold. All Israel will bow before you. All Israel will remember this day. And if they do not, then I will. Forever." He kissed me softly. "Lady of the *markab*," he whispered. "My best love."

What is love, but to hold dear without expectation?

What is love, but first given devotion?

What is love . . .

But freedom.

I meant to say all of this as he lifted me into the box. But the king was kissing my lips as my knees curled in against my chest. "I love you as the sun rises. I love you by the moon." His face twisted. "How do I let you go knowing that in saving you, you may yet pass to the afterlife? How do I leave you in the hands of any god?"

"Surrender," I said, and did so.

I remember the jostling of arms. The world closing in and going dark.

THIRTY-TWO

I saw them pull away like the fabled parting of the sea. How they fell away! Like the rains washing down two sides of a mountain.

Impossibly, I saw them.

There were so many of them, and so many armed men among them, enigma on their faces, and alarm, before they shielded their eyes.

They ran, scattering like leaves before a gale.

But all is well, I wanted to say. The sun rises, without our aid. And the moon will come in her wake. And there is one force that makes them rise and decline, and one that made them both.

I knew this now.

All the riddles were gone, only the husk of them remaining like the hard shells of locusts still clinging to the stem.

And then the shells themselves blew away.

Including mine.

Who am I?

There was no Bilqis and no Makeda or priestess. No daughter, princess, or queen. No lover, or unloved. There was only the name that I had always had, but forgotten. A name by which I was known to God, that is neither spoken or written. That annihilated self. A vessel that is full because it has first been emptied.

Yes. Freedom. Yafush was right.

The crescent was over the sun in the sky. Time and eternity, at once. How beautiful the world was. And heaven danced among us.

I had sought love. I had talked of love, not knowing that it is one step beyond wisdom into the face of God. And this was the only salvation.

The king was there when the lid was lifted away and the first gust of chill air roused me. It was he who pulled me from that golden box as though from a fist-tight womb.

"Does she breathe? Is she dead?" Yafush cried.

I had never heard that sound from him.

"She lives!" the king cried, pulling me into his arms.

Indeed. More than he knew.

He kissed me—a thousand times, he kissed me. How I wanted to comfort him with a thousand proclamations, to tell him to remember all that I had said, as I would remember all that he said when he answered my riddles with answers beyond even him.

And how I wanted to tell him that Yaweh had not forgotten him.

Yes. That, most of all.

Instead, I spoke one word, the one I saw now when I looked on his face—or that of Yafush, or Shara, or any man or woman known to me or not—as the draught, held at bay all this while, had its way at last.

I forgot to tell him he must finish our story. Somehow I must remember to tell him that.

THIRTY-THREE

The sand had left the air in its typical greenish haze. And so they said, when we put in at the best port that we could make, that the storm had come with the ships.

This is not true.

It took us two weeks to find suitable landing on the coast, to unload the camels and tents and the fodder that would see us inland the rest of the way south, to Saba—including that most precious cargo, covered in heavy woolen blankets. The strange misshapen thing carried on the poles by the Levites who had brought it out from the city and accompanied us to the ships. And two weeks, also, for me to recover and reconstruct all that had happened in the space of hours with any semblance of clarity.

They said I was incoherent when I boarded the ship. This, too, is untrue. I revived sometime beyond Jerusalem to hear the tale being told in camp of how I was smuggled out in plain sight as the people in and outside the city fell away from the ark in dread fear, the riot instantly quelled. Hadad, the king had claimed, was massing on the border in a show of force. So the king rode out with his men bearing the presence of Yaweh lest they attack during the feast.

No one would question the king—not with the ark before them. And no one would ride out toward Edom to find out for himself, though this, in fact, turned out to be true, and it was only the presence of the king and ark so nearby that sent them in retreat a day after we had sailed. This was confirmed by my men who took the land route south with the caravan.

They didn't believe that I had seen it all. How could I, shut away?

But a wise man once said that only a fool tries to defend vehemently what she knows is true.

The Levites came with the false ark all the way down to Eziongeber but once there would not turn back. I absolved them in good conscience; the true ark was in the temple. But they refused and said their fate lay in Saba, or wherever the box would go.

I took my leave of the king there, on the shores of his port to the sound of the workers, the prows of the remaining unfinished ships rising up against the sunrise on their majestic bows.

"You must take this ark with you to Saba," Solomon said.

"But we have no more need of the ruse. And your people will notice if you do not return with it."

"Give me the *markab* with a covering. Let me retain this part of you as you hold dear the symbol of my god, who has chosen you, in exchange far greater than any vow we might have made. Set me as a seal on your heart. And someday, when our son is a man, you must send him north so that I might lay eyes on him. Make me this promise, so that I may see the two of us together in him, until the day I rise from sleep and see your face before me again."

He gathered my hands, and kissed them through tears. "Remember me by the sun. Remember me by the moon. Remember me to our son," his voice broke, "and speak well . . . of this foolish king."

He was more lovely to me in that final moment than in a thousand before. We clung together before we parted and I stood, memorizing his face from the prow of the ship, until I could see it no more.

During the weeks at sea, Shara asked often if I was well. I said that I was, though I had not known until then that a woman might survive with the remaining half of a heart. I gratefully entered the tents of those who came out to greet us, whom we greeted in turn with news as we made our way south. To Marib, and the palace.

Wahabil welcomed me with joy and then surprise as I embraced him around my swelling belly.

He would have the heir he had hoped for at last and never know that the name housed in three temples all this time had been his.

"But where is the *markab*?" he asked me alone in my privy chamber.

"In Israel," I said, "in the palace of the king."

"But you have brought another in its place," he said, bewildered.

"I have exchanged a nation for God."

Three months later, a sandy plume wound its way down from the north. But when we went out to meet them, Asm was not among their number. His acolytes told me he wandered out of camp near the dead salt sea one night and never returned. I could only hope he had received his longed-for vision at last.

I feasted Tamrin in the palace where he delivered gifts and horses sent out to camp before the festival. There were shadows around his eyes and I knew he was already restless, though he promised to visit again in spring.

"The king has said it will never be safe for you to return," he said when we were alone. And I knew he, too, loved the king in his own way. "Not when it is discovered what you have brought south for safekeeping."

At the time I assumed he meant the son in my belly.

The spring rains came and the fields turned green. The Levite priests were uncomfortable in my capital, where there was far too much talk of Almaqah. That fall, I sent them across the sea with their cargo, to Punt. I did not understand their loyalty to that golden box, but the day I saw them carry it from the palace, I noticed for the first time that the poles seemed not as long as I remembered the night the king first took me down to the hidden room.

I bid them safe journey in the name of Yaweh and returned to the palace, at peace.

To raise a son, a nation.

EPILOGUE

The ships have come as they do every three years. One fleet south, to Punt. Another east, to Saba's port in Aden. They are majestic, but not like the caravans I looked forward to all these years. They have not been the same since Tamrin's passing on the incense road he loved so well. I hope often that he found his destination, somewhere on that journey.

It is the first year Menelik will receive them, I tell the captain proudly. The first fleet he will welcome as king.

The captain wants to know if I miss the throne I abdicated. No, I say, it is much quieter in Punt, except for the cicadas. Yafush, who sits, rather than stands, beside me these days, agrees.

But now, I ask, does he have something for me?

He delivers the scroll, as he has so many times. But this time he sighs.

The king has gone, he says, to walk with his fathers. This will be the last one.

My fingers tremble. I want to be alone.

When I am, I clasp the scroll to my breast before breaking it open. As I read his last song the tears come, but they are not sad.

He has remembered the garden.

He has finished the story, at last.

Set me as a seal upon your heart,
As a seal upon your arm,
For love is as strong as death . . .
Many waters cannot quench love,
Neither can floods drown it.

Make haste, my beloved.

AFTERWORD

Solomon's unified kingdom broke apart during the reign of his successor, Rehoboam, splitting the ten tribes of Israel in the north from the two tribes of Judah in the south. Jeroboam, returned from Egypt, led the rebellion of the northern tribes after Rehoboam not only refused to lighten the north's labor but proclaimed he would increase it tenfold. Jeroboam ruled Israel for twenty-two years, and Rehoboam in Judah for seventeen. The two rulers were at war for the duration of their reigns.

Pharaoh Shishak (Sheshonq I, founder of the Twenty-second "Libyan" Dynasty) invaded northern Israel in the fifth year of Rehoboam's reign, capturing several cities, including Megiddo, and reclaiming Gezer in the process. The famous Bubastite gate in the temple to Amun I in Karnak depicts Sheshonq I carrying off "the treasures of the House of Yaweh and the treasures of the royal palace," along with Solomon's golden shields. Jerusalem itself is not mentioned in the list of conquered cities on the gate, whereas it is the only city mentioned in the biblical account. Scholars theorize Jeroboam staved off attack on the capital by paying the items as tribute. Judah subsequently became a vassal state of Egypt.

The Ark of the Covenant seems to have survived Shishak's

invasion (as evidenced by King Josiah returning it to the temple in 2 Chronicles 35:1–6—its only other mention after Solomon's time), but disappears from scripture and history both sometime before or around the Babylonian siege of Jerusalem in 589-587 BC when Nebuchadnezzar burned the temple to the ground and razed Jerusalem. The ark, however, is not mentioned in the 2 Kings list of Nebuchadnezzar's spoils, even though items as small as dishes are. Nor is it listed among the items returned to Jerusalem by Cyrus in the Book of Ezra.

Menelik, the son of the queen of Sheba and King Solomon according to Ethiopian legend, became the first king in the Solomonic Dynasty of Ethiopia—a succession of kings who ruled for 3,000 years until the end of the reign of Emperor Haile Selassie in 1974.

After the sheer volume of research that went into the writing of *Iscariot*, I naïvely thought reconstructing Sheba's queen from fragments of history a thousand years earlier would be easy in comparison. In fact, unearthing the enigmatic queen proved a new adventure in hair-pulling for opposite reasons.

Sheba's queen appears in three major works: the Bible, the Quran, and the *Kebra Nagast: The Glory of the Kings*—the 700-plus-year-old origin story of the Solomonic kings of Ethiopia; Ethiopia's conversion from the worship of the sun, moon, and stars to the God of Israel; and how the Ark of the Covenant came to purportedly reside in Ethiopia. All three works are considered inspired by their devotees.* All three contain the queen's legendary journey to visit King Solomon in Israel. But their commonality stops there.

To Jews and Christians, the queen of Sheba is the unnamed Old Testament sovereign of the southern spice lands who visited Solomon with four and a half tons of gold, confirmed his power, and blessed his god—the same queen Jesus proclaims in the gospels will judge the generation of Israel that condemned him. To Muslims, she is the Arabian queen Bilqis, who traveled to pay homage to Israel's king and converted to the worship of Allah. To Ethiopians, she is Makeda, a woman tricked by Solomon into sleeping with him, who converts to the worship of Yaweh and becomes the mother of a 3,000-year-old dynasty of kings.

Sheba's queen is also mentioned by the historian Josephus as Nikaulis, the queen of Egypt and Ethiopia, despite the fact that there was no reigning queen in Egypt at the time of Solomon according to most chronologies. Apocryphal books list Sheba's queen as the product of a lineage of queens, but the historical and archaeological record give no indication of queens ruling in southern Arabia.

What can we truly know of this tenth-century BC queen? The short answer: very little. To believers of the biblical and Quranic accounts or Ethiopian legend, her life is fact. To the historian, her existence is dubious at best.

The Sabaean kingdom spanned the Red Sea from ancient Yemen to Ethiopia. The Sabaeans no doubt existed; the ruins of their temples, dams, and cities are the subject of decades of excavation and research. Sabaean script appears both in Yemen and colonies in ancient D'mt, which would centuries later become the kingdom of Aksum.

The veracity and longevity of the Incense Route is undisputed: Neo-Assyrian texts document trade between Southern Arabia and the Middle Euphrates as early as the beginning of the ninth century, with trade between Southern Arabia and the Levant probably originating a thousand years earlier. Scholars believe that the core account of 1 Kings 10:1–13 was likely written around the tenth century BC, well within this time frame. Pieces of a bronze Sabaean inscription dated ca. 600 BC depict the ibex heads so pervasive in Sabaean art and document trade between Southern Arabia and the "towns of Judah."

Tantalizing finds point to Solomon and Sheba. In 2012, an archaeological team in northern Ethiopia discovered a twenty-foot stone stele inscribed with the sun and crescent moon, fragments of

Sabaean script, and the columns of a temple to the moon god near the shaft to an ancient gold mine. Farther north, copper mines in Edom point to organized activity in the tenth century BC—and an interruption of that activity around the time of Shishak/Sheshonq I's invasion.

Even so, to say the archaeological record of Sheba's queen—and Solomon, for that matter—is scant would be generous. Findings specific to either sovereign have yet to be discovered.

In the 1980s, the Israel Museum purchased a 3,000-year-old ivory pomegranate from an anonymous collector. The thumb-sized ornament, carved of hippopotamus bone with a hole in the bottom, was thought to top the scepter of a priest. Its inscription read: "Belonging to the Temple of the Lord (Yahweh), holy to the priests," proving at last the existence of the first temple, built by Solomon. The inscription, however, was declared a forgery in 2004, with the pomegranate itself predating the first temple period.

According to the Quran, the queen was a worshipper of the sun. Shams, the sun goddess, was known and worshipped in ancient Yemen along with a host of other gods, depending on where one lived. The god Almaqah is widespread in surviving texts, and ruins of ibex-adorned temples dot the Sabaean territory. Scholars, however, do not agree on whether Almaqah was a lunar or solar deity.

Though we are given far more about the life of King Solomon (who reigned roughly 970-930 BC by most chronologies) than of Sheba's queen, he wears a slightly different face in each of the three major accounts that mention him. In the Bible, he is the all-wise king who ultimately failed to follow the dictates of Yaweh—who granted him the knowledge he asked for and the riches and power he did not. In the Quran, he speaks the language of animals and even insects, learns about Sheba's queen from the curious hoopoe bird, and commands jinns to deliver her throne to him before her arrival. Arabic legend says he forced her to reveal the true nature of her feet with a pool of water in his throne room.

In the *Kebra Nagast*, he is the wily king who resorts to trickery again—this time to persuade the queen to sleep with him. He later loses the Ark of the Covenant to the Judean honor guard he sends home with Menelik after his son's visit. According to lore, Solomon only intended to send a copy of the ark with Menelik so that he might worship Yaweh in his faraway home. But Menelik, concerned about Solomon's growing apostasy, has the guard smuggle the true ark out of Jerusalem, leaving the forgery in its place. Today many Beta Israel "Black Jews" of Ethiopia claim lineage from Menelik's Israelite cohort. (Others claim descent from the ancient tribe of Dan.)

Though evidence of a royal city near Jerusalem's Temple Mount and other buildings dating to the time of Solomon confirm biblical references to his projects, many scholars dispute the claims of Solomon's wealth and influence as inflated.

And so we turn from here to that mystical third player in this drama: the ark.

The idea of an ark as a battle standard is not unique to Israel. The *markab* served a similar purpose in wartime, though to my knowledge was never infused with the spiritual power of Israel's Ark of the Covenant—a veritable weapon of mass destruction. Gold chests containing sacred objects occur throughout ancient history. (Such a processional chest discovered in Tutankhamen's tomb elicited a flurry of sensationalism in 1922. The dimensions for the pylon-shaped chest, however, were not the same as those for the Ark of the Covenant, and Tutankhamen's "ark" bore the likeness of Anubis.)

What really happened to the Ark of the Covenant has been the subject of countless searches, legends, conspiracy theories—and of course Hollywood movies—ranging from locations in Israel, Egypt,

Arabia, Ireland, France, and even the U.S. by more than a few Indiana Jones look-alikes.

The obvious answer is that the ark was taken by Nebuchadnezzar in his 587 BC siege of Jerusalem. The ark, however, is not mentioned among the list of goods seized from the temple in 2 Kings 25:13–15 or Jeremiah 52:17–22—a list that details items taken from the temple columns and bronze sea cauldron, down to shovels, dishes, and wick-trimmers. Only the apocryphal 4 Ezra 10:19–22 mentions the plundering of the ark—a book generally thought to have been written 90-100 AD and in response to Roman invasion. I find it incredible that Jeremiah, the "Weeping Prophet," would fail to mourn the capture of the ark in his musings. Nor is the ark listed in the items returned by Cyrus to Israel in the Book of Ezra.

According to 2 Maccabees, Jeremiah buried the ark in a cave on Mount Nebo just east of Jerusalem prior to the invasion, keeping it "until the time that God should gather His people again together." In *The Lost Ark of the Covenant* (2008), Tudor Parfitt postulates it was later removed from Israel to Yemen.

Most interesting to me for the purpose of this book is the tradition of the ark and ark replicas in Ethiopia. Every Ethiopian Orthodox Church keeps a *tabot*—a stone slab representing the tablets of the ark or a replica of the ark itself. Without a *tabot*, the church is not considered consecrated. That said, the Ethiopian Orthodox Church also claims to have the real thing. Ask the guardian of the ark—a monk of no other name committed to the lifelong office of tending the holy relic in secret—at the Chapel of the Tablet in Aksum and he will attest that the ark is under his protection. The only downside is that he's the only one allowed to see it.

Given the tradition of ark replicas, one "conspiracy" theory caught my eye in particular—an idea based on the peculiar attention given to the length of the ark's poles when it was installed in the temple (2 Chronicles 5:9). Also, according to 1 Kings 8:9 and 2 Chronicles 5:10, there was "nothing in the ark" other than the two stone tablets of Moses, excluding mention of the jar of manna and Aaron's budded staff. The theory here being that a fake with much longer poles was installed in the temple and the true ark hidden, ostensibly, for safe-keeping.

Others believe the ark still resides in Jerusalem and that all questions will be answered the day the mount is better excavated—which may be very long in coming due to the extreme sensitivity of the site where the Dome of the Rock sits today. That said, the Temple Mount Sifting Project, dedicated to excavating the debris of a hole dug (to great criticism) into the temple platform in 1996-1999 to build the El-Marwani Mosque, has unearthed some spectacular finds in the 20 percent of rubble sifted so far. You can follow the progress of the project at: templemount.wordpress.com.

Jerusalem is rife with underground tunnels, including the one by which David famously took the city (possibly discovered in 2008 by Dr. Eilat Mazar), and a tunnel system adjacent to the Western Wall. No doubt many more tunnels lay hidden beneath the Temple Mount.

A couple of additional notes:

1. I've no doubt committed a cultural sin in eliminating the aleph (') and other notations from Sabaean proper nouns in order to spare readers (and myself) names such as Ammī'amar, Ma'dīkarib, dhāt-Ba'dån.

2. Bilqis' "fearless or reckless" ibex urn is imagined, though the statue of Astarte with the wax plugs in her breasts is based on a figurine of the goddess discovered in Tutugi, Spain, that dates to the sixth or seventh century and performs the same "miracle." Religious machinations were not unknown in the ancient world—and about to get more common.

In the end, even though Solomon and the queen of Sheba have yet to show themselves in the archaeological record, they are as vividly alive as though their palaces still stand to the Ethiopians who claim the queen of Sheba as a vital part of their national identity and to Christians, Jews, and Muslims, for whom the veracity of David and Solomon's unified kingdom underpins the unfolding story of their faith.

As for me, I assert that we don't need artifacts to know something of either monarch: their questions, foibles, hurts, joys, triumphs, and losses are not unique—they are, in fact, the same as our own . . . if only with a little more gold.

* Other sources that proved invaluable to me:

Queen of Sheba: Treasures From Ancient Yemen, edited by St. John Simpson (Trustees of the British Museum, 2002)

Sheba: Through the Desert in Search of the Legendary Queen, Nicholas Clapp (Nicholas Clapp, 2001)

Ancient South Arabia: From the Queen of Sheba to the Advent of Islam, Klaus Schippmann (Markus Wiener Publishers, 2001)

Arabia Felix: From the Time of the Queen of Sheba, Jean-François Breton (University of Notre Dame Press, 1999)

Arabia and the Arabs: From the Bronze Age to the Coming of Islam, Robert G. Hoyland (Routledge, 2001)

Solomon & Sheba: Inner Marriage and Individuation, Barbara Black Koltuv (Nicolas-Hays, Inc., 1993)

Arabian Sands, Wilfred Thesiger (Penguin, 2007)

Of additional interest:

From Eden to Exile: The Epic History of the People of the Bible, David Rohl (Arrow Books, 2003)

The Sign and the Seal: The Quest for the Lost Ark of the Covenant, Graham Hancock (Arrow Books, 1997)

ACKNOWLEDGMENTS

Every book is a journey of a thousand thank-yous and amazing companions—those who plan the route, travel alongside us, come to our aid, direct and encourage . . . and then, miraculously, do it all again.

Thank you to my readers for your intrepid souls, your encouragement, your bacon anecdotes, and for keeping me company through my marathon sprees. Every book is for you.

The pathfinders: Dan Raines and Meredith Smith of Creative Trust, who have yet to (visibly) flinch at my next harebrained idea. Jeanie Kaserman, who reads print so fine it cannot be seen by the naked eye.

My editor, Becky Nesbitt, and assistant editor, Amanda Demastus, who carve beauty from the storm of my early drafts. Jonathan Merkh, Rob Birkhead, Brandi Lewis, Jennifer Smith, Bonnie MacIsaac, Chris Long, Bruce Gore, and the entire team at Howard, thank you for your excellence.

Cindy Conger, who keeps me on track and sane. Mark Dahmke, who helped me search the ancient sky. Meredith Efken, who plodded through the early stages with me over Korean tacos. Stephen Parolini, who ran alongside me through the first draft with off-handed

Star Wars references—your hilarity keeps me from hating you for your brilliance.

The experts: Dallas Baptist University professor of Old Testament Dr. Joe Cathey, who never exhausts of my myriad weird questions. Professor of history at the University of Northern Iowa Dr. Robert L. Dise Jr., Pastor Jeff Scheich, and new friend Jon Culver—thank you for lending your experience, intellect, and time.

Thank you to my family, genetic and adopted, for not assuming me dead in my long periods of silence and giving my stuff away, friends for never pointing out that I've been wearing the same thing for days, Julie for playing hooky with me the last thirty years, and Bryan, Wynter, Kayla, Gage, and Kole for sowing love in this heart.

Greatest thanks of all to the God I used to say shows me great things, but these days just mostly freaks me out with stuff I never saw coming. I've learned to quit saying "I'm ready," because I never am.